PRAISE FOR THE
OF LORELEI J

"With *Unwound*, James once again proves she's the master of erotic romance. Filled with unforgettable characters, fiery passions, and an all-encompassing love story, it's a must read for anyone craving more kink in their romance."

—*New York Times* Bestselling Author Tara Sue Me

"Her sexy cowboys are to die for!"

—*New York Times* bestselling author Maya Banks

"Sweet, seductive, and romantic . . . an emotional ride filled with joy, angst, laughs, and a wonderful happily-ever-after. Lorelei James knows how to write one hot, sexy cowboy."

—*New York Times* bestselling author Jaci Burton

"The down-and-dirty, rough-and-tumble Blacktop Cowboys kept me up long past my bedtime. Scorchingly hot, wickedly naughty."

—Lacey Alexander

"Hang on to your cowboy hats, because this book is scorching hot!"

—Romance Junkies

"Lorelei James knows how to write fun, sexy, and hot stories."

—Joyfully Reviewed

"Lorelei James excels at creating new and evocative fantasies."

—TwoLips Reviews

"Incredibly hot." —The Romance Studio

continued . . .

"Beware: Before you read this hot erotic from Lorelei James, get a glass of ice. You are going to need it." —Fallen Angel Reviews

"Think it's impossible to combine extremely erotic and sweet? Not if James is writing." —*Romantic Times*

"Plenty of steamy love scenes that will have you reaching for your own hottie!" —Just Erotic Romance Reviews

"Smokin'-hot cowboys [and] lots of Western charm." —Fiction Vixen Book Reviews

"I honestly do not know how . . . Lorelei James keeps doing it, but every new book is a masterpiece, blending an incredible story line, sexy alpha cowboys, and strong women, plus luvin' so smokin' hot, you'll be stocking up on batteries!" —Guilty Pleasures Book Reviews

ALSO BY LORELEI JAMES

The Mastered Series

Bound

The Blacktop Cowboys® Series

Corralled

Saddled and Spurred

Wrangled and Tangled

One Night Rodeo

Turn and Burn

LORELEI JAMES

UNWOUND

The Mastered Series

New American Library

New American Library
Published by the Penguin Group
Penguin Group (USA) LLC, 375 Hudson Street,
New York, New York 10014

USA | Canada | UK | Ireland | Australia | New Zealand | India | South Africa | China
penguin.com
A Penguin Random House Company

First published by New American Library,
a division of Penguin Group (USA) LLC

First Printing, April 2014

LIBRARY OF CONGRESS CATALOGING-IN-PUBLICATION DATA:
James, Lorelei.
Unwound/Lorelei James.
p. cm.—(The mastered series)
ISBN 978-0-451-46731-7 (pbk.)
1. Martial artists—Fiction. 2. Bondage (Sexual behavior)—Fiction.
I. Title.
PS3610.A4475U59 2014
813'.6—dc23 2013045109

Printed in the United States of America
10 9 8 7 6 5 4 3 2 1

Set in Bembo
Designed by Spring Hoteling

PUBLISHER'S NOTE
This is a work of fiction. Names, characters, places, and incidents either are the product of the author's imagination or are used fictitiously, and any resemblance to actual persons, living or dead, business establishments, events, or locales is entirely coincidental.

UNWOUND

PROLOGUE

HIS head hurt like a motherfucker.

He couldn't see a damn thing in this dark alley.

Why the hell hadn't she come to the door yet?

He smacked his helmet into the steel three more times.

Please, baby, just let me in.

No lights came on. No clicking sounds of the door locks disengaging.

But he couldn't hear anything above the pain screaming in his head.

He rested his shoulders on the brick building. When he put his palm to his forehead to try to keep his brain from exploding, his fingers came away wet.

What the hell?

Why the fuck was he bleeding?

The steel door squeaked and opened only far enough so she could peer out. Playing it safe. Good girl.

"Who's there?"

"It's me."

"*Ronin?* What are you doing here?"

"I needed to see you."

"At two in the morning?"

"Yes. Please. Let me in." As soon as she opened the door, Ronin stumbled inside and his helmet bounced across the concrete floor.

She dove for him when he swayed. Somehow she kept him on his feet and maneuvered him against the wall. She gasped softly. "Your face. What happened?"

He swallowed the bile crawling up his throat. He dropped to his knees and hissed at the excruciating pain before he plopped onto the floor with a juddering thump.

"Ronin?" She crouched beside him. "You look like you've taken a beating."

"I have. Being beaten down has been my natural state since you walked out on me."

His response jarred her into silence.

So he kept talking. "The fight . . . rattled my brain."

"You were in a fight tonight? A real fight?"

"Yeah."

"Can I ask why?"

"Needed to numb the pain." He winced when he tried to shift positions. "But then I couldn't remember."

"What? Why you came here?"

"I came here because I didn't have any other place to go."

She picked up his hand. "You're bleeding."

"Sorry. I never wanted you to see me like this."

"Like what?"

"Broken."

He heard a soft gasp. "Ronin, you probably need a doctor."

It was getting harder to breathe and maintain focus. And balance. He slurred, "No. I just need to sleep." Then he half rolled/half fell to his side.

"You can't sleep."

"Have to. Fuck. It hurts."

"No, no, no, no, no, no! Don't close your eyes. Dammit, Ronin, stay with me. Come on! Where's the infallible martial arts master? You are freaking me out."

"Sorry." Then he was at the mouth of a tunnel. Her distorted voice echoed back to him from a point far away.

Or was this an illusion?

He raced toward the pinpoint of light, running faster when it began to fade.

Then he was engulfed in nothingness.

CHAPTER ONE

Six weeks earlier . . .

RONIN Black had thought his breaking and entering days were behind him.

But after the cold reception he'd received from Molly, Amery's receptionist at Hardwick Designs, and Molly's lack of information about where her boss had disappeared to, he'd opted for Plan B.

Since Amery had given him a key, technically his presence in her loft wasn't illegal. It wasn't as if he planned to read her journal or scroll through her private accounts on her computer. He just needed some idea of where she'd gone before he went out of his fucking mind.

It wasn't the *why* Ronin didn't understand, since Amery's parting shot twenty-four hours earlier replayed on a continuous loop in his head: *Don't bother running after me with the excuses you consider apologies or offering more lies masquerading as explanations because we're done this time. Done.*

Fuck that. They weren't even close to done. They'd barely begun.

Just thinking about how badly he'd fucked up . . . Ronin squeezed the key so hard it bit into his palm. So much for staying composed. After he'd calmed down last night, following their . . . blowup, his fuckup, or whatever the hell it was, he'd tried calling her. Her cell phone had kicked him over to voice mail every one of the fifteen times he'd called. He hadn't left a message. He needed to talk to her, not a machine.

He forced his hand to relax and jammed the key into the lock, twisting until the mechanism clicked. After he'd opened the door, he slipped inside the back room.

Since the offices at the front of the building were empty, he called out, "Amery?" just in case she was hiding out.

No response.

Ronin scaled the circular staircase as quietly as possible. But he had no reason for stealth; as soon as his foot hit the top tread, he knew she wasn't here.

The blinds were drawn in her main living area. If Amery were around she'd have the windows open, the curtains billowing in the breeze. He circled her couch and coffee table, noticing she'd tidied up more than normal. He found the same thing in the kitchen. Dishes drying on the drain rack, garbage taken out, wooden fruit bowl emptied. He checked the contents of the fridge. No dairy products or takeout containers, which suggested she planned to be gone long enough to worry about food spoilage.

Her toothbrush wasn't in the flower-shaped cup holder in the bathroom. Her cosmetics weren't strewn across the counter. No pajamas or workout clothes were piled in the hamper. He squeezed the bath towel hanging on the hook. Completely dry. But just touching it released the scent of her shampoo, and his stomach knotted with longing.

Fuck.

He didn't do this. He didn't know *how* to do this missing her and wanting her thing.

But you do know how to fuck something up beyond repair.

He had to fix this. *Had* to.

Ronin retreated from the bathroom. He paused in the doorway to her bedroom. Her rumpled bed looked exactly as he'd left it. Exactly. Bedding dangling off the end of the mattress where he'd thrown it back. Pillows shoved to his side of the bed.

But on her side of the bed . . . there were the two coils of black rope he'd forgotten to pack up before leaving yesterday morning.

Christ. Had it been only yesterday morning he'd woken in her bed? Only one damn day since everything had imploded?

At least she hadn't thrown them out in a fit of pique.

Now that he knew they were here, he had a legitimate excuse for returning.

BACK at the Black Arts dojo, Ronin wandered around like a ghost. No one engaged him while he observed classes from a distance. He saw everything yet nothing as his mind focused elsewhere—which is probably why he didn't recognize the woman at first.

Shihan Knox barked, "None of you have shown any familiarity with this technique, and I know this is not the first time you've worked with it."

Every student appeared to hang their head in shame.

Except for one.

Naturally Knox noticed her defiant posture. His eyes narrowed and he pointed to her. "You. Up here. Now."

The woman sauntered to the front of the class and bowed.

"You familiar with this technique?"

She kept her head lowered. "Yes, Godan."

"Good." Knox took five steps back. "Start from the defensive stance." He went at her, low and outside.

In that split second Ronin recognized Knox's mistake—as did his student.

She used the forward motion of his body against him, knocking him sideways. The move caught him completely off guard, and he took a knee—which was as good as admitting defeat.

Shihan Knox shot to his feet. He tried to appear unfazed, but Ronin recognized his annoyance. Knox said, "Reverse stances. You're on the offensive."

"No," the student said calmly.

"Excuse me?"

"I decline the challenge. I wouldn't come at you from the angle you've been demonstrating. That's why no one in the class has mastered it. With all due respect, Godan, this teaching method is ineffective."

Rather than show irritation, Knox grinned. Ronin knew he lived for this comeuppance shit.

"Since you have ideas on how our training time might be better spent, defend yourself any way you see fit." Then Knox rushed her.

She lowered into a defensive stance, allowing herself to get steamrolled, the equivalent of offering the alpha dog her throat.

That didn't make Knox happy. "Partner up at the heavy bags. We'll work on kicks for the remainder of class."

Ronin stayed in the dark corner, assessing each student's skills. Clearly they needed to put the screws to this class—he saw several students slacking on basic techniques. Their lack of discipline reflected on him as owner of the dojo.

Knox dismissed class student by student—as was his prerogative. He retained the female student until everyone had left.

"Please stand."

She gracefully propelled herself upright.

"Why did you refuse to demonstrate the reversal of the technique?"

"Out of deference to you, Godan."

She called him Godan, his belt rank, and not Shihan, a term used for the highest-ranking teacher besides the sensei.

"Explain that," Knox demanded.

"I am merely a visitor to your domain."

Knox loomed over her, but she wouldn't meet his gaze. "So

you let me win because you didn't want to show me up in front of my students?"

"Yes."

"Oh, hell no. We'll go again. This time? No holding back. And that is an order."

"As you wish." She fortified her stance.

For a big guy, Knox was fast on his feet, very adaptable in the moment. But he didn't stand a chance against the woman's speed and intuition.

She dodged, ducked, and knocked Knox down, immobilizing him against the mat with her elbow on the back of his neck. She held his wrist in a joint lock, which, if he moved the wrong way, would result in a fracture.

Ronin stepped forward. "Release him."

The woman immediately let Knox go. When she offered him a helping hand, Knox tugged her to the mat, trying to regain ground, but she merely pulled a reversal and Knox found himself in the same subservient position as before.

Knox swore under his breath.

"Ill-advised attempt at saving face, Shihan." Then Ronin addressed the woman. "I take it you didn't introduce yourself to my staff?"

She shrugged. "You gave me a guest pass. I used it. It didn't include *welcome to the dojo* instructions."

Such a smart mouth. "Let him go."

She glanced down at Knox. "Do I have permission to put him in his place again if he doesn't behave?"

"Shihan?" Ronin prompted.

Knox gritted out, "I won't engage her."

"Wise move." She stood and bowed to Ronin. "Sensei."

Ronin gestured to the petite woman, who failed to pull off an innocent look. "Knox, this is my sister, Shiori Hirano."

"Your sister? Fuck me."

"No, thank you." She sniffed. "I never fuck guys I can top."

"Shiori. Knock it off," Ronin warned.

Knox's gaze zeroed in on Shiori's plain black belt. "What's your rank?"

"Rokudan."

"You outrank me?"

"Yes, which is why I didn't want to engage you."

"You don't have that option with me." Ronin kept his eyes locked on hers. "Get dressed and meet me in the second-floor conference room. You'll know which one I mean. It's missing a window from when I threw a chair through it after your conversation with my girlfriend yesterday." He spun on his heel and exited the room.

Ronin made it halfway down the hall before Knox caught up to him. "I guess I expected your sister would look more—"

"Like a fire-breathing dragon lady?"

"No, more like you. Although I see the resemblance in your combative attitudes."

He bit back a snarl.

"Are you in the right frame of mind to deal with her?"

"Probably not. But it's been a long time coming." Years. Since everything that had gone down with Naomi.

Knox set his hand on Ronin's shoulder. "Then I'll stick around and run interference."

"Not necessary."

"I insist. You're a powder keg and she's a match. The dojo has sustained enough damage in the last day."

"Good point."

They stopped in the conference room. The window hadn't been replaced, but he'd cleaned up the mess.

"Any luck tracking Amery down today?"

Ronin shook his head. "Molly wouldn't talk to me. The state of Amery's apartment indicated she'd be gone for a few days."

"How'd you get into her place?"

"I've got a key."

"A key," Knox repeated. "As in . . . you two exchanged keys? Does she have access to your penthouse?"

"Yes."

"Jesus. We need to change the security codes to the building right away."

"No. I want her to be able to get to me. It'll show I trust her."

"Why should she trust you? When you weren't honest with her about anything?"

At the comment, Ronin turned to face Shiori, leaning in the doorway, still wearing her gi. "You're ballsy enough to speak of honesty to me?"

She tsk-tsked. "How quickly you've forgotten the importance of discretion." She gave Knox a haughty *be gone with you* gesture.

"Knox stays."

"We don't bring outsiders into family business."

"Guess you broke that rule when you introduced me to Naomi and fucked up my life. I trust Knox implicitly, and he might just be the only thing keeping me from killing you."

Knox leaned forward, blocking her from Ronin's sight. "Not helping. Take it down a notch."

Shiori sidestepped Knox and sat at the end of the table. "Don't feign surprise that you forced my hand and my appearance in Denver by insisting that the company hire your latest squeeze."

"I didn't force anything. I provided the name of a qualified designer for a project you discussed with me months ago. You want me to take an interest in the company, and when I do, you still question my motives."

She steepled her fingers. "So your interest in this specific Okada project is your way of telling me you're considering taking the reins?"

"That's always been your dream, not mine," Ronin stated. "How long are you here?"

"Undecided."

"I didn't think Grandfather let you out of his sight."

"You wouldn't know, since you haven't been around both of us together for a long time, have you?"

Zing. He deserved that. "Did you arrive with an entourage?"

"Just Jenko. He insisted on checking the security at the Ritz since I've leased the penthouse for the foreseeable future. He also interviewed potential security specialists, should I require one. I doubt that'll be necessary, and I'm looking forward to a little breathing room."

Jenko, Shiori's bodyguard, wasn't employed by the family company, Okada; therefore, he didn't answer to their grandfather. Hiring the former Sumo wrestler was one of the few things she'd done against their patriarch's wishes. "Jenko won't remain in Denver with you?"

A look of sorrow flashed in her eyes. "He has a wife and daughter. It's not fair to ask him to be away from them indefinitely." She inhaled a calming breath. "Look, I'll admit I didn't arrive in Denver with good intentions toward Amery. But I did have good intentions toward *you*, Ronin. I wanted to see if you were being taken advantage of by this woman."

"Because I'm such a fucking idiot and an easy mark when it comes to women?"

"No. I'm really sorry for the way I handled it, okay?" Shiori picked at her fingernails, a nervous habit she'd had for years.

Ronin had no response for that.

"Putting aside our personal differences, I'll need a place to practice while I'm in Denver. May I have your permission to train here, in whatever capacity best suits the dojo?"

"Who are you training with in Tokyo?"

"Masaman. A protégé of your sensei. The best I could get."

As far as Ronin knew, he was the last student his sensei had consented to teach—and that'd been twenty-two years ago. "In your defense, he's never taken a woman as a pupil."

"That seems to be a tradition you're following."

"Wrong. I have female students."

"Ah. But do you have any female instructors?"

"No."

Shiori cocked her head. "Because you don't feel women are as qualified to teach as men?"

Ronin did not want to get into a gender-equality argument with his sister.

But you can admit she has a point.

"I've not had any women apply for an instructor's position."

"But you do have female students at black belt level you could've moved up?" she pressed.

"A few. But like I said, none of them have expressed interest."

"Perhaps they're afraid to be the first to break the Black Arts glass ceiling. Along those lines, what is the protocol for my visitor's status?"

"Having a higher-ranking belt than my Shihan hasn't come up before, so we don't have protocol in place. I'll discuss options with my instructors and let you know." Maybe he'd have his sister put her money where her mouth was and assign her to teach classes.

"Thank you." She stood. "I'm not returning to Japan until things are settled between us. I screwed up. I've apologized. I don't expect immediate forgiveness, but I do expect you to acknowledge that the person you're angriest with is . . . yourself."

She walked out, regal as a warrior queen.

Unbelievable. His pesky little sister still had the ability to get under his skin.

Knox cleared his throat.

"What?"

"I hear you muttering. And not to be a dick, but I agree with your sister. While she stirred the pot, the shit stew that was already in it was all yours."

A sense of self-loathing rose again. Ronin closed his eyes.

"Let it go, my man. You can sort things out with Amery when she returns from wherever she's gone. Don't you always preach to control the things you can and ignore the rest? You can't control this."

"I'm a postulating asshole sometimes, aren't I?"

Knox grinned. "Only on the days of the week ending in Y."

IT'D been one week since Ronin had seen Amery.

One week.

Seven fucking days without a word from her.

He hadn't gone back to her loft. But he hadn't stopped calling her once an hour. His way of letting her know he thought of her every waking hour of his day.

Then maybe you should leave a message so she'll call you back.

"Ronin?"

He turned away from brooding out his office window and faced Deacon. "Hey. What's up? I didn't think you were coming in today."

"I hadn't planned on it. But I got some bad news yesterday."

"What's going on?"

Deacon ran his hand across his bald head and sighed. "You know my grandfather died a few months back and his estate is in limbo. My dad's been trying to mediate all this inheritance shit between his brother and sister. My aunt hired an attorney, which we all expected, and he's scheduled a meeting for next Thursday afternoon."

Ronin's gaze sharpened. "That's the night you're scheduled for a bout with Alvares Curacao."

"I know. And if the meeting were in Denver, it wouldn't be an issue. But it's in San Antonio. My dad . . ." Deacon started to pace. "He's had a rough go of it. On top of losing his father, he's dealing with his greedy siblings, who care only about the money they feel is owed to them as their birthright."

Deacon came from money. Old Texas oil money. So the legal summons wasn't something he could ignore, especially when his participation in MMA fights was more of a hobby. Their family situations were similar only in that they both had more money than they could possibly ever spend.

"Look, I'm really sorry—"

"No worries, Deacon. Be there for your dad. How much time off will you need?"

"I'll leave on Tuesday morning and take a late flight back on Sunday. In addition to putting you in a bind with missing the fight, that leaves four days' worth of classes uncovered."

"We can combine classes. I'll move Jon up to instructor level. Probably time I did that anyway."

"Fine, but four students in my Friday class are testing for black belts next week, remember? I don't have to be there to test them, but I promised to extend class time so they could work on techniques, and that requires an instructor."

Ronin reached for the printout with the month's class schedules. "Can we push testing back until next month?"

Deacon shook his head. "It's already been postponed once. These students have been working hard for the last year. I don't wanna disappoint them."

Since Ronin preferred to run his martial arts studio with a small staff of instructors, something like this could upend his system.

He glanced up. "There is one option. Since it doesn't appear my sister plans to leave Denver anytime soon, she could fill in."

"Will Shiori feel that's beneath her?"

"If she practices here, she's under my leadership. She'll do what I tell her." Ronin noticed Deacon's rigid posture. "Don't tell me both you and Knox have an issue with her?"

"Nope, not me. She pushes Shihan's buttons something fierce.

You've been . . . distracted the past week, but it's taken me, Ito, and Zach to keep them from takin' their issues to the mat."

Distracted was an impartial way of putting it. Ronin had been worthless this past week. Angry, melancholy, on edge—and those were the good days. His instructors hadn't mentioned the chair-throwing incident nor questioned Amery's absence.

"Anyway, I'll get outta your hair. I just wanted to let you know what was up."

"I appreciate it. If anything changes and you need more time in Texas, take it."

"Thanks, Ronin." Deacon stopped in the doorway and turned around. "Look. If you ever need to talk—"

"Yeah, yeah, I get that I can call you."

Deacon looked horrified. "Fuck that. I was gonna tell you to call Knox because he can be such a girl about that kinda emotional shit. But if you wanna flat-out forget your troubles? Call me. I've got a case of Jägermeister and VIP access to Jiggles Strip Club."

Ronin managed a smile. "I'll keep that in mind."

For the next hour, he dealt with dojo business, including trying to find a replacement fighter for the bout Thursday night. Normally he didn't mix with other dojos, but in the last couple months, he'd refereed events run by Alvares "Blue" Curacao, an MMA fighter who owned ABC, a Brazilian jujitsu dojo. Blue had proven himself different from the other Brazilian jujitsu practitioners in the area, and Ronin respected the man to the point they'd discussed bringing in ABC as part of Black Arts. He and Blue had met privately to talk about possible options before they each brought it up with their instructors. So not supplying a fighter for the main bout, especially against Blue, would give the impression that Black Arts didn't have a qualified fighter besides Deacon.

Why don't you just admit it? You don't have a qualified professional fighter.

Fuck that. He'd figure something out.

Feeling at loose ends in nearly every aspect of his life, he called Amery's cell phone for the tenth time and hung up when it kicked over to voice mail. He was getting tired of her dodging his calls.

That's because she's done with you.

With the voices in his head wreaking havoc, he decided to pursue a more productive mind-set, like spending time in his Zen garden, when two knocks sounded on his office door. "Come in."

Martel, his UPS courier, bounded in. "Afternoon, Mr. B. How's it hangin'?"

"Low. You?"

"High. I start my vacay tomorrow. A week in Cancun." He thrust the cardboard box at Ronin. "Same-day delivery. Signature required on this one."

He signed the electronic pad and missed the rest of what Martel said because the package was from Amery. He squinted at the block lettering. Jesus. Even her writing looked angry. Especially the PERSONAL notation in the corner—angrily outlined three times with red marker.

As soon as the door shut, he used a carton cutter to slice through the tape. His heart raced as he folded back the cardboard edges and yanked out the bubble wrap.

His heart stopped when he saw the contents: two coils of black rope. The rope he'd left at her place the last time they were together. The rope he'd seen on her floor last week.

He upended the box on his desk. No note. Just the rope. And a pair of scissors.

She'd made her message loud and clear. She wanted no part of him. No reminders of their time together. She was cutting all ties.

Ronin dropped into his chair and stared at the black bundles as fury hit him as hard and fast as a freight train. His current anger-management program—beating the fuck out of a speed bag—wouldn't dampen his rage this time. He needed something else. Something . . . real.

A plan took shape in his mind. It would require every bit of his focus, leaving him no time to think about anything—or anyone—else, which is exactly what he wanted.

After he retaped the box and shoved the package under his desk, he hit the intercom for the training room. "Shihan? A word in my office, please."

Knox walked in a few minutes later. "What's up?"

"Did you talk to Deacon today?"

Knox uncapped his water bottle and drank deeply before answering. "No. I saw him, but he didn't stop to talk. Is something wrong?"

"He's got family stuff going on next week in Texas, so he pulled out of the fight Thursday night."

"Shit." Knox flopped into the office chair across from the desk. "How much money is tied up in the event?"

"Twenty grand."

"Shit," he said again. "This is why we've stayed out of the fight-promotion business."

"I'm aware of that. I'm also aware that Blue runs events like this all the time, and we'll come across as unprofessional if we can't pull it together." Ronin didn't give a damn about the money. The dojo saving face was all that mattered to him.

"You worried advance ticket sales will drop off when we change the fight matchup?"

"Some. But that's why there's the disclaimer about fight matchups being subject to change without notice."

Knox gave him a contemplative look. "The easiest thing would be to drop the last bout altogether since it's the only pro matchup."

"We're not dropping the main bout. I've already got someone who can fight in Deacon's place."

"Who?"

"Me."

"Hilarious. And here I thought you'd lost your sense of humor in the last week."

"I'm not joking."

Knox's smile died, and he changed into that steely-eyed former soldier. "Fuck that, Ronin. You don't have to do this."

"Not a matter of have to. It's a matter of want to."

"With all the shit that's happened in the last week, you are not in the right frame of mind. Let me represent the dojo."

Ronin leaned forward and didn't bank the rage fueling him. "Are you suggesting, Godan, that I don't have the skills to adequately represent the dojo I own?"

"Jesus, no. I'm questioning why you're doing this."

"Because I can." Ronin shoved the updated schedule at him. "Find replacement instructors for the times I circled. I'll give Shiori a heads up and let her know she's taking over Deacon's classes."

Knox opened his mouth to argue but thought better of it. He asked, "What else can I do?"

"Call Clint. He owes me a favor."

"Maybe this is obvious, but Clint is retired from the UFC because his body couldn't take it anymore. And he's five years younger than you."

Ronin shrugged. "One fight won't kill me. But I'm not an idiot. I've no doubt I'll feel every one of my thirty-eight years and then some after the final bell rings."

"How long has it been since you've stepped foot in the ring?"

Hadn't been that long ago, but he wasn't sharing that information. "Between you and Clint . . . figure out a training regimen that will get me up to speed fast because Blue is one tough motherfucker."

Knox stood. "I wouldn't be doing my job if I didn't question your decisions."

"Noted."

After Knox left, Ronin headed to the training room.

Fuck finding Zen.

Six nights later

Fight night was a blur.

Ronin remembered getting in the ring believing he was the most impervious motherfucker on the planet. Acting like he'd bring the pain. Welcoming the physical punishment Blue Curacao would dish out.

But somewhere in the middle of the second round, Ronin's focus shifted. He fought back with minimal effort. He embraced the feeling of numbness after his opponent's blows connected with his body. Every drop of blood he lost cleansed him. Everything around him dropped into slow motion, so when he saw the powerful right cross headed for his jaw, he didn't bother to block it.

He hit the mat and the lights went out.

People poked and prodded him. He answered their questions by rote. He'd been in this situation enough times that he gave them the responses they were looking for. He made it out of the ring on his own steam and promptly passed out in the locker room with only Shiori and Knox as his witnesses.

"Ronin."

Go away.

"You managed to walk in here on your own after the medical team checked you out, so I know you can hear me."

Ronin opened his eye—the one that wasn't swollen shut. "What?"

"You're smiling? Are you actually happy that you got your ass kicked?"

He choked out a simple "Yes."

"Why? Brother, he knocked you out."

"Not until the third round." He slowly pushed up from the cot. Fuck. Every inch of his body hurt. The sadistic side of his brain smugly said, *Good.* The part of his brain with the pain receptors responded by kicking into overdrive.

"Why are you wearing that scary-ass smile?" Knox demanded.

"Getting beat means it's a perfect setup for a rematch. I'll probably have to fight a few other bouts to pump up interest."

"Bullshit," Shiori spat. "You said one fight, Ronin. *One.*"

"I changed my mind."

Knox shook his head. "Sensei, you're not a pro fighter. These twenty-something guys will be gunning to kick the shit out of an eighth-degree jujitsu master."

"They're welcome to try." Ronin chugged half a bottle of water and spit it in the bucket. "I'm going home."

"You had a knockout, which equals concussion," Shiori snapped. "You need to go to the ER."

"This wasn't my first fight. I've lived the doctor's advice: rest, painkillers, and alternate ice and heat for swelling." Ronin pushed to his feet and swayed.

Shiori caught him. "See? You are not all right."

"I just got up too fast." He tried to sidestep her, but she wouldn't let go. "What?"

"Are you doing this because of her?"

Ronin got right in her face. "You don't get to play that card. Ever." He dropped his arm. "My personal life is off-limits to you. Period."

"Not when you are beaten and bleeding."

"When I'm beaten and bleeding is the only time I really feel alive."

Shiori looked like she was ready to cry.

"Don't," he warned sharply. "I'm fucking fine."

"No, you're not." She took a deep breath and glanced at Knox before meeting his gaze again. "Ronin. Sensei. We can't stand by and watch you do this to yourself."

"Then don't watch. Because this is just the beginning."

He headed down the hallway, ignoring their shouts calling him back.

CHAPTER TWO

Five weeks later

BRIGHT lights, loud voices, a cacophony of noises bombarded him from every angle, jarring him from the blissful darkness where the pain had been dormant.

"Status."

"Thirty-eight-year-old male. In and out of consciousness. Symptoms indicate possible concussion. Lacerations on the face. Contusions on several parts of the body. Possible patella fracture. Possible cracked ribs."

"From a car accident?"

"No, from a mixed martial arts fight."

Light flashed across his face. "If he won, I'd hate to see the guy who lost."

"No kidding. Be warned: He's disoriented and volatile."

"Put him in the back while we wait for an opening in the diagnostic rooms."

"You got it, Doc."

The noise faded and his stomach roiled. This time he couldn't stop it.

"He's gagging. Get a bucket."

Hands tilted his head, and he expelled the contents of his stomach.

Then he went under again.

"MR. Black, can you open your eyes?"

Ronin winced when he shook his head. Felt like his brain was grinding against the inside of his skull.

"Sorry. I have to do this. Hold him still."

Someone pried his eyelids open with a crowbar and tried to sear his retinas with laser beams. Tears streamed out the corners of his eyes and down his neck. He tried to twist away, but rough hands held him firm.

"Almost done."

White spots danced behind his lids even after he slammed them shut.

"Tell me the last thing you remember."

Everything had been so fuzzy—shrouded by the pain in his head. "I was nauseous."

"Before that?"

Being in the cage. Existing in that state where he focused on inflicting maximum damage on his opponent. Then being on his motorcycle. Racing toward . . .

"Sir?" the voice interrupted. "Try to think back. The last image you remember."

"I was in a tunnel."

"Like tunnel vision?"

"Yes."

"Suddenly bright light? Or very dim?"

"Both. I saw a pinpoint in the distance; then my peripheral vision blurred and became dark." He remembered the hardness pressing into his swollen knee and the cooling effects of the flooring on his forearms before everything went black.

"Do you recall where you were?"

He squeezed his eyes as if that would help him concentrate. Why couldn't he remember?

"Places? People?"

Wait. He'd banged on a door. Not the door to the dojo but a door in an alley. He'd had a sense of urgency. Of anxiety.

Amery.

His stomach twisted. What had he done? Last time he'd had a memory lapse like this . . .

He'd hurt her.

He frantically attempted to sit up; the center of his body seemed glued down. His arms and legs were useless. Jesus. Was he paralyzed?

He clenched his hands into fists. Beeping machines, unidentifiable clicking sounds, the murmur of voices surrounded him as he jerked to free himself.

"Mr. Black. Stay still."

"Why the fuck can't I move?"

"The EMTs had to strap you down because you were agitated."

"Where am I?"

"Denver Memorial's emergency room."

"Undo the straps."

"I'm sorry. We have to keep you immobilized for your protection and ours."

He tried to roll his shoulders. "I didn't ask to be admitted. You can't hold me against my will."

"Ronin. Stop fighting." Cool hands pressed against his cheeks. "Please."

His heart raced and his body stirred. "Amery. Are you okay?"

"I'm better off than you are." Then her soft fingers smoothed his hair back. "Stay still."

Immediately, Ronin relaxed.

"You seem to have the magic touch," the persistent voice remarked.

"There's a first time for everything," Amery said.

"I need to check on something. You'll be okay staying with him?"

"Yes."

Her gentle touches calmed him but stirred his confusion. "Why are you here?"

"You asked me to come."

"Even after I—"

"Showed up in the dead of night, bloodied, beat-up, and confused? When I haven't heard from you in six weeks? Yes."

"Did I . . ." He swallowed hard. "Hurt you?"

"Physically? No. But seeing you like this?" She paused. "That definitely hurts. Especially since I don't think you'll remember much of what you've said tonight."

Even when he tried to open his eyes, he couldn't. He needed to see her. To make sure he wasn't dreaming. "I might not remember the past few hours, but I do remember the past few weeks have been hell without you."

"Is this where I point out it took a blow to the head before you reached out to me?"

"You reached out to me first. With that peace offering."

"Stop. You're making no sense." She trailed her fingertips across his hairline and down his temple. "I can't imagine how much pain you're in. What can I do?"

"Don't go."

"I may not have a choice. Shiori is on her way."

"How'd she . . . ?"

"I called Knox. He contacted her."

A shard of pain lanced his brain, as if trying to cleave his head in two. He groaned.

"Don't try to talk. Just rest."

With her soothing continual touch, he drifted off again.

NEW voices by his bedside roused him.

"How did he get there after the injury?" a man asked.

"Apparently he drove his motorcycle."

"Impossible. There's no way this man was capable of operating a vehicle."

"You don't know my brother," Shiori retorted. "He can block out pain, bend it to his will, use it to his advantage."

"Determined man, is he?"

"Very."

"Unfortunately determination is no match for trauma to the head. I see you've requested your own physician?"

"Physicians. I've contacted the medical team I want assessing and treating him. Nothing gets done without my permission, understand?"

"I'm right fucking here, Shiori," Ronin interjected. "Don't talk about me like I'm in a goddamn coma."

"But you're not really here, are you? You're drifting in and out of consciousness, which is why someone needs to make these medical decisions for you."

It took too much effort to open his eyes and glare at her.

"I know better than anyone how you get when you're injured. Case in point—you're strapped down. The orthopedist hasn't been in, nor has the neurologist, nor the plastic surgeon."

"Why the fuck do I need a plastic surgeon?"

"There's a nasty gash above your eye. A split in your lip. Your nose is swollen. It might be broken again."

"Like I give a shit about how I look? Get. Out. I don't want—nor do I need—you here."

"Ronin." Amery's soft hand brushed his cheek. "You aren't

thinking straight if you believe your sister has an ulterior motive besides getting you the best medical care as soon as possible."

He must really be fucked up if he heard Amery defending Shiori.

"We're ready for him in X-ray," someone said.

"So what's it going to be?" Shiori asked.

"I'll let you make my immediate medical decisions, but not personal ones. Amery stays with me as long as she wants to."

"All right." Shiori kissed his cheek, then whispered in Japanese, "I only want what's best for you, brother."

"She's what's best for me."

WHEN Ronin woke up the next morning, he half expected to be in his bedroom, the events from the previous night some sort of bad dream. But he was in a hospital bed, hooked up to an IV with a cuff thing on his arm.

He had a vague recollection of being X-rayed head to toe. A chatty doctor providing running commentary as he stitched Ronin's head and lip. Another doctor forcing him to do leg lifts to gauge damage to his kneecap. Amery's hand in his as they wheeled him into a private hospital room. Then nothing as pain and consciousness faded away.

He blinked his bleary eyes. The shades were drawn, and the only light in his room came from the fixture above the sink. But that scant light bathed Amery in an ethereal glow.

"You're awake."

"Your beautiful face is the very best thing to wake up to."

"Beautiful. Right. I look like hell."

"Still brushing aside my compliments."

She moved closer. "I'm chalking them up to your muddled brain. What do you remember from last night?"

"The very last thing?" He frowned. "Did you really ask me how *I* liked being strapped down for a change?"

She smiled. "Yes. I also said I could see the appeal of binding from the other side."

"Evil woman."

"Just an opportunist." She pointed to the strap dangling from the bed frame. "Did they release your restraints, or did the ninja master manage to undo them by himself?"

"Sometime during the twenty million times the nurse poked me awake, she freed me." Ronin shifted his arm, and the movement caused a sharp pain in his shoulder. "How long did you stay?"

"Until your pain drugs kicked in and you were down for the count. Knox gave me a ride home and moved your motorcycle into the back room. Which meant I had to stick around to tell Molly why your bike was there. I postponed a client meeting, changed out of my blood-spattered clothes, and grabbed these." She set his cell phone and his keys on the side table.

"Thank you for all that. But mostly thanks for coming back."

"I almost didn't." Amery ducked her head, and her strawberry-blond hair covered her face. When a drop of wetness landed on his arm, he realized she was crying.

"Baby. Can you look at me?"

She raised her head. Her blue eyes flashed a message of anger and fear. "Do you have any idea how terrifying last night was for me? Seeing you like that and then hearing you admit things were left unfinished between us? Dammit, Ronin. In the past five weeks, after you stopped calling, I assumed you were done with me."

"Done with you," he repeated. "Maybe I assumed after calling you sixteen times a day for seven days after you walked out on me and you didn't return a single phone call that *you* were done with *me*."

"You didn't leave a single message in all the times you called."

"And it never occurred to you to pick up the damn phone when it was ringing to see what I wanted?"

"I didn't know you'd called. After I left the dojo that day, I was in a daze. I charged my phone in my office while I finished up a few things. I didn't realize I didn't have it until three hours later, when I was on the road headed to North Dakota."

"You didn't have your phone for a week?" he asked skeptically.

"Evidently I didn't need it. I checked in with Molly once a day on the office line. When I called my cell voice mail, I didn't have a single message from you. In seven days."

His eyes searched hers. "If I would've left a message?"

"I would've returned your call."

"Instead you got pissed off and returned my ropes."

"Not even that garnered me an enraged visit from Master Black. Anytime before when I'd pissed you off, you showed up loaded for bear."

"Baby." He unwrapped her fingers from the metal side rail and kissed her knuckles. "We've both got a lot to learn when it comes to communication."

"Agreed."

"But thank you for reaching out to me."

She frowned. "What do you mean?"

"The package you sent."

"I sent the ropes weeks ago."

"No. The box I got yesterday. With a peace lily and an invite to come by so we could talk. I'm pretty sure that's how I got it in my head to show up at your place last night."

"Ronin . . . I didn't send you anything like that."

They stared at each other. "Somebody wanted to get us talking again."

"Now you babbling about a peace offering makes sense. But that wasn't—"

Three knocks sounded on the door, and a guy in a white coat walked in.

"Mr. Black, I'm Dr. Dainsworth. Your neurologist."

"I hope you're here with good news."

"I guess that depends on your idea of good." He glanced around the dark room. "Still having light-sensitivity issues?"

"Yes."

"It might take as long as a week before you're back to normal. If it takes any longer than that, you'll need to contact my office so I can coordinate with an ophthalmologist for additional testing." The doctor gave Amery a once-over, and Ronin bristled. Mostly because the young blond doc was the type of man Amery found attractive.

But her eyes were firmly focused on him.

"Can I speak freely? Or would you prefer we discuss my concerns in private?"

Amery released his hand. "I'll wait outside."

Ronin snatched her wrist before she'd even moved. "I want you to stay."

That shocked her.

"Why don't you both have a seat." The doctor pointed to the small table and chairs in the corner. "I'll be right back."

Ronin gritted his teeth from the sharp sting zipping down his spine when he simply rotated his body to set his bare feet on the cold tile.

"Do you need help?"

He tamped down his automatic response that he wasn't a fucking invalid. "No." As soon as he put pressure on his bruised knee, he nearly stumbled.

She said, "Careful," but didn't touch him.

Goddammit, he hated—fucking hated—how he shuffled the twenty feet between the bed and the chair like an old cripple. There wasn't a part of his body that didn't hurt.

Suck it up and be a man.

Ronin caught sight of himself in the mirror above the sink. His right eye was discolored red and purple. He had a bandage above his left eyebrow covering stitches. Bruises dotted his jaw. His bottom lip was busted up and also sported stitches. In his younger years, he would've shown pride in his injuries. Now? He was disturbed Amery had seen him this way.

Easing himself into the chair caused the hospital gown to ride up. To make his humiliation complete, Amery draped a blanket across his lap.

Dr. Dainsworth returned and sat on the rolling stool, getting in Ronin's face. "I did my homework on you, Sensei Black. Impressive that you've achieved the eighth-degree black belt level at your age. Aren't most jujitsu practitioners who reach Hachidan status in their fifties?"

"Yes. But my sensei in Japan factors other things besides mastering techniques into advancement. The belt system in Japan is different from the U.S."

"Understood."

"I imagine my sister contacted you because you're . . . ?" Ronin purposely left that vague to see how this doctor would fill in the blanks.

"A neurologist specializing in treating sports-related brain trauma for athletes who have a documented history of repetitive cranial injuries." He raised an eyebrow. "Need my other qualifications? Medical degrees? Internships? I can have my secretary send you a copy of my latest article in the *New England Journal of Medicine* on the four years of research I compiled on potential long-term effects of brain injuries in mixed martial arts fighters as compared to boxers."

"So you're the best of the best."

"Yes. And like you, I reached that level at a relatively young age, also due to dedicating my life to my studies."

Ronin respected warranted cockiness. "Hit me with the questions."

"If you had to guess, how many times would you say you've been knocked unconscious either during a match or in practice?"

"I honestly don't know."

"Because it's too high a number to count?"

He nodded.

The doctor jotted something down in Ronin's chart. Then he asked, "How many times have you been knocked out in the last month?"

"Twice." Ronin didn't look at Amery, but he felt her staring at him.

"Did you seek medical attention after the first incident?"

"No."

"What was different this time? Did you feel your injuries were more severe?"

"Not especially. I probably wouldn't have sought help on my own. But I had some . . . confused moments and showed up on Amery's doorstep and she . . ."

"Had no choice but to call an ambulance when you passed out on my floor," she finished.

Dr. Dainsworth focused on Amery. "Did you see him after his first concussion? Were his reactions and behavior similar?"

She shook her head. "We broke up a little more than six weeks ago."

The doctor directed his shrewd gaze to Ronin. "Did this breakup directly contribute to your need to compete on a more physical level?"

Here was a moment of truth between them. Ronin reached for Amery's hand. "Yes. Being in the cage forced my focus away from what was going on in my personal life."

The sound of the doctor scrawling seemed unbearably loud in the quiet room.

"Look. I'll be brutally honest here." The doctor's eyes searched Ronin's face. "You've suffered two major head injuries in the past four weeks. Have you heard of second-impact syndrome?"

"Of course."

"So you know that a second impact to the brain, while you're still symptomatic from the first traumatic concussion, can result in cerebral edema, brain stem herniation, cerebral hemorrhaging, and even death?"

"I'm aware of the risks, Doctor."

"But you disregarded them. Why?"

"Physical pain is something I know how to deal with." Even though Ronin wasn't about to start discussing emotional pain with the doctor, the topic seemed to hang in the air like a foul odor.

Walking like a cripple, complaining about your head hurting—why don't you just start crying so you come across as a total fucking pussy?

"After studying your CAT scan," the doctor continued, "your MRI, and your PET scan, my recommendation for treatment hasn't changed. Before I tell you what that is, I have to ask: If you were aware that one of your students had these same types of brain injuries in the same time frame, what would your recommendation be for recovery?"

"Medical tests. Rest. Observe the practices but zero physical participation until cleared by a medical professional and after all the risk factors for returning to the discipline were weighed."

"So you'll enforce that rule with your students but don't abide by the same rule yourself?"

Ronin hadn't seen that one coming. He glanced over at Amery, expecting to see a smirk, but she was horrified. "Amery—"

"Don't," she snapped. "Shut up and listen to your doctor for a change."

Fuck. "So what is the verdict?"

"If I thought you'd adhere to my edict of no more MMA-style fighting—ever—I'd issue it." The doctor furrowed his brow. "But I've dealt with your type for years—physical contact is in your blood. For you personally, it's a way of life."

"And my livelihood," Ronin pointed out.

"Teaching is your livelihood," Amery retorted. "Not fighting."

Being a fighter—whether in the ring himself or teaching

others, was what defined him. Who would he be if he didn't have that?

"My recommendation is one more week of rest. During that time, while you're working on physical therapy for your knee, you can start gentle stretches to maintain your flexibility. Then for the next month, no body-to-body impact. That means zero. If you can teach without physical demonstration, then return to teaching. But no jarring moves either against the mat, the heavy bag, or another person."

A month wandering around his dojo doing goddamn nothing besides observing?

"Then I'll see you in my office and we'll run follow-up tests to see what level of activity you can safely resume."

Despite the panic rising inside him, he managed a cool, "Even then, what are the chances my physical activity will be limited?"

"I guarantee if you don't follow my instructions for at least a month, it'll affect your recovery time. But beyond that? Time will tell. The best thing you can do as a teacher is to lead by example. Show your students that head injuries are serious—no matter what level of martial arts mastery you achieve. Don't risk your life and your long-term health because of pride."

"When can I go home?"

"Tomorrow. You'll need someone to stay with you, at least for the first few days. I'll call in a month's meds to the pharmacy on file. Any further questions?"

"No."

The doctor stood. "Give yourself time to heal. I've seen guys in car accidents who didn't sustain these levels of injury." He motioned for Amery to walk with him to the door.

What the fuck was he saying to her?

Take it easy. Getting angry put more pressure in his head. He closed his eyes. The thought of staying in this place another minute literally made him nauseous. He forced even, slow breaths to try to keep his heart rate steady so it wasn't obvious on the monitor just how much he felt like a caged animal.

"Ronin?"

"What?" When he realized he'd snapped at her, he said, "Sorry. It's just not what I wanted to hear."

"I get that, but on some level you had to expect this." She reached over and swept his hair from his eyes. "So are you going to ask me to stay with you and take care of you while you recover?"

No fucking way. She'd seen too much of his weak side already. "I don't expect that from you."

"Then why did you show up at my door?"

His soul screamed, *Because I need you,* but his mouth couldn't force the words out. What if she believed the only reason he said that was because he required a caretaker for the short term? What he wanted—no, what he needed—from her was far, far more than that. So why couldn't he tell her?

"Don't pull that silent macho attitude on me. We both know you need me there. We both know my presence wouldn't be like hiring a home health aide." She paused. "But that would be easier for you, wouldn't it?"

"Infinitely."

"You are seriously pissing me off, and I'm about three seconds from walking out the door for good."

"Please don't." Ronin grabbed her hand before she ran off. "Come here." He relaxed when she threaded her fingers through his.

"Why are you trying to shut me out?"

Ronin turned his face to the wall.

"Hey." She pinched his chin and slowly turned his head back toward her. "Last chance. Ask me."

"Fine. Please stay with me. I need you so goddamn much it scares the shit out of me, okay?" Ronin locked his gaze to hers, trying to retain some control in this situation. "But if you agree, you'll be in my home and in my bed for as long as my recovery takes."

"That's not—"

"Negotiable, Amery. Period."

She smiled. "See? That wasn't so hard, was it?"

Jesus. He'd fallen right into that.

"I'm practicing my bedside manner and telling you to get back in bed and rest."

Like hell. He'd let her take care of him at his place, but he was getting out of here today as soon as possible—even if he had to fucking crawl.

After he'd situated himself in bed, he said, "You don't have to hover."

Amery looked torn. "You sure?"

"Yeah." He touched her cheek. "Thank you for seeing past my bullshit and sticking around today."

"You're welcome. But as soon as you're out of here, we're having a talk about all the bullshit I can't see past, the things you kept from me that forced me to walk away from you in the first place." Amery kissed his wrist. "I'll see you later."

After she left, he picked up the phone.

CHAPTER THREE

DURING their conversation in the hospital, Amery had felt like the lines of communication had been reopened and Ronin wanted to establish trust and honesty between them.

But apparently that honesty didn't include sharing his plan to escape from the damn hospital.

The stupid, stubborn man needed to be hog-tied to his goddamn bed—and not for sexy fun and games. Imagining him in a straitjacket, his ankles bound to the bedposts and a gag in his mouth, didn't cool Amery's fury even a little bit.

As soon as the elevator doors opened to the penthouse, she barreled down the hallway. "Ronin Black, you lying asshole. Get your butt out here right now before I come in there and kick it!"

"No need to shout."

She whirled around and saw him reclined in the far corner of the dark living room. "What is wrong with you? Why did you sneak out of the hospital?"

"I left because I wasn't getting any rest anyway. I need the solitude of my own surroundings to help me heal."

"And a phone call informing me of that was too much to ask?"

"I wasn't thinking straight." He sighed. "The food sucked. I felt like I was suffocating."

Amery studied his face, seeing the lie in it. "Then maybe you should've heeded your doctor's advice after your freakin' head injury and stayed put for another day." She balled her hands into fists. Had *anything* changed with him? Or would he continue to feed her half-truths because she'd always swallowed them without question?

Fuck. That. "Who drove the getaway car? Not Knox, because he was with Shiori at the hospital. He was just as spitting mad as your sister."

"Did you go to the hospital?"

"Not after I got the angry phone call from her accusing me of aiding in your escape. I came straight here. Who helped you?"

"Zach. For the record, he wasn't happy either."

"Let me guess. You pulled that *I'm your sensei* bullshit."

"Pretty much."

"So why didn't he stick around?"

"Because I made him drop me off in the alley."

"Unfuckingbelievable. Why aren't you in bed?"

Ronin dropped his head into his hands. "Because my bedroom was too goddamn far away. Head injury, dislocated kneecap, sore ribs. Who knew walking that extra five hundred feet would be so difficult?"

She forced herself to quell her anger and reminded herself she was here to take care of him. "You're lucky I hadn't shredded the keycard you gave me."

"I didn't change the codes because I was holding out hope that you'd show up and ream me for being an ass—kind of like you're doing right now."

"I haven't even started to ream you."

"It'll have to wait. I need you to do something for me."

"What?"

"Inside the coat closet, on a hook above the light switch, is a key ring. Can you grab it?"

"Where's the coat closet?"

"End of the hall past the elevator."

In all the times Amery had been in Ronin's place, she'd never noticed the pastoral mural on the wall wasn't just a framed picture but a sliding door. She found the keys and brought them to him.

He selected a key with a circular end. "Below the call button on the elevator panel is a small open circle. This key fits it. Turn it until the word *lock* appears in red letters on the panel."

"And I'm doing this . . . why?"

"I'm locking the elevator car up here so no one else can get in."

"Good thing I planned to stay over." After locking them in, she returned to the living room to see Ronin hunched over, his head in his hands again. She crouched next to him. Even lying strapped on the gurney in the hospital, Ronin hadn't seemed this helpless. "Tell me the truth about how you feel or I swear I'm calling an ambulance."

When he whispered, "I'm in agony," she briefly closed her eyes, knowing that admission probably hurt him as much as the actual head injury.

She ran her fingers through his hair and he winced at the contact. "Where are your painkillers?"

"On the kitchen counter."

"I'll get them." After he downed the pills, she said, "Stretch out. I'll get a pillow and a blanket."

Ronin raised his head, and she saw it pained him. "There's not enough room for both of us on this couch."

"But I thought—"

"You said you'd be in my bed. I'm holding you to that."

"You are so stubborn. What if I roll over in the middle of the night and somehow hurt you?"

"It'll hurt me much worse if you're not right there beside me."

God. The man was relentless. "Stand up. I'll help you to your room."

Ronin was shaky and sweating by the time he rested against the platform bed. She eyed his clothes. Baggy athletic shorts and a baggier Denver Broncos jersey. "Where'd you get the clothes?"

"Zach brought them. Easy to get on."

"Let's hope they're easy to get off." She pulled the jersey, trying to free his arms.

Ronin murmured, "I love to get you off."

"Please focus."

"I am. Where I should be. Entirely on you."

She looked at him. Her stomach cartwheeled at the determination in his dark eyes.

"You're beautiful, inside and out. I've never had anyone in my life like you. I'd say I didn't realize that until it was too late and you walked out, but I knew it from the moment I met you."

Ronin Black saying that mushy stuff meant the pain pill had kicked in. "Hang on."

"That wasn't a lie when I told you the scar on your arm is the Japanese symbol for my name."

"I know. I only said that to hurt you."

"It worked." He briefly closed his eyes and shuddered. "I've been in fucking misery since you left."

"Hold still while I pull this over your head." Amery froze once she'd removed his shirt. Her first glimpse of the mass of bruises on his torso made her gut clench. "Oh, sweetheart. Look at you. Why did you do this to yourself?"

"Pain made me forget."

Just for a moment, she rested her cheek above his heart. "Crawl in before the pain meds knock you out."

He gritted his teeth and pulled himself onto the bed.

Amery curled up beside him, watching him closely until he'd fallen asleep.

But she was too keyed up to stare at the ceiling or to listen to him breathe. Happy as she was he was resting, the day's events had only muddied the waters and postponed their long-overdue conversation. Restless, she slipped out of bed and wandered through his apartment.

With the bright moon and the temperate night, she would've loved to sit by the pool. But with her luck, she'd screw up the elevator if she tried to get to the roof. So her entertainment choices were staring out the windows or watching TV.

She flipped through channels for what seemed like hours and then drifted off.

That's when the dreams started in again, and she didn't have the mental energy to fight to stay awake.

Some nights the dreams were so sex-fueled she rolled toward his side of the bed, searching for the warmth of his body, the scent of his skin, the familiarity of his hands. Only to feel an empty spot beside her. Then the longing was so potent she cried into her pillow upon awakening.

Some nights the dreams were sensual, featuring a cloaked figure wielding ropes. Although she never saw his face, Ronin's mesmerizing voice drifted from beneath the black hood. He praised her bravery and beauty as he tied her in elaborate configurations.

But tonight the dream took a different turn. She was naked and gagged, suspended above the floor.

Loud circus music distorted the silence. Then Ronin appeared with a flourish, dressed as a ringmaster.

She dangled above his head, out of reach, bound with black ropes that abraded her skin, but he didn't acknowledge her. Applause surrounded them, and he took bow after bow—deep, formal jujitsu bows. And every time he bent over to acknowledge the adoration, his mask would fall off. But just as quickly, a new one would appear.

It hit her like a fist to the stomach that she didn't know this man at all. She shouted at him to cut her loose, but with the gag blocking her mouth, no sound came out at all.

That's when she woke up. She blinked at the strobelike effect coming from the TV and had a flash of panic. Where was she?

Then she remembered.

Ronin's.

She ran a hand through her hair. Jesus. Talk about fucked up. Amery didn't buy into a lot of the new-age stuff, yet the dream unsettled her. The symbolism in it touched on too many of her fears about Ronin to merely be nonsensical.

Although she returned to his bedroom to check on him, she couldn't sleep with him. Not until they talked about everything that'd been hanging in the balance the last few weeks. So she slept on the couch.

THE next morning Amery crept into Ronin's bedroom to check on him. Judging by his peaceful expression, it looked like he did rest better in his own bed. Or maybe he'd doubled up on his pain pills. He hadn't moved from the bed in fourteen hours.

You needed it, baby.

Amery placed a soft kiss on his forehead and tiptoed from the room.

After brewing a pot of coffee, she wandered through the penthouse, unsure what to do with herself. That's how she found herself in front of the door to his practice room, wondering if he'd used it in the last few weeks. Prior to their split, Ronin had become more aggressive in his efforts to sway her into being his rope model for club demos.

She rested her forehead against the cool wood, her hand on the doorknob, her heart pounding crazily as the vivid memory of the last time she'd been in the practice room surfaced.

"*I want to do a suspension binding on you.*"

Amery had looked at Ronin with alarm. "Hanging me from hooks and stuff? Like a slab of meat?"

Then he wrapped his long, strong fingers around her throat and lower jaw, guaranteeing her undivided attention. "No. Like a piece of art. Like beauty suspended in time."

The intensity in his eyes had overwhelmed her to the point she'd felt her knees start to buckle.

"Do not move."

After she'd found her balance, Ronin had merely said, "You don't usually wilt at the first sign of heat, baby. Talk to me."

"I don't understand the suspension part of kinbaku. Why it appeals to you."

"Or why it frightens you," he countered.

Amery stared at him, this man who pushed her limits, this man who seemed to see right into the heart of her and refused to let her hide from herself. "It scares me to think I'll be dangling from the ceiling naked."

"I can assure you the riggings are completely safe. But it's not the riggings that worry you."

"No. It's the impersonal aspect of suspension that freaks me out. Maybe it's stupid to base that fear on the images I've seen in your bondage books."

"Neither how you feel or your fears are ever stupid." He gentled his hold and stroked his thumb along her jawline. "It's never impersonal when I bind you. The only way I can allay your fears is to show you. Will you trust me?"

She didn't respond immediately.

Ronin let her be indecisive. He didn't push. Or cajole. Or guilt her. He just continued to hold her in place, treating her to that maddeningly erotic stroking motion of his thumb.

Only when she softly said, "Yes," did his demeanor change.

He devoured her mouth, taking, conquering. He pulled away long enough to say, "Clothes off. Hair down."

She stripped slowly, needing the power in the moment when she bared herself to him.

As soon as she was naked, he centered his hand on her belly, signaling for her calmness. He murmured, "Beautiful," and placed a single, soft kiss on her lips. Then he stripped to the waist, laying his gi top over her clothing, another simple sign he'd shelter and protect her.

"Drop to your knees. Arms behind your back."

It was hard to focus on her breathing and letting the anticipation fill her when she heard a door being opened and closed, followed by a squeaking sound.

Then Ronin knelt behind her and stroked her hair. "I've decided against a full tsuri—suspension—today. I will need to blindfold you for the position."

Heart rate racing, mouth dry, she managed to nod.

Cloth covered her eyes. Ronin clasped her elbows and brought her to her feet. "I'm going to start binding you now." After planting a tender kiss on her shoulder, he positioned her arms into an elbow clasp behind her. He wound the rope from elbow to elbow, but somehow left her hands free.

A loop circled her neck, and she stiffened up.

"For the chest harness," he explained. "Your torso will bear the brunt of your weight, but the ropes will do the work."

Ronin's explanation calmed her, as did the constant contact of his skin to hers as he turned her body into his canvas. His intensity filled the room. He maneuvered her backward until her butt connected with something solid.

Then her upper arms were squeezed by ropes. As was her midsection. A thick band of rope pressed her lower belly all the way to her pubic bone, splitting into two sections that ran alongside the rise of her mound and became a single rope again, nestled in her butt crack.

"Ronin."

He was right there, touching her, nuzzling her neck. "I'm here."

"Are you going to fuck me when I'm suspended?"

His soft breath teased her ear, and she felt his lips curve against her cheek. "Of course. You are too beautiful for me to resist."

As soon as he stepped back, she felt ropes bisecting the flesh above her kneecap and high up on her thighs. Ronin pushed her forward slightly and began to add to the rope configuration across her back.

"Hold still. Here comes the lift."

Amery felt the tension in her arms and shoulders increase, gasping when she became airborne. The distinctive noise of a pulley echoed to her from both sides. Then her legs were raised simultaneously, and she was spread completely open until her knees were level with her hips.

The binding around her chest squeezed. The ropes on her legs pulled. Although her buttocks rested against a hard surface, the ropes held her in suspension.

Immediately, she squirmed, shifting her hips, and moved her shoulders, but all the movement did was allow the rope to dig deeper into her skin.

"Breathe. I'm here. Stay still. I won't leave you." His hands traveled the tops of her feet and the front of her shins, over her knees and her inner thighs, where he stuck two fingers to test the pressure of the ropes. Then his fingers followed the rope on her belly, stopping at her chest to twist her nipples. Ronin fit his palm over her neck as his other hand twined in her hair, pulling her head back so he could ravage her mouth.

The friction and pressure from the ropes was a constant throb. Ronin's kiss, packed with pride, gratitude, lust, and need turned the pain into pleasure.

Amery reveled in that moment, when Ronin's satisfaction surrounded her, flowed over her as warm as a summer breeze.

"My beautiful Amery," he breathed against her lips. "I need you to see yourself."

Ronin slipped off the bandanna.

She blinked against the sudden light. She first noticed the chest harness crisscrossing above and below her breasts, then the double wrap of rope around her rib cage, which changed into a thick section of braided rope snug against her belly. The tight binds on her thighs were attached to pulleys above her head. The object she was secured to by the ropes was a wooden X.

He was in front of her, stroking her cheek. "If I were to take a picture of you, I'd name it: Goddess—Bound Open.*"*

"Ronin."

He lowered to his knees.

Without another word, he worshipped her with his mouth and hands until she cried out and the climax swamped her. Then he shed his clothes and fucked her. Those rough and talented hands on her ass, his teeth on her nipples, his body driving into hers with heat and passion.

After he was spent, he murmured, "A better title is: Goddess—Bound Open. Goddess Mine.*"*

Amery shook herself out of the memory and returned to the living room. Even the flashbacks of the times she'd been bound by that sexy man made her knees weak, made her body heat, made her want him. Although she'd enjoyed that intense encounter, she still hadn't been convinced she could do a public demo. Her reluctance had fueled her fears, and those fears slipped in and distorted her dreams. During their weeks apart, she'd almost convinced herself she couldn't be with Ronin because she couldn't give him what he needed.

My, how things had changed. Maybe it made her needy, but she kind of liked that the infallible Ronin Black needed her right back.

"Morning, gorgeous."

She spun around to see a bare-chested Ronin leaning against the wall. She'd been so lost in thought she hadn't heard his approach. "Good morning. I'd ask how you're feeling, but the pinched look on your face pretty much gives it away."

The man didn't blink, but leveled her with his tough sensei stare.

Undeterred by it, she said, "I read the discharge papers. You're supposed to stay off of that knee, and you need to wear the brace all the time except during therapy."

He shuffled forward. "That's one doctor's opinion. I read online that other doctors advocate the more you work a sprained limb, the quicker the recovery time."

"I call bullshit on that. I know you weren't booting up your computer and checking medical facts last night. You were passed out."

"I'm curious as to why there's a blanket and pillow on the couch."

"Because that's where I slept."

His dark eyes pierced hers. "You were supposed to be in my bed," he said with a dangerous edge to his voice.

"We were supposed to talk, and until that happens between us, there's no chance anything else will." That blank mask covered Ronin's face, reminding Amery of her dream last night, and she suppressed a shudder.

"Fine. We'll talk now."

Ronin Black was back to being bossy and terse—big surprise.

When he eased himself onto the couch, she sat across from him.

"I don't know where to start."

Don't fall for his helpless act. "From the beginning. Why didn't you tell me?"

"About my family connections?"

She wouldn't put up with him hedging or answering her questions with another question. "About your status as a billionaire."

"I'm not a billionaire."

Amery looked at him suspiciously. "So you're not an heir to the Okada Food conglomerate in Japan?"

"I am, but I'm not."

"Well, that cleared things up a fuck ton. Thank you." She stood and started toward the elevator. "I can't do this."

"Do what? Give me a second to get my head on straight?"

She whirled around and faced him. "We were together for months prior to the breakup. So you've had plenty of time to devise a way to tell me, so it's not like I'm asking for something you aren't prepared for."

He played the silent card.

"Look, you don't need me here. You didn't want me here in the first place, and I pushed my way in, so it's best if I leave."

Ronin lifted his head and looked at her. "Don't go."

"Give me a reason why I should stay."

Very carefully, he pushed up from the couch and stepped into the path between her and the elevator. Curling his hand around the nape of her neck, he pulled her in, bringing her mouth to his for far too chaste a kiss. Then he rested his cheek to her temple. "Is that reason enough?"

"Ronin—"

"Look at me. I'm covered in sweat just from walking to the damn couch. Part of the reason I ignored medical advice and left the hospital when you weren't there? I hate that you're seeing me like this . . . like a fucking invalid. I'd rather take another beating than let you see me, even briefly, in a goddamn wheelchair." He broke eye contact.

Amery grabbed his chin and forced him to look at her. "Don't. I get you're injured. But you need to understand that I won't let you use it as an excuse; nor will I stick around if you keep avoiding the issues between us."

"I get that now. And I'll tell you everything—I will answer every single question you throw at me with complete honesty from here on out, but can we please sit down during this discussion?"

Then she felt like an ass. The man was wounded. "Pick a spot because we'll be there for a while."

He hobbled back to the couch.

After she sat next to him, she gave him a pointed look. "Start talking, billionaire baby."

He sighed. "Contrary to what my sister told you, I'm not a billionaire. The Okada empire is worth billions, but I'm not directly involved in it."

"Except for suggesting Okada use my company for a prime design gig."

"After you told me you were struggling financially, I tried to help you out because I know you're talented—not because we were lovers. But in my defense, I never knew Maggie Arnold followed through and contacted you."

"If she had, then you would've told me the truth?"

"Yes. But Shiori wields the corporate power. If she told Maggie to keep me out of the loop, she would. Why didn't you say anything to me when you were contacted?"

Oh, hell no. She was *not* taking the blame for this. "I signed a ton of nondisclosures. But that's not the point." She jabbed her finger at him. "You did nothing when I confronted you with the truth except treat me with disdain. There wasn't a single sign of the man"—*I'd fallen in love with*—"I knew when I showed up to talk to you. You'd never treated me like that, Ronin. It hurt. It scared me, and I lashed out."

"But you're not apologizing for your behavior," he said curtly.

"At the time, I wasn't sorry. Because you showed all the emotion of a goddamn parking meter." She inhaled and exhaled. "That's why I left. If you'd acted like you cared at all—"

"Five minutes after you ran out, I hurled a chair through the window. I'd gotten a good start on destroying the conference room when Knox stopped me."

Amery's mouth dropped open.

Ronin leaned forward slightly. "You think I'm scary when I'm trying to maintain control? Wrong. I'm scary when I lose it."

Holy. Shit.

"After you walked out? I. Lost. My. Fucking. Mind. Knox dosed me with an entire bottle of rum because passed-out drunk was the only way he could keep me from going after you. And trust me; you didn't want to deal with me in that state."

"I'm not being trite when I say thank you for telling me," she said softly. "I'm sorry for the shit I spewed. Some of what I said is a blur."

"What stung the most was your accusation that I'm a billionaire who plays at running a dojo." His hands clenched and unclenched. "Direct fucking hit to the one thing in my life I'm most proud of. Everything I've built? I've earned. Every drop of blood I lost fighting, every sketchy thing I did to make a buck went into building this business. The only exception?" He gestured to the room. "My living space."

"Your grandfather offered to pay for it?"

Ronin shook his head. "He'd set up several trusts to be paid at various milestones. I never touched a penny until the year I turned thirty-two. I'd been living in an office on the third floor for years—I didn't need more than a futon, a TV, and a hot plate."

Hearing him describing how he lived and looking around this place . . . It was hard to reconcile those two images and maybe even those two men.

"I'd convinced myself there was no shame in living a minimalist life. But something . . . clicked right around that birthday, and I decided I deserved to use some of the cash to create a living space with all the amenities. As soon as I withdrew money to pay the architect, I got a call from my grandfather."

"What did he expect from you?"

"It's not important now. But at the time? I had so much resentment toward him. He disrupted my business to attend to his, and he meddled in my personal life." He shoved his hand through his hair. "He manipulates Shiori with this same shit. She's been trying to prove herself worthy of taking over since she started working in the Okada offices at age twelve. She'll follow any instructions he gives her."

"Still?"

"She's been in Colorado for more than seven weeks. I don't know if she has an agenda—besides fucking up things between us." Ronin's eyes bored into hers. "That's not me refusing to take responsibility for not telling you about my familial ties, but what Shiori freely admitted to me." He reached for her hands. "I'm sorry I didn't tell you about any of this. But being an heir isn't something I'm proud of because I didn't earn it. I hate that you questioned your own judgment because of me. I know what that feels like."

"I'm sure you do."

"I'd really like to have you back in my life, because it's been empty without you in it." Ronin stroked her cheek. "I missed you."

"So you've said."

He lifted an eyebrow. "You don't believe me?"

"I think that you actually showing me this sweet side of you is the result of your concussion."

"I'd turn you over my knee for that smart-ass comment, but it hurts too fucking much."

"Speaking of . . . You are putting on that brace as soon as we're done talking," she warned him.

"When did you become such a hardass?"

"When you asked me to take care of you. That entails more than fluffing your pillows and administering your meds."

"Yes, ma'am. So now it's your turn to talk about fun family stuff." He blinked at her with confusion. "I know in the past I've been lax about remembering details of things you've told me, but I'm positive you never mentioned you were planning a trip back to North Dakota."

Amery's cheeks heated. "I needed to get away. And since money is tight—not that you'd understand what that's like—I couldn't jet off to a tropical island for a few days. I ended up in my car, heading north. Ironically enough, my father's thirty-fifth anniversary as an ordained minister was that weekend." She twisted her fingers. "I wasn't going to go. In fact, I'd told them I wouldn't be attending. Then all that happened with us, and I couldn't leave town fast enough." She looked away. "Pathetic, huh? That the only place I had to go was the last place I ever wanted to be."

"Jesus, Amery. How—"

"I'm glad I went if for no other reason than my brother, Aiden, got seventy-two hours' leave from the army and surprised our parents, which worked out for me because I didn't spend much one-on-one time with Mom or Dad. They were pleased that I showed up more for how it looked to my father's congregation and the community than from joy at seeing me. So it was a miserable trip with the exception of spending time with Aiden."

"Baby. I'm sorry."

"It is what it is."

After an uncomfortable moment, Ronin asked, "Are we done talking about this?"

"For now. But I reserve the right to ask other questions as they occur to me."

"Anything, anytime. From here on out, I'm an open book for you, Amery."

As much as she wanted to believe him, unless he proved that statement true, he was just paying lip service to what she wanted. "Good. But for now, you need to get back in bed. I'll grab the knee brace."

He slowly rose to his feet but still had to slap a hand on the wall to keep his balance as he started down the hallway.

His knee buckled, and Amery made it to his side before he hit the floor. "Sweetheart, you need to remember I'm here to help you."

"God, I missed hearing you call me that." Breathing hard, he sagged against the wall.

"Are you okay?"

"No. I'm exhausted. Feels like I got hit by a truck while running a marathon. But that's not the worst part."

Amery waited as his eyes roamed over her face.

"The worst part is, after six goddamn weeks without you, I can't even kiss you like I want to."

Maybe it was reckless, ignoring the warnings to take it slow, but she closed the gap between them and slid her hands up his chest to cup his jaw. Meeting his gaze, she said, "Then how about if I kiss you?"

Those soulful brown eyes watched her with hunger and relief. She swept gentle kisses across his upper lip, placing an extra-soft kiss on the stitches. Then she moved to the corners of his mouth and his lower lip, dipping her tongue inside that pouty lower swell. Keeping their eyes locked, she pressed her lips to his fully, letting the moment linger.

Watching his beautiful banged-up face, she knew her tenderness soothed more than just his bruised mouth. "Let's get you tucked in."

WHILE Ronin was resting, she raced to her loft and showered. In her overnight bag, she packed clothes, her laptop, a few client files, and her e-book reader.

At Target, she bought the bare necessities for groceries. Just because Ronin hadn't shown much of an appetite didn't mean it wouldn't suddenly appear. She picked up a bottle of over-the-counter painkillers, an extra ACE bandage, and two more ice packs. In the clearance section, she noticed a single wooden crutch. That would allow him to keep weight off his knee. She threw it and a pair of foam pads in the cart.

The universe smiled on her when she found a parking space close to the dojo. Trying to get all the bags carried to the front door in one load made for slow going.

She heard angry footsteps and looked up to see Knox bearing down on her.

"Goddammit, Amery, are you really too stubborn to ask for help?"

"I didn't know you were at the dojo today or I would've asked."

He took all the bags except her suitcase and the crutch. He didn't speak until they were in the elevator. "How is he doing?"

"He's in pain. And tired. Cranky. Frustrated with himself."

"I can't fucking believe he locked the damn elevator."

"Yes, you can. He's got way too much pride. Couple that with a head injury . . ."

Knox sighed. "Thank you for being there for him. I hope it means you're working things out."

"We're trying."

They switched elevators. The doors opened, and she immediately saw Ronin poke his head out of the den. "Did you invite my sister up too?"

"Don't get your panties in a twist, Ronin," Knox said. "I figured Amery would need provisions, so I waited her out. Not her fault."

"Provisions. Spoken like a true soldier."

When Ronin started down the hall, she said, "Not so fast. I brought you something."

"A crutch? Jesus, Amery. I'm not that bad off."

She marched up to him and shook the crutch in his face. "I imagine if you would've remained in the hospital like you were supposed to, they would've discharged you with a pair of these. You need to stop aggravating your knee. This, at least, will allow you to take the pressure off. I assumed you'd rather have this than my original idea of locking you up in your practice room."

His eyes bled from brown into the molten black that indicated he was turned on.

A curl of heat unfurled in her belly.

"Careful, baby. That sharp tongue, those fiery eyes, and your pouty lips are a potent combination."

Backtrack. Backtrack now. "Really? You're freshly out of the hospital, Ronin. You are injured. *In. Jured.* Get that through your head."

"The big head hears you. The little head sees you and wants you."

The man took advantage of her distraction and brushed his mouth across hers. His tongue even snaked in for a little taste before she snapped out of it.

She stepped back and fiddled with the crutch, attaching the foam pads to the top and the bar in the middle. "Try that."

He headed down the hallway. "You're right. Much easier. Thank you."

"This is not the first time you've used crutches."

"No, but I hope it's the last."

Knox was messing with his phone when they walked into the kitchen. Without looking up, he said, "I texted your sister and assured her you were being looked after and hadn't taken a header off the roof in your doped-up state."

"Since when are you and Shiori texting pals?"

"Since we realized we had the same goal. Trying to keep you out of the ring. Obviously, we failed on that front."

Amery hid her smile.

"I'm also here to inform you that I'd better not see you downstairs for several days. Trust that your staff can step up to the task of running the dojo in your absence." He pocketed his phone. "I'll let myself out. But I strongly suggest you don't lock the goddamn elevator again. I know you're an island and all that shit, but straight up, Sensei, you fucked up. If not for Amery letting me know you were all right after your hospital escape, I would've had the fire department here using an emergency override to get to you."

Ronin said nothing.

"You need anything, holler. I'll bring it up." Then he walked away without saying another word.

AMERY forced Ronin to rest for the remainder of the weekend. They sat by the pool, stretched out in the shade of the garden, and napped. One moment they'd be holding hands, enjoying the easy silence, the next Amery would feel the tension rolling off him. She figured out his tension came when he'd overexerted himself and was in pain. Or if she wasn't right by his side.

"What was that sigh for?"

"Did I sigh?"

"For the third time. Are you already bored?"

"No. Why? Are you?"

"I'm never bored with you."

She set her laptop on the coffee table. "What show are you watching?"

"Hell if I know. I've been watching you."

Amery rolled her eyes. "How's your head?"

"Sore. Before you ask, it's no longer a constant pain. It comes and goes."

She grabbed a pillow and draped it across her lap. "Maybe lying flat will help."

Ronin nestled the back of his head against her stomach and stretched out. "That is better."

Amery ran her hands through his hair from scalp to the ends, over and over, just because she could. She'd take this rare intimate indulgence while he allowed it.

"God. That feels so good."

She remembered that the last time he said that he'd been buried inside her. His breath in her ear. His body sliding against hers, all heat and hardness and urgency.

"You tensed up. What's wrong?"

"Just thinking about work," she lied.

"I haven't asked about that. How's it going?"

"Pretty much the same. No major client losses, but I haven't been hired by anyone either. I pounded the pavement the past two months, but all that's yielded me is sore feet."

"And Molly?"

"She's still working for me part-time and going to school. Emmylou has been traveling with the Colorado Rockies, so she hasn't been around. Chaz is Chaz. He does his own thing."

"That was short and sweet."

"Not a whole lot has changed." Amery twisted small sections of his hair, amusing herself by how fast the curl reverted to straight. "We never really did this, did we?"

"What? Lounge around?"

"Yes. I mean we did lounge by the pool, but we ended up fucking on a chaise or in the water."

Ronin shifted to face her. "Not every time."

"Most every time. Once we started having sex, that was pretty much all we did." Amery put her fingers over his lips. "Not that I'm complaining."

"But?"

"No buts. Although I am sorry that you're hurting, I'm content to spend time with you like this. Without the pressure of sex."

"Just because I haven't pinned you down and fucked you like we both want doesn't mean I haven't thought about it."

"I know." She continued to stroke his hair. "Even if you were one hundred percent healthy, I still wouldn't be all in for sexcapades."

Ronin looked at her quizzically. "Why not?"

"Because I'm not ready to resume a sexual relationship with you. We need to reestablish intimacy first."

"The sexual pull between us hasn't diminished at all since we've been apart, and fulfilling those needs is the ultimate intimacy, Amery."

"It is in part. Intimacy means sharing. Bodies, minds, thoughts. Parts of the past. Fears for the future."

He stared at her. "My biggest fear is you don't believe we have a future."

She said nothing.

"Your silence is not reassuring."

"I know."

"So maybe I need to reassure you first. I swore when I got the chance with you again I wouldn't hold back. On anything. Thoughts. Feelings. Actions. Words."

Her heart raced.

"Maybe I need to start with the words and tell you that I lo—"

Amery put her hand over his mouth so fast his teeth connected with her skin. "Don't."

Ronin didn't bother to hide his frustration.

"The only reassurances I need right now are that you're taking your meds and giving your body time to heal."

He pushed himself upright. "I am healing. But fair warning, baby. Just as you wouldn't let me use my health issues as an excuse not to talk, I won't let you use my health issues as an excuse not to rekindle our physical relationship. Because we both know we would've ended up fucking each other like crazy the first damn night after we talked things through, if not for my—"

"Visit to the hospital because of your fight injuries?" she supplied. "That's a crap reason because we wouldn't be here if not for that."

"Wrong. I wouldn't have let this break between us go on much longer."

"Let?" she repeated.

Ronin caged her against the back of the couch. "Yes, *let.* This is not a temporary thing between us. Never has been, never will be. So I'll let you try to push me away. I'll let you try to convince yourself that you're holding back from fucking me blind because I don't understand intimacy. But we both know differently. And I'll do everything in my power to prove you wrong." He dipped his head and ran his lips along the edge of her jaw and down her throat until she shivered. "I want you. I need you. And in the end, baby, I *am* going to have you. All of you."

Her will to resist went as mushy as her heart. Damn him.

He stood and grabbed his crutch. "Now, are you coming to bed, or what?"

CHAPTER FOUR

THE next two days passed in a blur of boredom.

Early the third morning, Ronin woke up annoyed that Amery had turned away from him during the night again. He spent an hour in the practice room working on katas. He blanked his mind to everything except maintaining the proper breathing and stance as he moved through the forms. For the first time in a week, he completed his usual routine without any breaks.

He climbed out of the shower, and the cold air chilled him to the bone. But Amery's heated look when she handed him a towel set his blood on fire. "Thanks."

"You're welcome. The scrapes on your arms and knuckles are healing."

He wanted—needed—more than just her eyes on him. He craved her touch. "Can you check the ones on my back?"

"Sure." Amery moved in behind him, and he closed his eyes when her soft fingertips brushed his spine. "You've still got discoloration from bruises." She swept her thumb across his left scapula. "How did you get injured back here anyway?"

"Probably from a takedown. Are there marks anywhere else?"

She lightly pushed on his neck until he dropped his head. More gentle touches across his shoulders. "One here. It's on a bone, so it's still a big lump. Does it hurt?"

Not when you're touching me like that.

"You've also got a big knot in this muscle."

As soon as her fingers connected with that sore spot, his skin broke out in gooseflesh. It'd been a lifetime since she'd put her hands on him.

"This tension is probably from how you're holding the crutch." She rubbed a few more times. "Any other tight spots?"

The skin covering his dick was getting tighter by the second—he couldn't tell her that, but pretty quick it'd be obvious. "No."

She moved to stand in front of him and placed her palms on his rib cage. "Does this hurt?"

"A little."

Amery's scent surrounded him so completely he couldn't think of anything except pulling her into bed with him and holding her captive until she promised never to leave him again

"Will any of these marks scar?" She inched her fingers down his belly.

His cock nearly leaped into her hand, and he willed the motherfucking thing to stand down. "Doubtful. They're just bruises."

"Just bruises, he says." She traced the contusions with such tenderness he ached for more. "Such a tough guy."

"I don't know about tough, but today I almost feel back to normal." When she looked up at him, he said, "Being this close to you and not being able to touch you like I want is killing me."

Just like that, Amery sidestepped him. "I wanted to talk to you before I left for work."

Allowing her retreat, he briskly towel dried his hair. "What's up?"

"I think it might be best if I stayed at my place tonight."

Ronin didn't answer. He just waited.

"You're getting better, and you don't need me—"

Before she could finish, he wrapped his hand around the back of her neck and brought her against his body. "Do you really believe the only reason you're staying with me is because I needed you as my nursemaid?"

She blinked those big blue eyes at him.

"Answer me."

"I don't know."

"Yes, you *do* know, and that's why you're running. Guess what? That's not happening." He slanted his mouth over hers and kissed her. Not bothering to hide his hunger, not allowing her to retreat. Holding her in place until she responded with the passion she still felt for him but tried to discount.

The taste of her was hot and sweet. Heaven and hell because he wanted so much more from her than this small taste.

And he knew she wanted more too when she plastered her body against his, not caring he was wet. Fisting her hand in his hair with the possession he'd missed.

He forced himself to end the kiss. He brushed his lips over her chin and down her throat, holding her tighter when she trembled. "Amery, I need you. If I haven't made that clear, then allow me to do so now. I need you in my life every day. Not just for the short term." He nuzzled her ear and whispered, "Please. Stay with me." He tipped her head back and smiled at her. But his smile dried when he noticed her tears. "Baby. What's wrong? I thought we—"

"I'm scared. I trusted you once, and that nearly broke me."

Ronin wiped the moisture from her face. "You walking away did break me. I threw myself back into those fights because I wanted the outside of my body to hurt as badly as the inside."

Her eyes, her posture, everything about her softened toward him.

He had no problem taking advantage of that. "We're working through this. The only way we can do that is if we're spending time together reestablishing intimacy and trust, right?"

"You are so damn smooth." She traced his lips with the tips of her fingers. "And so gorgeous. Sometimes I look at you and find it hard to breathe."

"You humble me." He dropped another kiss on her mouth. Then he parted his lips and followed the curve of her neck on a slow glide from top to bottom. Then bottom to top.

She shivered.

Rather than get greedy and push for more, Ronin withdrew, but he had secret satisfaction in seeing that Amery trembled from just the brief touch of his mouth on her skin. "It's too damn cold in here. I'm freezing my balls off."

"I thought it was just me." She raised an eyebrow at him. "There's no excuse for you not to turn on the heat since you've got the funds to cover the higher cost of winter utilities."

That was the first time she'd joked about his financial status. Had to be a good sign. He smiled at her. "That is an upside."

THROUGHOUT the day, Ronin's determination that they'd re-unite as lovers grew. He'd made his intentions clear this morning; tonight, he'd drive the point home.

After he left the dojo, he stopped in the penthouse long enough to grab a beer, a towel and to tell Amery he was going for a swim.

On the pool deck, he rolled back the thick plastic cover, leaving three quarters of the water covered. He popped off his knee brace and shed his gi pants and T-shirt. The brisk wind blowing over his nakedness forced him to get into the pool quickly.

The water warmed him, but it wasn't as warm as he'd like. His outdoor spaces designer had assumed he would use the area for entertaining and had set it up accordingly. But half the lounge chairs hadn't ever been used. The tiki bar looked cool in theory, but in reality, he'd rather have a hot tub.

Sipping his beer, Ronin stared up at the sky, wondering if it'd take a helicopter to get the heavy tub portion up here. The bad thing about downsizing the cargo elevator was he lost the ability to haul big pieces past the fifth floor. He could've opted for big, symmetrically shaped plastic pieces for a cover, which, once assembled, encompassed the entire roof. But he'd had no place to store them in the summer months. He'd chosen extreme weather-resistant plastic, which made a tight enough seal around the area that some of the heartier trees on the garden side didn't have to be moved indoors when the temperatures dropped below freezing.

Wouldn't be long before that happened. He'd better get the guy here to set up the winterization kit next week.

That decided, he performed water therapy exercises on his knee. Something in the movement caused the pain in his shoulder to flare. He did push-ups against the side. One arm, then both arms. Then he raised his arm over his head like he was swinging a hammer.

"Are you supposed to be doing that?"

Ronin jumped. Then he spun around. "Were you trying to sneak up on me?"

The smile on her face said everything. "What goes around, comes around, ninja."

"I deserve that."

Amery shoved her hands in her pockets. "Are you all right?"

"I'm fine. Why?"

"I don't know. I thought you were mad at me or something."

"What gave you that idea?"

"You hardly said anything to me when you came up from the dojo."

He slowly moved his arm across the front of his body, then pulled on his wrist with his other hand. A loud popping sound echoed.

Her eyes widened. "Was that a body part?"

"Yeah. But it feels remarkably better now."

"Oh. Well. Good."

"I'd invite you to join me, but I know you'll decline. I'll probably stay in another half hour."

"Why don't you think I'll join you?"

"Because I'd demand you strip to skin. And if you decided to thwart me and jump in in your swimsuit, I'd take great pleasure in tearing it off you." He let his wicked intent show in his eyes. "With my teeth. Then I'd probably tie you up with your bikini strings."

Clearly torn between defiance and desire, Amery blinked at him.

"So, baby, what's it going to be?"

"Ronin—"

"That's what I thought." Ronin turned his back on her and resumed his exercises.

It took twelve reps of lunges before she stomped into view. Her pink-tipped toes twitched with anger.

"Do you know how much I hate that dismissive tone of yours? You assume a lot sometimes, Master Black."

"Arguing with me about why you won't get in the pool isn't getting you into the pool, so why do it?"

"Infuriating man."

Ronin swam to the opposite side.

"So you invite me into the pool and now you're getting out?"

"No. I'm just grabbing my beer." He drained it. "And I didn't invite you, remember?"

"*Rude*, infuriating man."

And it was about to get a whole lot worse. He waggled the empty bottle at her. "Babe, since you're probably stomping off anyway, would you mind throwing this away on your way back downstairs?"

If that wouldn't get her in the pool, anxious to dunk his ass, nothing would.

"Babe?" Off went her jeans as she spoke. "Babe?" Then her panties. "Babe?" Her T-shirt was next. Hey, wait a second; that was *his* T-shirt.

Her escalating use of the word *babe* culminated in an angry jump into the pool. Amery splashed him while flinging phrases like *sexist pig* and *bossy bastard* at him.

Eyes flashing, her tits bouncing, her nipples rigid points . . . goddamn, the woman was a fucking goddess.

"Ronin! Are you even listening to me?"

"No." He caught her wrist before she splashed him again. "Nothing registered after you started coming toward me, those perfect perky tits leading the way."

"Omigod, you are such an ass."

Ronin hauled her against his body. "Thanks for joining me in the pool." His lips started at the spot below her ear and moved across that stubborn jawline, tasting her skin beneath the chlorine. "I miss that breathy sigh you make when I kiss you right here." He zeroed in on the spot two inches below her ear.

She made the sound.

"I could spend the next hour telling you everything I missed in the past seven weeks, but I'd rather show you." Holding her head in place, he kissed her with all the need he felt for her, with fire, with impatience.

Amery kissed him back, but her hands were wrapped around his forearms, holding him back.

Like. Hell.

"Need my mouth on you," he growled against her throat.

"Ronin—"

"Now. Tell me you don't want my mouth between your thighs." He sucked on the spot below her ear that made her moan.

"I can't think when you do that."

"So stop thinking and give me what I want." He pushed her backward until they reached the folded pool cover. "Lie back."

"Won't I sink?"

"Not if you hold still."

"But I can't hold still when you . . ."

"That's never a bad thing. Arms above your head like you're floating. That's it. Beautiful."

Ronin lowered himself into the water and raised her pussy to the level of his mouth. He licked her slowly, searching every soft fold for the sweet taste of her.

There it was. Goddamn. There it was. He greedily buried his tongue inside her.

"Oh, god."

He pulled back and rubbed his lips over the inner swell of her mound. "Tell me you missed this."

She moaned.

"Tell. Me."

"I missed you."

You. Not this.

"I missed you too, baby. I . . ." Ronin's attempts to tell her that he loved her were met with resistance, so here was his chance to show her.

He was too starved for her to slowly drive her to the detonation point. He pushed back the skin hiding her clit with his lips and settled his mouth over the hot spot. "You taste so fucking sweet."

"You're so amazing at that."

His response was to suck harder in precisely the way she liked.

Wasn't long before she started to rock her hips into his face, and he felt that first spasm against his mouth.

He sucked and swallowed those sweet juices, growling against her tender flesh. When her legs stopped trembling and the pulses ended, he kissed the inside of her thigh. As he eased her off the pool cover, he kissed straight up her belly. He latched on to her nipple, which had gone tight in the cold night air.

Amery wrapped her legs around his waist. When she was fuzzy from orgasmic bliss, worrying about his injuries appeared to be the farthest thing from her mind.

Ronin feasted on her nipples. Warming them with his mouth, wanting to slide her body down to where he ached and slip inside her. He kissed his way up her chest to her chin. "Amery, baby, I lo—"

She slanted her lips over his and kissed him with deliberation.

"I do taste pretty sweet on you," she murmured between soft pecks on his mouth.

Once again, she'd stopped the words in his heart from passing through his lips. Why?

Because she's scared.

Then she proved it by pushing away from him. "I'm cold. Let's go inside."

AFTER they crawled into bed, Ronin said, "I should let you know that Shiori will be calling you to have lunch tomorrow."

"Did she say why?"

"No."

"Huh. That's weird."

"You don't have to go."

"I know."

"In fact, I wish you wouldn't."

She turned over and gave him a cool look. "Why's that? Afraid she'll ask me how your injuries are healing since I doubt you're being honest with her either?"

"Either? It's been a week since the fight. I'm nearly back to normal."

"Then there's no reason for me to stay here and tend to you, is there?"

Goddammit. Why was she baiting him and then moving closer to taunt him?

Amery touched the bruise on his chest. She ran her hands across his ribs. "Are you so insistent I see you as bounce-back Black that you'd rather I leave than admit that you aren't one hundred percent?"

"Would you rather I pretended my recovery time is taking longer than I expected so I can keep you here?" he countered.

She sighed. "You are such an exasperating man."

Ronin plucked her hand from his chest and ran his thumb over her knuckles. "You aren't going anywhere."

His declaration didn't seem to bother her because she didn't argue. "Will you start driving tomorrow since it's been a week?"

"Maybe. I'd thought about taking you to lunch, but my sister beat me to it."

"How about if I cut out early and bring you food? Then, if you're feeling stir crazy, we could go for a drive." A wide smile spread across her beautiful face. "I'd love to get behind the wheel of your Corvette."

"No chance." He kissed the inside of her wrist. "And the only time I'm stir crazy is when you're not here."

"What happened when you went down to the dojo today?"

"Are you asking if I overexerted myself? I didn't. There were a few business things I needed to handle. All in all, I wandered around and felt pretty useless." *Jesus. Why don't you just blurt out all of your fears? That with limited physical contact, your students will see you the way you've seen so many other martial arts instructors—as washed up? As a teacher who knows the techniques but can no longer employ them?*

"You're not useless." She scooted even closer. "You're *so* not."

He wanted to show her just how useful he could be to her.

But then the crazy woman shocked him by pulling his mouth to hers and kissing him. She never let it get to the combustible stage, keeping it slow. A gentle exploration. A sweet communion. A promise of more.

After she'd incited him and soothed him with her kiss, she didn't sleep on her side of the bed for the first time in five nights. She curled her body into his and fell asleep in his arms.

CHAPTER FIVE

AMERY arrived at the bistro early, scoring the prime spot in the corner, where she could keep an eye on the door. Since her last formal meeting with Shiori had been at the Ritz, she wanted the familiarity of her home turf.

Gigi, her favorite server, sauntered over with a smile. "Where have you been keeping yourself? I haven't seen you in ages."

"I've been working through lunch most days." A lie, but confessing she couldn't afford to eat out seemed pathetic. "Someone is joining me, but I'll start out with a Moscow mule."

"Is Emmylou your lunch date?" Gigi asked hopefully.

Her office mate had flirted outrageously with Gigi the last time they'd eaten here, and the poor girl had eaten it up. "No. She's traveling this month."

"Oh. I'll put that drink order in for you."

After Gigi flounced off, Amery noticed other neighborhood business owners scattered throughout the restaurant. She waved at a couple and then scanned the menu. The lunch special, turkey salad on homemade molasses bread with a side of Colorado peaches and mountain huckleberries, caused her stomach to rumble. They hadn't had time for breakfast this morning, and she was starved. Ronin would be too, and this sandwich looked healthy enough that he'd eat it.

Her thoughts drifted to last night in the pool . . . Ronin's hunger for her, his skill at driving her to the edge and then making her fly—familiar sensations, yet somehow they felt new. Maybe it was the gently lapping water as his tongue greedily devoured her. She'd wanted her hands on his head, pulling his hair, guiding him, controlling him, but no. Once again he'd controlled her and the situation. Like he always did.

Gigi dropped off the drink, and Amery stirred it without taking a sip.

After the spectacular orgasm, and later, as they were entwined in bed, she'd wondered how much longer she could hold Ronin off on resuming their sexual relationship. But mostly she wondered *why* she was holding back. Now that he was on the mend . . . why wasn't she jumping him?

Right then it occurred to her the physical side of their relationship renewal was starting out the same way as their first intimate encounters had. Ronin giving all to her and not allowing her to reciprocate. What had she done last night as soon as those skilled hands of his touched her flesh and his tongue stroked her? She'd gone mindless. But even if she'd tried to return the favor, he would've found some way to distract her.

No more. She'd let him know, in no uncertain terms, that his body was hers to play with, pleasure, and control.

Amery just happened to glance up as Shiori started toward her. The woman's graceful glide reminded her of a sleek panther. There was a sense of beauty and danger with a coiled edginess that warned you not to take your eyes off her or you'd feel the slice of those sharp claws and the bite of deadly teeth.

Shiori had dressed in a short jade-colored skirt that showed off her legs. Over a lavender silk shell, she wore a long-sleeved black jacket that nipped in at the waist and ended above her hips in a wide peplum. Of course the outfit was chic, sexy, and completely professional. Amery bit back a jealous sigh. And of course she finished the outfit with the perfect accessories—lavender suede pumps and an oversized satchel color-blocked with jade and black.

Thankfully Shiori didn't expect the fake kiss-kiss and half-hug reception. She simply smiled and slid into the booth. "Amery. It's good to see you. Thank you for agreeing to meet me today."

"My pleasure. And without it seeming like I'm fawning, can I just say that outfit is outstanding? You look amazing."

Shiori grinned. "Thank you. I've been filling my free time shopping."

"Shopping here in Denver?"

"Some. New York City is too far to fly to justify a couple of hours to shop, so I've found the most darling boutiques in Chicago, Las Vegas, and Dallas."

"You hop on a plane just to go shopping for a few hours?"

"Oh no. I charter a plane and attend to business while I'm in the air. I'm all about multitasking."

Amery couldn't hide her shock. Ronin and his sister really did live in two different worlds; she couldn't imagine Ronin doing something so frivolous.

Don't judge. Her money, her life, her choices.

Shiori leaned over and peered at Amery's drink. "What is that?"

"A Moscow mule. Lime, vodka, and ginger beer."

"I don't usually drink cocktails at lunch, but I'll try one."

Amery gestured to Gigi to bring Shiori a drink.

"Have you decided on what you're having?" Shiori asked.

"The lunch special. But everything here is very good."

Gigi dropped off Shiori's drink. "Are you ladies ready to order?"

"Yes, I'll have the special," Amery said. "And I'll need another order to go."

"And you, ma'am?"

"The cheesesteak, extra cheese, onions, and mushrooms with steak fries. And an order of Rocky Mountain oysters with a side of wasabi." Shiori handed over the menu. "Save me a slice of the piña colada cheesecake too."

After Gigi left, Amery asked, "Where exactly are you going to put all that food?"

Shiori shrugged. "I have a high metabolism. And yes, I know my brother would be having a fit right now. He lectures me on my bad eating habits." She sipped her drink. "That is good. Speaking of my brother, he wasn't happy when I told him I planned to ask you to lunch."

"Does he have a reason to be concerned this time?"

"Depends on if you can move on from the way I mishandled our initial meeting."

"At least you can admit you screwed up. What happened between Ronin and me . . . while I hated that you were the messenger, it didn't change that he should've told me himself."

"Agreed. I'm happy that you two are trying to work things out. I only wish he hadn't taken that path again to find his way back to you."

Given Shiori's comments and her own observations, Amery suspected whenever things went wrong in Ronin's life, he turned to fighting. She'd accidentally overheard a conversation between him and Knox, where Ronin admitted he'd been fighting in the underground club scene. That he'd hidden how deep he'd sunk his roots into that world of violence, even from those closest to him, had broken her heart. It also scared her to think that no matter how physically and emotionally she'd open herself up to him, he'd always withhold parts of himself from her.

"How do you feel his recovery is coming along?"

"More slowly than he'd like. But he's been more patient than I expected." With the exception of resuming their sex life.

"He's less patient in the dojo. He's filling his time practicing katas."

Amery frowned. "What's a kata?"

"A series of flowing defensive movements that puts the art in martial arts. Since traditional jujitsu doesn't have specific kata forms, Ronin memorized forms from judo, karate, and aikido. Crazy man. Who does stuff like that?"

A master. A man who wouldn't ever be satisfied with mediocrity. A man who needed art and beauty in his life.

Gigi dropped off a plate of golden fried Rocky Mountain oysters.

Shiori said, "Please. Help yourself."

"I'll pass. You do know what those are, don't you?"

"Yep." She popped one in her mouth and chewed. "Calf nuts. Now I can truly scare my associates in Japan with the statement that I eat balls for lunch."

Amery laughed.

She polished off the appetizer in no time and shoved the plate aside. "Now that we've cleared the air, let's get down to business."

"Business?"

"Yes. I tend to be brutally honest, so bear with me. I'll get to the point, after I've made a few pre-points."

Sounded like Amery might need another drink. "Okay."

"Your company working on the packaging for the new line of Okada frozen foods wasn't just a toss off to give you busywork at Ronin's request. Maggie Arnold hadn't been happy with our usual graphics team, and she needed an excuse to cut professional ties with them before they got wind of this new product line."

"So I became the scapegoat?"

"To some extent. So in addition to sending you all the information, she chose five other companies she'd heard positive feedback on and sent them the specs too."

"Where are these companies located?"

"Los Angeles. Chicago. Houston. San Francisco. Minneapolis."

All major players with unlimited resources. How much would it suck if their proposals made her mock-ups look like grade school art projects. "And?"

Shiori stirred her drink. "And when I became aware of the situation and Ronin's request of your company to submit ideas, I felt a little smug. Surely your state school college education and small company in a smaller ad and PR market would produce inferior results."

Amery waited, expecting the most insulting portion of this conversation was yet to come.

"I expected to show my brother proof of your inability to design products for major international markets by having a comparison to the other companies' samples. But the strangest thing has happened in the past few weeks after you left your designs with me."

"What? You spilled tea on them and improved them or something?"

She smiled. "So defensive and paranoid. Not that I blame you. I forwarded your designs to Maggie. Once we had all of them, I flew to Seattle. Maggie and I pored over every single concept. And every single one was unoriginal, boring, or just plain lazy. None of the companies had followed the parameters; they'd given us what *they* envisioned instead of working with our vision." Shiori locked her gaze to Amery's. "The graphic artists with MFAs and MBAs and art school degrees can't compete with a company that doesn't have anything to lose and puts everything on the line. Your designs did that. They were far, far superior to anything we'd seen and surpassed our expectations."

When Amery drained her drink, Shiori laughed.

"I'm not dragging this out to make you uneasy, but you deserve to know what you were up against and how the selection process works for a global conglomerate. We showed all six designs to Maggie's team without any indication of what company had done which product. They unanimously chose your vision. We then forwarded the proposals to the team in charge of branding, concepts, and marketing, and once again, your designs were picked. So then we put it to the ultimate test."

"Your grandfather."

"Yes, the big, bad CEO, the man who hasn't met an idea he can't crush."

Amery found herself holding her breath.

"He approved the proposal."

"Omigod." She swallowed hard. "Does Ronin know?"

Shiori leaned forward. "No. I wanted to make it very clear to you that this is all you. Your concept, your designs. Ronin put you on our radar, but that's it. I don't want you to believe that Ronin has any part in Okada offering you a contract."

"A contract?" Before she could ask specifics, the food arrived.

Shiori immediately dug in and left the conversation hanging.

Amery was too keyed up to politely nibble on a sandwich and a plate of fruit. Ideas spun around in her head. So did fear.

"Amery," Shiori said sharply. "I can hear your stomach growling. Eat."

"You sound like your brother." But she ate all of it. She even asked Gigi to bring her a slice of chocolate-chip cheesecake.

When she couldn't stand it any longer, she blurted, "So you mentioned a contract?"

"We've come up with a couple of contract options because Okada definitely wants your designs. We pay very well. Yet, if you feel you've been overpaid because of your relationship with an Okada heir, I can let you see other, similar contracts."

"I'd appreciate that. And forgive me if I'm acting spacey, but this is a huge shock. After everything that happened, I literally put the work I'd done on the project out of my mind and focused on my existing clients. I never imagined that you'd do anything with my proposal besides toss it in the trash. Not that I didn't think it was good. I just believed the whole thing had been a setup from the start and I'd never really had a chance."

"Understandable."

"What are my options?"

"A one-time lump sum. You turn over ownership of all the existing designs to us."

"Okay. What else?"

"Okada puts you under contract. Lump sum for the finished designs and you work on other concepts for the company—not limited to this new product line. While you'd have guaranteed income during that time, usually two years, whatever you design in that time we'd own."

"No more lump sum payments with that option."

"Correct."

"More than likely, I'd have to give up my existing clients due to time constraints." And limited manpower. But with a new income stream, she could hire more employees to pick up the slack.

"Yes. I should also warn you that if you're under contract, you'll have to give up all other clients with food-based businesses. Okada won't chance our brand being recognized on another competing company's products."

"That makes sense. But some of my clients have stuck with me when they could've jumped ship."

"Which is why you need to think this through. It is a great opportunity, and the exposure will change the future of your business. Other competing Asian food companies will mimic your designs and try to hire you away. That's part of the game. I trust that you'll handle that part just fine."

"But the other parts?"

"Working for Okada means you'll be tied to Ronin even if things don't work out between you two. I don't want resentment from you in case things go south. I don't want resentment from Ronin because you're involved in the company. I'm asking you to take a couple of days or even a week to weigh the pros and cons."

"Can I talk to Ronin about this?"

"Of course. It affects both of you. Don't be surprised if he isn't very enthusiastic."

They finished their desserts in silence. When Gigi dropped off the bill and the to-go order, Shiori handed her a hundred-dollar bill. "Keep the change."

"Oh. Wow. Thank you."

But Shiori was already engrossed in her phone.

Amery left the remainder of her drink unfinished and stood. "I appreciate your candor and the opportunity, Shiori. Thank you for lunch."

"You're welcome." She pointed to the Styrofoam box. "Want me to take that to Ronin?"

"No. He's expecting me."

Shiori unfolded from the booth as sinuously as a feline. She reached into her bag and pulled out a sealed manila envelope. "Here are copies of both contracts with the proposed remuneration. Any questions at all, just call. My cell and my hotel numbers are both listed."

"Are you still staying at the Ritz?"

"Yes. They're accommodating and discreet."

Why would Shiori need discretion?

She followed her outside.

"I'll look forward to hearing from you soon."

A black limo pulled up to the curb. A beefy, good-looking blond guy in a suit exited the passenger side and opened the rear door for her.

According to Ronin, they hadn't grown up in luxury, surrounded by servants attending to their every whim. Amery wondered at what point Shiori had started acting the part of the billionaire heiress.

And at what point Ronin had rejected it.

CHAPTER SIX

RONIN was finishing his grocery order when he heard the elevator engage.

"Yes. Go ahead and fillet the tilapia. Whole-grain English muffins. Canned coconut milk. The light kind. Pine nuts. Three pounds of baby sweet potatoes. Five pounds of seasonal fruit—but not all apples or pears. Mangos are fine. A bag of whole Kona coffee beans. Yes. That should do it. Tomorrow after nine is fine. Thank you."

Amery stopped on the opposite side of the serving bar. "Who was that?"

"Harvest Table."

"Ronin, I told you I can pick up groceries."

"And I told you after I felt better I'd feed you." He noticed her furrowed brow. "Did lunch with my sister give you indigestion?"

She glanced up. "No. It was very . . . enlightening." She slid a to-go box toward him. "Brought you a sandwich. Don't worry. It's healthy."

Ronin moved in beside her and curled his hand around the back of her neck. Their mouths met, and she leaned into him, letting him lead the kiss. But when he tried to break their lip-lock, she growled and chased his mouth until he was kissing her again.

"Baby," he said between tiny love bites, "I have only so much control. Keep kissing me like this and I'm fucking you against the refrigerator."

"But I love kissing you."

"My lips are yours, anytime you want them. Right now, though, I need them to eat."

Amery was distracted as she plated his food.

"What did you and Shiori talk about?"

"She brought pictures of your dorky teen years and filled me in on all the crazy stuff you used to do."

Ronin stopped chewing and looked up at her.

She laughed. "Kidding. But your guilty look means there are things to tell."

"Not much. I was an exemplary child."

"Says you. I'd bet that was because you've always been such a damn control freak."

He ignored the comment and continued eating his lunch.

Amery poured two glasses of lemonade. "I've been thinking about what you've been harping on the past few days."

Harping on? Really? Bullshit. "And?"

"And you're right." She picked up his hand and traced the backs of his fingers. "We need to reconnect sexually because it is a big part of who we were together."

"Were?"

"Yes, were. We have to take the past into account to go forward. And I realized something else today."

Why wouldn't she look at him? "What's that?"

"Things are starting out between us exactly the same way they did last time. We—I—need to break the cycle."

"Amery, I'm lost."

Her gaze collided with his. "Last night you went down on me.

Yes, it was as great as it's always been. So that is the same type of scene as when you poured candle wax on me and got me off with your hand."

"That's not the same thing at all. And if you're looking to even the score—although god knows I'm not keeping track—I'll drop my pants and you can blow me right here, right now."

She dropped his hand so fast it smacked into the countertop. Then she stepped back and glared at him. "Omigod. Are you even listening to me?"

Shit. "I'm trying, but apparently we're having a miscommunication. Tell me exactly what you want from me."

"I want to tie your hands, blindfold you, drip wax on your chest, and then jack you off."

Ronin spit lemonade halfway across the kitchen.

Then an evil laugh accompanied the knowing twist of her lips. "Surprised, Master Black?"

"Yes, and I hope like hell you're joking."

"I am not joking. You expect me to jump right back into your bed like nothing ever went wrong between us. Plus you demand that I trust you, and I always have. In bed and out and whenever you bind me. So I want *you* to show *me* that same level of trust."

Fuck. The woman was serious. And there wasn't any way he could say no. He could try to play the injury card . . . But one glimpse into those determined blue eyes of hers and he knew he was totally fucked.

Totally. Fucked.

Except . . .

"All right. I'll agree to prove my trust in you, but I have a couple stipulations."

"Of course you do," she muttered. "Fine. Name them."

Ronin rose from the chair and started toward her. "First, you truss me up, tease me with wax, and get me off in my practice room."

"Okay."

Did the woman have any idea how much it turned him on when she backed away from him with that sexual fire in her eyes? "You are sweet sin, and I cannot wait to get my fucking hands on you again."

"Is that a stipulation?"

"Yes. Feeding this craving I have for you won't be a one-time thing. After we break the ice that's settled between us, I can fuck you anytime I want."

"Or I can fuck you anytime I want," she retorted.

"Fair enough." He caged her against the wall and placed an openmouthed kiss on the sweet spot on her neck. "You let me bind you again. Starting tomorrow night."

When she trembled, he knew she'd missed that intimate connection as much as he had.

"I look forward to your rope tricks," she whispered against his throat. "Is there anything else?"

"Yes." His heart rate quadrupled, but his fear wasn't holding him back this time. Ronin nudged her chin up and gazed into her beautiful eyes. "You let me tell you that I—"

Lightning fast, her fingers pressed against his lips, stopping the flow of words. "You don't have to—"

Equally fast, he pulled her hand away. "Yes, I do, and it is a stipulation or this is a no-go, understand?"

She nodded.

He captured her face in his hands so she couldn't look away. "Amery, I love you. I've been in love with you since the moment you kissed my bloodied hands and asked me to put them on you. I don't know why you haven't let me say it to you whenever I've tried to in the last week, but you need to know before you let me make love to you again that I do love you."

"Okay."

Okay? That was it? That was all he got from her?

This is not about how she feels; it's about you manning up and telling her how you feel.

Then Amery smashed her mouth to his and kissed him with the unbridled passion he'd missed.

She put her hand on his chest and pushed, breaking the kiss. "You . . . Damn. You completely fried my circuits."

"Just imagine how mindless I'll make you when I'm inside you."

"I can't wait. But first I need to know where you keep your candles."

Ronin stepped back. "We're doing this right now?"

"You have other plans?"

"Now that you mention it, I think I'm out of candles."

"No problem. The citronella ones from the pool area worked on me. Guess it'd be poetic—or would that be ironic?—if I used one on you."

"Maybe I have birthday cake candles somewhere in the kitchen."

Amery raised both eyebrows. "Birthday cake candles? You aren't afraid of a little burning-hot pain, are you, Master Black?"

"No," he scoffed. "Just trying to improvise. Isn't there a red candle in the guest bedroom?"

A horrified look crossed her face.

"What?"

"Red wax would look too much like blood, and I've seen enough of your blood to last me a lifetime." She swallowed hard. "Red wouldn't be sexy at all—"

"Ssh, hey." He tugged her against his chest. "Bad idea. We'll figure something out."

Amery clung to him for minute and retreated. "I'll go up to the roof and get those. You can go into the practice room and get ready."

"Get ready?"

"Strip and meditate or whatever you do to prepare your mind

for when you go into rope master mode." She grinned. "Oh, and pick out the rope for your hands and a blindfold."

"You are enjoying this far too much, Amery."

She pecked him on the mouth. "I hope you enjoy it too."

Ronin stared after her, hoping he didn't freak out from the loss of control. He'd never allowed a woman to master him. For some reason, that'd always been a point of pride with him.

Pride goeth before a fall—and heaven knew he'd fallen for her hard since he'd agreed to put himself in her hands.

He unlocked the practice room and turned on the lights. Then he headed down the hallway to his bedroom. Getting naked wasn't an option. Amery had worn pants during that encounter, and so would he. He stripped off his gi and dragged on a pair of nylon athletic shorts.

After washing up, Ronin strolled into the practice room. Amery was already there, standing in front of the picture of herself bound in red ropes.

Ronin moved in behind her. "Have you forgotten how stunning you are when I bind you?"

"Do I really look like that to you?" she asked softly.

"Yes." He brushed his mouth across her ear. "You look like you belong in here, don't you?"

"You mean the picture looks like it belongs in here."

"That too." He retreated and went to the small chest of drawers in the corner, which held miscellaneous items. He selected a simple black eye mask. When he turned around, Amery was right behind him.

"I believe it's my right to select the blindfold. And nice try with that one, but no." She ducked around him and rummaged through the pile until she found the one she wanted. She faced him, and a long black silk scarf dangled from her fingertips. "Oh, and FYI, I found a black candle on your sacrificial altar."

He'd forgotten about that since he'd been lax in his meditation practice the past few weeks.

Amery snapped her fingers in front of his face. "Focus, sub."

He lifted a brow. "Sub?"

"Kidding. Now, which rope do I use for the binding?"

Ronin picked up a fifteen-foot length of black cotton rope, half an inch in diameter. "Hold out your wrists so I can show you a fast and easy binding." He folded the rope in half. "Where it's folded is called the bight. Move down about twenty inches and hold it as you start to wrap the wrists. Make sure the wrists don't touch, or you can't finish the binding." He wrapped the rope three times. "Now twist them together. Then drop the bight end and the end of the rope between the gap in the wrists. Pull both back up and tie a square knot."

"Ronin, I don't think I can do this."

He smooched her lips. "Yes, you can." He tugged, and the knot came free. Then he unwound the rope. "It doesn't have to be perfect or tight. I'll put out the rope scissors so if you do have a tying issue you can cut me free. Okay?"

"Okay." She ran her fingers over the rope. "You trust me with this?"

"Yes."

"I have to ask you something else."

"What?"

"Will you let me take pictures of you if I feel the shots are right?"

That'd come out of nowhere. But it played into his need to document the art she let him create on her body with his ropes.

"I mean, it'll be just like the shots you took of me. No one will see them unless you give me your permission."

He tipped her chin up because she wouldn't look at him. "Why are the pictures important to you? As proof that I surrendered myself to you?"

"No!" She placed her hand over his heart. "You are such a stunning man. Your face is a work of art. So is this sculpted body. I'd like to capture your strength and raw masculinity. Because, like you told me, the submissive has all the power. Call it whatever name you like, but when you're bound and blindfolded, you will be submissive to me. I'd like to see if that dichotomy of strength and surrender is visible in photographs." Amery gestured to the photo of herself. "Kind of like you wanted to show the innocence and passion in me."

"You make a compelling argument. And I'll agree. With one stipulation."

"You and your damn stipulations," she grumbled.

"That you allow me to photograph you bound again."

Amery bit her lip, clearly torn. Finally she said, "All right."

He smiled. "Now that we're through negotiations, where do you want me?"

"Sit on the bench. Arms behind you."

Ronin was oddly nervous.

"Close your eyes," she said behind him. She tipped his head back and ran her fingers through his hair. "I love your hair. It's perfect. Thick and dark and so soft to the touch." She pulled it all back and gathered it at his nape. "I love that you wear it long. It's your rogue samurai warrior side showing. And I really"—she breathed in his ear—"really love how your hair feels brushing across my skin. Sexy and naughty and hot.

"When you made me come last night? And you turned your head to rub your damp lips on the top of my thigh? The ends of these silky strands teased across my leg and I almost came again."

Jesus. He might not survive her sweet dirty talk. Tingles shot down his spine whenever her breath flowed over his skin.

"Every time you go down on me and you do that soft kiss and nuzzle thing on my inner thighs? Like you can't get enough of the taste of me or the scent of me . . . I melt." She kissed the top of his ear. "You own me in that moment, Ronin."

His cock was fully erect by the time she finished securing his hair in a ponytail.

"Now for the blindfold."

Cool silk covered his eyes.

She knotted it below his ponytail. "Is that too tight?"

"It's fine."

"Good. Now your hands."

And like when he bound her, Amery's fingers caressed his arms from shoulders to wrists. He jumped when her sassy little tongue snaked out and followed the cut of his triceps on the back of his arm. He heard her drop to her knees on the mat and he remained still as she worked the rope.

Ronin couldn't tell when she started to wrap his wrists whether she was doing it right or not. He didn't feel anything until the rope ends trailed over his fingers and she pulled them up and jerked them into a knot.

"Try that."

He attempted to leverage his wrists by bowing his elbows, but he couldn't make them budge. "It's a good wrap. Not too tight either. But could you do me a favor? Take a picture of the binding, so I can see what you did."

"No way, rope master. Just keep the image in your pretty little head that I achieved perfection on my first attempt."

His grin turned into a groan when she cupped his face in her hands and kissed him stupid.

She whispered, "Your tap-out word is . . . ?"

Clever girl, using a martial arts term as a safe-out. "Red."

Amery kissed his jawline, his throat, his collarbone while her fingers mapped his pectorals and gingerly swept down his ribs to his abdomen. Then her hot mouth engulfed his nipple, and he hissed. He automatically tried to bring his hands to her face, but he couldn't move. A feeling of panic arose, and he jerked hard.

She stilled. After a few seconds, a soft, lingering kiss landed on his sternum. "Don't forget to breathe, baby."

Unaware he'd been holding his breath, he inhaled deeply, and that eased some of his anxiety.

The woman destroyed him with more sweet kisses and tender caresses.

Then she kicked it up a notch. Licking, biting, and sucking random spots on his chest and neck. Nails scraping down his back and fingers teasing the ridges of his stomach between brutal kisses.

Ronin was utterly lost in her. Deprived of sight and touch, his other senses made up for it. The scent of her hair and his own musk. The sound of her mouth on his skin and his soft groans reverberating in his ears. The taste of her lips—sweet and salty. And those hands of hers. Constantly touching him. His dick was so fucking hard he figured three pumps and he'd be spilling in her hand.

Although her fingers veered close to his groin, she hadn't touched his cock.

With the sensory overload, he'd forgotten about the candle wax until the first hot drop splatted on his left pectoral. "Christ!"

"Hold still." The next time she dribbled wax on him, she slammed her lips down on his in a bruising kiss.

And Amery was an absolute master in the art of anticipation. Ronin teetered on the edge of saying his tap-out word when she coated his nipple in wax, arching closer when her warm lips and heated breath grazed his sweat-dampened skin.

"Ronin."

Her voice in his ear caused gooseflesh to erupt.

"You look incredible. Your muscles are gleaming and trembling, your chest dotted with black wax. The arch of your neck and spine is stunning." She trailed a fingertip from behind his earlobe up over his shoulder and down his spine. "Hold this pose, lover, and think dirty thoughts because I'm going to snap a few pictures."

Ronin held the pose as she walked away. He counted twenty long breaths before he heard the first whirring click of the camera. The blindfold blocked light so completely he didn't get a glimpse of the flash.

"Lift your chin. More. God, you are gorgeous."

He smiled.

"No, no, no. As much as I love that panty-dropping grin, I need you to look fierce. Like you're in the throes of ecstasy."

Jesus. Now he felt like an idiot.

Then Amery was right there, soothing and enticing him, her lips teasing his, her tongue dipping in and running across the bottom edge of his teeth. Kissing him, tasting him, swallowing his breath until he felt dizzy. "There's the look. Like you're waiting for more. Like you don't know when your lover will add more wax. Or suck on your nipples. Or slowly slide her hand between your legs."

The woman made him so damn hot.

Between more camera clicks, she kept him on edge. Fleeting caresses and little love bites. Whispering praise and naughty nothings.

Ronin was so anxious and scrambled that he almost didn't register when Amery's hand cupped his cock.

Almost.

Her fingers enclosed his shaft, and she stroked. The nylon material of his athletic shorts added an additional layer of friction.

"Baby, where do you want my mouth as I'm getting you off?" she murmured in his ear.

"Anywhere you want to put it. Please don't stop. I need . . ."

"I'll give you what you need." Her tongue zigzagged down his neck to the spot in his throat where his pulse pounded. She sucked, licked, and scattered kisses around that area as she jacked his shaft.

Ronin pumped his pelvis, and her hand sped up.

Yes. Yes. Fuck. Almost . . . He ignored any embarrassment about being a two-pump chump when his balls drew up. He couldn't make a sound when come pulsed out of his cock in hot waves. Each firm pull . . . Fuck. His eyes rolled back in his head as he came for what felt like a solid minute.

As soon as his head and his balls stopped buzzing, he sighed.

He heard several shutter clicks.

When had she let go of his junk and grabbed her camera? "Amery—"

"That shot was strictly for me." She swept soft kisses across his lips as she spoke. When he attempted to deepen the kiss, she retreated. "Have I mentioned how dangerously sexy you look even all tied up, Master Black?"

"Several times. Now it's time to untie me."

"Oh, I don't know. Maybe I like having you at my mercy."

A rumbling noise started in his chest, and he realized it was a growl. "You trying to get me to tap out?"

"No. But there is a second part to my plan."

Ronin wiggled impatiently. A length of rope brushed his thumbs. He maneuvered the rope between his index finger and thumb and tugged. He felt the knot give and the bindings loosen.

Oh, sweetheart, rookie rope mistake.

Somehow he managed not to grin.

Amery stepped between his legs and placed his chin between her breasts. Then she slipped the blindfold off.

He blinked at her. He angled his face and put his lips on the upper curve of her breast. "Take your shirt off. Bra too. I want my mouth on you now."

"I believe I'm calling the shots."

Not for long. He'd undone the first rope wrap.

"You know how you always wanted me to masturbate for you? I think now would be the perfect time, don't you?"

Ronin swept another openmouthed kiss on her breast. When he tried to snake his tongue into her bra cup, she jumped back, and he used her distraction to tug the second wrist wrap free. "Why are you ready to do that for me now? Have you been practicing in the weeks we were apart?"

"No." Amery framed his face in her hands and kissed his forehead. She slid her palms over his skull and freed his hair from the ponytail. She messed with the damp strands until she'd arranged it to her liking. "In fact, I didn't touch myself at all while we were apart."

"Why not?"

She ducked her head away.

"Amery. Look at me."

"I couldn't even put my hands on my body. All I could think about was how badly I wanted your hands on me."

"Baby."

"The memory of you was more potent than a thirty-second buzz with my vibrator."

She undid him with her honesty. As soon as he removed his bindings, he'd give her a hot new memory to add to the others.

"Right now, after all the things I've done to you, I'm wet and achy and I need . . ." She kissed his furrowed brow. "Now seems to be the right time to give you something you've always wanted from me."

"All I ever wanted was you."

"You're sweet."

Like hell he was sweet. He wanted to pin her to the floor and fuck her hard.

"Don't judge me too harshly since this is my first public show."

When she stepped back, Ronin said, "No peep show. If you're doing this, do it naked. That way I get the full effect of your quivering girl parts and the breathtaking blush that spreads across every inch of your skin when you get off."

Unabashed by his demand, Amery whipped off her tank top, reached behind her back and unhooked her bra.

He finally unwound the last wrap. He inched his arms apart,

and the rope fell to the floor. Rather than launching himself at her, he figured the element of surprise would work in his favor. He threaded his fingers together and clasped his hands behind his back.

Amery impatiently flipped her hair out of her face after she'd shimmied her yoga pants to her ankles.

"I love your body, baby. Keep going."

"Wouldn't it be sexier if I left my panties on?"

Ronin shook his head. "What would be hot is if you draped yourself across my lap. Your legs spread, your tits in my face. All I'd have to do is look down for a birds'-eye view of you stroking your pussy. And my mouth is right there, if you need extra lube."

"Handy."

"I thought so." *Come on. Come just a little closer.*

She squinted at him. "You're wearing an awfully wolfish grin for a man who's covered in wax with his hands bound."

"I'm just happy to see you naked." His gaze dipped to her mound. "And wet and walking toward me."

"Hmm." She glanced at his crotch and then back into his eyes. "Are you hard again?"

"Yes. What part of *hot, naked woman in front of me* is confusing to you? Because my cock sure gets it."

"I assumed you need recovery time."

"When have I ever needed recovery time when it comes to you? Besides, you're not the only one who went without."

She froze. "What do you mean?"

"I didn't spank the monkey or grease the pole when we were apart either." Ronin couldn't tell her he'd always been a fight-or-fuck guy. If he was training to fight, he didn't expend energy fucking.

Amery draped her legs over his, and he pressed his knees together, providing her more stability.

It took every ounce of his control not to just grab her.

She set her forearm on his shoulder and dropped her other hand between her thighs.

When Ronin glanced down to watch, she yanked on his hair and tipped his head back.

"Huh-uh. Keep those beautiful eyes on mine."

"Why?"

"The only time I can read you is when we're intimate like this. The rest of the time, you are the unflappable Master Black."

"Does that bother you?"

"It used to. Until I realized I get to see part of you that no one else does. So I feel a bit cocky about that."

"You're acting cocky today too. Driving me fucking crazy."

Amery kept an intense eye lock with him as her hand moved between her thighs.

Jesus.

Then her fingers were in front of his lips. "Think I'm wet enough to start the show?"

Ronin opened his mouth and sucked her fingers inside, losing his head at the tangy taste of her. After sucking every sweet bit of her juice, he said, "You're wet enough for what I have in mind." He unclasped his hands and clamped them on her ass. "Surprise."

CHAPTER SEVEN

"OMIGOD! How did you get free?"

"Rope master secret." Then he fisted his hand in her hair and pulled her head to the side, baring her throat to him.

The symbolism in that action wasn't lost on her.

His mouth teased the spot on her neck that shut down all of her brain functions.

He muttered, "On the mat or against the wall?"

"Ah. What?" How was she supposed to think when his wet tongue was flicking . . . Oh, sweet mother of god. Right. Fucking. There. She trembled violently.

"Where I'm fucking you. On the mat or against the wall?"

"Wouldn't the impact on the mat hurt your injured knee?"

Ronin made an agitated noise. Next thing she knew, she was briefly airborne before her back hit the mat with a hundred and eighty pounds of Ronin Black on top of her.

"The mat it is." He reached down, yanked off his shorts, and was back above her almost before she blinked.

"Ronin—"

"Wrap your legs around my waist, baby, and let me in."

If he didn't give a damn about his injuries, why should she? All she could think about was how much she needed him.

Amery widened her knees and canted her hips. He slammed inside her so fast and hard she gasped.

"I'm sorry," he panted as he began to fuck her with fast, deep strokes. "Sweet and slow next time, okay? Been dying for you."

That confession sounded like it'd been ripped from the depths of his soul.

She pushed her hips down to meet his powerful thrusts, throwing her arms above her head like he preferred so he could restrain her with his hands. Or just his will.

"No. I want your hands on me, Amery. Your scratches on my back. Your nail marks on my ass. Your teeth on my throat." Ronin kissed a line down to her nipple. That warm, firmly sucking mouth latched on to the tip, and he didn't miss a beat as he continued to hammer into her.

Amery hooked her heels on the inside of his thighs, using his body motion as leverage to grind her clit against him. She twisted her fingers into his damp hair, slipping her other hand between them to feel that sexy flexor muscle tightening as he fucked her.

Ronin slowed down a little, letting his body abrade the magical spot on hers longer on every stroke. So in tune with what she needed.

She rubbed her lips across the shell of his ear. "I missed you."

"I never want to be without you again."

Her emotions were on overdrive because she had that urge to cry again.

His rapid breath drifted across his neck. "Baby, I am not going to last long."

"Do that hip twist thing, and I'll be right there with you."

And he did.

One second she was clinging to him as he bucked hard and poured himself into her; the next, her pussy clamped down on his shaft. Every pulse in her clit and tightening pull of her soft tissues reverberated through her body like distortion bouncing off feedback from a microphone. When the throbbing stopped, her hearing was muffled as if she'd been at a loud concert.

Ronin found her mouth and kissed her with the familiar sweetness, fire, and satisfaction she'd missed.

Afterward, when they were lying side by side on the mat, Amery asked, "How's your knee?"

"Ready for round two."

She slid her hand down his belly and cupped his softening cock. "Yeah?"

"Keep it up and we won't make it to the bedroom."

She propped herself up on her elbow and started to peel off the wax droplets.

"Leave them."

"We don't need wax in the sheets. Especially since they're what? Two thousand thread count?"

"Point taken."

She remembered when he'd removed the wax he'd left a soft kiss on each spot. So she did the same, using her mouth and the gentle rub of her fingers.

By the time Amery finished, Ronin was ready for round two.

They didn't make it to the bedroom.

And the second time wasn't slow and sweet either.

AFTER they ate a light supper and were lazing around, talking, touching and just existing in the same space, Amery knew Ronin needed to rest. He kept yawning, and every time he shifted positions, he made a pain-filled huffing noise.

She crawled into the big bed and watched him flexing his leg. "You put too much pressure on your knee when you fucked me from behind in the practice room."

"I'll take the twinge of pain if I can be naked with you.

Besides, it's sore no matter what I do—or don't do." He seemed annoyed with himself after that admission and reached out to touch her cheek. "And I've had a few hours' recovery time, keeping it elevated, thanks to you."

Amery kissed his fingertips. "Is that your way of telling me you're up for a third round?"

"While hard and fast always appeals to me . . ." Ronin followed the V of her pajama top from the edge of her collarbone to the swell of her cleavage. "I haven't put my hands on you with slow deliberation for seven weeks."

"You are a menace with those hands."

He pressed kisses across her collarbone, stopping to run his tongue in the dip between her neck and shoulder as his rough-skinned hand caressed her belly. "I missed this. All the different ways I can worship you."

When she twisted her fingers in his hair and tried to pull him away, he continued his maddeningly erotic exploration of the sensitive skin on the side of her breast.

"You know what I do with hands that get in my way," he warned, rubbing his soft lips across the same spot.

"Tie them up."

"Don't pretend you don't like that."

"I do like it. It's just . . ."

Ronin raised his head, stopping his delicious torture. "It's just what?"

"I'm really sore from earlier." She tried to say it without blushing but didn't quite manage it.

"So touching you automatically leads to fucking you?"

"It always has in the past. Not that I'm complaining," she added quickly.

"Sounds to me like you are." Ronin pushed upright. His eyes were dark with that you're-in-for-it now look. "It's up to me to prove you wrong. Hands above your head."

"I didn't mean . . ."

He got nose to nose with her. "I won't repeat myself."

Shit. Amery raised her arms and grabbed on to the headboard.

Ronin reached into the nightstand and pulled out a length of rope.

"You keep rope in here?"

"Baby, I keep rope everywhere. I never know when it'll come in handy."

She watched with total fascination as he folded the rope. Then he straddled her chest, and within thirty seconds, he had her wrists bound and secured to the headboard. "What was that?"

"Hojojutsu quick bind." Those wonderfully callused hands skated down her arms from below the wrist binding to her shoulders. "That's the only thing that'll be quick about this. One of my greatest pleasures is getting to put my hands on you whenever I want." He circled her nipple with the tip of his finger. "Not just the obvious parts."

Her stomach performed a little flip when he brushed a velvety-soft kiss on the edge of her jaw.

"And using my mouth to taste and tease is another pleasure."

His warm breath and deep voice sent tingles down the left side of her body.

"You've voiced your concerns about establishing intimacy outside of sex." He nuzzled beneath her chin until she arched her neck, giving him the section of skin he wanted. "Let me establish it right now. I will touch you, taste you, tease you—but I will not fuck you. This isn't about seeing how hard I can make you come. It's about you understanding how much I enjoy the journey of getting you there."

Amery gave herself over to him.

His hands and mouth were in constant motion. Sweet, powerful words were whispered against her skin. He stayed true to his word; no part of her body went unattended. When he reached her sex, he touched, licked, nuzzled, and kissed with no more reverence than he'd given the flare of her hips and the curve of her outer thighs.

When he finished the front side of her body, he turned her and started over. By the time he finished, her skin felt electrified.

Next Ronin kissed her—a kiss unlike any other. Kissing her as if her mouth should never be parted from his. The only place he touched her was on her face and neck with achingly tender caresses as the kiss heated up and cooled down. Finally he broke his lips free and sighed softly into her hair.

Yeah, she didn't need to lecture him on the meaning of intimacy.

Then he untied her hands and pulled her into his arms. "Sleep."

And she did.

AMERY woke alone.

She slipped on her robe and went looking for Ronin. She found a note in the kitchen.

> *Handling oversight on Saturday-morning classes. Then working on PT. It'll be mid-afternoon before I'm done. Groceries will be delivered today—I'll bring them up. Stick around. Please.*

No signature.

At loose ends, she brewed a pot of coffee and opened her laptop to check her e-mail. She forwarded a couple things to Molly and clicked on the e-mail from Cherry Starr—the erotica author she'd created a sexy book cover for.

> *Amery,*
> *The book reviews have been awesome so far—fingers crossed sales will reflect that! The cover has been getting serious buzz. Like,*

serious buzz. I've had several author friends ask who designed the cover after they've failed to find out more information online about Hard-Edge Designs.

I know you weren't sure whether this type of sideline would be worthwhile, so I haven't given out your contact information. A really selfish part of me wants to keep you all to myself, but I realize that's unrealistic ☺.

She laughed and sipped her coffee.

If you're interested, let me know—I'll let you contact them. One of my friends has a sideline giving sex toy parties, but the kicker is, she's teaching her customers how to make their own toys out of everyday household objects. And yes, this is classier than carving a dildo out of a cucumber. But she'd like a professional brochure done, and I immediately thought of you.

Last thing . . . I don't remember if I told you I'd planned a three-books out of these characters, and I've already started writing the second book. I'd really love for you to design the next two book covers in this series. I'm envisioning a man in bondage on the next cover—something sexy and edgy like you do so well. No rush. Let me know . . .

Cherry Starr~

A man in bondage. That could have some really interesting possibilities. A hot guy, bound up. . . .

She'd snapped a couple of pictures of a really hot guy yesterday.

Ronin.

They'd gotten so involved last night that she hadn't even looked at the shots. Not that she expected they'd be any good. Ronin was a beautiful subject matter, but she'd been so high on binding him and being in control of his pleasure that she'd more or less taken snapshots.

Still, she couldn't wait to see them.

The door to the practice room was shut. She felt strange even briefly popping in because the space, more so than any other place in the house, was entirely Ronin's domain. She saw the camera on the floor, grabbed it, and scooted out.

Back in the kitchen, she found the first picture of the session and clicked on it.

Holy shit. Her heart skipped a beat when she scrolled through the images. They were fantastic—Ronin couldn't take a bad picture. The darkness in the background made the light glow on his tawny-colored skin. The flexing of his arm showcased the cut of his biceps and triceps. His well-defined chest was arched, leaving the candle wax hidden in shadow. The stubborn angle to his jaw and the way his head fell back allowed his hair to cascade over his shoulders like black silk.

Ronin Black was a fucking god. Any one of the images would create a stunning cover. Too bad she'd promised him no one would ever see the pictures but them.

After she fixed herself toast and eggs, she looked around the cluttered kitchen and living area. Ronin's housekeeper hadn't come this week, and it was testament to how out of it he'd been that this mess hadn't bothered him. The man hated clutter.

Turning off the snarky voice in her head about nesting in a place that wasn't hers, she started to tackle cleaning the penthouse since they'd probably be staying in all weekend.

SUNDAY afternoon, as they were lazing in bed after another mind-blowing "lesson" in reestablishing intimacy, which included her being bound to a chair, Amery released a soft sigh.

Ronin trailed his fingers up and down her spine. "Something on your mind?"

"This has been a great weekend, just relaxing and hanging out."

"You mean locking us in the penthouse so you could make me rest."

She peered at him over her shoulder. "Your idea of rest is vastly different from the norm, Master Black."

"We spent most of the weekend in bed. That counts as rest." He smiled unrepentantly.

"Still, I should probably go home. I have to be in the office early tomorrow—"

Ronin moved in closer. "Then we'll go to bed at a decent time so you can be up early. But you're staying here."

She hadn't expected that vehement response.

"What's going on that you have to be there early?"

"I've gotten behind in the last week and need to catch up." Not entirely untrue. She'd scheduled an early coffee date with Molly to run the Okada deal past her. Amery couldn't take the job without her only employee's support. Since Molly was in grad school, Amery needed a better idea on Molly's future plans. She probably should get Ronin's input, since he ran a successful business, but for now she wanted to weigh her options outside of her lover's purview.

"I realize you're behind because of me. But I don't feel guilty enough to let you leave tonight. And that brings up something I wanted to talk to you about anyway." He rolled on top of her and pinned her down. "I want you to move in with me."

Stunned, she couldn't think of a single thing to say.

"This isn't a temporary thing between us. We were headed that way before I fucked it up." He rested his forehead to hers. "I love you. I need you in my life. I don't want to be apart from you for even one night."

By the way his body tensed up, she knew that wasn't easy for him to admit. Even though he had been using the L word at every opportunity. But she couldn't make this decision in the space of one week. She kept it light. "You sure you wouldn't rather move in with me? There's a great organic foods grocery store within walking distance of my cramped hovel."

Ronin laughed—like she'd hoped.

"It's a big step for us. I'll think about it, okay? But I need some time before I can answer you."

"Okay. In the meantime, I'll give you another reason to make this permanent." He pushed up. "I'm cooking dinner. Pulling out all the stops to wow you with my culinary expertise."

"You're making hot wings?" she asked hopefully.

He sighed. "I'll make spicy chicken breasts."

She smiled. "Close enough. See? I'm willing to compromise on some things."

A dangerously possessive look flitted through his eyes. "Understand that when it comes to what I want from you, I'm not willing to compromise. At all."

AMERY picked up croissants and fruit tarts on the way to her place Monday morning. The coffee had just finished brewing when Molly yelled, "Amery?" from the bottom of the staircase.

"Come on up."

Molly looked professional in a western-cut tweed blazer, a dark brown A-line skirt, and tan riding boots. Something had prompted her employee to care more about her appearance both on and off the job in the past two months. With a flattering new hairstyle, different makeup, and age-appropriate wardrobe updates, she'd transformed herself from geek to chic. Molly had also lost the baby fat in her cheeks, and overall she was much more toned since she'd started taking classes at Black Arts.

"Hey, woman, what an awesome outfit."

Molly blushed. "Thanks."

"Seriously. You look great."

"I credit kickboxing at the dojo three times a week. Deacon is a mean bastard, but I won't let him chase me off or convince me I'm too soft." She checked out the food on the counter. "Wow. Now, here's a breakfast spread. What's the occasion?"

Amery filled two cups and slid one across the counter. "I wanted to—" She glanced up sharply when Molly gasped. "What's wrong?"

"You're firing me, aren't you? This is a goodbye breakfast."

"God, no. Take a breath, okay? This is just breakfast."

Molly nodded and wrapped her hands around her coffee cup like it was a lifeline.

"I needed to talk to you about something before we tackle the Wicksburg Farm project."

"What's going on?"

"I had lunch with Shiori Hirano on Friday."

"No wonder you were so distracted."

"I wasn't sure what she wanted. I'd suspected she wanted to clear the air since I'm involved with her brother again."

"But?" Molly prompted and reached for a blueberry tart.

"It ended up being a business meeting." Amery sipped her coffee. "About the pitch I made to Okada Foods."

"Please tell me she asked you to pitch something again?"

"No need to. Long story short, the multiple major design companies they checked out for the same project we worked on were bypassed in favor of our designs."

Molly's jaw dropped. Luckily she slapped her hand over her mouth before blueberry filling spilled out. She swigged her coffee and blurted, "Omigod. Amery, that's huge! And this is not one of the times to cut the story short. I need details."

So Amery filled her in on everything, and Molly still wore a look of shock.

"I knew our designs rocked because they were so different, but I kinda worried that might be a detriment."

"Evidently not. Here's where we stand and what Okada offered." She pulled out the contracts. "Try not to get blueberry stains on them."

Molly stuck out her tongue.

Amery finished three cups of coffee and sorted her laundry while Molly scoured the documents. She'd pulled a notepad out of her purse and jotted down notes.

"Okay. You can stop pacing now," she called from the kitchen.

"What's the verdict, MBA candidate?"

"Well, the contracts are specific, and extensive, but they seem fair. I'd definitely have a lawyer look them over and see if any loopholes show up."

"So which, if any, option do you think is best?"

Molly looked taken aback. "Why are you asking me? You're the owner."

"But you've got a stake in this too. You worked on the project for free. You haven't cut your hours back even when I've cut your paycheck. You're very much a team player. I need to know if you want to be on my team and, if so, whether it's long-term." She held up her hand when Molly opened her mouth. "Hear me out completely first.

"You're in school. This job was supposed to be part-time, no pressure, a way to give you a chance to work with your creative side. Not everyone can get an MBA, and your business classes are just going to get harder in the next two years. I'm not implying that you can't do both—I just want you to ask yourself if you think it's worth it."

"What? Getting my MBA? Or working here?"

"Either. Both. If I decide to sign the contract, I can't do all the work myself. I need help. I'd love for that help to come from you. But then again, this is my business, and I'm not sure if you want to be invested in my vision. I hope you understand I'm saying that with zero malice, Molly. You are a bright, fantastic young woman with a thousand roads open to you. I don't want you to feel you've gotten stuck on this one with me." Amery stopped to take a breath.

"Well, if you're done listing all the reasons I should cut tail and run, maybe you'd like to hear my perspective?" Molly said curtly.

"By all means."

"I applied to graduate school in Denver because I knew if I didn't, I'd be stuck living at home, working as a number cruncher for my uncle Bob's insurance business for the rest of my life. So I never had a burning desire to get an MBA as much as I had a burning desire to get the hell out of Norfolk, Nebraska.

"I spent my whole life goal oriented. My nose stuck in a book. Believing the world I lived in with my family would always be enough. I think I still sort of believed that even after I moved here. But my ideas began to change after I went to work for you. You never made me feel dowdy or like a hick girl in the city. You took the time to teach me, to build up my self-esteem, to show me that yes, maybe someday I could be as cool as you—working in a job I love, having friends to hang out with and not just wacky relatives. I could have a better future than I ever imagined for myself."

"Molly, you're going to make me cry."

"Suck it up because I'm not done. So while I'd like to continue taking business classes, if I have the chance to go to work for you full-time, earn a good salary, help you grow and expand your business, then I'll drop out of school tomorrow."

Amery laughed and discreetly wiped her tears. "Okay, then. You're on board. Before we dissect the contract options, I want to say my goal, while making money and doing work I'm proud of, isn't to become obsessed with this and work myself to exhaustion or to the point I hate it. Finding balance in life is key."

"I never understood what that meant until the last couple of months, when I've actually built a life outside of school, books, and bad TV." Molly smiled. "I don't know if I can ever thank you enough for chewing me out for my shit attitude."

"I just wish I could've done it without you being physically assaulted first."

"But you wouldn't have met Ronin."

Amery smiled. "There is that."

"How are things going with him?"

"Good. He's almost back to his normal pushy, bossy, impossibly perfect self."

"I'm glad to hear that. I know his instructors at the dojo were really concerned about him after you guys broke up. Every time I saw him, he looked like crap. Like he'd been on the receiving end of . . ."

Her gaze zoomed to Molly. "Of what? Did you know Master Black had started fighting again?"

"I didn't know specifics, but all you had to do was look at him to see something was up."

"Why didn't you tell me he was a mess?" Amery demanded.

Molly gave her a defiant look. "Because you didn't ask me, Amery. Not once. You knew I went to the dojo, and you never asked me if I'd seen Ronin or how he was doing."

"And if I had?"

"I would've told you the truth. He was a wreck. You were a wreck."

"I was not," Amery protested.

"Puh-lease." Molly rolled her eyes. "Within hours of your breakup with Ronin, you ran away for an entire week. You spent the next week in your loft eating ice cream and crying while you watched martial arts movies and romantic tragedies."

She blushed.

"You snapped out of it a little in week three. The beginning of week four, you burst into tears when the cover you did for Cherry Starr went live on the book vendor sites, and you were worthless the rest of that week."

It'd seemed so surreal looking at that cover and the image of herself. Almost like it'd never happened. Adding in that Ronin hadn't called her or chased her down had made her believe maybe she had been under some kind of spell.

"Week six—"

"Jesus, Molly, how the hell do you remember all this when I don't?"

Molly offered her a smug smile. "I wrote it on the calendar. Chaz and I took bets on how long you and Ronin could hold out and stay away from each other. I said six weeks, he said eight. And since I always lose, I had to cheat—" She slapped her hand over her mouth.

That's when Amery knew. "You're the one who sent the package to Ronin with the peace offering and the note, aren't you?"

"Yes, I did and, please, please don't be mad. It got you two to talking again and to see that you are so perfect for each other—"

"Stop. I understand why you did it. I knew I was falling apart during that time, and it pissed me off because I swore I'd never be one of those women who can't function without a man in her life." She laughed. "I thought I'd done pretty well at hiding it from you."

"You sucked at hiding it. It was hard for us to watch and do nothing. Chaz swore after the stuff had gone down with Emmylou and her issues with Ronin last time that he wasn't meddling in your love life again."

"But Chaz encouraged you to."

"Yep. I don't regret it, because you're happy, Amery."

"I am."

Molly tapped the contracts. "So what does Ronin think of you going to work in the family business?"

"He doesn't know."

"What? Why not?"

She twisted a hank of hair. "Because it's his family's business. I need to make the decision on my own—what's best for my company. He wouldn't consult me on a business decision for the dojo. I have to draw that dividing line because I don't think he can be neutral when it comes to Okada."

"Probably true."

"So let's keep this between us for now." She picked up the

contracts and dropped them back in the envelope. "I'll make copies before I take this to my lawyer."

"Cool." Molly slid off the stool. "And in my downtime, in my new role as office manager—"

"Office manager?" Amery repeated.

"If you take the Okada job, you'll need to hire another graphic artist. I'll have seniority, and I'm good at balancing the creative and business side. Anyway, I'll check out the actual profit and losses for your existing food-based customers and see if letting that part of your business go will be a financial blow."

"Awesome. But I want you to wait until this is a done deal before you drop out of school."

"Damn. And here I was totally going to blow off my homework."

"Smart-ass. Let's get set up for the Wicksburg Farm Halloween bash." Amery made it halfway to the sink with the empty coffee cups when she remembered she'd left her camera in Ronin's practice room. She couldn't take a chance on Molly seeing those photographs even if she swapped out the memory cards, and if she and Ronin continued to take risqué pictures of each other, they'd need a camera at his place anyway.

"What's wrong?"

She turned around and smiled. "On second thought, let's head to the electronics store first. I've been meaning to upgrade my camera and get one of those headset thingies."

CHAPTER EIGHT

THE following week, Alvares "Blue" Curacao showed up at Black Arts on time with his instructors—two men and one woman. He bowed and then offered his hand. "Hachidan Black. Thank you for this opportunity."

It seemed strange to hear his belt rank mentioned since Ronin was used to being called Sensei at the dojo. "My pleasure. Have a seat, and everyone can introduce themselves before we get started."

The tension in the room was palpable.

That's when Shiori walked in.

Ronin could feel Knox and Deacon's questioning looks, but he kept his focus on his sister. He'd asked her to mediate this meeting. Personal issues aside, Shiori was a shrewd businesswoman, and he wanted her involvement in this situation.

"Gentlemen." She nodded to the other woman in the room. "Sophia. I'm Shiori Hirano, a visiting instructor from Japan. Since I have no personal stake in the outcome of this meeting, I'm here as an impartial mediator. Anything that is said in this meeting is confidential, agreed?"

"Agreed," Blue said.

"Agreed," Ronin said.

"Let's start with you, Mr. Curacao. Tell us about your dojo. Number of students, qualifications of instructors, monthly fees."

"Currently we have three qualified instructors besides myself, black belt levels sanctioned by BJJA—Brazilian Jujitsu Association. We teach seventy-five students. The majority of them are below blue belt ranking since the Brazilian method moves slower through the belt ranking system than traditional jujitsu. Our requirements are a minimum of three paid classes a week. We do not charge higher-ranking belts higher fees."

Everyone around the table nodded approval. Several martial arts disciplines charged higher fees for brown and black belt levels—which created a problem because the instructors moved the students up the ranks faster to collect the significantly higher class fees.

When Blue revealed his hourly class fee, Ronin quickly did the math. They were making a nice chunk of change every month.

Shiori looked to Ronin to offer the same information.

After he finished speaking, she opened up the discussion to the instructors from both camps. Ronin was really impressed that his guys asked things he hadn't considered. And Sophia asked why the Black Arts staff wasn't utilizing female instructors. Then she questioned the boy-to-girl training ratio. Something that had never crossed his radar—until Shiori had questioned him along those same lines.

When Shiori began speaking of the different philosophies, Ronin discreetly shook his head. Always a pointless discussion.

Knox stood. "Let's look at the training rooms."

At that point, everyone left Blue and Ronin alone.

"I thank you for opening the door to this discussion, Sensei. Especially after—"

"You knocked me out? I don't hold grudges."

Blue cocked his head. "So I shouldn't hold it against you that you let me win?"

Ronin said nothing.

"I'm an excellent fighter, but it shouldn't have been that easy. I have to ask, why did you want the punishment?"

He would've been disappointed if Blue hadn't picked up on it. "Ever done something so unbelievably stupid that you want to kick your own ass?"

"Of course."

"Since I couldn't do that, and no one here would help me out, I let you kick it for me."

Blue laughed.

"I appreciate you following up on my physical condition after the fight."

"No problem. I never asked if you made any money from the event."

Ronin paused and studied the guy. Blue's face carried scars from his fighting years. He was one intimidating motherfucker in the ring. But he had a decent head for business—Ronin had checked him out thoroughly before setting up the meetings. "It's a nonissue at this point. Do you make money from events?"

"I make enough to tempt me into wanting to make more. I'd like to bring something up before we get into the possible dojo merger. Because if that doesn't work out, for some reason I think this idea might."

"I'm listening."

Blue leaned forward, resting his forearms on his knees. "We both know mixed martial arts fighters' goals are to get into one of the big organizations and fight on a professional level. But if amateurs have no place to fight, how will they establish a record and move up the ranks?"

"It's impossible. Or close to."

"The major players are bypassing this market. I figured out that the way to make money is to pack the fight card with amateur fights. That brings in friends and family. Put women in the ring for one match. Then close the evening with a pro match, or what passes as a pro matchup. If we combine our resources, in very little time we would be the go-to promoters for amateur fights in this area."

Ronin cocked his head. "How many fights are you promoting a year right now?"

"Three or four very small ones that are barely a step above smokers. How about Black Arts?"

"Officially? None. I personally set up . . . underground bouts a few times a year. I keep it off the radar. Pay the purse out of my pocket."

Blue gave him a narrow-eyed look. "So you fight in these unsanctioned matches?"

He fought the urge to squirm. Before he'd returned to the cage, he'd had to come clean with Knox. It'd been fucking embarrassing to admit that in the past three years, he'd hidden his compulsion to fight like it was some dirty secret. He'd convinced himself he needed to test his skills outside of the dojo, outside of being Sensei Black. But the truth was, after all the years he'd spent earning his reputation with his fighting skills, he couldn't just . . . stop. He loved to fight. It was the one thing in his life that he was good at.

"Hachidan?" Blue prompted.

"Yes, I've maintained a presence in the underground fighting world. Seventy percent of the time I referee. The other thirty percent?" He met Blue's gaze head-on. "I fight."

"Dangerous hobby, my friend, and one I'd require you give up for good if we join forces."

Ronin nodded. He'd already been forced to give it up, and his respect grew for the man across the table for expecting they'd keep things on the up-and-up.

"Back to the topic at hand. I'd like to pursue a partnership with you for the major amateur event we've scheduled in three weeks."

"Here in Denver?"

"Yep. And you're thinking . . . why haven't you heard of it, right?"

"Right."

"That's what I'm saying. You're involved in the fight world, and you're unaware of the event. Think how many other martial arts studios with MMA training programs are in the same situation. They have no place to put their fighters to the test. Between us, we've got the network to make it happen. We've got the diversity. We've got the money."

Ronin had to slow down the gears churning in his head and focus. "Expenses?"

"Everything fifty-fifty. From the overhead to the venue to the staffing. This first event could be a trial run to see how well we mesh. A lot of the logistics are already in place. It'd just entail swapping a few things out. And you kicking in some cash."

"I'll admit you've piqued my interest." Really piqued it. If Ronin couldn't participate in the fighting world in the cage or host fights in dive bars that catered to a rougher crowd, he could be an active part of it from a different angle. God knew he needed something to occupy himself while he was supposed to sit around twiddling his fucking thumbs.

Blue smiled. "Good. I didn't mean to steer you away from the real reason I'm here."

"Let's cut to the chase. I think we can come to a workable agreement as far as absorbing your dojo into mine, while letting you keep some autonomy. What is your biggest issue right now?"

"I do not own my facility. I moved into the location last year. In the last nine months, I've been approached by two guys offering me protection. I initially declined."

"Let me guess. After declining their offers, your place has been vandalized."

"Three times. Renter's insurance didn't begin to cover the replacement costs. I contacted the rental property company to ask for assistance with paying for new windows, and they informed me anything involving 'malicious intent' isn't covered."

"Did the protection guys warn you about the vandalism?"

He nodded. "Being from Brazil and growing up on American TV, I thought those types of business practices were for effect. Or they only happened on the East Coast."

"Sadly, no. How long is your lease?"

"I've got one year remaining on it. I'm the only tenant left in the building."

"Is the building for sale?"

"No, but every other building on the block has changed hands in the last two years. As far as I know, the owners weren't interested in selling."

Sounded like the owners were being pressured to sell by a third party harassing the existing leaseholder into breaking the lease and cutting off the owner's income stream. Easy to hire muscle, use scare tactics and property damage to convince the tenants to leave. He'd seen it happen over and over. And in the not too distant past, he'd been the guy doing the persuading.

"You don't believe me," Blue stated quietly.

Ronin glanced up at him. "No, it's not that. A few organizations around here still get results by those tactics. Are you paying for protection?"

Blue's face turned red. "I have no choice. But it's sucking every bit of profit, and I'll have to close my dojo before too much longer. I'd much rather be under the Black Arts umbrella and pay you rather than lose everything I've worked for in the last three years."

"I understand. Is there a chance the property management company would relax the penalties for breaking your lease?"

"I'll ask."

"Let me do some checking around. I know some guys in the business." Denver mover and shaker Thaddeus "TP" Pettigrew owed him a favor, so the real estate angle would be easy to check.

"You'd do that before we signed any formal agreement?"

"Let's put it this way: I'll feel better signing an agreement with you if all of that stuff is already taken care of." Ronin stood. "Let's join the tour. And if you're all right with it, we can get Shiori started on the transitional paperwork."

"As long as she's willing to work with Sophia. She handles the business end of ABC."

"You should know that Shiori is my sister. She's here temporarily handling some family business and filling in as an instructor."

Blue grinned again. "A sure sign that this arrangement is meant to be, no? Because Sophia is my sister."

THE next evening, Ronin said, "I think I might go back to teaching next week."

Amery lifted her head from his chest. "I know the bruises have faded, but are you really ready? Or are you just feeling guilty?"

"Teaching is what I do." Fuck. That's all they'd let him do.

"What classes are you usurping? Poor Sandan Zach's women's self-defense class?"

He slapped her bare ass. "I did my penance teaching you."

"Hey!"

"Don't pout, baby." Ronin dropped a quick kiss on her forehead. "I'd be helping Ito with the younger kids."

"Why? Aren't your highly advanced skills wasted there?"

"I should be accessible to all students, not just those in advanced classes. Plus I need to assess all levels more frequently to ensure their skill sets are up to par."

"Will you have time to do that, given how much time you've already committed to the new promotion company?"

Ronin would be going fucking crazy if he didn't have that. In just one day, he'd expanded on Blue's original idea and he'd become a little obsessed with it.

"What are you calling the promo company?"

He frowned. "No idea."

"I have one. My creative little brain has just been cranking."

"And?"

"What about . . . Black and Blue Promotions?"

Ronin laughed. "That is perfect. Damn, woman, you are brilliant."

"I know." Amery's lips started a southerly path down the center of his chest. She detoured to his right nipple and sucked so hard he nearly bowed off the bed. So when she slid her wet lips across his sternum to his left nipple, he expected the same treatment. But she flicked just the tip of her tongue around the flat disc until it puckered. Then she reconnected with the line bisecting his belly and licked straight down to his cock. Anytime her hot tongue teased his skin, his cock took notice. It'd begun to stir, but was still soft and curled on the inside of his thigh. No sweet nuzzling like he expected. Amery's mouth enclosed his cock.

That time he did arch up.

She sucked gently as blood filled his shaft. When her mouth couldn't contain the swelling flesh, she changed her position. She started bobbing her head.

Ronin closed his eyes and groaned. His thought processes grew hazy, and his pulse jumped as her hot, wet mouth worked him. She drew the length in and out rapidly, not sucking, but keeping his shaft slippery. So slippery that moisture seeped down and coated his balls.

Usually he preferred to be in control, even when Amery was blowing him. He liked keeping a tight grip on her hair. He liked pushing his cock to the back of her throat and holding it there when he came. He liked binding her hands and holding her face between his palms as he directed how fast, how hard, and how long he plunged in and out of her addictive mouth.

But he kept his hands by his sides, allowing himself to feel all the nuances of how she wanted to please him. Her soft tongue. The scrape of her teeth. Heat and wetness and pressure.

He tensed when she reached between his legs and fondled his balls. But she didn't stop there. She rubbed his perineum with her thumb. Up and down until she brushed his asshole. She swept around and around, the wetness making the pucker slippery enough so she could press the digit in slightly.

Jesus, that felt amazing. He'd started to pant as she brought him closer to the edge.

Amery switched her hand position, easing a finger past the sensitized ring and into his ass. She sucked his cock with shorter, tighter strokes, and she rubbed the tip of her finger across his gland.

Ronin felt every other muscle in his body going equally rigid, desperate for the explosion of orgasm. When he glanced down at Amery's beautiful face, her sexy look of determination had him relaxing into the mattress, allowing her to give him the orgasm rather than chasing after it.

As much as he tried to focus on her, he squeezed his eyes shut in ecstasy as his cock and balls tightened with a warning tingle. Then his ass clamped down on her finger, and liquid heat pulsed out of his dick so violently he felt the pulling sensation in his lower abdomen.

"Fuck. Yes. Jesus, don't stop."

Amery kept that magical mouth and finger connection going, dragging out his climax until he saw spots behind his eyes and his entire being floated in a quiet void. As the pulses faded and he became aware of his surroundings, he decided the bliss of orgasm defined a Zen moment.

She removed her finger and her mouth. Took him a second to figure out the vibration on his lower belly was actually Amery's chuckle.

He grabbed a handful of her hair and caught her attention. "What was that giggle for?"

"I believed you called out nirvana at one point." She offered him a sly smile and tongued his belly button.

"That it was." He ran his knuckles down her cheek. "Goddamn, woman, I love you."

Amery pushed up and away from him. "Of course you say you love me after your dick has been in my mouth and I just blew you to nirvana."

What the fuck? Rather than call her on her bitchy comment, he calmly said, "I tell you I love you all the time, not just after sex." He stared at her, letting her unspoken words, words he was so desperate to hear from her, hang in the air between them, almost like a dare. *Tell me you love me, Amery. Come on. It's not that hard.*

His response didn't prompt her to do anything but retreat. She rolled off the bed, slipped on her robe, and announced, "I feel like making popcorn," and fled from the room.

He resisted all of five seconds before he punched the pillows. Maybe she didn't love him, but her discounting how he felt about her wasn't fair and it sure as hell wasn't happening again.

NOTHING on the sports channels caught his attention.

Amery wandered in munching on popcorn and plopped beside him. "Anything good on?"

"Not really. Was there something you wanted to watch?"

"What's on the classic TV channel?"

"I don't think I can sit through another episode of *Bewitched*."

She shot him a sideways glance. "I know you're secretly hoping *Kung Fu* is on."

He groaned.

"Maybe I'll check out your DVDs."

That would take her all of two minutes.

So when she was still pacing in front of the bookshelves ten minutes later, he knew she was nervous—which caused his heart to skip a beat. Was she about to tell him that he'd have to make room for her DVDs and stuff when she moved in? "Something on your mind?"

"Yeah. But I feel stupid bringing it up now."

"Why?"

"Because I don't want you to think I sucked your dick in hopes it'd soften you up."

"Baby, you sucking my dick makes me harder, not softer."

"You know what I mean."

Ronin stood, removed the popcorn bowl from her hands and set it on the table. "No bullshit between us. What's going on?"

"I need a favor."

He kept his face blank and banked his disappointment. Why did it always boil down to this? When he'd called TP earlier to ask about the protection business around Blue's dojo, TP said he needed a favor and insisted on setting up a meeting to discuss it. "What kind of favor?"

"You know those supersexy pictures I took of you blindfolded that day?"

"Like I could ever forget that," he murmured.

"I know I told you they'd be for my eyes only. But I heard from Cherry Starr, and she wants me to do another cover for her. Evidently the book has been really popular, and she's decided to write a series. So for the next book, she wants a bound guy on the cover. She isn't in any rush, so I do have time to set up another photo shoot. But I figured it wouldn't hurt to ask you first."

No, immediately jumped into his head. Given his level of expertise in two disciplines—jujitsu and rope bondage—it'd be . . . embarrassing if anyone recognized him. Especially if they believed he was submissive behind closed doors.

Letting silence distort the mood hadn't been intentional on his part. So when Amery said, "Forget it," and tore out of the room, he realized he'd been so lost in possibilities that he hadn't answered her.

Of course Amery would assume he'd hedged because he intended to say no.

But don't you plan to say no?

Ronin found her at the bar fixing herself a cocktail.

"I'm driving you to drink?"

She shook her head. "It's just been a crazy day. And you dragging me to bed two seconds after I walked in tonight and trussing me up to ravish me made me forget the stress of my day. So now I'm making the stress reliever I intended to." She pulled out another lowball glass. "Want one?"

"What are you making?"

"A White Russian. The sweet goes very well with the salty."

"I'll pass."

After measuring out the booze, Amery headed to the kitchen, adding ice and cream to the glass. She stirred, sipped, and sighed.

"Look. About the photo for the cover . . ."

She held up her hand. "Forget I mentioned it."

Ronin ran his hand through his hair. "I didn't say *no*."

"But you didn't say *yes* or *maybe* either. Which sounds a lot like *no*." She took another sip of her drink. "It's fine, Ronin."

"Where's your folksy North Dakota–ism that reminds me that what's good for the goose is good for the gander?" he prompted.

"It had crossed my mind. But I'm not going to harangue you. I'll find another way. Shouldn't be hard to find another male model. Of course, whichever young hottie I do find and convince to get half naked in front of me won't be nearly as hot, sexy, and compelling as you."

She'd be in the same room with a half-naked guy?

Fuck that.

"It'd actually be a relief to have a rope novice as a model since I'm pretty sure the way I bind him won't matter. But it'd be cool if you gave me a few tips to put him at ease." Her gaze went a little . . . dreamy. "Or maybe it'd be easier for him if I blindfold him first. That way he won't know that I don't know what I'm doing with ropes."

His woman really believed he'd allow her to put her hands all over some strange naked guy? And then make the moment even more intimate by binding him?

Fuck that.

Ronin crowded her against the counter. "No. Fucking. Way."

"You don't get to decide that." Amery poked him in the chest. "End of discussion, so back off."

"How about if I give you a lesson in binding right now?"

She shook her head, but he'd already clamped his hands on her ass and lifted her onto the countertop.

A startled *eep* escaped her, followed by, "You can't just—"

"I can, I will, and I did. Don't argue, or I'll gag you."

He reached for the cotton dish towel the same time his other hand latched on to her throat below her jawline. "Stay just like this. Palms flat, wrists together behind you."

Amery threw her shoulders back and glared at him—but she obeyed him.

"Lose that surly look and get with the program. You brought it on yourself." Ronin took advantage of her rigid pink nipple peeking out from her robe and sucked it hard while his hands worked. This basic hojojutsu tie was child's play; he didn't need to watch as he bound her wrists.

But Little Miss Feisty tested the binding anyway.

He placed her heels on the edge of the counter. She was stable, but it wasn't a comfortable pose she could relax into.

"Hold still." Ronin tugged on the ends of her robe tie and pushed her knee out as he wrapped the silk around her ankle. Then he did the same thing on the other side. With the belt anchored in the small of her back. When he looked up at his smart-mouthed lover, her jaw hung open.

"You tied me up that fast?"

"Baby, I *am* a professional. Technically this is called a crab tie, and your hands should be attached to the ankle binding, but I improvised."

No defiant look entered her eyes. Just heat.

"Now, if you attempt to move your feet, you'll just pull yourself forward. Wouldn't want you to fall off the counter. Not with what I've got planned for you." He permitted a smile. He peeled back the edges of her robe and feasted his eyes on her. Then he flattened his palms on her chest and slowly slid them down her torso. "I love this flush on your skin. Heat and dew. Wonder where else you're dewy?"

Keeping his gaze fastened to hers, he dragged his thumb up and down her slit. "You wet because you love blowing me? Or because I showed you I can tie you up anytime I want?"

"Both."

"Good answer." Ronin brought his thumb to his mouth, sucking her juices. "Tangy. A little salty. Delicious." He snagged her drink and curbed his smile when her eyes widened. "Didn't you just say sweet goes well with salty?"

"What are you doing?"

"Adding a little more cream." He held the glass below her chin and tipped it over her chest.

Amery expelled a loud gasp when the cold drink hit her skin.

The white liquid ran down her body pretty fast but not in the path he wanted. So he poured more.

She gasped louder when the cold drink flowed over her mound and her pussy.

It was tempting to fish an ice cube out of the glass and torture her nipples until they were icy and then suck the sting away with his hot mouth, but he needed to taste her like this.

Ronin tilted the glass one more time. But this time he chased the white line with his mouth. Sucking the tiny bit that'd pooled in the hollow of her throat, straight down between her breasts, over her quivering abdomen. Sucking the sticky cream from her small patch of pubic hair, getting a full taste of her musk sweetened by the drink.

He tongued her clit ruthlessly until the inside of her thighs trembled. Then he spread her pussy lips with his thumbs and buried his mouth in her.

Amery's soft cries barely registered; he was so lost in sucking every bit of sweetness from her cunt. The more he licked and flicked his tongue over her every soft, sensitive fold and her tight opening, the more cream poured from her.

When she arched hard against his mouth, he pushed open the hood hiding her clit with his teeth and suckled that swollen nub until her entire sex pulsed and she screamed.

And it was the scream and panting moans that had him growling against her throbbing tissues. His cock throbbed in response.

As soon as her orgasm ended, he said, "Baby, look at me."

She tilted her chin down and opened her eyes.

Ronin pressed his mouth to hers, sharing the taste of her passion and her drink.

Amery licked the inside of his lips. Sucked his tongue. Turning him fucking inside out with the need to have her—be in her, be on her—again and again.

After he broke the lip-lock, he murmured, "You're so fucking sexy. I can't get enough of you. Hold on."

He ditched his pants and turned her so she was completely on the counter. Then he climbed up between her thighs and balanced on his haunches, ignoring the throb in his knee. He scooped her ass cheeks into his hands, keeping her body angled, raising her up just high enough so he could lean forward and lodge his cock into her.

At the first thrust, he watched her, expecting she'd ask if he was in any pain, given their position. But all he saw was dark desire in her eyes. Her tits bounced with every hard plunge.

The quiet between them added to the eroticism. Sometimes silence spoke louder than any play-by-play. They were so in tune—breathing, heart rate, and their movements—that Ronin began a tantric rhythm. Putting only his cock head inside her, then pulling out, then slamming deep and holding himself at full penetration for two seconds. He built that short-long-hold tempo, starting at one stroke and building to nine. By the time they reached the seventh set of nine, they were both covered in sweat and the need for release pulsed in the air.

During the eighth set, Amery made a soft whimper, and Ronin placed his hand on her heart—the anahata chakra.

At that pinnacle moment when they climbed up to the last set of nine, he slid his hand down and stroked her clit.

She shattered.

Being seated inside her to the root, without moving, he felt every contraction of her pussy muscles clear into his balls as she milked his orgasm.

And even in the intense moment with the pulsing and connection consuming him, his head counted to nine.

Nine pulses of her clit beneath his finger.

Nine pulls of her inner muscles.

Nine bursts of heat shooting from his cock.

His head fell back. He seemed to float outside his body, yet he'd never been more grounded.

When his senses returned, he glanced down at her.

She blinked at him with sated, sleepy eyes. "What the hell was that, Master Black?"

Heaven. "Tantric circle of nine."

Ronin lowered her butt to the counter and broke the connection of their bodies. Then he ran his palms up her torso, gently cupping her breasts. "You're beautiful."

"So are you." She tried to level out her breathing. "Is there any eastern philosophy or discipline you're unfamiliar with?"

He swept his thumbs over her nipples. "I lived in a monastery for four years. I studied and trained. That's all there was to do."

"That tantric thing cannot be learned from reading a book."

"Do you really want to talk about those lessons now?" A piercing pain shot through his knee, and he ducked his head to hide his wince, focusing on undoing the knots at Amery's ankles. "Any pain?" he asked as he gently rubbed her anklebones and her calves.

"No, because I can't feel my arms."

He slowly pulled her upright by the shoulders and unbound her wrists. "Tell me when it starts to tingle."

"Now."

Fuck. He should've paid more attention to—

"Ronin, I'm fine."

He nuzzled her neck, filling his lungs with the scent of her skin as he rubbed circulation back into her arms. "I'm sorry."

"Don't be. That was so intense I forgot I even had arms."

"We were sort of on another plane, weren't we?"

"You've got lots of . . . sex moves that I've never heard of, don't you?"

"Doesn't that make you want to move in and stay with me forever?"

The way she stiffened beneath him bothered him. He pulled back and looked at her. "What?"

"But I don't have an encyclopedia of fancy sex tricks to keep you interested in me forever."

"As long as you're enjoying what we do together, I don't care. It's not a competition. There won't be a test." He swept his thumb across her lips. "If we never do anything except make love face-to-face in our bed, baby, I'm good with that. I love you. And you know that's not just the afterglow of hot sex talking. It's all me."

Her big blue eyes softened, but she didn't respond in kind—either that she loved him or she couldn't wait to make his bed theirs by moving in. Yet she did wrap herself around him and kiss him with a perfect mix of desire, sweetness, and gratitude.

Since he suspected he had a ways to go in establishing trust between them again, he had to put himself out there first. "So back to our original discussion."

"Which discussion was that? Because you completely scrambled my brain with your tantric sex moves."

"About the book cover. I'll let you use a picture of me, as long as I'm not recognizable."

"Really?"

"Really."

Amery's telling smirk ruined her feigned look of surprise. She'd riled him up on purpose, talking about hiring a male model.

His thoughts flashed back to when his ex had pouted and lied to manipulate him. But he couldn't draw parallels between the two women when they were polar opposites. Amery was a terrible liar—too honest almost to a fault. He couldn't remember any instance when she'd used manipulation to get her way.

But then, you wouldn't know until it was too late, would you?

"I promise you won't regret this." She leaned forward to hug him and made a sour face. "Ouch. My butt is sticking to the counter."

"We did make a mess."

"*You* made a mess."

"Good thing the cleaning service comes tomorrow."

Amery lightly whapped him on the chest. "Ronin Black, we are not leaving this for your housekeeper to clean up! That's just . . ." Her eyes narrowed. "You're yanking my chain. You'd never leave a mess for someone else to clean up just because you can. You sure don't act like I expected a billionaire would."

"You sound disappointed."

"Not hardly. Grab a rag, moneybags, and start wiping."

CHAPTER NINE

RONIN understood why Thaddeus Pettigrew preferred to conduct meetings in his private executive dining room at his high-rise office building. The real estate, restaurant, oil, and timber magnate couldn't go anywhere without being approached by business associates, wannabe business associates, the media, or critics.

Yet Ronin knew agreeing to TP's parameters put the power in his hands. He suspected from their very first meeting that TP recorded their conversation. Since many of their discussions included what could be considered criminal activity, Ronin had configured a scrambling device he kept in his pocket whenever they held a meeting. If TP was aware of it, he hadn't mentioned it. Ronin believed his business relationship with TP survived and thrived because Ronin looked after his own best interests first.

He took the elevator to the thirtieth floor and was met by a curvy brunette who proclaimed herself TP's personal assistant. Funny how fast TP went through assistants; in ten years, Ronin hadn't seen the same one twice.

And if Amery was impressed with his private elevator, she'd really be blown away by the one that led to TP's office. A glass elevator on the inside of the building. Given how much she loved his rooftop garden, this three-story glass atrium, which had been designed to mimic a rain forest, would be right up her alley. Even when the snow flew and the temps dipped below freezing, it felt like the Amazon in here.

The assistant led him into the executive room where TP held court. He stood and held out his hand when Ronin approached.

"Ronin, I was glad you called. I've heard some interesting tidbits in the past few weeks that no one will confirm, but I know I'll get the truth from you. Before we delve into that and the favor I need to ask you, care for a cocktail?"

"Sure. I'll have whatever you're having."

TP beckoned his personal assistant closer. "Bambi, be a dear and fix us a drink. Chivas and water."

"Right away, Mr. Pettigrew." She stepped to a well-stocked bar, mixed the drinks, and had them on the table almost before Ronin took a seat.

"Is there anything else, sir?"

TP shook his head and blew a big puff of cigar smoke in her face.

She didn't even blink or cough before she tottered out of the room.

"Bambi?" Ronin repeated. "Is that her real name?"

"The guy at the strip club who lent her to me for a few weeks swears it is."

Don't ask.

"So what's this I hear about you getting the fuck beat outta you in the cage?"

"Which time are you referring to?"

TP's shaggy gray eyebrows rose. "Jesus, Black. It happened more than once? What? You getting soft or something?"

"Just old and stupid. I filled in for a fighter, and my brain forgot to remind my body that I'm thirty-eight, not twenty-eight."

"Don't you train every goddamn day so you're ready to fight anytime, anyplace?"

"Yes. But like in the business world, theory and practice aren't always copacetic." Ronin shrugged. "Still hurts like a motherfucker to get knocked out. That aspect hasn't changed. The recovery time is longer too as I've aged."

"So the rumors aren't true? You weren't a last-minute add-on as a dare?"

"No. My only pro-level fighter backed out of a scheduled bout. It was a rare foray into official fight promotion for us, and rather than lose more money, I fought." He grinned. "Ended up getting my ass handed to me—at least during the fight."

"No one else would be grinning about that, Ronin."

"Yet you are."

"Yep." TP grinned widely. "Like you, I hate bein' predictable. Pays to keep people guessing."

"And it always pays well for you."

He grunted. "Not always. Let's get the first business discussion out of the way. Why'd you want to know about that property on Baldwin?"

"The lone tenant is a friend of mine." Ronin explained the incidents, ending with, "I hadn't heard of those organizations moving into that neighborhood. Figured you'd know something about it."

"I'd heard a blip or two over the past few months but nothing solid. I'll be keeping a better eye on it now. I'll also pass the info to Stanislovsky. I know that won't sit well with him."

"How is Max?"

"Headed for divorce court again. This marriage lasted barely three years. He set her up in business, some healthy frozen yogurt chain. She had some success with it, so she figures that entitles her to a bigger piece of all of his business." TP sighed. "He could've saved himself two divorces and ten million bucks if he'd listened to my advice."

"Which is what?"

"Keep your woman—or women—out of your business."

Surely he'd misheard that.

"I see by the look on your face you think I'm sexist." TP shrugged and puffed on his cigar. "Maybe I am. I've been married thirty years. Not once have I ever asked my wife's opinion on a possible business deal. Not once have I given her the details on how I make the money she's more than happy to spend."

"So you don't share anything with your wife?"

"Businesswise? Nope."

Maybe that's why rumors abounded that TP had multiple mistresses. Just like Ronin's grandfather—but at least he didn't have a wife literally overlooking his affairs.

"I never fooled myself into believing I was a handsome son of a bitch like you, Black. I'm fat. Obnoxious. Cocky. Crude. I don't score with the ladies because they're getting a night with Brad Pitt. I'm rich. That's my appeal. I knew it when I married my wife. I know it whenever I hire a new assistant. I'm good with that."

"Does that throwback attitude keep you from doing business with women?"

"No. I know women are highly capable of running their own businesses. I just don't want them running mine. Men like us? We do what we have to do. We don't piss and moan about it and wring our hands. We don't hold a focus group to determine the best course of action. We just do it."

Ronin wasn't anything like TP . . . Was he?

"Can't go back and change the past, Ronin. Only thing you can do is move forward."

"I fail to see how asking me to do you a favor—given the types of favors I've done for you in the past—is allowing me to move forward."

"So tell me no."

"Jesus, TP, are you off your meds?"

TP grinned. "You paid your debt to me years ago, Ronin. It's your sense of loyalty that keeps you doing the occasional favor for me. I'm not above taking advantage of that for no reason other than I trust you. And you can be guaran-damn-teed if I've asked for your help it's because I've exhausted other options."

There was a compliment in there somewhere. "What's going on?"

He sighed. "My daughter Katie. She's twenty-three, beautiful, sweet, and dumb as a post. I say that with pure fatherly love and no malevolence."

"What's she gotten herself into?"

"Three months ago, she called her mom, claiming her boyfriend was holding her against her will. Prior to that, we hadn't seen the girl for damn near two months, so we had legitimate reason for concern. Katie has fallen for every dirtbag to come down the pike since she turned sixteen. When these guys figure out who she is, they swear it's true love." He snorted. "She even married one of these bastards. It lasted one month. That cost me a chunk of change. Every time she's been in a situation, I've bailed her out."

"Of jail?"

"Not so far, knock on wood." He rapped on the table. "Like our other kids, when she turned eighteen, she started receiving monthly dividends from her trust fund. For the past five years, at the beginning of every month, the balance on the account is close to zero because she—or her douche bag boyfriend of the moment—has emptied the account. But during those three months, she hadn't touched the money. Long story short, my PI found her, and my security team dragged her out of the roach-infested place she'd been held. The wife picked out a rehab place in California that specializes in rebuilding or re-creating self-esteem in poor little rich girls or some such new-age shit. After she completed the program, she returned to Denver, and she's been driving me batshit crazy ever since."

"While I'm glad it sounds like everything worked out, why are you telling me this, TP?"

"Come to find out, the guy she'd shacked up with was an MMA fighter." He blew a smoke ring. "Evidently you refereed one of his amateur underground fights."

"Still not seeing where you're going with this."

"Katie discovered you and I are acquaintances. Somewhere along the way, she's convinced herself she belongs in the MMA fight-promotion business. Specifically building one with Black Arts."

Ronin couldn't stop his look of shock.

TP laughed. "Exactly my reaction when my daughter demanded I set up a meeting between the three of us to discuss options."

He fought the urge to look over his shoulder to see if TP's kid was joining them.

"Don't worry. I ain't gonna foist my ditzy daughter on ya without your permission. I like you too much. But my wife, who is not privy to my business, is riding my ass about this. So I gotta come up with something besides losing a shit ton of money."

"Jesus. I need another drink." Ronin walked to the bar in the corner of the room and grabbed the bottle of Chivas, bringing it back to the table. "I don't know what to say."

"Like I said, tell me no." TP refilled both their glasses. "I won't hold it against you."

Ronin knocked back the scotch. "Christ, TP. This feels wrong."

A sheepish look crossed TP's face. "Look, I don't want you to get the wrong impression. I adore this kid—she's sweet and she's got a damn good heart. It's the first time I've seen her excited about anything besides a man in years. She did manage to finish a two-year community-college degree in administrative business."

An odd notion occurred to him.

"What? I see the wheels turning. If you've got an idea—no matter how damn crazy it sounds—I'd consider it."

"It is crazy. But do you think she'd buy that being a ring girl for an event is the best way to learn the fight-promotion business from the inside?"

"Possibly. The girl's got the body and the looks for it."

Most fathers thought their daughters were beautiful. What if Katie . . . wasn't? Ronin needed a backup idea. "Would she be willing to enroll in martial arts classes?"

"You could make it a stipulation." His eyes turned shrewd. "How'd you come up with that?"

"Black Arts is adding on Brazilian jujitsu. I'd like to have a newcomer in the classes as a way to keep an eye on things."

TP's eyebrows rose. "Whose idea was that?"

Since TP freely admitted he never took his woman's advice, Ronin opted to keep Amery's suggestions out of it. "Makes financial sense to expand. I found an instructor who is qualified and has an established dojo."

"What's this guy's name?"

"Alvares Curacao. He owns the ABC dojo. Oddly enough, your timing is"—*suspect*, but Ronin soldiered on with—"good because he and I recently decided to combine resources and start a fight-promotion company that focuses on the amateur circuit. Katie could work as a ring girl, and train in the dojo to see firsthand what the MMA fighters do to prepare."

"Keep going."

"She'd have to understand she starts on the bottom, doing grunt work like anyone else." Ronin gave TP a contemplative look. "Will it mean more to her if she thinks she got the job on her own?"

"It'd be a first." TP poured himself another shot. "I appreciate you doing this, Ronin. And don't worry; I'm fully prepared to pay her salary."

Ronin laughed. "Not happening, Daddy Warbucks. She works for me; I pay her. Won't be much. Nor will it be full-time. I'd put her on probation for the standard six months to see if she's serious. Because I don't think you really know how long her interest in this will last."

"Understood. I'll tell Katie I talked to you and you have an opening, but she has to apply for the job like everyone else. If she doesn't follow through, neither of us are out anything." TP grinned. "Think I oughta tell her to keep it on the down low that she's my daughter? She kept the last name of the asshole she married. Hiding your family connections has worked well for you."

"Not always." Definitely not with Amery.

"Count yourself lucky you were born with the looks that make it an option for you. An ugly guy like me? No choice but to flash money around." He put out his cigar. "When do you want Katie to interview?"

"Have her send a résumé to Black and Blue Promotions. Same address as the dojo."

"Clever name."

Another one of Amery's ideas. "I'll probably sit on it for a week or so before I call her in."

"Good plan. And just so we're clear. You do this for me? We're square. For good. No more favors."

That right there made it worth doing.

"Deal."

THURSDAY afternoon, Ronin was rearranging teaching schedules when his cell phone rang. "Ronin Black."

"It's Blue. I don't know what kind of pull you've got, but man, thank you. I spoke to the property rental company on Monday right after our conversation, and the guy pretty much guaranteed it'd be a hefty enough penalty for breaking the lease that I'd end up staying. So today I had a message from him, and he said there'd be no penalty at all for breaking the lease early except for losing first and last month deposits and incurring a cleaning cost."

Ronin had figured either TP or Max would step in. "I'm glad to hear they saw the light."

"The kicker is we have to be out of here by Saturday."

"How much equipment do you have?" Ronin jotted down items as Blue rattled them off. That was less stuff than he'd anticipated. But it'd take a crew to load and unload. "How many guys you got helping make the move?"

"Five."

"I can add"—he did a quick calculation—"six more. Shouldn't take too long. When is final inspection?"

"Saturday afternoon at two." He paused. "But here's the thing. I worry the protection dudes will vandalize the building before the lease company signs off."

"They might make an example of you, so protect yourself."

"How am I supposed to do that?"

"Set up a perimeter around the building and get enough guys to stand watch from sundown to sunup. They show their faces, make sure none of your guys engage them in any kind of physical altercation and call the cops."

"What if the cops don't show up?"

"Just say shots have been fired, and I guarantee you'll get a response."

Blue got quiet. "I'd ask how you know all this stuff, but then I'd know, and I'm not sure I want that."

"Smart choice. Call me if you have any problems. I'll have people there at six a.m. with a truck. I want you there keeping an eye out, not loading stuff."

"Thanks, Sensei. Anything else I need to know?"

"You'll have legal documents to sign on Saturday afternoon, as soon as everything is unloaded here. We'll go over scheduling and all that the first part of next week. I'm giving only you a keycard and the security codes until we decide who else will get access."

"I appreciate everything, and I'm looking forward to being in business together."

After Ronin hung up, he rummaged in his desk for something

to eradicate the pounding in his head. But he couldn't even find a damn aspirin, and it was too much trouble to head up to his place for a pain pill.

Fifteen minutes before classes were scheduled to start, Knox came into his office without knocking and closed the door.

"What?"

"Please tell me that the hot fucking blonde out there applying for a job is one of the female black belt instructors you've been talking about hiring?"

Ronin shook his head. "I haven't set up any interviews."

"Maybe it's our lucky day because she's here for a job interview. Said you were expecting her."

He rubbed his forehead. "No. Send her—"

"Jesus, man, don't send her away. I'll hire her for something."

"I was going to say send her in, you fucking pervert."

Almost as soon as Knox opened the door, a six-foot blond bombshell sashayed in wearing a low-cut shirt that showcased a big pair of tits that jiggled too perfectly to be fake. She offered her hand. "Ronin? I'm Katie Pettigrew Gardiner."

This was TP's daughter? He glanced at Knox—who had his gaze glued on this chick's ass in her painted-on jeans. "Shihan, close the door on your way out."

"Ah, sure."

Ronin pointed at the chair across from the desk and didn't take Katie's hand. "I received your résumé. I intended to call you next week to set up an interview."

"I couldn't wait. I'm just so excited to be part of the team." Her gaze encompassed the room and frowned. "Will my office be smaller than this one?"

"Ms. Gardiner. You need to take a step back."

"Excuse me?"

"I haven't hired you. And with the way you've shown up,

assuming you've already got the job? I'm leaning toward ending this interview right now."

Katie blinked with confusion. "But didn't you talk to Daddy and come to an agreement about this?"

"No. I agreed to read your résumé and call you for an interview. That's it. Unlike most people in this town, I do not jump through hoops for Thaddeus Pettigrew."

"But you've had it since yesterday! I sent it by special courier."

Was this woman for real?

Yes. She's had the kind of spoiled upbringing your mother refused to give her children.

Ronin said a silent thank-you to his mother.

"Have you read my résumé?"

"I skimmed it."

"And?" she demanded.

"You have zero experience for the position." He paused. "You are aware of the job requirements?"

"I'd be heading up the Black and Blue promotional team for MMA events."

Ronin flashed his teeth at her. "Wrong. You are applying for an entry-level position—a part-time position. Your main responsibility? Ring girl."

Her jaw almost hit her cleavage. "Are you kidding me?"

"No. We're hiring a ring girl, a gopher, and a lackey—all-in-one. Those would be your job duties and in that order, plus you'd be enrolled in classes and report to me."

Katie's eyes cooled. "My father knew this was the type of job after he spoke to you."

"Yes. And you would've known it too if you would've waited for the callback. But since you're here, and you've been apprised of what the job entails, I imagine you're not interested?"

"Ring girl," she muttered. "I should've known he'd pass me

off as some brainless twit." Determination shone on her face. "Of course I'd be happy to represent Black and Blue Promotions as ring girl. I'll even fetch coffee and file."

If she expected Ronin to backtrack, the girl was bound to be disappointed. "We'll need help setting up the office next week. I'll have to get back to you on specific times. Your classes here will be free. The job pays minimum wage for office work. The dollar amounts will vary for your work as ring girl, depending on sponsor commitments, size of the event, and the venue. Clothing is provided. Any questions?"

"Is my father paying you to hire me?"

"No. He is not paying your wages, either. If you take the job, you will have six months of job probation."

"Which means you can fire me at will."

"Yes. I'll warn you—I'm demanding, and I will not treat you like a delicate flower. You'll either bloom on your own or wither and die. Your choice."

She looked confused—and maybe a little scared.

Good.

She rose to her feet. "Thank you for this opportunity, Ronin."

"Not Ronin. Call me Mr. Black."

"Absolutely, Mr. Black." She stood and bowed with a flourish before she spun on her heel and exited the room.

His screaming headache had just gotten worse.

Normally he'd head to the workout room and pound on a speed bag, or a heavy bag, or a sparring opponent and give himself something else to focus on besides the pain. But that wasn't an option, because he was heeding the doctor's warnings. Ronin had to admit his body wasn't fully healed. So he detoured to the Crow's Nest to brood and pace. Up here, his anxiety would be hidden. Up here, he'd be spared from his instructors treating him with kid gloves.

Over the years, he'd packed his working hours with so much he had no idea what to do with himself when he had free time. So what had he done when he had free time? Started a new promotion company that occupied his every waking hour spent in the dojo so he didn't have to worry that he'd finally irreparably damaged his body and he'd never bounce back to the man—to the fighter—he was.

As much as he tried not to think about the repercussions of a lifetime spent pushing his body past normal limits, he couldn't help it since he had a doctor's appointment scheduled for tomorrow.

A loud *ki-yah* brought Ronin's attention to the class of yellow belts. He barely remembered being in that stage of his training. He'd accelerated quickly because his father had drilled him continually, both in class and outside of it.

Maybe it was Shiori's constant presence, or maybe it was because he'd been dodging his mother's calls, but his family had been on his mind a lot lately. He'd been thinking about his grandfather's expectations, which had somehow segued into his questioning his father's motives in enrolling him in jujitsu at such a young age.

Had his father seen that something extra special in his son that caused him to constantly push Ronin to the next level? Or had his father merely lived vicariously through his child?

A long-buried memory surfaced of being with his father in the tiny backyard of their house on base, practicing kicking strikes. Ronin couldn't have been older than five, and all he'd wanted to do on that sunny afternoon was roll in the grass, chase his little sister around, and dig in the dirt with his toy trucks. He'd heard the happy shrieks of the boy next door and his friends and experienced his first taste of envy. His father believed a purposeful life meant a structured use of time. So while kids his age learned to have fun, Ronin learned how to tune out those sounds and concentrate on achieving greatness.

That jarred him. Been a while since that phrase surfaced: *achieving greatness.* Those were his father's favorite words to explain why Ronin's life wouldn't be like other kids.' He was meant for more.

Ronin heard the bottom door open and played the guessing

game of who'd breached Master Black's ivory tower. Then Amery's sweet cherry scent wafted toward him, calming him.

She pressed her chest to his back and wreathed her arms around his waist. "Hi."

"Hi."

"I had this crazy idea you were hiding from me when you didn't answer your phone, and you weren't in the penthouse or in your office or punishing yourself in the weight room. So I set out on a quest to find you."

"And find me you did."

"So whatcha doing up here, Sensei?"

"Taking stock."

"And how are the kiddos performing?"

Ronin launched into details of training errors he'd seen. When Amery didn't respond, he realized his explanation had turned into a diatribe. "Sorry to go off on a tangent."

"It's okay. I could complain about my horrible day, but luckily, I got to manipulate shadows and light on an image of this really hot guy who is gracing the cover of a very naughty book."

He didn't even crack a smile.

Amery moved in front of him. "Is the pained look in your eye because of me? I know I'm not supposed to be up here."

"No, baby, I'm very glad to see you."

"Doesn't seem like it. Do you want me to bail so you can continue glaring at the yellow belt class? Because that redheaded kid in the second row? I think he's looking up here and purposely taunting you with his very sloppy half-guard technique."

That did bring a smile. "You are such a smart-ass."

She placed her cool hands on his cheeks.

He closed his eyes and sighed.

"Ronin. You're not well."

"Was it my lack of charming conversation or that I didn't immediately try to seduce you that gave it away?"

"Come on. Tell me where it hurts. Maybe I can help."

He glossed over her concerns. "I'm having light-sensitivity issues, which is why you found me sitting in the dark, with a screaming fucking headache. I've been spending time picking apart my youngest students' techniques when I'm not fixating on Black and Blue Promotions and what it'll mean in the long run to absorb ABC into Black Arts. I'm not getting shit done." Ronin softly smooched her mouth. "That makes me unpleasant to be around."

"I beg to differ. I find you very pleasant to be around. Especially when you're naked with that wicked gleam in your eye." She kissed him. "So since you're not getting shit done down here, why don't you come upstairs and do me?"

He gathered a handful of her hair and pressed the softness against his lips, breathing her in. Just being close to her chased away his shadows.

"Ronin?"

"You don't have any idea what you do to me, do you?" he murmured. "You bring such joy and light into my life, Amery. Can you blame me for wanting to wake up with that every morning? To surround myself with it every night?" Her reluctance to officially commit to moving in with him was just another thing he'd been obsessing about.

For once she didn't look away from him when he brought up taking that permanent step. She reached up and brushed away a few hairs that were stuck to his forehead. "Let me take care of you tonight."

"I wouldn't mind if we just crawled in bed and you wrapped yourself around me."

Amery gasped with mock horror. "You don't want to wrap ropes around me? Just your arms? You must really feel like shit." She kept running her hands through his hair. "When is your appointment with the neurologist?"

As much as he wanted her at his appointment tomorrow . . . he didn't want her there. Telling her that would piss her off, and she deserved better after trying to improve his mood. He wanted her to see his physical improvement, not dwell on whatever limitations his doctor would set. He'd been enough of a whiny, brooding ass lately.

"Ronin?"

"Can we just drop it and go upstairs? My brain is throbbing."

"Poor baby with a throbbing need. Once we're upstairs, I'll give you a little head . . . massage."

Damn woman always made him feel better.

AMERY did drop it, but she didn't forget about it. And she wasn't sure whether it was a blessing or a curse when she saw the doctor's appointment card with today's date and time tossed in the garbage. It wasn't as if she'd been pawing through the trash looking for clues; the postcard had fallen out of the bag when she'd removed it from the garbage can.

So maybe if she'd found it in a stack of mail or with the magazines in the den, she'd think Ronin had left it lying about, hoping she'd find it and ask him about it. But since he'd stuffed it in the trash . . . that told her he was hiding the appointment from her.

Why? Especially when he'd insisted she was an integral part of his life and his recovery process?

Because he's back to the same old keeping things from you bullshit.

Amery didn't want to believe it, but with the way he'd been acting the last couple of days? She couldn't stop the niggling worry that there was more to it. She'd hoped last night, confronting him in his private space, cajoling him, keeping things light and showing her total support of him with gentle teasing and soft kisses would encourage him to confide in her. But that hadn't happened. He'd just remained tight and closed off even during his massage. Directly after that he'd conked out.

Maybe he wanted to hear the doctor's diagnosis first before he involved her. That she could understand. Still, she couldn't help but feel shut out.

Nothing you can do about it now but wait and see if he wants to talk later.

She ditched the trash in the Dumpster and headed to work.

After working late, she didn't have the energy to drive to the penthouse. As much as she loved being there, she felt the need to be in her own space for a change. That was another indication she wasn't ready to move in with Ronin. Her phone pinged with a text message.

RB: Where are you?

I'm at home.

RB: At the penthouse?

No. My loft. Where are you?

RB: Dojo. You didn't stop in, so I figured you're working late. Are you about done and on your way?

I'm done, but I'm tired. I'll probably just stay here tonight.

RB: Fine. I'll be there in a bit. Have you eaten?

I was just about to make a sandwich. Should I make two?

RB: Please. See you soon. I'll let myself in.

Twenty minutes later, the high-pitched whine of a motorcycle echoed from the alley. The back door slammed. He didn't clomp up the stairs. The next thing she knew, Ronin was standing next to the breakfast bar looking at her.

"Hey."

Maybe she was being paranoid, but he didn't cross the room to kiss her. "Hey, yourself. Have a seat. Food's almost ready. Can I get you something to drink?"

"I'm good." He sat on a barstool. "What did you work on today that kept you in the office so late that you're crashing here?"

Rather than point out that she lived here, she focused on assembling the sandwich. "A new campground contacted me about designing promotional material. They've got a unique concept, so that'll be a fun project."

"What's unique about it?"

Amery placed two slices of thick-cut twelve-grain bread on the cutting board. Then she spread brown mustard across each slice. "It's a winter campground close to the slopes that offers modern tent camping but in the snow. A cheaper option for winter sports enthusiasts to enjoy the ski season in the Rockies instead of staying in pricey hotels in Aspen and Vail."

Ronin watched as she piled on sliced turkey, tomato, avocado, and alfalfa sprouts. She drizzled balsamic vinaigrette over everything. Then she slathered hummus on the top pieces of bread before layering them on top. She cut each in half, plated them, and slid one in front of him.

"Eat up. And yes, all the ingredients are organic." She cracked open a small bag of veggie chips—slices of baked beets, sweet potatoes, and spinach. "I seriously eyed the jumbo bag of kettle-cooked salt-and-vinegar chips, but opted for healthy. You should be proud you're rubbing off on me."

"I'd like to rub you off," he said with a wolfish smile before taking a bite of his sandwich.

Amery laughed and relaxed at seeing the glimmer of the Ronin she hadn't seen for a few days. "Maybe for dessert." She filled two glasses of water and slid into the seat beside him.

Ronin must've been hungry; he finished his entire sandwich before she'd eaten half of hers. Sheepishly, he said, "I forgot to eat lunch."

"I can make you another one," she offered.

"I'm full. But thank you. It was delicious."

After several long moments of dead air, Amery's sandwich seemed to be lodged in her throat. Or maybe it was the awkward silence between them that was choking her. She asked, "So what did you do today?" and inwardly cringed at her lack of subtlety.

"I was out most of the day, and then I hung around the dojo. Why?"

So suspicious. Instead of zeroing in on the vagueness of his response, she said, "I'm surprised you didn't eat. Doesn't Shiori bring you lunch most days?"

"There was a to-go box in the fridge when I returned from running errands, but it was late afternoon and I didn't have time to eat. Why?"

It was hard not to bristle at his accusatory tone. "I just find it weird that she brings you food but the two of you don't eat it together."

"We don't eat together because she uses it as an opportunity to harangue me, and that gives me indigestion."

Now she was getting somewhere. "Haranguing you about what?"

"To stop ignoring our mother's calls. Jesus. Every time she nags me, it makes me feel like a delinquent teenager again."

Amery poked his arm. "Don't deny you've acted like a surly teen the last couple of days." She sipped her water. "So are you telling me that by-the-book Sensei participated in wild teenage behavior in his younger years and lied to his mom about it? Or did you just not tell her?"

He faced her, his gaze suspicious. "Where'd that come from?"

"You don't talk much about your formative years, so I'm curious. Did you sneak out of the house to meet a girl? Or did you sneak a girl into your room? Did you swipe candy from the corner market on a dare? Did you and your buddies rip off a bottle of booze and get barfing drunk?"

"I didn't have a typical upbringing, by Japanese or American standards. The focus of my school from the age of twelve on was jujitsu."

She frowned. "You didn't study Japanese history, or government, or language, or literature, or take computer classes while you studied martial arts?"

"Of course I did. My mother insisted on a private tutor. He taught through pop culture, so Shiori and I became fluent in switching back and forth between English and Japanese fairly young. At age sixteen, when I started training with a jujitsu master, he taught me more about Japanese history and culture in two years than I learned in all the time I spent in a traditional classroom. Also during that time, my grandfather insisted I take business classes."

"Did you enjoy them?"

He shrugged. "More than I was willing to admit. That knowledge helped when I started my own business."

"And yet you still sidestepped the question, Master Black. Any getting-a-girl-drunk, copping-a-feel, pulling-pranks-with-your-buddies stories?"

Ronin's puzzled look said, *Why are you pressing me on this?*

Because this is what a man and a woman in a serious relationship do—share pieces of their lives. Open up to me, Ronin, like you promised you would. You can trust me.

When he realized she wasn't backing down, he sighed. "I didn't have a group of buddies, just boys I went to school with. We were so disciplined that if one of us would've admitted to breaking a rule, or even asked another student to help break a rule, even in fun, most likely that infraction would've been reported to the headmaster."

She whistled. "Harsh. No wonder the Japanese educational system is superior to ours."

"But it's hell on maintaining individuality."

"Even with the way you look?" she cooed. "Sweetheart, I'd bet you broke hearts being such an exotic-looking hottie with all those muscles from hours of practicing jujitsu."

"Exotic looking might be a benefit for a woman, but not for a boy." He traced the edge of his water glass, lost in thought. With the way his cheeks flushed, she wondered if the memories caused embarrassment. "The reason I didn't have a gang of friends growing up was because I didn't fit in, not just because I was the only mixed race kid. My mother further alienated me by keeping our family affiliation from everyone in the school even when she knew it'd provide me with more acceptance from my peers."

Was that the genesis of him hiding who he was from everyone? Because that's how he was taught to act? No wonder he had identity issues. "Maybe she worried that people would want to be your friend only because your family was filthy rich."

"My grandfather was filthy rich, not us. We lived modestly. And during my surly teen phase"—he offered a slight smile—"I didn't understand why my grandfather wouldn't pay for my jujitsu studies after I finished regular school. It wasn't like he couldn't afford it. But now I'm grateful because I've had to make it on my own."

Amery cupped the side of his face and urged him to look at her. "While I admire all you've accomplished and you have a right to be proud that your drive got you to where you are today, I'm still sad that you were a lonely little boy."

He kissed her, and the sweetness in it curled around her heart.

"So what happened when you grew into these amazing looks of yours?"

"I've never been a player. But I did lose my virginity in a Japanese bathhouse to an older woman who swore she was a trained geisha."

Her mouth dropped open. "Is that true?"

"Absolutely. While I remember thinking wet, naked bodies sliding together was the greatest invention ever, the best thing to come out of that"—Amery groaned at his pun—"was the woman warning me not to neglect my sexual skills because I was easy to look at."

"That you are," she murmured. "Leave it to Master Black to have a metaphysical cherry popping."

He laughed. Then he kissed her again.

She ran her fingers through his hair. "Is your head better today?"

His face became that blank mask she hated. He immediately retreated physically and emotionally.

That freaked her out. What had the doctor said about his recovery? Why didn't Ronin want to discuss it? She opened her mouth to give voice to those questions, but the annoyance in his eyes kept her lips closed.

"Don't nag me, Amery. I'm not in the mood."

Nag him? She never nagged him and resented the implication she did. "I'm not Shiori. And I see you're still as cranky as you were yesterday."

"Cranky is for kids who need a nap." Ronin invaded her space. "And, baby, I'd be happy to crawl in bed with you, but we sure as fuck won't be sleeping."

Amery ducked away from him. "Nice try. Watch TV or something. I need to put this stuff away."

"So you plan to shoot down my advances now that I *don't* have a headache?"

Tell me why you don't have a headache for the first time in a week. Tell me if you're on different meds. Tell me what the damn doctor said. But once again, she voiced none of that.

Unhappy with her hesitation, Ronin threw up his hands. "Fine. I'll watch TV."

She finished the dishes, silently cursing him because he hadn't offered to help. He always helped, which was just another indication that something was distracting him.

Amery wasn't being petulant, or testing him, but she wasn't going to ask him—nag him—about what was wrong. If everything in his life truly was an open book, as he often proclaimed, then he should be willing to share—the good and the bad. In fact, he should *want* to share it.

But she wanted to do something for him that'd get him out of the weird funk he'd been in. With Blue and crew moving into the dojo this weekend, he'd be busy, which would be good for him. She'd allow him a few days to settle in, and then she'd pull out all the stops to remind him she trusted him implicitly with her body. Maybe that would spur him to spill the secrets he was keeping.

After cleaning the kitchen, she snuggled into him on the couch.

He didn't say anything; he just kissed her on the forehead and returned to watching reruns of *The Big Bang Theory*.

When Amery began to drift off, she pushed upright and stifled a yawn. "I'm going to bed."

"I'll be in shortly."

Another oddity. He usually went to bed when she did, although rarely because he wanted to sleep. Come to think of it, he hadn't touched her last night. Or the night before that. A tiny kernel of panic lodged in her belly. Maybe his attraction for her had cooled? Maybe that was why he'd been so damn distant? It also occurred to her he hadn't pressed the issue of her moving in with him. What if he already regretted the invite?

Not knowing the answers to any of these questions cemented her decision to keep things as is.

She completed her bedtime rituals and eased between the sheets. Her bed wasn't as comfortable as Ronin's, but she sighed anyway when her head hit the pillow.

Sometime later, the mattress dipped, alerting her to his presence.

Then he switched on the bedside lamp to ensure he had her attention. He said, "I love these baby doll nighties you wear."

Amery gave him a sleepy-eyed glance over her shoulder.

Ronin had propped himself up on his elbow, and his hungry gaze drifted over her body.

"Why do I feel like Little Red Riding Hood about to be pounced on by the Big, Bad Wolf?"

He slowly ran his finger down her bare arm. "Maybe because you look very tasty." He tugged on the ties of her nightgown. "I want to lift you to your knees and bind your hands with these. I know how warm your skin feels against mine as I fuck you from behind. I know how much you like my breath in your ear as you shatter beneath me."

Amery faced him and glanced at the tent pole imitation his cock was doing against his boxers and then back up into his smoldering eyes. "You're hard, and you haven't even touched me yet."

"That's about to change." He leaned over so his lips brushed the skin below her ear. "I need you to surrender to me tonight."

She trembled from the heat and intensity pouring from him. She said "yes" and gave herself over to him completely.

But even though the sex was spectacular, as soon as they were both sweaty, sated, and spent, she felt him disconnect emotionally. And she was at a loss as to what to do about it.

CHAPTER TEN

ONCE again Ronin was in the Crow's Nest. No one thought anything odd about him being in there. He used to spend a lot of time up here.

He half listened as the students counted during warm-up exercises. His father had considered it a point of pride that Ronin learned to count to ten in Japanese by age two.

What would his father and his sensei say about the students upstairs counting to ten in Portuguese and not Japanese?

Not that he'd gone up to the ABC dojo and watched the Brazilian working with his students.

His thoughts bounced all over the place, and he worried about what his lack of concentration might mean as far as permanent damage.

The stairs squeaked and Ronin knew who had violated his inner sanctum before he saw her reflection in the dark glass. His body responded to her as it always did—heart rate jumping, shaft thickening. His primal male need to mark her seemed stronger than usual lately, which had made it doubly hard to ignore it.

Her hands slipped up his belly, and she latched on to his shoulders from behind. "I know something is wrong and I've tried not to push, but things aren't getting any better."

That she'd recognized his melancholy and listlessness spoke volumes.

"I've thought a lot about what could be causing this reaction. It's not your students' lack of progress. I don't think it's solely about your recovery process. I don't think it is entirely about the recent changes with the dojo and starting a new promotion company. Your family issues might play a small part in the restlessness I see in you. I don't believe it has to do with me and your invite for me to move in with you. Yet I do think it's a combination of all those things."

Ronin said nothing; he just turned his head and dropped a kiss on her knuckles.

"So here's my theory. You're bored. You can't train like you used to. At least when you were fighting, you weren't quite sure of the outcome. When you were teaching, it broke up your day and forced you to concentrate outside yourself. Even that's been taken away from you. So knowing all these factors, I took it upon myself to find a challenge for you."

"Amery—"

"Hear me out completely before you interrupt. I like rope play, Master Black. As much as it pleases you that I'm your willing partner, it's not a challenge for you. Figuring out which technique to use on me has its challenges, but nothing like the test of capturing and punishing a disobedient partner."

Interest stirred his brain and his cock.

"So I'm here to make a confession."

"What did you do?"

"I broke your 'no observation' rule. I've watched classes. I even interrupted a class Knox was teaching last night—he's probably still wrestling with the best way to tell his boss that the boss's girlfriend has been openly violating rules."

"That is pretty blatant."

"And I haven't learned my lesson. Case in point? I'm up here.

Civilians aren't supposed to enter your domain during class hours. This is the second time I've done it in a week. You never let that shit slide."

"True—I've always been adamant about enforcing the rules."

"So what are you going to do about it? Pull down my panties, bend me over your desk, and spank my bare ass? Huh-uh. We'd end up fucking for sure. And, hot man of mine? Fucking you is always a reward, never a punishment."

"Are you trying to piss me off or turn me on?"

Amery stood on tiptoe and murmured, "Both," in his ear. "*You* know you have to punish me. *I* know you have to punish me. But there's no way I'll be on my knees in the practice room waiting for you to finish up your day to dish that punishment out."

Ronin whirled around and, shockingly, Amery was already halfway across the room.

"This is where the challenge starts, Samurai," she cooed sexily. "You'll have to find me before you can exact the punishment of your choosing."

"Find you," he repeated.

"After the dojo closes, I'll be somewhere in this building except for the penthouse level. I bet I know some really great nooks and crannies that you aren't even aware of. Or maybe I'll be plotting my escape back to my place. I'll give you an hour to find me. If you're unsuccessful, your bed will seem big and lonely without me in it tonight, don't you think?"

Ronin started to stalk her. "When I do track you down? What then?"

"You'd better have a plan in place to capture me because I won't go easy."

"Baby, throwing down the gauntlet is what I live for. The fact that it's you issuing the challenge?" His greedy gaze raked over her from head to toe. "Even better. But I'll give you a warning. If you're my prisoner? I get to do anything I want to you. *Anything*."

"Guess we'll see about that, won't we?" Amery smiled and said, "Catch you later."

"You can count on it."

She slipped out of the room.

RONIN warned his instructors they needed a speedy shutdown.

He'd tied a coil of hemp rope from his gi belt. Normally he worried about the burn ratio of the size and texture of the rope against bare skin when he tied her, but not tonight. Tonight when he caught her, he'd give her a taste of the hojojutsu side of bondage. Chase, capture, and bind for the reward.

For the past two hours, since she'd issued the challenge, Ronin had created a defensive and an offensive strategy, breaking down possibilities. After her hint about sneaking off to her place, he knew she'd try to escape from the building. He wasn't falling for her red herring warning him to search every nook and cranny of the place.

There were two exits from the building where the door lock was automatic and she wouldn't have to rearm the system. All entrances into the building were locked after five p.m. So she'd either try to sneak out with the other dojo students leaving through the main entrance, or she'd leave by the back door.

Ronin didn't consider it cheating that he could cover both entrances at once by watching the security camera feed, because guaranteed Amery would try to disguise herself. Still, maybe she'd be bold and not bother. He scrutinized every head for that distinctive strawberry-blond hair until the last remaining instructor killed all the lights and exited the building.

Since the students tended to congregate out on the sidewalk after class, Amery would avoid that side.

Or maybe she'd wait until they were gone, hoping he'd watch the alley while she slipped out the front.

There was no way he could prepare for every contingency.

But he really, really looked forward to the chase.

He left the security monitors for a couple of minutes to send the elevator up to the third floor. Would that flush her out?

Ten minutes after the dojo emptied, there she was exiting the back door to the alley.

Gotcha, baby.

Now his adrenaline was really pumping.

Ronin left via the front entrance and kept his footsteps light as he crossed the street to the parking garage. Another thing to factor in; Amery showed up after work, which meant she'd have to park on either of the top two levels.

So while she snuck into the structure via the back alley, probably cocky enough to ride the elevator, Ronin hauled ass, sprinting for the stairs. He stopped on the fourth level to catch his breath.

He welcomed the chill in the night air as he listened for her. Was that the ping of the elevator? He peered around the edge of the stairwell and watched as the doors opened.

No one exited.

Son of a bitch. She'd pulled the same fake elevator car ride trick that he had.

Or maybe she's in the corner of the elevator car where you can't see her.

Either way, when the elevator moved to the lower floor, so did Ronin.

Hurling himself down two sets of metal stairs, three stair treads at a time, tested the stability of his knee. It also played hell on his stealthy ninja attempt because Amery could hear him coming.

He reached the third level of the garage the same time the elevator doors opened and Amery stepped out. She made the mistake of stopping and looking around.

That's when she saw Ronin.

That's when she started to run.

Oh, I really gotcha now, baby.

Even though half a garage length separated them, Ronin kicked his stride into sprint stage and grabbed her from behind about ten feet from her car.

He had to give her credit; she didn't scream, but she did try to employ some of the self-defense tactics he'd taught her.

Tried and failed—but tried nonetheless.

He pushed her against the closest vehicle, keeping her wrists together as he freed the short length of rope and quickly tied her hands. Then he put his mouth to her ear. "Don't scream."

"What are you going to do to me?"

"Punish you."

"But I didn't do anything wrong!"

"Then why did you run?"

"Because I was scared."

Ronin spun her back around and wrapped his hand around the front of her throat. "You claim that you didn't do anything wrong, but I got you dead to rights. You confessed to breaking my rules at the dojo. Blatant violations result in punishment as your Sensei sees fit. Do you understand?"

That hot little pink tongue of hers darted out and licked her lips—a sure sign of her arousal. His cock was already hard—hell, he'd been semihard since she'd sauntered into his office and challenged him.

"I said, *Do you understand*?" he repeated.

"Uh, yeah."

Ronin got nose to nose with her. "The correct answer is *yes, sir; yes, Sensei; or yes, Master Black. Uh, yeah* is not one of them."

"Yes, Master Black. I understand." She pulled back from him and tossed her head. "Now, can we get on with it?"

"Such a sassy mouth." Ronin crowded her until she didn't have anyplace to go and her back bowed over the car's trunk. He traced the seam of her mouth with his tongue and then brushed whisper-soft kisses across her pouty lips. "I'm torn between gagging you and keeping your jaw hinged open so I can use your mouth however I want."

Amery's eyes widened. "What do you plan on doing to me?"

"Punishing you. But, baby, I will make sure the punishment fits the crime." He kissed her with brutal possession.

She pressed her chest to his, trying to get closer, and ravaged his mouth with equal ferocity.

Ronin slid his palm to the nape of her neck and pulled her upright as he continued to kiss her. Then he ripped his mouth free. "I'm taking you back to the dojo. I'm not sure if this garage has working surveillance cameras, so I can't do the full restraint here. Don't try to escape."

"And what if I do?"

"Escape?"

She nodded.

Ronin laughed. "Won't happen. But if you even try? Punishment is double. And for you that means double the amount of rope and twice the time I'd keep you bound. Let's go." He kept his hand wrapped around her binding as he steered her toward the elevator.

As soon as they were in the elevator, Amery said, "Is that a length of rope in your pocket, or are you just happy to capture me?"

Although inside he was laughing at the boldness that reminded him of the first night they'd met, he didn't crack a smile. "Gag it is."

Amery cranked her head around to glare at him.

"Keep it up and you'll just add to your punishment."

She immediately faced forward with a huff.

Once they were almost out of the parking garage, she said, "May I ask you a question, sir?"

"Yes. Doesn't mean I'll answer."

"How did you find me so fast?"

"Secret ninja stealth tricks." He helped her over the concrete embankment and stopped. "Did you really think you had a chance of getting away from me?"

"Yes."

Ronin kissed the back of her head. "I love that you're an optimist." He directed her to the back door.

She didn't speak until they were in his private elevator. "Why aren't you meting out my punishment in the dojo, since that's where my alleged infractions occurred?"

"Because there are cameras everywhere, and I didn't think you'd want anyone seeing you bound, punished, and fucked."

"That's how you knew where I'd gone! You just watched the camera feed. That's cheating."

"No, a modern-day samurai uses every technological edge to gain the advantage. Besides, even without the visual assistance, I'd guessed correctly in which way you'd attempt to escape."

"So I was screwed either way."

Ronin rubbed his lips over the shell of her ear. "You like being screwed by me."

"Not fair."

He pulled her hair to the side to access her neck. "Should I mete out your punishment in the practice room? Or the bedroom?"

"Why are you letting me choose?"

"I'm not. Just musing aloud."

"I hate it when you're cryptic like this."

"Practice room it is," he said, leading her inside. "In front of the mirror." Ronin pointed to the camera on the bench. "I'll make sure to get a few photos in."

She vehemently shook her head.

"Tough shit. I will have pictures of this if for no other reason than to remind you who is in charge." He wrapped his fingers around her jaw. "They are for our eyes only. I can promise you that."

Amery nodded.

"Do. Not. Move." He retreated to his supply drawer and pulled out the things he'd need. Standing behind her again, he gathered her hair on top of her head and secured it with an elastic tie. "Pity this sexy dress got torn in our scuffle." He tugged the pocket flap and it ripped, leaving a large tear that exposed her bra.

Her mouth hung open.

Then Ronin did the same thing to the other side, but with more force. The lace hem ripped easily, and he let it hang drunkenly above her knee. The side seam had more give than he expected, so when he rent the two pieces apart, the split almost reached Amery's armpit.

She still hadn't torn her gaze away from the image in the mirror, so Ronin faced her forward.

He unhooked the rope bundle from his belt. "You will be bound like a criminal in the hojojutsu style. This binding requires several sections of rope wound around your neck. The most important thing for you to remember? This is a punishment binding. It won't be comfortable. And if you move your neck?" Ronin traced the cord in her throat. "It will hurt. It will leave marks because this rope has a high burn rate."

A couple of beats passed before she babbled, "I don't want to be punished. I made the whole thing up about breaking the dojo rules."

"No, you didn't. I double-checked." He bestowed a lingering kiss on her mouth. "You issue a challenge, and it won't go unanswered. And I need a challenge like I need air. So thank you for giving me exactly what I needed."

That softened some of the panic in her eyes.

Ronin held up the rope and folded it in half. "I'll need to rebind your hands. Do I need to issue another warning about what will happen to you if you attempt to escape?"

"No, sir."

"Clasp your elbows behind your back." He secured her wrists, leaving the tails long enough to attach to the back binding. He stepped in front of her and folded another section of rope in half. "Open your mouth."

Amery blinked at him and shook her head.

"I'll ask one more time. You were warned that gagging you was a consequence, and you chose to ignore my warning. Now, open your mouth, or I will fashion the chopsticks gag, where your tongue is pressed between two chopsticks and the ropes from the gag are tied tightly at the base of your skull."

She parted her lips.

"Smart choice." Ronin slipped the rope between her lips and tied a square knot at the nape of her neck. That would allow him to attach the gag to the main binding.

"Normally I don't give a play-by-play, but since this is new and you can't speak"—he tugged at the gag—"I'll tell you what I'm doing. This is *nijyuu-hishi nawa*—a double diamond samurai tie. It looks precisely as it sounds. Hojojutsu binds are meant to be done quickly with a minimum amount of rope."

Ronin started with the double neck wrap and split the two sections, tying a knot at the top, pulling the rope down and straight across her arm. He wrapped beneath the arm on both sides and then added another knot at the base of her spine above where her hands were tied. He wound another section midway between her shoulder and elbow. Back up to the knot at the top, he tied another knot below it and crossed to her opposite arm and then down to her wrist binding.

"Done." Keeping his eyes on hers in the mirror, he used his first two fingers to trace the double diamond, wishing he had her naked. But the power of the binding was such that Amery shuddered anyway.

He picked up the camera and shot several rearview photos. Full length. Close up. Then, since the staged resistance looked so real, he snapped a couple of photos of that. Before he set the camera down, he said, "Struggle to get out of the bindings."

She thrashed and twisted, but the bindings held.

He snapped a few shots. "Stop."

When Ronin moved in front of Amery, her gaze fell to the floor.

He crouched, forcing her attention. He slipped his hands beneath her dress until he reached the crotch of her panties. Hooking a finger between her cunt—her wet cunt—and the silky fabric, he yanked hard until her underwear was around her ankles. "Kick them off."

Ronin grabbed the box holding his surprise and dropped to his knees in front of her.

Amery's eyes went big. Her response was garbled by the ropes in her mouth.

"What's this? It's called a lotus blossom. Similar to the butterfly sex toy in that it has a remote control. But the petals contour more to the curve of your sex." The straps were thin, and with the way Amery flailed around, he'd have to readjust them.

Once he had the lotus blossom situated, he turned the vibrator on.

"Oomgld! Wtrooglooee?"

"Ever heard of orgasm torture?"

She shook her head wildly.

"That's where I make you come. Over and over. As many times as I want. Until you can't take it anymore. Until you beg me to stop." Ronin traced his fingers up and down the insides of her thighs, watching that pretty pale skin tremble. "But you can take a lot, can't you?"

Another violent head shake.

Ronin stood and held the remote. "Let's test that. Better brace yourself." He flicked it on, keeping it on low. He grabbed the hook he used for rigging assistance and attached the wide belly strap on the Y chain.

Amery had cranked her head to see what he was doing.

He turned the vibrator to high. Then he stood behind her, holding on to her bound wrists so she didn't pitch forward when the orgasm hit. "Look at yourself. Any second, the vibrations will take over and you'll be helpless to do anything but watch how beautiful you are when you come." His mouth brushed her ear. "Close, baby?"

She nodded.

He nibbled on her neck. Gifting her with soft little bites and tiny sucks until her breathing was labored. When her eyes drifted to half-mast, he said, "Watch yourself. Watch me watching you."

Their gazes connected again, and he saw her bite down on the rope. Ronin could feel the pulse in her throat against his lips, and he growled against her skin. "I can almost taste you. Sweet. Salty. Creamy."

She unraveled. As soon her orgasm abated, she slumped against him, and he turned off the vibrator.

"I am so crazy about you. Crazy scared about all the things you make me feel." He wrapped his hand beneath her jaw. "Look at what you do to me. I'm about to crawl out of my damn skin from wanting you."

"Den dake mee."

"Oh, I'll take you." He nuzzled her temple. "I'll take you someplace you've never gone. As soon as you can't take it anymore." He swept his thumb over her distended lip. He leaned close enough to press his mouth to hers. His tongue snaked out and followed the rope. He sucked in her shallow breaths as he let the very tip of his tongue tease the underside of her top lip and the ridge of her teeth. "One more and I'll take the gag off," he murmured against her mouth. Then he turned the vibrator back on.

Good thing he'd held on to her because her knees buckled.

Amery tried to get away from the vibrations, but thrashing caused the rope to saw into her neck and the corners of her mouth.

Ronin's eyes met hers in the mirror. "Don't fight it. Let it happen." He placed his hand in the center of her chest and slowly moved it up to slip a finger underneath the rope at the hollow of her throat. "You look breathtaking in my ropes. Regardless of whether you're naked, or clothed, you're as regal as royalty and yet . . . you still wear the blush of innocence. Neither is an act with you. That *is* you, Amery. It's beautiful and compelling and mine. I do this to you. No one else."

"Oomgld. Leez." Almost against her will, she released a muffled wail. Her body trembled.

Ronin latched on to the sweet spot below her earlobe and sucked, making her tremble harder. After the climax ended, he clicked off the vibrator and untied the gag. As soon as her mouth was freed, he kissed her with gentleness and surety. "You're doing good, baby." He kissed the corners of her lips. "So good."

"You weren't kidding about orgasm torture," she panted. "My whole body is jumping like a live wire."

"This time I'll keep it on low longer."

"What? Again? Why?"

"Because you knew what I needed—to step a foot off that ledge. You gave it to me. I've always sated that need with violence. But now I can sate it with you." Ronin murmured, "How many more orgasms until you beg me to stop?"

"I—I don't know!"

"Do you know how fucking sexy it is knowing that your pussy is completely under my control? I can do this"—he flicked on the switch and she gasped—"and watch you fly apart."

"Ronin. Please. I can't. What . . . oh, god, is it pulsating?"

"Guess I hit the random switch." His mouth cruised down the slope of her neck. "Like that?"

"Yes. No. How can I be coming again . . . oh, oh, oh." Amery threw her head back, and her soft wail curled around his body like a silken ribbon.

When she came down from her climax high and was panting softly, he put his mouth right on her ear. "This hot little ass of yours? Is mine tonight."

Amery seemed too blissed out to answer, so he reiterated, "Tell me what I want."

"To fuck me in the ass."

"Beg me to fuck you and give you a break from this."

She shrieked when he cranked the vibrator on again. "Please, Ronin. Make it stop. Then take whatever—fuck me however you want. Please."

Ronin fed her hungry kisses. "*My* reward for capturing you? I will fuck you as long and as hard as I need."

"Yes." Amery turned her head and rubbed his cheek. "But I don't think I can stand up."

"I have a suspension rigging set up." He moved to the side, pulling the strap over her head and settling it in her midsection. "Lean forward, baby. That's it. Now slide your heels out."

"I feel like I'm floating."

"You will be by the time I'm done with you."

She closed her eyes and moaned softly.

"Eyes on the mirror. Watch me." Ronin stood behind her, heart and cock pounding with anticipation as he scraped his fingertips up the backs of her thighs. Then he smoothed his palms over those soft buttocks and pushed the dress up her back.

"You look like some conquering hero about to take the spoils of war," she said, her voice a rasp of awe tinged with fear.

"I am." He reached for the lube and squeezed a generous amount on his fingers. "Relax, and it'll go a little easier on you."

"But not much."

"Make no mistake; it's gonna hurt." He swirled the slickness around the tight pucker of her anus and eased the tip of his finger in.

Their gazes remained locked as he prepared her. One finger, then two. The intensity increasing every time he pushed deeper. "But that's what you want, isn't it?"

Amery whispered, "Yes. Do it."

Ronin shed his gi pants and stroked his cock, adding more lube.

Her ragged breathing, wide eyes, swollen mouth, and her binding fueled his need in a way he'd never experienced. He pressed the head of his cock between her ass cheeks, following the line of her crack until he met that resistant little hole. Grabbing her hips, he pushed past the ring of muscle trying to keep him out. He did pause momentarily, loving the tight squeeze of her muscle at just the head of his cock.

Amery bit her lip and tried to drop her head.

"Look at me." He eased inside her fully.

Jesus fucking Christ. *Hot and tight* repeated on a loop in his brain. He began to move, slowly and steadily, so he could feel the anal passage clamped around every inch of his cock. He worked in and out of her virgin ass in a modified version of seven samurai. Five slow strokes; on the sixth stroke, he pulled all the way out, keeping the head of his dick against that tiny spasming pucker, then counting to seven before he slammed into her fully.

"Oh, fuck."

Ronin didn't speak. He watched his cock disappearing into that small rosette and grunted with satisfaction every time his cock bottomed out.

Amery kept her head up, her gaze hot with desire as she started tightening her inner muscles around his cock when he was fully seated inside her.

That's when he lost all track of his counting and his need to make this last. His hips connected with her flesh with a hard, fast slap. Perspiration glazed his body as he raced toward the tipping point.

But Ronin wasn't going over that edge alone. He reached for the remote and cranked it to high.

"Damn you. That's not fair. I can't take . . ."

"Hurts so good, doesn't it?"

She lowered her lids and arched her neck, purposely giving herself a mark.

"Look at you," he growled. "So sexy and defiant. You don't want to come again, but you will."

"Ronin—"

"Give it to me. This one is mine."

He felt the vibration from the lotus every time his cock bottomed out and his balls swung up. When he pulled out fully and rammed home with each thrust, she shuddered.

"Yes, like that." As soon as she said, "Don't stop," her inner muscles began that rhythmic spasming, and she cried out.

Ronin let her body pull the climax from his as each pulsating spasm milked his cock, almost in slow motion. The heat of his seed against the hot tissues of her anal walls eased his every short, fast jab.

His head nearly split from the pleasure—the visual of her body bound as he fucked her mindless and the orgasm that nearly had his knees bucking from the sheer magnitude of it.

When his brain finally stopped spinning, he realized he'd rested all his weight on her as he slumped over her body. His cock was still buried in her ass and the lotus kept buzzing away.

And he felt the power of it again as another orgasm rocketed through her. He fastened his mouth to the side of her neck, tasting her sweat and feeling her pulse pounding beneath his lips. As soon as Amery sucked in another breath, he switched off the lotus.

"I can't—"

"I know, baby. I've got you. We're done."

He pulled out of her. Then he unhooked her hand binding from the body binding. He gently hauled her upright, away from the rigging. "Can you stand?"

"I think so."

Keeping one arm banded around her hips, he worked the knots free. The last piece was the neck rope. After he removed it, he ran the tips of his fingers across the rope burns. He had a momentary pang of guilt until Amery said hoarsely, "I wanted the marks tonight. I earned these marks."

He pressed kisses from one side of her throat to the other. "You wear them beautifully." Then he slipped his right arm behind her knees and lifted her into his arms.

"Ronin, don't. Your knee—"

"Is fine. And as the victor in tonight's challenge, it's my right to bring my prize into my bed."

"You haven't undone my hands," she said softly against his neck.

"Because I don't want you pushing away from me when I'm carrying you." He kissed the frown lines in her forehead as he strolled down the hallway. "I'm running on a lot of adrenaline right now, so I'm good."

But he became a little concerned when his neck got wet. With her tears?

The easiest way to undo her wrist wrap was to place her upper body on the mattress and get at her from behind. But her emotions were high, so he took her to the chair in the corner, keeping her cradled to his chest. Luckily the binding was such he could undo it with one hand. Even with both hands tied behind her back.

Ronin brought both wrists into her lap and began to rub. "Any numbness?"

"Yes. But no pain. Not yet."

"Soreness anywhere else?" He rubbed her forearms and up to her biceps.

"Just my ass," she mumbled.

A soft laugh escaped. "No apologies for that."

"It's not funny. I'm going to feel it for the next day."

"Good. I want you thinking about me."

She traced the edge of his jaw.

Ronin snagged her hand and kissed her fingertips. "Thank you for tonight. But, baby, why are you crying?"

"A rush of adrenaline makes you stronger. It makes me weepy. Sorry."

He tipped her chin up. "Don't apologize. You are beautiful, honest, and real. And you are also completely mine." He kissed her until she sighed and relaxed into him. Then he undressed her and tucked her in his bed where she belonged.

CHAPTER ELEVEN

"WE'VE got to stop meeting like this," Shiori deadpanned.

"Are you afraid people will start to talk?" Amery joked back.

Shiori peered over the top of her sunglasses. "That's the question of the day, isn't it? Why did you summon me to your lair?"

"To go over my questions on the contracts. In private." Amery had set up this meeting after everyone in the office had gone for the day. She still hadn't shared with her friend and officemate Chaz why she and Ronin had broken up in the first place. Now that they'd reconciled, Ronin's family connections didn't matter—at least not to her. But if sexy, mysterious Shiori Hirano sauntered into the office, Chaz would grill her. So the best way to deal with the potential headache was to avoid it.

At least for now.

While Shiori wandered around Amery's apartment, Amery filled the two lowball glasses with ice. "What would you like to drink?"

"Just water. I'm teaching the late class tonight."

"How's it going?"

Shiori took a seat at the breakfast bar. "I enjoy teaching far more than I thought I would."

"I'm surprised you have time with all the responsibilities of someone in your position."

She shrugged. "I'd be training there anyway if I weren't teaching. My sensei in Japan reminded me that teaching is just another way to learn."

"Philosophical. Are all masters of martial arts like that?"

"The good ones are."

"You sound like Knox."

"The only thing Knox and I have in common is our desire to beat each other unconscious."

Amery raised an eyebrow.

Shiori pointed to the contracts. "What have you decided?"

"You said the terms are negotiable."

"To some extent. But to be blunt, Okada walks away if the terms aren't to our liking. Then all negotiations are permanently over."

"I understand that I need Okada more than Okada needs me. But along those lines, I don't think I can work for one company exclusively, no matter how well they pay."

"Forgive me if I don't quite grasp this. Your company is dangerously close to shutting down because of lack of revenue, and Okada is offering you a permanent, steady income, and you're turning it down?"

Amery fiddled with the ice in her glass before sucking down a mouthful of booze. "I know it sounds crazy. And believe me, I've wrestled with this, but I like the diversity of what I do. Being contracted for a specific project line with Okada would provide me with enough income to keep Molly on and maybe hire another employee. Yet at the same time, I could retain my other clients. They've stuck with me, so I don't want to ditch them when a bigger company waves a big, fat check in my face." She met Shiori's confused gaze. "You do get what I'm trying to tell you, don't you?"

"You're about loyalty. You'd rather fail on your own than compromise your integrity."

"Exactly."

"I can respect that." Shiori rifled through the contracts. "I believe the language in this one is case specific. I'm fairly confident Okada will agree to those terms, but they will expect you to forego design work for your clients in the restaurant business." She offered a small smile. "We would prefer consumers were at home eating our line of healthy frozen meals."

She laughed. "Done. My design work for them is minimal anyway. What about the organic food markets?"

"As long as you're not creating ads for our competition, I don't believe that'll be an issue."

Amery exhaled slowly. "Then I'll sign on the dotted line."

"Good. Have you discussed this with Ronin?"

"No. I'd like that nondisclosure agreement to go both ways."

Shiori frowned. "You don't plan to tell him?"

"Of course I'll tell him. But I want it to be on my terms, when the timing is right. We're still working through things." It wasn't like he wasn't keeping things close to the vest himself. Case in point: She still had no idea what the doctor had told him. Amery finished her drink. "Like you reminded me, it might've been my relationship with Ronin that got my foot in the door, but the work speaks for itself."

"All right. But if my brother asks me point-blank if you're working for Okada? I will not lie to him. I've done that often enough, usually without choice, that I fear our relationship can never be repaired. Anytime I try to talk to him . . . he shuts me down. Or ignores me."

"Neither of those are my favorite traits of his either."

Shiori nodded. "Last business thing. Given our history and your relationship with Ronin, you won't be dealing directly with me at all."

"Really?" she said skeptically.

"Yes. You're in North America, which means you're under

Maggie Arnold's purview anyway. I told her I'd be in Denver and would meet with you to save her the trip, but all information, payments, and problems will be handled by the Seattle office." She smirked. "So if you fuck this up, don't expect me to bail you out."

"You're hilarious."

"So because I'm nosy, I have to ask what other projects you're working on that are exciting enough to keep you from becoming Okada's lackey?" She laughed. "Sorry—I couldn't resist the shot at the family business."

At least she had a sense of humor. Amery was finding the more time she spent with Ronin's sister, the more she liked her. "Give me a second." She scrolled through her folders and clicked on the cover she'd designed for Cherry Starr. "Check this out." She spun the laptop toward Shiori.

Shiori leaned closer. "You did this?"

"Yep."

"Graphics too?"

"Yep."

"That is stunning. The red rope against the paler skin. Everything about this is sexy. *Tied to Him*." Shiori looked at her. "Did you come up with the title?"

"No. The author has written several books in this vein."

Then Shiori pulled the laptop closer. "Beautiful binding. It's perfect. I assume this is rope master Black's handiwork?"

"Since it's no big secret to your family that Ronin is a rope master, I can say yes, Ronin did the binding for this shot."

"Do you know the model?"

Amery felt her neck getting warm. "Yes."

"You didn't take issue with him doing kinbaku on another woman right in front of you?" Shiori's gaze snapped to her. "That's because *you're* the model."

"What gave it away?"

"Nothing in the image screams, 'body by Amery Hardwick,

binding by Ronin Black.' But it's easy to make the leap since I'm aware that you two have this type of relationship." She peered at the image again. "I want to read this book."

"She's working on the other two books in the trilogy."

"Did she ask you to do the covers?"

That stupid blush moved from her neck and warmed her cheeks.

"You did! Show me."

"I've only done the second one. We're still debating on what to do for the last book." She angled the laptop, then opened the image. "Here's the cover for book two."

"Holy. Shit. That's Ronin."

Amery's jaw dropped. "How did you know?"

"I guessed. Was it a case of 'I'll let you bind me if I can bind you'?"

"No. We were messing around and I snapped a few pictures. After I promised that no one would know how sloppily I bound the rope master, as well as assuring him I'd never tell anyone the rope model's name, I showed it to Cherry and she loved it."

"*Undone by Her.* Another great title to go with the image. He does look to be hanging by a thread."

You have no idea. Amery loved that she and Ronin were the only two who'd ever know what really happened at the photo shoot to put that look on his face.

"Dammit. Does this mean I can't tease my big brother about being featured on the cover of an erotic novel?"

"No!"

Shiori laughed. "Kidding. On a serious note, it shows how much he trusts you, Amery, that he let you bind him."

Amery absentmindedly touched the image on the screen. "I guess. But it's not his trust in me that's the issue. It's whether I trust him." The second the words exited her mouth, she wished she could take them back.

"I don't fault you for how you feel. I'm happy you're giving him the chance to earn that trust back. Maybe he'll figure out I'm trying to do the same thing." Shiori's slip into melancholy vanished. "What are your ideas for the third cover?"

"I'd love to do a shadowed image of Ronin and me. Keeping with the rope theme, either him holding a coil before he binds me or after, right before he unties me. It'd take the series full circle. And the title for the last book is *Tangled Together.*"

"Have you run the idea by the author yet?"

Amery groaned. "I haven't run it by Ronin yet. It'd be a difficult shot to achieve without having a third person with us. I don't know if he's down with that, but we'll see."

"Without sounding creepy, if you need someone to help with the shot, I'm a decent photographer."

"Thanks for the offer. I'll definitely let you know."

"Either way, I want to see the third cover." Shiori took her phone out and dialed. "I'm ready. Pick me up in the alley. Thanks." She smiled. "My ride. Time for me to get to the dojo."

On the way down the stairs, Amery said, "I find it strange there aren't any pictures of Ronin's family anywhere at his place."

"I didn't see pictures of your family among your knickknacks either," Shiori pointed out. "But that reminds me." She reached into her oyster-colored Chanel handbag and pulled out the wrapped package Amery had given her at their first meeting. "I don't think this was meant for me, was it?"

"No."

"Give it to him. He needs reminders of you and how you feel about him everywhere."

"Clashes with your decor, huh?" Amery said lightly.

"Raunchy is more my style. I'll show you my Hello Kitty whip collection sometime." Shiori smiled, slipped on her Versace shades, and stepped out the back door.

Yes, she was really starting to like Ronin's sister—even when she suspected Shiori hadn't been kidding about the anime whip thing.

"I don't think it's necessary. In fact, if you looked at my proposal, you'd see . . ." *Blah, blah, blahdedy, blah.*

Ronin stared at Katie, imagining four or five different ways he could choke her out to get that damn mouth of hers to stop moving.

TP had neglected to mention his daughter was a know-it-all pain in the rear who came to work dressed like a hooker, flirted with any male that crossed her path, smacked her gum like a cliché teenager, and wasn't nearly the dim bulb her father portrayed her to be.

Katie Pettigrew Gardiner was the antithesis of what he wanted in a promotional lackey for their upstart company. The girl needed humility in a bad way, and since he was her boss, it was up to him to dish it out.

He hated this shit. Hated it.

TP, you bastard, we are more than even after this.

"Ronin, are you even listening to me?" Katie demanded with a pout.

"How many times do I have to tell you not to call me by my first name? I am your boss. Which means you call me Mr. Black, or sir, understood?"

"Yes, sir."

"Second, you do what I tell you. Nothing more and definitely nothing less. While I appreciate your initiative, I don't need it. I need you to put on the ring-girl outfit."

"But—"

He held up his hand. "No buts. Ever. Meet Sophia down in the dojo locker room. Handing out free tickets for the upcoming event is your job. A job which you are still on probation for."

Katie pushed herself out of the chair. "I will prove to you that I'm more valuable than being a bimbo ring girl."

Two raps sounded on the door, and Amery walked in. "Hey, Ronin. I just . . ." She froze, and her gaze flicked over Katie.

A sneaky smile curled Katie's mouth. "Okay, boss man. Do you want me to come back up and model the outfit? I know how much it means having your approval."

"No. Get moving. You're already late."

"It was hard to tear myself away from such fascinating conversation with you, even when we've spent most of the day together," she practically cooed. "Until tomorrow." She whirled around and strutted out of his office.

"Who the fuck is she?" Amery demanded. "Is she lost?"

He did not need this today on top of every fucking thing else. "No. She works for Black and Blue Promotions."

"So she came with Blue's crew?"

"No. I hired her."

With the way her eyes turned into lethal arrows? He'd given the wrong answer. "Just how closely will you be working with her in this new promotion company?"

"Why are you acting like this?"

Amery seemed to take a deep breath to try to compose herself, then stalked over and slapped her hands on the desk. "A six-foot-tall Amazon with perfect tits, a perfect ass, perfect blond hair, and a predatory smile just sauntered out of your office, after making it perfectly clear to *me* that she planned to be around *you* all the damn time."

"You're reading too much into this. Katie is a kid."

"You're kidding yourself if you don't think that *kid* has designs on you. And she's not a kid. I'll bet I'm not that much older than her."

Ronin counted to ten. "You've misread the situation."

"Then explain it to me."

"We agreed to stay out of each other's business. This is business, plain and simple."

She looked ready to argue, but changed her mind and stepped back. "You're right. I forgot my place for a moment."

"Jesus, Amery. Stop with this."

"You betcha. Wouldn't wanna speak up when something bothers me. I'll just let the big, strong man handle it and put it out of my empty little head." She granted him a fake smile, along with two cheesy thumbs-up, and stomped off.

He would not chase her down.

Would. Not.

Right. Who the fuck was he kidding? He always chased her down.

Ronin smacked his sore knee on the side of the desk and bit back a curse when it slowed him down. When he reached the hallway, Amery was nowhere to be found.

Blue came around the corner. "Hey, do you—"

"Did you pass Amery?"

"Yeah. She was not looking too happy."

"Where'd she go?"

"I don't know. So do you have time—"

"Not now. I have to deal with this first."

Blue clapped Ronin on the shoulder. "Hope you have a cup on, man."

He heard the elevator *ping*, so he reversed course and opened the door to the stairwell. In Amery's present mood, she wouldn't head for the penthouse, so he started downstairs. She'd have to get off at the second floor since classes were in session in the dojo.

So when the elevator door opened, Ronin was leaning against the wall waiting for her. When she saw him, she frantically poked buttons, trying to close the door in his face, but he was too fast. He snagged her wrist and hauled her out.

"Hey! What the hell? Let me go."

Ronin didn't respond; he just towed her down the hallway.

"You are pissing me off."

He tightened his grip on her wrist in warning.

"Don't make me use kung fu on you."

Jesus. The shit she said sometimes . . .

The conference room door was open. Ito, Terrel, one of Blue's instructors, and Knox were lounging around the table. They all looked up.

Ronin bit off, "Get. Out."

Ito and the other dude were gone lightning fast. But Knox said, "Fair warning. I hear you throwing furniture around and glass breaking again, and I will come in."

"Lock the door," Ronin said to Knox without taking his eyes off Amery.

Knox grumbled, but he left.

Ronin slammed his mouth down on hers as soon as the door shut. One hand holding her head in place, his other hand locked around both of her wrists as he literally pushed her into a corner.

After returning his kiss with equal voracity, Amery must've remembered she was mad at him and kissed him angrily. If he hadn't moved his mouth, she would've sunk her teeth into his lower lip hard enough to draw blood.

"Not nice, baby," he panted against her throat.

"I'm not feeling very nice toward you right now, *baby*."

"What has gotten into you? You're never this insanely jealous."

"What has gotten into you? You've never put a porn star on the payroll."

Do. Not. Laugh. "This is all about Katie?"

"Yes. When did you hire her? While we were broken up? Because I will be screaming banshee mad at you if you already had my replacement picked out. What did—"

"Stop talking. You're just getting yourself in deeper."

"Make me stop talking, hotshot. Just because—"

Ronin put his hand over her mouth. "Calm down, and listen, because I'm going to say this one time."

She blinked.

"We are together. That means I don't look at another woman the way I look at you. I don't touch another woman the way I touch you. I don't feel about any woman the way I feel about you. Got it? Don't ever think I'd throw away what we have for a cheap, meaningless fuck. You either trust me, or you don't. So what's it going to be?" He moved his hand from her mouth and released her wrists.

She studied him without speaking, which was so unlike her. Then she slapped her palms on his chest. "Goddamn you. I worked up a really good mad and then you say something like that."

"I should've said something like . . . Do you know how fucking hot it is that you're jealous?" He pressed his dick into her hip.

Amery tossed her head. "Oh, that hard-on is for me? I thought maybe . . ."

"What?"

"That you were hard before I walked into your office."

Ronin growled. "Now you're just provoking me. The only woman who gets me this hard is you." He put his mouth on her ear. "I'll prove it. Right fucking now."

"Ronin—"

"I warned you not to throw down a challenge in my dojo because it will be answered." He used his teeth on the cord in her neck as she strained to get away from him.

"Master Black—omigod you are *not* doing that here."

"What? This?" He zeroed in on the sensitive section of skin between her collarbone and shoulder that made her squirm, made her wet, made her moan.

When she called out his name, it came out on a long wail.

"Tell me to stop."

"I can't! You know I can't."

"Because you want this."

Amery angled her cheek into his. "I always want you. It makes me crazy when I see other women wanting you too."

Ronin took her mouth hungrily, giving her every ounce of passion she brought out in him. He eased back, looking into her lust-glazed eyes as he brushed whisper-soft kisses across her lips. "Crow's Nest. Now. The penthouse is too goddamn far away."

She swallowed hard and nodded.

He stepped back and she tried to duck past him, but he snagged her upper arm. "Stairs." He didn't touch her at all as they left the conference room.

Inside the stairwell, Ronin pushed her against the wall, sliding his leg between hers so she rode his thigh. Then he slipped his hands underneath her shirt, letting his thumbs sweep across the arc of her rib cage. "Undo the buttons."

Her hands shook as she unbuttoned her blouse.

As soon as she'd exposed her camisole, he lowered his head and dragged his mouth over the mounded flesh spilling from the white lace. Her skin was so soft. So warm. Smelled so fucking sweet, like cherries, that he wanted to take a big bite. So he did. Sinking his teeth into her flesh and sucking hard.

Amery's head fell back, and she groaned.

"Someday I'll tie you to my bed and leave these marks everywhere. I want you to see that every part of you is mine."

"Are you trying to make me come before that big cock of yours is inside me?"

"No, baby, just stating a fact." He dipped his tongue beneath the lace, trying to reach her nipple.

Then her fingers were there, pulling the stretchy fabric aside. "Suck hard. Make me feel how much you want me."

Goddamn he loved this woman. He circled the rigid point with his tongue. Then he nipped just the tip hard enough that she released a sharp gasp. He suckled the hot flesh strongly, drawing as much as possible into his mouth.

"You're gonna make me come," she panted.

"Not. Yet." He removed his hands and straightened her blouse. "Stop tempting me."

"Then stop stalling."

Grabbing her hand, he towed her down the stairs to the first floor. The door to the Crow's Nest locked only from the inside, so as soon as they were in, he locked the door. He turned and hauled Amery against him, kissing her crazily while his fingers worked the button and zipper of her skirt. "Off."

Amery's blouse fluttered to the floor and she kicked off her shoes.

Ronin shucked his gi pants. He stroked his cock, watching as Amery shed her skirt and panties. "Are you wet?"

"With the way you've been using that dirty mouth on me? I'm dripping."

He clamped his hands on her ass and lifted her, pressing her back against the brick wall. "Put me in you."

Her fingers circled the root, and she swirled the head of his cock around her wet entrance. "Say pretty please."

Ronin canted his hips and drove into her with one hard stroke. "I'm too impatient to say please. Holy fuck, woman, you are drenched."

"Stop being so chatty and fuck me."

Chatty? Jesus. Not even on his best day was he considered chatty and definitely not when he was balls deep inside this sexpot who made him so insane to have her he was fucking her in his dojo, for christsake. He never did that.

"What are you muttering about?" she asked.

"You." He buried his lips in her neck. Keeping one hand on

her ass, he moved the other beside her head for better leverage. "How goddamn much you own me." He plowed into her, his cock withdrawing completely and slamming back into her hard.

One of Amery's hands was gripping his hair; the other clutched the back of his neck. "Grind more," she panted. "Yes, like that."

Ronin flicked his tongue across the pulse point in her throat when he felt her legs tighten around his hips.

"Harder."

"I won't last long, if I start doing that."

"Do it." Five more hard strokes and Amery detonated. Her pelvis grinding into his. Her fingers digging into his shoulder. Biting her lip to keep herself from crying out.

Somehow he managed to keep focused on giving her what she needed rather than letting her orgasm pull him over the edge with her.

A sigh, a full-body shudder, and then her soft lips brushed his damp forehead. "You fuck like a dream, man of mine."

Ronin would've laughed, but he was too goddamn close. "Lift your tank top; I'm coming on your belly."

"What? Why?"

"Because I'm eating my fill of this hot cunt after I'm done fucking you." He rubbed his lips below her jaw. "I want you to look at yourself and know you're sticky beneath your shirt, wearing my seed."

Amery's fingers inched between their chests, and she maneuvered her camisole up while Ronin continued to pound into her.

"Almost. Fuck!" When his shaft tightened from his cock to his balls, he pulled out and rubbed the length along her slit, angling up on every stroke so his cock head connected with her clit.

When he started to come, he threw his head back as his cock jerked against her belly with every hard pulse.

She yanked him to her for a voracious kiss. A hot clash of tongues, lips, and teeth. After a dizzying minute of her onslaught, he tried to break free, but she refused to release his mouth. With the kiss, she helped him slow his heart and respiration rate, breathing with him, letting their lips part for only a moment to change angles. Only when he'd regained his balance did she let him go.

Amery nuzzled his temple. "Your semen was so hot when it marked me, but now it's drying. Sticking to my skin."

A rumble of satisfaction filled his chest. He looked into her eyes. "I'm not done with you."

"Ah. Okay. What—*eep*!"

Ronin pulled her away from the wall and carried her to the stairs that led to the observation deck. "You'll need that yoga balance." He set her on the fourth stair tread. "Hook your feet against the half-walls and rest on your elbows."

"You're serious."

"About eating your pussy? Yes." When she hesitated, he said, "Do it. Get your hips in the air and give me what I want."

Her eyes darkened. Yeah, his sexpot liked being bossed around.

As soon as her feet were in place and she raised her hips, he scooped her soft buttocks into his hands, pulling her into a forty-five-degree angle, leaving her no choice but to balance on her elbows.

"Ronin!"

"What? You're always worried about me putting too much pressure on my knee. This way I can stand and the pressure is on you." The woman was such a visual fucking feast, wide open to him, her pussy wet and swollen. He lowered his head and licked her. One long, thorough swipe with the flat of his tongue. She tasted good. Like sex and woman. He pushed her hips up higher and met her gaze across the slope of her upper body. "Seeing my come still glistening on your belly turns me into a wild man, baby. So be warned."

He settled his mouth over that hot, slick flesh and tongued her clit until she came in a thigh-clenching, chest-heaving orgasm.

"That's one," he whispered against the inside of her thigh. "One more."

"I can't."

"I know you can." Ronin backed off from direct contact. He pressed his lips to every inch of her bare mound; she'd gone full Brazilian last time. He nibbled her softest tissues. Teased her with his breath and the very tip of his tongue. He soothed the nip and scrape of his teeth with soft smooches. He licked every fold and swell, jamming his tongue in and coating his face with her juices. He backed away when she started to pump her groin into his face. Rubbing his five-o'clock shadow on her inner thighs as they trembled. Then sweeping his razor-stubbled chin across her clit just to test her reaction.

Her hips nearly shot to the roof—good to know. He'd test her limits on that another time.

Ronin switched his focus to her clit, suctioning his mouth to the plumped pearl, using his tongue until she arched harder and moaned his name.

Her cunt pulsed against his mouth, and he swallowed every spasm, every bit of sweet slickness, growling against her soft tissues because he wanted more.

"Ronin. Stop. I can't hold this pose anymore."

He gently set her butt on the stairs before leaning forward and running his hands up the inside of her legs, from her ankles to the creases of her thighs. "Come on."

Amery still had that slightly vacant post-orgasmic look in her eyes. "Where are we going?"

"Up," was all he said. He lifted her over his shoulder in a fireman's hold.

"What are you doing? Your knee—"

"Is fine." He slapped her bare ass. "You should worry about my cock, because I'm still not done with you."

"You are insatiable."

Upon reaching the observation room, Ronin headed for the small desk. He swept everything off it before letting Amery slide down his body.

He flipped her around onto her belly across the desk and hiked her hips in the air. He pushed between her thighs, his cock hitting her warm wet center on the first attempt, and he slowly slid inside her.

Amery moaned. "You're trying to break me."

Curling his fingers around her hips, he layered his chest to her back, wishing they were skin to skin. "No, I'm proving to you you're the only one who gets me this fucking hard." For a moment he stayed right there, inhaling the scent of her hair, and then he exhaled slowly, feeling her shudder beneath him as the air tickled her ear. "Not once in the ten years I've owned this dojo have I ever fucked a woman in it. Never. And I'm fucking you *twice*. So what does that say about you, baby?"

"Oh god. You're killing me with this, Ronin."

"Say. It."

"It says you love me. Just me. You want me. Just me."

"Goddamn right I do." He pulled out of her pussy and eased back in. His cock wanted to hammer into her tight, wet heat, but he forced himself to go slow. To draw out the pleasure of this joining.

She pushed up and turned her head, capturing his mouth. The angle was wrong, yet somehow, the glide of lips on lips was more erotic than an openmouthed tongue-thrusting kiss.

When Amery squeezed his dick with those strong inner muscles, he moved faster until his orgasm blasted through him.

The muffled sound of *ki-yahs* roused him from that other plane. He murmured, "I'm yours just as much as you're mine," before pulling out.

Ronin half staggered back to her after picking up their clothes. She sat on the desk facing him, watching him. After they dressed, she snaked her arms around his waist and held on tight.

As intense as the last half hour had been, it hadn't escaped his notice that Amery still hadn't admitted she loved him. But he did have some pride; he wouldn't ask her.

The intercom buzzed.

He disentangled from her and reached for the handset. "What?"

"Reminding you of the meeting," Knox said. "Five minutes."

"Thanks. Be right there."

"What's going on?" Amery asked him.

"Meeting to discuss the upcoming event."

"Have you always spent this much time pushing paper?"

"More than one might think. Why? Does the fact that I have to plan shit instead of using my fists take away from my manliness?"

Amery laughed and jumped down to zip up her skirt. "You just fucked me twice and I came four times, so your manliness is not in question, Ronin Black. I asked because I don't see you until the end of my workday, and you're already into the physically demanding part of your job."

"Not lately."

Her gaze sharpened. "But you are taking it easy?"

"Too easy." He reached out and smoothed the pieces of her hair sticking up all over. "Sorry about the sex hair."

"No, you're not. And you're changing the subject."

Which he did again. "Sit in on the meeting with me."

"Why?"

"You have great insight. Maybe you'll pick up on something I'm missing. Some of my MMA instructors have been less than enthusiastic about this promotion company."

"Ronin, I don't want to be that clingy girlfriend who horns in on everything."

"You're not." He kissed her. "You're in my life. This is part of my life."

She set her hand on his cheek. "There's more to it than that."

Again Ronin held back on telling her he felt useless in his own dojo. Being restricted to inactive status. Amery knew his limitations; she'd been babying him along as much as everyone else. He wanted her to see him in a take-charge business role, especially since all his instructors would be at this meeting. "So is that a no?"

"I'll sit in if it's really what you want."

"I do." He kissed her again, holding her head in place. He murmured, "But it'll give me another hard-on, looking at you and knowing you're wearing my seed beneath this prim-and-proper blouse."

"He says with a caveman growl."

He quit crowding her. "Let's go."

Amery slipped on her shoes and fussed with his hair before they left the Crow's Nest.

He didn't hold her hand as they headed down the short hallway. He felt Amery's questioning look as he retreated into his Sensei Black persona, but she didn't comment.

"Before we go in, do I need to know who teaches what in the MMA classes?"

"Deacon is the kickboxing leader. He studied Muay Thai for a few years. Fisher, who you've never met, is from a boxing family, and he was nationally ranked champion. He didn't start training in jujitsu until two years ago, and he's on the fence about MMA fighting. But he's great at working boxing drills. Ito also has an advanced black belt in judo; he works with throws."

"And you? What's your area of expertise?"

Ronin punched the elevator button. "Submission holds. Getting out of holds. I'm usually the grappling partner. But I'll admit it took me a while to get used to no-gi grappling."

Amery frowned. "What's no-gi grappling?"

Sometimes he forgot she hadn't been around martial arts her whole life like he and his instructors had. "In jujitsu we train students to use the gi in fighting situations. It's an added advantage to use your opponent's lapels, or sleeves, or even the back of the gi for takedown techniques. It's much easier throwing a guy to ground when he's wearing clothes than when his chest is bare. But we do spend time on no-gi grappling in class."

Before they exited the elevator, Amery put her hand on his chest. "So the scratches I sometimes see on your chest?"

"From grappling. Once in a while I'll get a mark from a gi that looks like a rope burn."

She smiled. "I've dealt with the rope burn issue recently."

When they stepped into the hallway, several guys were loitering outside the closed door. "What's going on?" Ronin asked Gil, Blue's second in command.

"Blue and Sophia are fighting. I tune them out because this is not unusual with them."

Great. Ronin knocked twice before opening the door. "You two about done? We're ready to start."

"Of course," Blue said. "Sophia was just—"

"I'm not leaving, brother."

"Fine. Everyone find a seat." Ronin took the chair at the head of the table. Amery sat beside him. He scanned the room. "Who are we missing?"

"Shiori," Sophia said, plopping next to Blue at the opposite end of the table.

"She's teaching," Ito said.

"Blue?" Ronin prompted. "Where are we on things?"

"The first event is set. I didn't have to jump through many hoops to get the name of our new company switched over. Not much to report." Blue smiled at Amery. "I believe Hardwick Designs is handling the flyers and print promotional materials?"

"Yes. If you have previous playbills—matchups, whatever they are—hand them over along with all the details I'll need and your deadline."

"Are any of the Black Arts fighters going up against ABC fighters in this event?" Knox asked.

Blue shook his head. "Deacon is in the pro fight. Sophia is representing ABC in the lone women's bout. We've got to decide how many amateur bouts we want on the card. Ideally we should represent as many weight classes as we can, and I think eventually that won't be a problem. But right now, we've got no amateurs in the heavyweight or super heavyweight divisions."

Ronin took the piece of paper Blue offered him. "What's this?"

"My recommendation on joint promotional goals versus individual dojo goals. I realize we both want to get our amateurs experience in the cage, but by putting too many guys from Black Arts and ABC on the Black and Blue Promotions fight card, we run the risk of becoming incestuous. What we don't want are other MMA clubs thinking we're only interested in furthering our fighters' records. Then they'll stop submitting fighters for events. The only way to accurately judge whether our club fighters are up to snuff is by fighting guys from other clubs."

"Agreed." He looked at Deacon and Knox, then Blue and Gil. "You guys see other options?"

Knox rested his elbows on the table. "If we limit entrants, we'll still have to find other fights for them."

"Also, why would they stay with our training program if we're not putting them in events we sponsor? They'd be better off training elsewhere. So we lose income and fighters. How is that beneficial for either club?" Gil asked.

Blue pointed to the piece of paper. "That's why I brought it up. Why would we help other amateur fighters but not our own?"

No one said anything out loud, but Fisher and Ito were speaking in low tones.

Amery cleared her throat. "Can I suggest something?"

Ronin didn't miss the annoyed looks sent her way—like why the fuck did Sensei's girlfriend get to speak?—and now he understood her reluctance to attend the meeting. "No one else has jumped in with ideas, so go ahead."

"Use the event as a carrot for your fighters. Tell them you're picking only one fighter to represent the club. If the guys are serious, won't they work harder to be the guy chosen?"

He checked out the reactions around the room. Everyone seemed surprised. "Not a bad idea. That'd also encourage them to find other amateur fights on their own to up their game."

"Makes sense," Deacon said. "Especially since I've gotta go lookin' for my own pro fights."

"So at least for the first few events, we'll limit the bouts to one fighter from ABC, one from Black Arts. That means we'll need two pro division fighters and sixteen amateur fighters to fill the other slots?" Blue asked Ronin.

"Sound fair?"

"Does to me." Blue prompted Sophia and Gil. "You guys all right with that?"

Gil nodded.

Sophia said, "We are going to feature at least one women's bout?"

"What's the crowd reception been on that? Because we've not had experience with it," Ronin asked Sophia.

"I could claim half-naked chicks beating the crap out of each other and rolling around on the floor really speaks to the type of people who attend MMA events, but I wouldn't want to be called sexist."

Everyone laughed.

"Seriously, even if we have to add a tenth match, I believe we should strive to have a women's bout on every card. Not all promo companies do this, and it would set us apart."

More murmured agreement.

"Blue, put the call out to other clubs. Since Deacon didn't fight last time, he'll be our one fighter."

Blue grinned. "You sure you don't wanna have a rematch, Sensei?"

"My fighting days are over for a while." Ronin felt Amery's stare, but he couldn't claim his fighting days were behind him for good.

"It's been some time since we've participated in a smoker," Gil said. "We haven't been keeping up with who's running them on a regular basis. Have you?"

"We used to hold them a few times a year," Knox said. "Sensei would ref. But the last time he ended up with a heel to the head."

Blue sucked air in through his teeth. "I heard about that."

Amery asked, "What's a smoker?"

"When MMA clubs hold matches against each other. There aren't winners and losers. It's just a chance for fighters to compete outside of their clubs," Sophia said. "The more you're around the fighting life, the more lingo you'll pick up." She stood. "We done here? I gotta see if Katie stuck it out in Terrel's class after she bitched about putting on the ring-girl outfit."

"We're done," Ronin said.

"You are. The rest of us have classes to teach," Knox grumbled.

After everyone was gone, Amery stood and paced to the window, then came back.

"What?"

"You didn't deny that you're going to fight again. Are you planning on it?"

"It's what I do."

"And if I asked you not to fight?"

"You won't. You accept all parts of me, remember?" Ronin picked up her right hand and nibbled on her fingers. "Let's go upstairs. It's your night to cook. What are we having?"

"Something unhealthy like spaghetti. For having such a kick-ass kitchen, you don't have all the tools I need to cook like I'm used to. So be warned: I'm bringing my stuff into your domain."

"Bring it all. Then it'll already be there when you move in with me."

"I'm thinking about it." She squirmed until he let her loose. "Tell me about Katie."

And . . . she had sidestepped the issue once again. "This can't go further than us."

Amery poked him in the chest. "I knew it! She is a porn star you're trying to reform."

He laughed. "No. She's Thaddeus Pettigrew's daughter." He explained the situation. "She'll be Blue's headache most of the time."

"Will she have access to you?"

"In limited amounts."

"Good." She nipped his chin and then flicked the sting away with a sassy flick of her tongue. "I'd hate to have to give that little bitch the beat-down. I have had training from the best."

"That you have."

"I brought you something." She reached inside her purse and pulled out a package. "Not as fancy of a tie as last time . . ."

"What is it?"

"A gift."

Ronin ripped open the paper and saw a framed tin-type picture with Asian influences that they'd seen at a Renaissance fair several months ago. She'd refused to let him buy it, evidently so she could go back and get it for him. "Amery. This is . . ." So fucking sweet and personal. He was undone once again by her thoughtfulness.

"Your desk is decidedly bare. Maybe it makes me territorial, but when you see it, I know you'll think of me."

"Always." He kissed her. "Thank you. It's perfect. I'll just grab the box of black ropes from under my desk before we go upstairs since we have a tradition of me tying you up after you present me with a gift."

Amery leaned back to look at him. "A tradition? This is only the second time."

"A tradition has to start somewhere."

CHAPTER TWELVE

"ARE you acting nervous because of the skimpy outfit?"

Katie peered at him over the top of the promotional poster she held, her blue eyes piercing. "No. I wore skimpier clothes than this to the club last weekend."

Ronin forced himself to continue the conversation. "Then why the nerves?"

"Actually, I'm more anxious than anything."

"Anxious for what?"

"Anxious to get this stupid thing over with."

He looked at her sharply. "If you're not willing to do this, then I will find someone else who is."

She crossed her arms over her chest and slumped back in the chair with a heavy sigh. Luckily she hadn't offered him that simpering little-girl pout or he would've booted her ass out the door—no matter what promises he'd made. "I said I'd do it."

"Then act enthusiastic. My reputation is at stake here."

Three knocks sounded, and Amery poked her head in. "Is this a bad time?"

Ronin smiled at her, grateful for the interruption. "No. Katie was just complaining again about her role at tonight's event."

"Please explain to me what being a ring girl has to do with learning the mixed martial arts fight-promotion business?" Katie demanded.

"A, ring girl is your *job,* so suck it up and do it or quit—your choice. B, while you're waiting to prance around the outside of the ring, reminding attendees which round it is and who our sponsors are, you will be sitting next to Sandan Zach, paying very close attention to how the fighters are scored."

"I dated an MMA guy. I know how to score."

Amery said, "I'll just bet you do," with such sweetness that Katie didn't recognize the sarcasm.

Ronin forced his face to remain blank, but inside he was laughing. "Regardless, pay attention to everything. The scoring, the judges' actions, the crowd's reactions, what the sponsors are doing in front of the crowd and behind the scenes. You will be tested."

Katie opened her mouth and snapped it shut before she stood. "You've got it, Sensei."

After Katie slunk out the door, Amery said, "Can I trip her as she's walking around the cage?"

He chuckled and pulled her onto his lap. "That'll fuck with my liability insurance, so no."

"She annoys me."

Although Amery had gotten over her bout of jealousy, she still eyed Katie with distrust. "I know she does, baby. She annoys everybody."

Amery ran her fingers through his hair. "Is it worth it? She's still sporting that spoiled rich girl attitude. Even Ito, who is more Zen than you, wanted to drop-kick her into next week."

"Katie's brattiness is a defense mechanism. She's a scared kid who's never been accountable for anything in her life, and she wants to be taken seriously."

"So that's why you're making her walk around the ring in front of a thousand people in booty shorts, a boob-baring halter top, dolled up with pageant queen hair and makeup? So sponsors will take her more seriously?"

Ronin slapped her ass. "She needs to learn ringside protocol. If I gave her a clipboard and put her next to the judges? She'd act like she was in charge—her pride wouldn't allow anything less. These next-level promoters would treat her like a bimbo and think our organization was unprofessional."

"So while she's dressed like a bimbo, she's learning humility as well as learning the business." Amery grinned. "Such a wise grasshopper you are, Sensei."

"Jesus."

"What did TP do for you that resulted in this huge favor you're doing for him?"

"He fixed Blue's lease issue. After this, regardless of how Katie does working for Black and Blue Promotions, all chits will be cashed in and I'll have a clean slate with TP. For the first time in more than ten years."

"You've never told me your history with TP."

He reached up and twined a hank of her hair around his finger. "After I earned enough money to buy a place to establish my business, I found out no bank would loan me money because of my credit history."

"The billionaire heir had bad credit?"

"I had *no* credit history. I paid cash for everything after I moved to the US. I had no official income because fighting was a cash-only business. Even when I had three bank accounts totaling more than three-quarters of a million dollars, no financial institution would lend me money to buy the piece-of-shit building in a crappy section of Denver." He continued to twist her rosy-gold hair. The soft curl reminded him of the silken ribbons he'd bound her with last night. "Also at that time, the trust funds Grandfather had set up in my name across the globe were worth seventy-five million dollars."

Amery's mouth dropped open. "Are you kidding me?"

"No. So technically I had the cash to buy the building outright—but I wanted to make my own way."

"Technically?"

"My name is on the accounts, but I've never considered it my money. I did research on various banks and came across TP's company. He had a reputation as a wild card, and the Denver financial establishment didn't like him, painting him as a liar, so I chose him."

"Why?"

"Because if he was a risk taker, he'd take a risk on me. If he blabbed the information about my family connection, I could chalk it up to him being a liar and a blowhard. Win-win."

Ronin remembered how cocky he'd been demanding a meeting with the CFO of Pettigrew Financial. Luck or karma or serendipity had been on his side that day because TP agreed to meet with him privately.

If Amery thought Ronin was tight-lipped now, it was nothing compared to how he was back then. But something about TP had prompted Ronin to spill every detail of his life, his family and financial connections, the reasons why he didn't use them, the resulting struggles because of that decision, and his business goals. TP had coolly taken the information and sent Ronin away with the promise he'd get back to him.

TP made him sweat it out an entire week before he showed up at the dive martial arts studio Ronin had been renting on a month-to-month basis. And truth was, if TP hadn't taken the time to thoroughly check out Ronin's backstory, then Ronin wouldn't have done business with him. But they'd had an odd connection from the start and hashed out details of their "deal" with just a handshake—unheard of in this day and age.

"So what happened?" Amery prompted, bringing him back to the present.

"He signed off on the loan for the building personally. He had two stipulations. One, that if I ever cashed in any of the trust funds,

I'd put the money in one of his banks. Two, that I'd do a favor for him from time to time." He frowned. "But the favor issue didn't come up until after I had problems with the construction company I hired for the building remodel. Within two weeks, a group of Russian construction workers showed up, and the guys trying to extort cash from me for 'protection services' vanished."

"Did TP help you handle it?"

Ronin laughed. "Yes. Which is how I ended up owing Max Stanislovsky a favor too."

Amery placed her hands on his cheeks and tilted his head to gaze into his eyes. "You don't have to go into detail, but are the thug-for-hire rumors about you true?"

"Yes."

"Tell me about it. About all of it."

"At this point, some guys would say they're not proud of what they've done, but I have no regrets. If I didn't believe in the favor I'd been asked to do, I passed. TP never had an issue with that. Neither did Max." Ronin peered into Amery's eyes, half afraid of what he'd see. But those beautiful baby blues held interest and love, not a hint of disdain. "Are you satisfied now?"

"Did you ever put money in TP's bank, or is he still waiting?"

"Remember when I told you I withdrew funds from a small trust account to finish my penthouse?"

Amery nodded.

"One beneficial thing my sister told me about my grandfather? It didn't matter if I took out a single dollar or a million. The amount of money wasn't the catalyst, just that I'd used any of it. As soon as I knew that, I cashed out every fucking penny of that trust. First thing I did was pay off my building." Ronin sensed she wanted to ask him how much that was, so he told her. "That one small account had more than ten million dollars in it."

"Oh. My. Fucking. God. You have ten million dollars in the bank? Right now? Right here in Colorado?"

Ronin smiled. "With TP's investment guy looking after it, it's closer to twenty million. And before you freak out, I live on what I make from the dojo. That money sits there. I'm happy without all the trappings of worrying about how to spend that much disposable cash. Most people don't understand that. I'm really happy my bank balance doesn't matter to you."

"I don't think I could be so cavalier about money. Maybe that attitude is the privilege of people who have it."

He forced himself to ask the question, wondering if he should be afraid of her answer. "So, has hearing all this changed how you look at me now?"

"No." Amery curled her hand around the side of his face. "Anything you did, even if you bloodied your hands doing it, wasn't done lightly or without good reason. I know you're a man of integrity." She slipped her hand down to the left side of his chest. "You have a good heart."

Ronin pressed his forehead to hers. "Baby, you own it."

Amery kissed him with the sweet comfort and acceptance he'd only ever gotten from her. Those soft lips trailed along his jaw, stopping at his ear. "I'm surprised we haven't been interrupted yet. Is there anything else you need to get off your chest?"

Just then Blue burst in and skidded to a stop. "Sorry to interrupt, but there's some pre-fight stuff we need to go over."

Amery whispered, "Later." Then she slid off Ronin's lap. "I need to track down my seat anyway."

"Ringside to the left of the judges table. Fifth row, outside seats," Blue offered.

After Amery left, Ronin said, "What's up?"

"The local affiliate for a national sports channel wants to interview someone from the Black and Blue promotion team. We never finished the discussion about who's handling media."

"That'll be Katie's job—provided she survives her probation. But for now . . . fuck. I don't want to be on camera. Do you?"

"Fuck no," Blue said. "TV interview shit is my least-favorite thing about fighting. Especially post-fight. Reporters sticking a damn camera in your face. Half the time I don't know my own name, never mind talking coherently about fight strategy."

"We're on the same page there. You want one of your guys and one of my guys?"

Katie stormed in through the side door. "Who's representing Black and Blue Promotions in the segment with KNNR?"

Blue's eyes nearly bugged out of his head and his tongue almost smacked into the floor at seeing Katie in her ring-girl getup.

"That's what we're discussing. Knox and Gil?"

"No, no, no. This is the first promotional event, so it has to be the owners, if for no other reason than to show a solid front after Mr. Curacao's public beat-down of you, Mr. Black."

The woman did have a point.

Then she opened the door. "Get on with it. Smile, but don't be goofy. Don't be aloof either. Talk about the exciting amateur matchups tonight, but also about all the exciting matchups we've planned over the next few months. Then mention that mixed martial arts bouts are great entertainment for the whole family."

Ronin and Blue exchanged a look.

Katie made the shooing motion again. "Go!"

Out in the hallway, Blue said, "Who knew the hot ring girl also had a brain?"

"Jesus, Blue."

"Her brain ain't bigger than her tits. Did you see those? I mean, how could you miss them, spilling out of that teeny top, no?"

"Maybe you should be thinking about this interview rather than Katie's sizable . . . contributions to the company."

AFTER the interview, five minutes before the event was slated to start, Ronin and Blue were in the hallway discussing last-minute details with their fighters, when Knox jogged up the hallway, Shiori hot on his heels.

"Sensei, we've got a problem."

Never fucking failed. "What?"

"The chick who's matched with Sophia is drunk. Like passed-out drunk in the women's locker room."

"You've got to be kidding me."

"Nope."

"Where in the hell did you find her?" he demanded of Blue.

But Sophia started hammering away at Blue in Portuguese before he could answer.

Then Shiori got in his face. "Ronin, I can do this."

"Do what?" Ronin scarcely paid any attention to his sister as he was trying to figure out why Sophia was so pissed off at Blue.

A shrill whistle split the air.

All arguing stopped and they faced Knox. "Three minutes till show time. I'll tell the announcer the women's bout is off."

"No. I'll fight in her place."

Shocked, Ronin looked at Shiori, dressed to kill in some slinky dress with sleeves that made her look like a butterfly. And she wore five-inch stilettos. "You're not prepared."

"That's what I told her," Knox said hotly.

Then Shiori went to stand in front of Blue. "You own half of the promotion company, and this was originally set up as your event. You need a fighter and I want to fight. I'm Rokudan. I've been teaching for two months and training in jujitsu my entire life. I'm not exactly unskilled. Or unprepared."

Blue gave her a considering look.

"Goddammit, Blue, you can't seriously—"

Sophia cut Knox off with, "Let her fight me. Then at least I'll know I have a worthy opponent and not a drunken whore you used to fuck. You owe me this, brother."

Blue said, "This is exactly why I didn't want you on the card tonight. Or any night."

Sophia cocked her head at Shiori. "We need these men making decisions for us? People paid good money to see a fight. Let's give them one."

Both women turned simultaneously toward Blue.

He threw up his hands. "Fine! Fight. But the win-lose outcome better never affect either of you at the dojo. Understood?"

"I'll already be ringside with Deacon, so who will be ringside with She-Cat?" Knox asked.

"Me," Ronin said, slipping his arm around Shiori's waist to keep her from clawing at Knox for his obnoxious nickname for her.

"Thank you."

"I see a streak of stupid runs wide in the Black family," Knox said.

Sophia's gaze moved over Shiori. "You have any gear with you?"

"None."

"I've got extra." Sophia grinned evilly. "Or we can just rip it off my drunken former opponent. Serve her right to wake up naked."

They headed to the women's locker room.

"Wonder if they're doing each other's hair, too?" Knox said snottily.

"If you ask me if you can watch, I'm knocking you the fuck out," Deacon drawled.

Blue met Ronin's gaze. "Look, I had no choice. Sophia accused me of rigging her fight."

"Did you?"

"No. But I did sleep with the woman she was supposed to meet in the cage tonight."

Ronin's eyes narrowed. "Please tell me you don't have a problem keeping your dick in your pants."

Blue blushed. "I'm discreet. The one time I'm not? Came back to bite me in the ass."

The announcer started his spiel and they headed into the arena.

THE event center was packed to capacity; they'd had to turn spectators away so as not to violate fire code. It'd be tempting to book a bigger venue next time, but word of mouth about the sold-out status of tonight's docket would pretty much guarantee early ticket sales for the next matchups.

The lights started swirling and the music crescendoed. Pageantry was Ronin's least-favorite part of MMA events. The fighter picking a theme song to enter the arena, a posse following behind him, while the crowd alternately booed and cheered.

In the amateur fights, held in boxing gyms and private back rooms at dive bars, the participants were patted down, put in the ring, given a reminder of the rules, and then the round began. Usually the ref was someone like him, a former fighter past his head-knocking prime who still loved a good, fair fight.

While Ronin liked to see professionalism and well-prepared fighters in the amateur division, something about the underground fights rang truer. Many guys in those bouts were in it for the money. Physical prowess played a part in it, but the chance to win a few hundred bucks for a few minutes' work made it easier to clock in for their blue-collar jobs come Monday morning.

Ronin scanned the Black and Blue seating section. Amery's beautiful hair shone like a beacon, and he moved down the aisle, taking the empty seat next to her.

Her eyes lit up when she saw him. "I thought you'd be in Deacon's corner, coaching him."

"Knox has it covered."

She leaned over. "I'm glad I'm sitting beside you during my first ever MMA fight and not watching you fight."

He brushed a kiss over her temple.

Katie vaulted onto the edge around the cage—easy to do with those mile-long legs of hers—and held up the round sign, moving from corner to corner, making sure to turn around and give the mostly male audience not only a look at her ass, but a reminder of the round sponsor's name on the back of the card.

Amery whapped Ronin's arm to get his attention.

"What?"

"Good thing I'm fairly secure in our relationship, Master Black, or I'd be worried you'd fall for Katie's holy-fucking-shit body."

"Fairly secure?" he repeated. "Guess I'll have to tie you up later to make sure you're very secure in the way I feel about you."

The announcer read the opponents' names, trunk colors, corners, and which MMA club they represented—if any—before going over the rules.

Ronin automatically tensed up when the fight started. His sweet Amery noticed and reached for his hand.

The crowd was all about cheering for the Denver native. So when the opponent's first kick connected with the guy's knee, loud boos echoed through the arena.

Denver wrestling guy took his opponent to the mat.

Ronin glanced at the judges. Then he focused on Zach and Katie seated at the promotions table. Blue switched between watching the fight and flipping through paperwork.

As soon as the round ended, Katie leaped onto the edge of the ring and did her thing.

"Who do you think is winning?" Amery asked.

"The Denver guy. I'd put his points around twenty and his opponent's at thirteen," he said absentmindedly while scanning the surrounding area.

"Am I cramping your style or something?"

Ronin's gaze zoomed to hers. "Why would you say that?"

"Although you're sitting here, you're not really here."

"Maybe it's because I don't know how to act when I'm not in the cage."

"Do you miss fighting?"

"Yes. I've no doubt even when I'm an old man—hopefully not suffering from *dementia pugilistica*—that I'll still miss being in the ring." Ronin tucked an errant hank of hair over her shoulder. "Are you worried I'm going to climb back in?"

"Yes. It's in your blood."

Ronin couldn't disagree. "I found out tonight it's also in Shiori's blood."

Amery's gaze darted to the empty seats in front of them and back to Ronin. "Where is she?"

"Warming up. The other female fighter passed out. Shiori volunteered to fill in."

"She's fighting Sophia?" When she realized how loud her voice had gotten, she leaned closer. "And you let her?"

"I had no say in whether or not she fights." He knew if he would've argued, Shiori would've thrown back her lack of influence in his choices about fighting. "And now I'll be coaching her."

"Ronin. How can you sit there and watch her without wanting to jump in and save her?"

"Shiori has never been the type to need saving."

The second round started, but Ronin paid no attention. He'd been coached his whole life and done plenty of coaching himself, so he should know how to coach his sister. But his mind had gone blank.

Focus. Find the calm.

But he couldn't when everything was in chaos.

After the second round ended, Amery rested her cheek against his upper arm. "What can I do?"

"Cheer for her."

"Will you be okay?"

He deflected answering by kissing her. "I'm glad you're here.

I'll meet you in the ready room after Deacon's fight and we'll head to the party."

IT was more of an out-of-body experience trailing behind his sister as she entered the arena than when he walked in himself. She carried herself with feminine grace. After the official patted her down, checking to make sure her upper-body clothing didn't have zippers or buttons and nothing had been hidden in her gloves, she ducked into the cage.

Ronin took his spot in her corner behind the netting. Ito brought the bucket of supplies and the stool.

Shiori approached him, calmer than he'd expected. In that moment, he had a punch of guilt that he had no clue whether she'd ever fought in an official fight before. During their teenage years, he'd participated in tournaments, but at a different level from his sister, so he'd never seen her compete.

"You good?" *Brilliant question, Ronin.*

"Yes." She looked at him expectantly.

He had to give her some kind of advice. "It'll be a ground fight."

"I know."

"Watch the arm bar. Watch those fast reversals. She'll be aggressive with the takedown and the mount. But don't let that stop you from using short jabs, elbows, anything in guard position to keep her off balance."

"Noted."

He patted her shoulder. "Put her in her place, Rokudan. You got this."

Shiori grinned and slipped in her mouth guard.

"In the red corner, we've got our replacement fighter in her amateur debut, all the way from Tokyo, Japan, weighing in at one hundred and twenty pounds, representing Black Arts dojo, Shiori 'She-Cat' Hirano."

She-Cat? Jesus. Shiori was going to kill Knox after this.

"In the blue corner, weighing in at one hundred and thirty pounds, with an amateur record of ten wins and zero losses, representing ABC dojo and originally hailing from Brazil, Sophia 'Stinger' Curacao."

Shiori and Sophia stepped into the center of the ring and listened to the rules. They bowed to each other rather than bumping fists.

When the bell rang, Ronin's entire body seized up. It was harder sitting here waiting for someone he cared about to get smacked around than to be in the cage himself.

Thank god Amery hadn't ever watched him fight.

Shiori came out swinging, which surprised both Ronin and Sophia. As the women circled each other, he noticed that Shiori held herself more like a boxer, hands up, body turned. She dodged a couple of Sophia's kicks. She managed to bob and weave enough to keep Sophia from taking her to the mat.

Every second of the three-minute round ticked by like an hour. At the thirty-second mark, Shiori switched tactics and charged for a takedown.

"That's it. Get her down and keep her down." Ronin's jaw tightened when Shiori sustained a strong blow to the side of her head. Didn't appear to make her loopy, just more determined.

The ten-second warning sounded and the first round ended.

He set the stool in her corner, grabbed the towel and the bottle of water.

Shiori removed her mouth guard. "How'd it look?"

"Good. I have you ahead. You kept her on her feet longer than I expected."

Breathing hard, she nodded and took a drink of water.

"I sensed some hesitation on her part," he said, mopping her face.

"Me too. I think she's holding back."

"Why?"

"I've got ten years on her and it's supposedly my first fight."

"Supposedly?" Ronin repeated.

Shiori patted his cheek. "As you say here in the west, this ain't my first rodeo."

Ronin grinned. "Goddamn. You've been holding back too."

"Not anymore."

During the second round, Shiori toyed with Sophia. Their ground game wasn't evenly matched. Several times Ronin saw where Shiori could've ended the bout, but she opted to stay in taunting mode.

But the first minute of the third round, Shiori zeroed in, knocked Sophia to the mat, and got her to tap out by putting her in a rear naked choke.

After Shiori was announced as the winner, Ronin accompanied her back through the gauntlet. Knox and Deacon leaned against the wall, not speaking as they waited for the main event to begin.

Knox said, "Look at you, She-Cat. Not a mark on your face. I'll admit I was hoping for at least a swollen lip."

Shiori sauntered up to Knox, swaggering in that supremely confident and yet wholly feminine manner. She stood on tiptoe and spoke directly into his ear.

After she stepped back, Knox seemed flustered for a beat or two. Then he said, "I'll pass."

Shiori bumped fists with Deacon. Then she headed to the women's locker room.

Ronin looked between Knox and Deacon. "Need anything?"

"Nah. We're good."

"I'll head up to the balcony level and watch from there."

He cut through to the side door and scaled the stairs. The seats were packed, and people were rowdy, ready for the final fight.

Since Deacon's opponent had a less-impressive win-loss record, he entered the event center first. His theme song was Pink's "So What," which was just wrong on so many levels. A dozen people followed him in. He stopped and kissed a woman and a baby; then he did the "man hug" thing with guys outside the ropes.

Cut to the entrance again, where they announced Deacon as Deacon "Con Man" McConnell—which was just fucking stupid that all these fighters had nicknames. When he'd fought, they'd forced a nickname on him too, calling him Ronin "the Master" Black. Better than someone's other suggestion of Ronin "Jet" Black. At least Ronin's entrance music had been tongue-in-cheek—when "Back in Black" by AC/DC blared from the speakers.

Deacon's entrance tune was old-school and a sly wink too—"Enter Sandman"—the same song he'd been using since he was Sandan belt rank. Two people followed Deacon—Knox and Ito. Deacon didn't kiss babies. He sure as fuck didn't hug anyone on his way into the cage. After the pat down, he retreated to his corner and conferred with Knox and Ito.

The announcer spent way too much time blathering—nothing new, that's what they were paid to do. Once the fighters had been introduced and Katie did her thing, the bell rang.

If Ronin had the chance to study his fighters from higher in the arena, he took it. Sometimes critical errors, especially repetitive critical errors, were better seen from above.

Deacon owned the match from the start. Ronin felt a stab of annoyance that the main pro bout had such mismatched fighters.

But as he watched, he realized Deacon's ground game wasn't up to par—surprising for a jujitsu MMA fighter. That showed Deacon had been spending too much training time on boxing and not enough on grappling. He needed to get back to basics.

The first round ended, and Ronin had a sense of dread that had nothing to do with the rest of the fight. Everyone had convinced him that because this event launched Black and Blue Promotions, they had to host an after-party. He'd grudgingly agreed. But now the idea of glad-handing sponsors, discussing upcoming opportunities with other promoters, rehashing fights with fighters and their families, plus the

Black Arts and ABC crews . . . he wanted to fake a setback injury and bow out.

Katie's appearance signaled the start of the second round.

After the bell dinged, Deacon came out with extra aggression. Two kicks, one fake punch, and then he executed a spinning back fist to his opponent's head and the match was over. He knocked the guy out cold.

Ronin had a phantom pain in the back of his skull—he'd been on the receiving end of that move recently.

The referee called the fight, the lights came on, and Ronin headed to the ready room.

CHAPTER THIRTEEN

AMERY had to admit it was cool to flash a pass for the private after-party. Black and Blue Promotions had gone all out, securing a large private banquet room at a local brewpub.

But it was cooler yet to walk in on Ronin Black's arm.

The man defined hot and sexy. And intimidating. Women eyed him. Other fighters wanted to be him. The man was constantly surrounded. But that was okay since she liked to admire him from afar too.

During the party, his eyes met hers across the crowded room, and the punch of lust tightened everything inside her even as her knees went weak. He allowed himself that I-own-you smirk and then refocused on his conversation.

She sighed.

"That is one sigh-worthy man, *ma chérie*," Chaz said behind her.

"Will I ever get used to the fact that he's with me?"

"Watch this." Chaz draped his arm over her shoulder.

Ronin's eyes immediately lasered onto Chaz. Although nothing changed on his face, his displeasure pulsed through the air like a sonic boom.

"See? The man is insanely jealous of even a gay man touching you. So your shock and awe that he's with you is reciprocated one hundred percent." He gave Ronin a little finger wave and dropped his arm.

"Thanks for coming tonight."

Chaz sipped his beer. "It's so not my thing, but I'm a supportive friend."

"I know. We've both been so crazy busy with work, we haven't had our Friday-night happy hour for ages."

"That's a shame for you, sugar lips, because I am fun. I think playing nursemaid to the billionaire made you forget that."

Last week, Amery had managed to sneak in a lunch date with Chaz and Emmylou, and she'd told them the truth about what'd happened. It spoke a lot of Chaz's loyalty that he understood her sense of betrayal about Ronin's nondisclosure regarding his family connections. Emmylou's reaction was harsh, and the lunch had ended on a sour note. "Ronin's pull is such I forget everything when I'm around him."

"Sweetie. Put the hottie who freakin' adores you out of his misery and just move in with him already."

It made no sense to others, why she was dragging her feet on packing up her stuff and moving in with him. It wasn't a power play—exactly the opposite. Ronin's nondisclosure about his recovery status convinced her he'd reverted to the share-nothing-unless-they-were-naked man. It wasn't wrong to wait. It wasn't wrong to expect more from him.

"Besides, it's not like you're not at his penthouse most of the time anyway." Chaz sighed. "Penthouse. I'm letting my bitchy jealous side show for a minute. Hot. Sexy. Rich. Mysterious. Tough. Yeah, hating on you that your man is all that."

Amery leaned over and whispered, "And he fucks like an animal, so there is that too."

"Hate you," he trilled. "Oops, here he comes."

Ronin stopped in front of Amery. He curled his hand around

the nape of her neck and pulled her to his mouth for a kiss that made her lips tingle. A very possessive kiss. A very unlike–Sensei Black display of public affection. When he eased back, so their lips were only a breath apart, he kept his thumb on the pulse point in her neck. "You okay?" he murmured.

"I am now."

"Well, I'm not," Chaz huffed. "I think I need a cold shower and a cigarette after that."

Ronin smiled at him. "Just making sure my woman doesn't feel neglected while I'm part of the dog and pony show. Thanks for coming to the event tonight, Chaz."

Chaz waved him off. "Sweaty half-naked guys rolling around the mat? I'm there."

He laughed. "I have to make the rounds." Ronin kissed Amery again, this time softly.

She sighed.

"Hate you," Chaz singsonged. Then he threaded his arm through hers. "Let's hit the buffet."

They were filling plates when Chaz said, "What's up with the ring girl still wearing her costume to the after-party?"

"Part of her promotional duties. And if I had a body like that? I'd flaunt it too."

"She certainly isn't lacking for male attention."

Amery glanced at Katie, holding court with half a dozen guys. Knox stood behind her, arms crossed, acting like her bodyguard. "She's supposed to be mingling with the sponsors, not trolling for dates."

They gossiped about some friends as they nibbled on way-too-healthy appetizers. Amery's gaze swept the room, and she spied Shiori looking a little disheveled. Something didn't fit. Shiori never went anywhere less than one hundred percent put together. Amery said, "Excuse me for just a minute," to Chaz and then headed toward Ronin's sister.

But Knox intercepted Shiori, and Amery caught the tail end of their heated conversation.

". . . sporting that just-fucked look."

"Not your concern," Shiori retorted.

"What's going on here?"

Knox retreated. "Nothing." He executed a military turn and was gone.

Amery studied Shiori, staring thoughtfully after Knox. "You plan to lie and say nothing is going on either?"

Shiori faced her. "The truth? After I spar, grapple, or fight, adrenaline charges through me. I get horny. Evidently it's all right for guys to take the edge off, but not a woman."

"So you . . . ?"

"Just fucked some hot young guy out in my limo. Without apology. Which I explained to Ob-Knox-ious."

Ouch, not a nice nickname. "Good for you. And no offense, but you are looking less uptight and a lot more rumpled."

Shiori smiled. "Good. And I also hope to have the glassy-eyed look of a drunk soon." She sauntered to the bar.

Amery caught Ronin's eye and gestured with her chin to go talk to his sister.

"I sure as hell wouldn't want to tangle with her after watching her fight tonight," Molly said.

"Hey! I hoped you'd show up. Sorry we didn't get to sit together."

"It's okay. Chaz kept up a raunchy commentary."

"I bet it was very entertaining."

"That it was. I never thought of the dirty connotation of the phrase *rear mount*."

She laughed. "Are you and Sandan Zach still avoiding each other?"

"I don't believe he's looked past Miss Perky Boobs all night to notice who else is here," she said dryly.

Amery had noticed Zach in the throng of Katie admirers.

"Anyway, I'm not avoiding him. I'm avoiding—shit, shit, shit, I gotta go." Molly turned her back to Amery. But before Molly could skulk away, Deacon's hand circled her upper arm.

"Goin' somewhere, darlin'?"

Molly blushed. "Ah, hey, Yondan. Great fight tonight. You looked amazing, like, really amazing." She blushed harder. "I mean your fighting skills were something else."

Deacon stared placidly at Molly in that ninja-master manner that Ronin used on Amery.

Even Amery fought the urge to fidget and run the hell away.

Molly blurted out, "When are you going to teach me the spinning back fist technique?"

"You've missed class the last two weeks."

She jerked her thumb at Amery. "Boss lady is keeping me late. We're really busy with some, ah, stuff."

Amery cringed. Molly was such a bad liar.

Deacon—beefed-up, bald-headed, tattooed badass, never-smile Deacon—threw back his head and laughed.

Several ring bunnies turned and gaped; Deacon's deep laugh was as sexy as his slow southern drawl.

"What?" Molly said testily. "It's true."

"No, darlin', it's not remotely close to the truth. Since Amery and Sensei are joined at the hip, I know she was in the dojo during those last two classes, which means you weren't workin'."

Molly raised her chin and glared at him.

"Need a repeat of the rules? Every class you miss requires a private makeup session. So you are now four classes behind. I will expect you in the training room next week. You do not want me to track you down."

"You wouldn't dare."

"I suggest you don't test me on that." He started to walk off.

"Doesn't matter, Yondan. I quit," Molly said to his back.

Before Molly blinked, Deacon was nose to nose with her. "No one quits my class without my permission. Including you. Maybe especially you."

Not surprisingly Molly didn't have a retort that time. But rather than huff and complain to Amery, she hightailed it in the opposite direction to Chaz.

When Amery turned to gauge Deacon's reaction, the man had vanished.

Damn these guys and their stealthy ninja tricks.

Ronin's warm hand settled on Amery's lower back. "Problem?"

"What is it with your instructors tonight? They all need an attitude adjustment."

"Maybe they're high on victory." His lips touched the top of her ear. "You look beautiful tonight."

She smiled. "So you've said. Thank you. You are smokin' hot yourself." Didn't matter what Ronin wore; her mind conjured up the image of him in his black gi pants with no shirt. Sweaty. His damp hair brushing his shoulders. Or pulled back in that sexy little ponytail.

Ronin tilted her face up to peer into her eyes. "You made the sexy hum that makes my dick hard."

"I was just thinking about you almost naked."

"I'm tempted to say screw it and haul you out into the alley and fuck you against the brick wall until you scream my name."

"Why don't you? It'd take me two seconds to ditch my panties."

Ronin traced the upper bow of her lip. "But the small, sane part of me that's not already mentally dragging you outside is reminded why I swore off sex in public."

"You fingered me under the table at the sports banquet," she reminded him.

"Not the same. I'm talking full-out pounding-into-your-wet-pussy, leaving-suck-marks-on-your-neck-and-feeling-your-nails-digging-into-my-ass sex."

"Hard and fast with no time for romance and silken ribbons?"

"You'd get bored with me if I didn't mix it up. And, baby, you loved being bound in softness."

"That I did." He'd artfully wrapped her mummy style with a long silk ribbon, winding the single long strand from her shoulders to her ankles. The colors morphed from mustard to pumpkin to scarlet to reddish black, so it appeared she'd sprung out of the embers as an undulating flame. Amery could admit she'd looked so amazing that she'd allowed him to take pictures. After he'd completely unraveled her, he'd made love to her in the pile of silk. She bit back another sigh. She loved when he showed his romantic streak.

"What in the hell is going on now?"

She turned in the direction Ronin was racing to see what'd snagged his attention. Sandan Zach and Deacon's losing opponent were in each other's faces. Amery scanned the crowd. No sign of Blue, Deacon, Knox, Ito, or Gil.

When Zach and the other dude came to blows, no one stepped in because hello? Martial arts guys throw elbows and kicks, and plenty of both were flying.

But that didn't deter Ronin. After he warned them to stop, and neither did, he jumped in. He blocked a blow from Zach and twisted his body until Zach fell to his knees. Then he faced the other guy, and when he moved to strike, Ronin performed a hip throw and the dude hit the ground hard.

Ronin's moves were so precise and well executed it seemed as if they were on the set of a martial arts movie.

"Out. Both of you." He stood between them. "Separately." Ronin angrily pointed to Zach as Ito and Gil raced up. Ito said something to Ronin, and then Gil handled getting Deacon's opponent out of the room.

A shiver of want rolled through her as he strolled back to her. With his graceful don't-fuck-with-me gait, the annoyed way he jammed his hand through his hair, and the tiny sneer on those full lips, the man epitomized sexy.

"This is why I fucking hate after-parties," Ronin said when he reached her. "The winning fighters are pumped up and the losing fighters are pissed off. Add booze and it's an unavoidable disaster."

"Especially when you're forced to deal with it alone because your minions are off doing . . . what?"

"Breaking up another fight in the hallway."

Her eyes widened. "Seriously? Why?"

"Who the fuck knows?" Ronin reached for her hand. "Remind me of these incidents next time it's suggested Black and Blue hosts a post-fight party."

"But it's been a good turnout. I saw you schmoozing with potential sponsors."

"I hate that part."

"But you're so smooth with that silver tongue of yours."

"I'd like to use my silver tongue on you," he murmured.

"Fights make you horny."

He smiled wolfishly. "It's an added bonus of the extra testosterone."

Amery set her free hand on his chest. "How long before we can leave?"

"Let's go. Grab your stuff, and I'll tell Blue we're heading out." He steered her toward the door. Halfway there he stopped. "You've *got* to be fucking kidding me."

"What?"

"Just stay close."

Three guys approached them. The two men flanking the guy in the middle had to be some type of personal security, odd because the middle guy—a good-looking blond in his mid-fifties—was the biggest of the three. He wore a suit and a capelike topcoat. He didn't smile as he approached. "I'm hurt you don't invite Max to your party." He tsk-tsked loudly. "Poor manners, my *drugh*."

Ronin bowed slightly and offered his hand. "My apologies, Max. I wasn't aware you were a fan of mixed martial arts."

The man took Ronin's hand, clasping it in his own and pulling Ronin to his chest before releasing him. "Why wouldn't I be fan? Russians invented it. Of course, we kept it big secret from the west."

"Of course." Ronin placed his hand on the small of Amery's back. "Max Stanislovsky, Amery Hardwick."

She knew that name—another one of Ronin's mysterious contacts—and held out her hand. "Happy to meet you, Mr. Stanislovsky."

He took her hand and kissed her knuckles. When she met his gaze, she melted a little. His eyes were a piercing steely gray.

"The pleasure is mine. What beautiful surprise you've been hiding from your friend Max, eh?"

Ronin tugged her closer to his body. "Can you blame me for keeping such fire and beauty to myself?"

"Nyet."

"Cut to the chase, Max. Did you really show up to chew my ass for forgetting your party invite?"

"I heard rumor. Came to verify." His gaze moved to the corner, where Katie was in conversation with Blue and Sophia. "I see the truth for myself."

"Of what?"

"The favor you're doing for TP. I need same type of favor too." Stanislovsky smiled at Amery. "Please excuse us."

Ronin shook his head. "Amery is aware of the terms of the favor for TP, even more so than Katie is."

"She is also aware of your past?" Stanislovsky addressed the question to Amery.

She inclined her head. "I know some of it, not all."

"And it doesn't bother you?"

"The past made him the man he is today. I can't have him as he is now without it."

"Beautiful, smart, and loyal. You're lucky man, and it's time you found worthy woman." He clapped Ronin on the shoulder. "But I digress! I need favor. For my son."

Ronin said, "I'm listening."

"My son's mother." He sighed with gusto. "Beautiful, passionate Russian woman. So passionate we have child together."

"Did you marry her?"

"*Nyet*. Discovered crazy passion often just masks crazy."

Amery withheld a laugh.

"But good thing to come from that crazy woman is my son, Ivan. He loves to fight. He lives to fight, which makes me happy. His mama? Not so much."

"Still waiting for the punch line, Max."

"Ivan would like to train as MMA fighter. Your dojo is best; you have program for amateurs, and he perfect fit."

Amery felt the tension pouring off Ronin, but nothing in his demeanor gave it away to Stanislovsky.

"You do TP favor for his daughter—poof, no more favors."

"You're offering me the same deal?"

"I'm telling you; I took care of your pest problem on Baldwin Street. As favor to you. This? What I ask in return."

"Black Arts trains your son."

Stanislovsky nodded. "Ivan is good boy. He needs guidance. Focus isn't problem since he's trained in sambo in Russia. He needs a challenge."

"Why not put him to work in one of your businesses?"

"No interest at this point in the . . . what you call it? Family ball and chain? Like you and Okada, eh?"

"Not exactly," Ronin said wryly.

"Ivan has time to learn business later. Only young and tough for so many years. Which I hear you recently learned firsthand, my *drugh*?"

"Yes."

"Here's my offer. You take my son on. He pays MMA fight club fees same as others. Pays for personal training same as others. Earns his place on team same as others. He wants to prove himself. I respect that. I believe you respect that. He respects you as much as I do."

Wow. Serious flattery.

"How old is Ivan, and will he need an interpreter?" In an aside to Amery, Ronin said, "I don't deal with Max's Russian compatriots because few of them speak English. Max knows this about me."

"Ivan is twenty-two. He's American citizen. His mother returned to Russia when he was ten, so over the years he's had boot on American soil half year and boot on Russian soil half year. He is fluent in English and Russian."

Ronin let a minute-long pause linger, where neither he nor Stanislovsky broke eye contact. Talk about a mind fuck.

"All right. You have a deal. With two stipulations. You don't interfere. Ever. This is between Black Arts and Ivan—not me and you. Also, make sure Ivan understands he won't be training only with me in the MMA club."

"Of course."

"Have him call next week and set up an interview time."

Stanislovsky grinned. "Done. You good man, Ronin Black. I look forward to watching my son's dream come true." They did the Russian hand clasp, chest bump thing again. Then his eyes flitted over Ronin's shoulder and his gaze filled with lust. "Such a lovely flower gracing your party. Introduce me." A demand, not a request.

Amery and Ronin both turned. Amery expected Stanislovsky's slavering gaze to be on Katie, but his focus was entirely on Shiori.

"No fucking way, Ruskie. That's my sister."

His gray eyes lit up. "Ah. Perfect. The Okada heir won't be after me for my money since she has no need of it."

"Not. Happening. Ever."

"Why not?"

"Because I know you're in the middle of *another* divorce."

"Then I am free to pursue her with all the romance we Russians are known for, eh?" He adjusted his tie. "Take me to her."

"Not on your life. Jesus, Max. You're too fucking old for her."

"Love knows no age, my *drugh*."

Ronin snorted. "Lust knows no boundaries when it comes to you."

One of the bodyguards leaned in and spoke to Stanislovsky. He nodded. "Sadly, it will have to wait. Other matters need my attention." He offered Ronin a salute and a bow before whipping around and marching out the door.

Amery stared after him. "Is he for real?"

"Yes. He's more eccentric than TP, but both men wield an insane amount of power in this town."

"And you're friends with them. You've done favors for both of them." She paused. "You told me how you ended up knowing TP, but how'd you end up on Stanislovsky's radar?"

Ronin looked around to make sure no one was within earshot. "Because of TP. Those two have a . . . friendly rivalry. They back each other, but they're also fierce competitors. So when I started having problems with the construction crews I'd hired to gut the dojo building, Max's crew just showed up and took over. They did the work for half the money in half the amount of time."

"But then you owed Stanislovsky favors."

He nodded. "Max has little tact. He bulldozes his way into things and can't figure out why he's gotten stuck. I've helped him get unstuck a time or fifty."

"Dangerous stuff?"

"Not bad. He has his own Russian leg breakers on his payroll, but there've been times when he's needed security with discretion. Or he's needed a diversion from his activities and certain businesses. I've assisted him with that."

His explanation sounded too pat. She slid her hands up his chest. "I wasn't kidding when I said I accept your past. But I don't want to be in the dark about it. Better for you to tell me than for me to find out from someone else."

"You're right." Ronin sighed. "Max runs prostitutes. It's how he started out. And although he's got his fingers in many more lucrative pies, he still controls the high-end escort service agencies in Denver. I don't agree with what he does, and he knows that. But every time he's asked for my help getting his girls out of a bad situation, or if they need protection, I haven't hesitated." His eyes locked onto hers. "And no, I've never traded my services for those services his girls offer."

Don't judge. This isn't about Ronin running hookers; this is about him protecting them.

She could wrap her head around that. Ronin Black as a white knight.

"And to finish this conversation so it doesn't stop us from getting on with our night, Max owns many clubs. I've trained his security and bouncers. That part all on the up-and-up."

"Hey. Wait. Does Max own . . . ?"

"BDSM clubs? Yes. Does he own the clubs I've belonged to? No."

"This is a lot to absorb."

"I know, baby. But it's in the past. Since TP and Max have this bizarre competition when it comes to my favors, I assumed it wouldn't be long before I heard from Max. I just wasn't expecting him to foist his kid on me too. Just what I don't need—to be known as Black's Babysitting Service."

Amery laughed.

Molly and Chaz approached them.

"Is it safe to talk to you now that you're done whispering naughty nothings to each other here in the middle of the room?" Chaz asked.

"We're just trying to decide the best avenue of escape before anything else happens," Ronin said.

"If you need a distraction, Molly could start a striptease."

"Chaz!"

"What? I'd offer, but this isn't really my crowd."

"And with that"—Ronin intoned dryly—"we're going."

"Wait. We left my car at the arena, remember?" Amery said to Ronin.

"Leave it. It'll be fine until morning."

"If Chaz can drop me off, I'll drive it to my apartment tonight and then to work tomorrow," Molly offered. "It'll save me bus fare."

"Mol, that would be great."

"You're working on a Saturday?" Ronin asked.

"Yes. We're behind on a few things. I'll get my keys." Amery wended through the thinning crowd and ducked downstairs to the coat check. No one was around. "Hello?"

Seemed like an hour before the coat check girl showed up, although it'd probably been only five minutes. But by the time she returned to the party, she saw the change in Ronin's demeanor, even from across the room.

Molly and Chaz were silent when she rejoined the group. "Now what happened?"

"Why didn't you tell me you were working for Okada?"

He'd said it with such sharpness it sounded like Al Qaeda. Freudian slip, maybe? Amery looked at Molly.

Her eyes were filled with regret. "I'm sorry. I thought he knew."

"Yes, one would think the subject would've come up since you've been working on the project for several weeks."

Chaz slipped his arm around Molly's shoulders and pulled her back. "We'll leave you two to work this out."

For the first time since they'd reconciled, Ronin wore that unyielding mask, and her heart sank. She'd fucked up.

"So even after I warned you about her, you still allowed my sister to manipulate you?" Ronin demanded.

"It's not like that. I'm not even working directly with Shiori—she just relayed the terms and options since she was here in town."

"Terms," he repeated. "Am I part of those terms?"

Amery blinked at him with confusion. "What are you talking about?"

"I've been a carrot, a stick, a wedge, and a damn doormat for Okada. What options were you offered if you returned to me?"

"None! My contract with Okada has nothing to do with you. Nothing. My designs beat out all other designs, even from big agencies across the country. Those are some powerful career-changing opportunities, Ronin."

"And you didn't think to discuss them with me?"

"You would've told me not to take it! You're so damn suspicious that your family is trying to get at you through me."

His eyes held a dangerous edge. "I have good reason to believe that, Amery."

"Well, you're wrong this time. And maybe this reaction was exactly what I feared and why I didn't tell you."

"Bullshit."

They hadn't raised their voices, but they were both angry. She noticed Ronin had blocked her from the room and backed her into a corner.

"Didn't you just say to me, not ten minutes ago, that it would be better for you to find out the truth from me about my business dealings and not from someone else? Didn't it occur to you how hypocritical that statement is?"

Telling him that she hadn't expected Molly to blab would only piss him off more. Really, what could she say at this point? She'd fucked up. But she wasn't the only one. "So what's your excuse for not telling me what the neurologist said?"

Ronin looked shocked by that . . . and not the least bit contrite.

"Yes, I knew about your appointment, and I waited for you to talk to me. I gave you many opportunities, and you didn't take a single one. So much for me being an important part of your recovery process. So much for us maintaining open communications about everything. You shut me out again."

He crowded her. "Is this about payback? I didn't tell you one little thing that happened in my life, so you use that as an excuse to hide a big goddamn secret from me?"

"First of all, your health isn't one little thing. Second of all, how can you even say that to me? I'm not like that."

"I didn't think you'd keep something this fucking important from me either. Since we decided—together—to try to make this work, I have laid myself open for you. You know things about me that no one else does. Not only in our intimate relationship, but in my business relationships. What I've done for TP and Max? Very privileged information. It's a testament to how much *I* trust you that Max spoke so freely in front of you tonight."

Shit.

"I'm not surprised Okada chose your designs, because you have the talent and drive to get to the next level. But since this is my family in the mix, and I know what my family is capable of far better than you, you need to understand that I don't trust it. I don't want you to be beholden to them."

"Excuse me, but you're the one who suggested my company for the project in the first place. After all the bullshit that went down between us, I put it out of my mind. So it's a huge ego boost that Shiori didn't toss the designs in the garbage. She passed them on to the appropriate people in the company, and those designs stood on their own merit. That is completely different from you throwing your girlfriend a bone because you're feeling sorry for her and you had the means to contribute to her self-worth."

"Did you ever consider that I'd like to be a part of celebrating your achievements? Since you're helping me celebrate mine tonight?"

"What are you talking about?"

"You are the reason I asked ABC Brazilian jujitsu to become part of Black Arts. You suggested I needed to think outside of my little dojo box and I did. I value your opinion. But I see now that you don't value mine."

Her eyes searched his. "Ronin. That's not even remotely close to true."

"You're always asking me to share my feelings? Well, here it is. I'm pissed off at you. I don't even rate the courtesy of you telling me that you're working for my family's company. I'm pissed off that you were concerned enough about my health to snoop around for answers but not ask me directly. I'm pissed off that you've been goddamn hedging about moving in with me. I'm pissed off you still haven't told me that you love me even when we both fucking know you do. This has become a one-sided fucking relationship, and you know it."

Dammit. Don't cry. He's right, and your tears will just aggravate him further and come across as manipulative.

"So either accept that I want a long-term, open and honest intimate relationship with you on every level, or don't. Your choice."

For the first time ever, Ronin walked away from her.

And not for the first time, she slunk away, embarrassed by her behavior.

CHAPTER FOURTEEN

TWO fucking days since Ronin had heard from Amery.

Two. Fucking. Days.

Since he'd left it up to her to contact him, it'd been torture not storming over to her place. Not calling her. Not tracking her down in a parking garage and doing a hojojutsu capture on her for real.

He'd spent all day Saturday with Blue, Knox, and Gil, hashing out revised class schedules. They'd gone over the receipts from the night's event. Charted what worked and what hadn't. Devised a strategy for the next event in six short weeks.

That's when his train of thought jumped the track, wondering if that much time would pass again before Amery approached him.

Maybe you won't hear from her again. Maybe she got what she wanted—a lucrative contract with Okada—and she doesn't need you anymore.

His logical side tried to stamp down the ridiculousness, but a small niggling fear remained.

Sunday he worked out—swimming, weights, hand work, foot work, cardio on the treadmill—until Shiori arrived late in the afternoon. As the highest belt rank in the dojo, her continued training fell on his shoulders. She was a tireless pupil, and they spent two hours working on what she called drills, skills, and thrills.

Then, at Shiori's request, they'd gone over the DVD of her match, dissecting the high points and the mistakes. Although she'd insisted the only reason she fought was to keep the fight card full, Ronin understood that she had the same need he did to physically prove herself. She admitted that she and Sophia had discussed starting a women's MMA basics class, just to see if it garnered interest. When he questioned if her time in the dojo was interfering with her position at Okada, she changed the subject. He assumed any questions about Amery's project with the company would elicit the same response, so he didn't bother to ask.

Ronin had been tempted to invite Shiori to his penthouse for dinner, but he decided it would be awkward if Amery showed up.

Wishful thinking on his part, as it'd turned out.

A shower and an hour of meditation centered him.

Still, he'd slept poorly, so Monday started off on a bad note. Katie's constant chattering got on his nerves, and he passed her off to Blue.

He thought he'd found solitude in his office when Knox barged in. "You have got to keep me in the loop on some of this shit, Ronin. There's this big dude out there who swears he has an appointment with you."

"Be nice if one of these kids actually *made* an appointment," he muttered. "Send him in."

Knox returned with a young man nearly Knox's height, which put him close to six foot three. He was solidly built, but not excessively bulked up like some gym rats who equated brawn with strength. He'd dressed appropriately—khaki pants, short-sleeved polo, shined shoes. His hair and eye color were all Max.

Ronin stood and offered his hand. "Ivan?"

"Yes, sir."

Manners too. "I'm Ronin Black. That's Knox Lofgren. He also runs the MMA club. Knox, this is Ivan Stanislovsky. He's a prospect."

"Pleased to meet you, sir," Ivan said.

"Same. We do use formal titles at Black Arts, so as Sensei's second-in-command, call me Shihan."

"Yes, Shihan."

Ronin pointed to the chair for Ivan and the edge of the desk for Knox. "I spoke to your father Friday night. I wasn't expecting you so soon."

He frowned. "Really? He assured me I had an appointment with you first thing this week. I'm sorry if I misunderstood."

Not the kid's fault that his father was a pushy bastard. "Luckily I have time right now. He mentioned your interest in training in an MMA program. What is your athletic background?"

Ivan blushed. "My mother put me in dance when I was four years old. She had visions of me becoming the next Baryshnikov. I trained in classical ballet in Denver, New York, and Russia until I was sixteen."

"Ballet training is incredibly rigorous and requires a lot of dedication. Why did you quit?"

"I got tired of defending myself. I'm not homosexual—I have nothing against those who are—but there is that perception from outsiders. I ended up in many fights. Got my butt kicked, so I asked my father if I could learn to fight. When I was in the US, he signed me up for tae kwon do. When in Russia with my mother, I studied sambo. Sambo," he repeated, "not samba, the dance."

"Thanks for the clarification. Any amateur fights?"

"Besides getting called out in the nightclubs? No, sir."

"The reason you want to become an MMA fighter? To have the skills to win those nightclub fights?" Knox asked.

Ivan shook his head. "I want to train to become the best fighter in my weight class and have the chance to earn a world title."

He'd said that without cockiness—bonus for him. Guys who showed up, claiming to be good enough to win a world title, were promptly shown the door.

Knox commented, "You sound confident."

"I know how to train and can push my body beyond normal physical limits. Some assume because my father raised me with the advantages he didn't have that I would act privileged. I do not. I learned my work ethic from my father."

His English wasn't as accented as Max's, but it held the same Russian inflections. "You're proud of your father?"

"Yes. He is a great man. We have philosophical differences, but I know he expects me to run his businesses when I'm ready, at least a decade down the road. Those are his words, not mine."

"Well, Ivan, if you'll sit tight for a moment, I'll get Deacon to show you around the dojo, the training rooms, and go through requirements, expectations, and costs." Ronin hit the intercom to the training room and asked Deacon to come to the office.

"Thank you, Sensei, for this opportunity."

"You'll earn it; trust me."

Deacon strolled in. Introductions were made, and they exited the office.

Of course Knox stayed. He plopped in the chair Ivan had vacated and propped his feet on the desk. "Didn't know we were actively building up our MMA roster."

"I meant to talk to you about it first. It came up Friday night, and the meeting was supposed to happen later this week."

"He seems solid."

"I hope so. We need a heavyweight fighter, and I plan to use him as an interpreter." Ronin gave Knox a sly smile. "I wouldn't mind getting a couple of those other Russian fighters on our roster."

Knox grinned back. "You sneaky dog. I bet you played it cool with Max too, acting like you're doing him a favor. But damn, Ronin. That's Max's kid. Does he know the kind of shit his dad is into?"

"I assume that would be the genesis of the 'differing philosophies' comment."

"Why don't you ever talk about your old man?"

Ronin's gaze sharpened. Where had that come from? "Why would I? He's been dead thirty years."

Knox shrugged. "He started you in jujitsu. It impacted you enough you've made it your career."

"So?"

"So, like Ivan, you have a family business that you could join anytime you wanted. Have Black Arts be a . . . hobby."

A hobby? What the fuck? "If you have something to say, Shihan, spit it out."

"Whoa, don't bite my head off. It's just I've noticed you're different since Amery came into your life. And before you fry me with that deadly stare, different in a good way. Mostly."

"Mostly?"

"Except for the reverting back to fighting shit, but I think you're done with that now. Anyway, you want to spend time with Amery, so you've relinquished some of your control. You've delegated, which needed to happen, but it wasn't like any of us were gonna bring it up with you." He mock shuddered.

"Fuck off."

Knox laughed. "So, I, for one, am happy about the changes. The students like it; the instructors like it. We're expanding in a positive way. ABC is a great fit. The promotion company is a brilliant idea."

"Do I sense a but?"

"Two things. Is something going on with Okada that I should know about since She-Cat has been here for so long?"

"Something going on . . . how?"

"You tell me. I have to wonder with you flipping Black Arts on its head, if the reason you're sharing control here is because you're about to take control somewhere else. Namely in Tokyo."

Ronin leaned back in his chair. "If that'd been part of my game plan, I would've clued you in. My grandfather hasn't brought up my ascension to the Okada throne for more than a year. The last three or four times I've spoken to him? We've discussed Japanese sports and American politics. As far as why Shiori is still here? No idea. If I ask her outright, she hedges. If I call up my grandfather and ask him, he'll think I have an interest in the company. So I've let it be." Ronin's mother probably knew what was going on, but they hadn't connected and it wasn't the type of conversation to have over e-mail.

"I wish she'd let me be. Man, she rides my ass about everything," Knox grumbled.

He refused to get in the middle of Shiori and Knox's multitude of personal issues. "You said there were two things. What's the other?"

Knox set his feet on the floor. "It's been mentioned to me that you've been to Twisted only twice in the last five months."

Ronin knew being a member of a sex club who didn't indulge in many sexual activities made him an anomaly. He'd joined because women in the BDSM world were open to rope play.

"Are you done with the place?"

"I don't know. It seemed . . . wrong to be there last time."

"Does Amery know you went there during the weeks you weren't together?"

"How do I tell her that I bound someone else? Not because I was teaching, but because I thought I needed to find the balance I was missing?" Ronin felt idiotic talking about this shit, but Knox had asked, and it wasn't like Ronin had other guys to talk to. "I remember thinking about the wrongness of it. I almost had to call it off. As it was, I had to cut the session short. That's never happened to me in almost two decades of tying."

"Because Amery is so much more to you than just a rope model, Ronin."

"I've been sexually involved with my rope partners and not sexually involved with them. It's always been about aesthetics, skill, sensuality, and connection in the moment," Ronin said defensively.

Knox just stared at him.

"What?"

"You're not an idiot. Even I know you've never been in love with any of your rope partners. The difficulty of the pattern, the amount of body-to-skin contact, the sexual pull—you can no longer compartmentalize any of it because it's all there when you bind her. And it's there only with her. The fact you were so off balance during those six weeks the two of you spent apart had nothing to do with you missing shibari or kinbaku in your life. It was about you missing her."

Ronin was truly stunned by Knox's insight.

"Maybe you've been binding so many women over the years because you've been looking for someone like Amery. Now you've found her and it's changed you. That's why it felt wrong to tie someone else." Knox popped to his feet. "I'm guessing your demo days at the club are over."

He wasn't sure how he felt about that even when he suspected it was true. Not that he and Amery had discussed it. That was just another thing hanging over his head. Was he ready to give up public bondage demonstrations?

Ten minutes later, Shiori waltzed in. "We're still on for tonight?"

"On for what?"

"The sporting goods trade show at the tech center. You agreed to meet with some of the equipment guys for possible sponsorship for Black and Blue Promotions since Blue is teaching tonight, remember?"

"I must've blocked it out. Aren't you teaching tonight?"

"Knox is taking over my class."

Ronin gave her a skeptical look. "How hard did you have to beg him?"

"Not at all. I outrank Godan. It's my responsibility to provide him with additional teaching opportunities."

Jesus. He'd get an earful about that.

"You want to ride with me?"

"I'll meet you."

"Okay. I'll be there around six. South entrance."

Shiori hesitated in the doorway.

"What?"

"Have you heard from her yet?"

He shook his head.

"You will."

"Do you know something I don't?"

"Just that she can't stay away from you any more than you can stay away from her."

He hoped to hell Shiori was right.

AFTER two hours wandering around the vendor spaces, Ronin was ready to leave. And the first place he intended to stop? Amery's. Her silence made him crazy.

He'd just pulled out his phone to text Shiori when he heard, "Hello, Ronin," from behind him.

Every molecule in his body seized up.

No. Fucking. Way. She couldn't be here. Had to be a hallucination, or he'd fallen asleep and was dreaming of hell.

Go away.

"I can make a scene to get you to pay attention to me."

Ronin slowly turned around.

Naomi stood less than five feet away.

She didn't look any different than she had almost four years ago. Same conservative business suit, same pixie haircut, same understated makeup—she'd even worn the same color of red lipstick. Normally he wouldn't remember things like that, but Naomi had glossed up her lips only when she'd gone down on him. She claimed it was to leave her mark as a reminder of how much she loved him. Afterward she'd placed fresh lipstick marks down his thighs. But he knew the truth; she wanted him to fear—just for a second—that she'd made him bleed.

Sick fucking woman.

Her siren-red mouth curved into a smile. "I know what you're thinking about."

He moved his gaze up to her eyes and kept his face impassive. "That it's obvious you've resorted to using Botox?"

"Insulting me? Not nice, pussycat."

Since she'd always preferred to speak Japanese with him, her use of English meant she wanted people to overhear their conversation. "When I insult you, you'll know it," he said in Japanese.

"Where's your new girlfriend? Shiori assured me you'd both be here tonight so I could pay my respects."

She was such a liar. "Wrong. How did you find out where I'd be?"

"Ronin-san, I know where you live."

So she'd followed him. Really fucking creepy but completely her style.

"I'm in Denver on unfinished business."

"Why would you think I'd care?" He started to back away.

She edged closer. "Aren't you curious about who I'm here with?"

"Some lowlife wannabe Dom you're trying to make jealous? You hoping he'll beat you and fuck you in front of everyone in the arena?"

Malice glittered in her eyes. "Sounds like jealousy, pussycat."

"Yes. You know me so well," he sneered.

"I know you better than you think." She pursed her lips into a pout. "I've missed you. All the great times we used to have together. In your penthouse, at my apartment, at the club. Don't you miss those days?"

As much as he missed an oozing boil.

"I do," she said dreamily. "Especially the club. Not that I could relive old times there after you had me banished for life."

"You made your choices, and you knew there'd be consequences."

"You don't feel guilty at all for such an extreme reaction? It was a sex club! You really can't blame me for taking a sample of what was freely offered."

Enough. Ronin turned to walk away.

But Naomi grabbed his arm. "Don't leave in a huff, lover. You'll want to hear this."

"Let. Go. Of. Me."

She dropped her hand. "So upon my return to Denver, without a club of my own, I visited your new club . . . Twisted? The manager is lovely. Of course I name-dropped you like crazy, and the man was very eager to dish on your rope skills. You do have a fan in him. Anyway, he indicated it's been quite some time since you did any public rope demonstrations at the club. I had to ask myself why that was. And then I asked him. Do you know what he told me?"

Ronin didn't react.

"The manager told me your new girlfriend refuses to be part of a public bondage scene. The information shocked me. A master who lets his lover impose the rules? Has pussycat become pussified?"

First thing tomorrow he'd contact the club owner and get the manager canned for breaking the confidential terms of service.

"Don't bother getting the man fired. I already did. He shouldn't have been so willing to discuss a certain club member's . . . problems with a potential new member."

"Why are you telling me this?"

"To remind you that I look out for you, Ronin. Even when you aren't aware of it. We were so good together." She reached out, and Ronin jerked back, away from her deadly claws.

"You baited the manager and got him fired, making sure you got the satisfaction of reminding me how psychotic you are."

"Aw, pussycat, don't be upset. After I learned of your girlfriend's phobia, I tracked you down to see if there was anything I can do to help you. I know the ropes, so to speak"—she winked lewdly—"so if you want to remind club-goers that you are the rope master, I'd gladly offer my services as your partner again."

"Pass."

"You sure? I'm only trying to help you save face. Your girlfriend's unwillingness to be publicly bound speaks of her shame of the act. It undermines your expertise, Master Black."

"Bullshit."

"Is she ashamed in private too?"

Don't respond.

"Didn't you always remind me that teachers don't let students impose limits on the lessons?"

Ronin's jaw tightened. As did his fist.

"Sounds to me like you've gone soft." Her gaze zeroed in on his groin, and she lifted her eyes back to his. "You were never soft in any area before. Does she prefer you make sweet, sweet love to her? Instead of binding her and fucking her like a beast?"

"I'm done listening to this."

"But you didn't answer." She pouted and stepped in front of him to stop his retreat. "Do you let your student dictate the rules to the master, pussycat? Or maybe I should stop by Hardwick Designs in Lodo and ask for the truth. Mention I'd be happy to be her stand-in at the club."

Ronin got right in her face. "No fucking way, no fucking how, never fucking happening. Stay away from me; stay away from Amery; stay away from my club."

"Not so Zen now, are you, Master Black?"

"Leave Denver, or I will fuck with your life in ways you can't even imagine."

"You already fucked with my life. Getting returned to Japan like a defective toy humiliated me on more levels than you can comprehend. So paybacks are a bitch, Ronin-san. And I plan to be around until I get mine."

He expected her to create a bigger scene, but he wasn't prepared for her to lean in and wipe her lipsticked mouth down the left side of his white shirt.

She grinned at him, red smeared across her chin, as she turned and vanished into the crowd.

CHAPTER FIFTEEN

"I'M not sure on that font," Amery said. "Too curved. Too fat."

Molly laughed. "Think a fat font on low-calorie snack packaging would be considered creating a subliminal message?"

"I can't believe people get paid to think about this stuff. Did you know that Okada has fifty food scientists on staff?" Amery shook her head. "Do some kids grow up with the goal of having a career in food science?"

"I don't know. But I hear getting a job in Hershey, Pennsylvania, is a sweet gig."

Amery groaned. "Let's call it a night."

Molly stood and stretched. "It's weird working this late because you leave a vapor trail as soon as five o'clock rolls around. What are you and Ronin doing tonight?"

Nothing, since she hadn't contacted Ronin yet.

After he'd pointed out her admittedly selfish behavior Friday night, she'd had every intention of calling him first thing Sunday morning after spending Saturday working, pretending everything was peachy. But on Sunday, Emmylou had a meltdown after her breakup with Sasha and had sounded near suicidal.

As much as Amery had appreciated Emmylou's friendship over

the years, it occurred to her as she listened to her friend complain and cry that Emmylou's friendship was one-sided. She'd never asked about Amery's state of mind during her breakup with Ronin. She'd never asked how things were going after they'd gotten back together. Since they hadn't spent much time together recently, Amery had invited Emmylou to the MMA fight—and then had to listen to Emmylou's diatribe against men's need to prove their dicks were superior through violence and then recite stats on physically abused women who were involved with those types of men who used steroids and their fists.

Seemed Emmylou's personality had undergone a drastic change in recent months, and Amery didn't like the changes. She'd keep their landlord and tenant relationship businesslike from here on out. Then she vowed it'd be the last time she'd waste an entire day trying to make someone else feel better about herself at the expense of fixing her own problems. By the time Amery had returned home, she'd been in no frame of mind to offer Ronin the apology he deserved.

Four loud raps on the front door had Amery checking to see who'd show up so late. Ronin? No. He'd use his key and come in through the back door.

Shiori was impatiently tapping her foot on the other side of the glass. Amery unlocked the door and Shiori walked past her with a brusque, "We need to talk."

Then she stopped abruptly upon seeing Molly.

"Shiori Hirano, VP of Okada Foods, this is my assistant, Molly Calloway."

Molly offered her hand. "It's good to finally meet you in person. I'm excited to work on the new Okada line." When Shiori stared at her blankly, Molly added, "Oh, I enjoyed watching you fight the other night."

"The feeling is mutual," she said, obviously not really paying attention to the conversation, and headed toward Amery's office.

When Molly raised both eyebrows in a silent, *Is she always this self-absorbed?* Amery shrugged.

"I'll lock up," Molly said, grabbing her coat and purse. "See you tomorrow."

Amery waited until Molly left before approaching Shiori as she prowled in Amery's office like a caged cat. "Not that I'm not happy to see you, but why are you here?"

Shiori whirled around. "I need a drink."

"Did something happen to Ronin?" Amery asked sharply.

"Not in the way you think."

"Start explaining. Now."

Those beautiful golden eyes, identical to Ronin's, were a little wild looking. "Naomi is in Denver and she confronted Ronin tonight."

Amery froze. "Why?"

"I don't know. I didn't hear their conversation, but I saw her smug fucking face as she walked out. When I tried to talk to Ronin, he cut me off and bailed. So I know you want to go to him, but there's more to the story with Naomi and it's time you knew the truth." Shiori looked more miserable than Amery had ever seen her.

"Now *I* need a goddamn drink. Come upstairs." She shut off all the lights as they headed to the back room.

Shiori took one look at the circular metal staircase, then slipped off her spike heels.

Amery hadn't spent much time in her loft in recent weeks. Since she practically lived with Ronin, it shouldn't be such a big deal to make it official and tell him yes, she would move in with him. But what if she rented out her loft and everything with Ronin fell apart? Where would she go? She'd suffered through something like that with her ex Tyler and had no desire to repeat the experience.

In the kitchen, she opened the cabinet where she stashed liquor.

"Your booze choices are gin, whiskey, vodka, and Baileys. My mixer selection is limited."

"I'll have Baileys."

Amery set out two lowball glasses, filled them with ice, and poured the creamy liqueur. "Here you go."

Shiori knocked back the entire glass before she poured herself another.

Not a good sign.

But Shiori relaxed a little and slid onto a barstool. Then she spun it around to check out the space. "This place has a great vibe. Like you, I lived in the same building where I worked in Tokyo. I could never really get away from work."

"That is the downside. Ronin has the right idea about keeping his work space separate from his personal space."

"He's always been able to compartmentalize."

"Quit stalling and tell me what happened tonight."

"Ronin and I met at the conference hall before we split up so he could meet with equipment sponsors. I was chatting with a guy who sets up trade shows in Tokyo when I saw her."

"Naomi."

She nodded. "At first I thought my eyes were deceiving me. I followed her and got close enough to see her face smeared with red lipstick. I'll admit I panicked, thinking she'd already found Ronin and baited him."

Amery's gut clenched.

"But then I saw her nasty grin . . ." Shiori briefly closed her eyes. "When I tracked Ronin down, he was in that state between shock and fury. Naomi told him that I'd told her where to find him."

"Did you?"

"No! I haven't seen Naomi for years. But I can see where my brother would believe it because I introduced them in the first place. I told you that Ronin and Naomi met at a Japanese social club. What I didn't tell you? It wasn't a random meeting. My marriage . . ." She looked away. "Wasn't good. I married against my mother and my grandfather's wishes and against my own common sense. Anyway, when it became too unbearable to endure, Grandfather promised to handle my divorce and all the legal stuff if I did one thing for him."

"Set Ronin up with Naomi."

"Yes. In Japan, arranged marriages aren't unusual between families with similar interests. We knew Ronin wouldn't ever agree to it, so we had to take a different tack. Since Naomi's family owns banks in Japan, Ronin would know Naomi wasn't after him for his money. But those banks were in trouble—I don't know the exact details, but Okada Foods transferring twenty percent of their financial business to a different bank would have a tremendous impact."

"But why Naomi?"

"She's beautiful. Cultured. She's from a respected family. It appeared she was successful in business in her own right—but that was just another family fabrication. She lived modestly—which also appealed to my brother, although he didn't know it wasn't Naomi's choice to live that way. My grandfather understood my brother would suspect anyone he introduced him to. And since I was supposedly in Denver on business, Ronin promised he'd escort me to official Okada functions. The only reason Ronin went to the Japanese social club with me that night was because they were holding an auction of shunga art."

"Naomi was there."

She nodded. "He and Naomi struck up a conversation about the pieces and ended up in a good-natured bidding war. Ronin won, but he asked Naomi out for dinner. Within two months, they were seeing each other exclusively. They swapped one kind of club for another. His rope expertise isn't a secret in the jujitsu martial arts world—he's a record holder in Japan for the second-fastest time for a hojojutsu tie."

She'd been on the receiving end of that particular skill. "Did Naomi know about Ronin's rope mastery before they met?"

Shiori nodded. "Naomi took to the club lifestyle quickly—as I'm sure Ronin told you. During the time they were together, she kept up the pretense of their relationship—volatile as it was—and I'd secretly hoped they'd fallen for each other for real. But then . . ." She picked up her drink and drained it. "Ronin tried to break it off with her after she'd disrespected him. Then Naomi told him everything had been set up by his family. She only wanted his money and the status she'd get by being married to an Okada heir."

Amery closed her eyes when the sick churning in her stomach made her dizzy.

"My brother cut off all contact with me, with our grandfather and our mother. No phone calls, no e-mails, nothing. For one year. He believed we'd infiltrated his dojo and planted spies, so he released all his instructors except for Shihan."

"I can't even fathom his sense of betrayal and animosity toward you."

"It's the worst thing I've ever been through. Realizing what I'd done and how much I'd lost by betraying my only brother's trust. I'd known it was wrong at the time, but I went along with it because I was so desperate to get out of a marriage that was suffocating me."

Amery couldn't feel sorry for Shiori—she'd made her choices. But their grandfather had manipulated Ronin, which would make Ronin question the loyalty of everyone around him and trust no one.

So by not telling him she'd taken the Okada offer, she'd given him reason to fear her feelings for him weren't real.

When have you ever told him how you really feel anyway?

"I don't know what happened or why Naomi returned to Denver, but the truth is she's the psycho type who'd show up here just because she's heard Ronin is happy and she wants to fuck with him and fuck that up for him." Shiori took her hand. "He will try to close himself off from you, and you can't let him do that. You should go to him. He needs you."

Amery shooed Shiori out the door and got in her car.

AFTER Ronin's run-in with Naomi, he returned to a private practice room at the dojo and worked on kata forms for two hours, until he was drenched in sweat. Reaching the exercise high dulled some of his rage. But it wasn't enough. He headed up to the roof, ditched his gi, dove into the pool, and started to swim laps.

The water temp cooled more than his hot head. In the repetitive rhythm of his strokes and the silence, he found his calm center. Where maintaining breath work required every ounce of concentration. Where time was irrelevant. He could've been in the pool ten minutes or four hours. His existence boiled down to *stroke, stroke, breathe, stroke, stroke, breathe.*

When he had depleted all the oxygen in his muscles, he stopped and floated on his back, arms and legs spread out in an X, still aiming for sensory deprivation.

Then he heard footsteps across the concrete deck.

A rush of happiness, of completeness, of need, of relief flowed over him.

Amery.

He let his feet sink to the bottom and he stood.

She waited at the edge of the steps, holding a bath sheet.

Ronin slowly exited the pool and let Amery wrap the big towel around his body. He remained still as she wrapped herself around him.

They stayed like that, bound together by unspoken words until the night chill caused him to shiver.

Amery eased back and stood on tiptoe to kiss his cheek. "Let's get you warmed up. I turned the fireplace on."

Inside the penthouse he noticed she'd moved a chair directly in front of the fire. After swapping the wet towel for his favorite stadium blanket, she settled him in the chair and swaddled him in fleece. Once she'd gently towel dried his hair, she ran her fingers through it, gifting him with the soothing touch he craved.

Warmth from the fire and her TLC seeped into his muscles and bones, turning his blood sluggish and his breathing slow. Physically and mentally exhausted, he dozed off.

A loud pop awoke him.

Startled, he glanced over at Amery sitting in the chair next to him, staring into the fireplace. Since she appeared to be brooding, he watched the golden glow of flames flickering across her beautiful face.

"Didn't your mother teach you it's impolite to stare?" she asked softly.

"She taught me to appreciate beauty."

Amery looked at him. "Are you warmed up?"

"Yes. Thank you." He paused. "I need—"

"To go to bed. It's late. And you've had a trying day."

Not the answer he wanted.

"But it seems a shame to waste this ambience."

She pushed her chair back and spread another blanket on the floor in front of the fire before she started stripping off her clothes.

"What are you doing?"

"I'm apologizing with my body tonight. We'll get to the talking stuff tomorrow."

Ronin stood and tried to kiss her, but she gave him a sultry laugh and ducked her head.

"I'm the seducer here, Master Black." She playfully tugged the blanket. "Lose the cover."

He let the blanket drop.

Amery's eyes ate him up. "Handy that you swam naked." She moved in to him, rubbing her bare skin against his, teasing his lips with flirty kisses. Reaching between them, she stroked his shaft, which had already gone hard. "You like the idea of me being on top."

"I like the idea of us naked together any way I can get you."

She slid her soft lips over his jaw, eliciting a sigh, and then down his neck, eliciting another. "There's no sexy, romantic way to get us on the floor. So you first."

He crouched down and rolled to his back.

Amery followed him down. Her knees bracketed his hips, and she hung above him on all fours. "How is it possible you look even more beautifully fierce by firelight?"

"Baby, you don't have to sweet-talk me. I'm a sure thing."

"As a gorgeous specimen of manliness, you should be able to take a compliment because you should be used to it." He shivered when she pressed her lips in the hollow beneath his ear. "If you're cold, I can get the blanket."

"No." Ronin pushed her hair over her shoulder. "I want to watch you moving on me."

Her teeth grazed his earlobe. She zigzagged her tongue down to his nipples. Sweetly tormenting them with her mouth while the silky ends of her hair swung against the side of his body like a hundred ghostly fingertips.

She didn't tease him until the point he begged her—but almost. Finally she circled his cock at the base and adjusted her hips, drawing the tip across her wet entrance before pushing down on a slow glide. She slanted her mouth over his and swallowed his groan.

So good. Every damn time. He felt enveloped by her completely—she'd caged him in, her chest against his, her forearms by his head, her elbows above his shoulders, her hair a veil of softness around his head. Every time he breathed in, his lungs were filled with the scent of her.

Ronin palmed her hips, feeling the muscles in her ass flexing as she rode him. The heat from the fire warmed his left side, but the fire she'd started inside him turned his blood white hot.

But she kept the pace slow. Steady. The perfect mix of passion and comfort. She was the perfect mix of everything he'd ever wanted in a woman and had lost hope that he'd ever find.

She broke the kiss and sighed against his lips. "You make my head spin, Ronin." She used her teeth to scrape the razor stubble on his jaw. "Even when I'm the seducer, I am utterly, completely, and totally seduced by you."

"Baby."

Amery kissed his chin. The curve of his lips. His cheeks. The corners of his eyes. His temples. Then she pushed back and balanced on her knees. Keeping her eyes on his, she lifted and lowered onto his cock.

"You're beautiful." The curves and planes of her body were a golden delight, bathed in the firelight.

She grabbed his hands, placing one on each of her thighs. "Touch me with these hands and make me feel beautiful."

Ronin stroked her legs, her arms, her shoulders, her belly.

When she arched back, wrapping her hands around his shins, his thumb delved into the heart of her.

"Yes, do that." She rode him harder, and he knew her orgasm was close.

The moment her body stiffened, he pinched her nipple and her clit simultaneously.

She gasped. Her head fell back and her nails dug into the outside of his calves.

Ronin couldn't take his eyes off her. Her abandonment to the moment and so openly sharing her joy were breathtaking.

As soon as she floated back down and began to move again, a challenge in her eye, he jackknifed up and took her mouth in a brutal kiss.

Skin on skin, mouth on mouth, heat and passion ratcheted up his need. Hips pumping, one hand bunched in her hair, one gripping her ass, he came fast and he came hard.

Her cunt clamped around his shaft with a hot pulse, her tongue stabbed into his mouth in the same rhythm she fucked him. And she didn't relent, driving harder and harder against him until she came again.

Ronin panted against her neck. Her hands stroked and soothed him as he tried to find any coherent thought beyond, *Goddamn, that was fucking good.*

They stayed locked together, hearts thundering, light and shadows dancing across their bodies.

"I was right," she murmured against the top of his head. "The fireplace does add ambience."

He wrapped his hand around her throat, holding her chin so she couldn't squirm away. "What you bring to me is more than I ever thought I'd have." He kissed her once. "Thank you."

She eased back and pushed to her feet. She folded the blankets and picked up her clothes. Then she clicked off the fireplace and held out her hand. "Let me take you to bed."

In his bedroom, Amery tucked her body into his, her cheek against his heart, her belly pressed into his hip, her left leg over the top of his.

He could actually feel her eyelashes sweep over his pectoral every time she blinked, so he knew she wasn't asleep. So why wasn't she pushing him to talk?

Because she didn't want to ruin this time together. Nothing would get solved tonight anyway.

DESPITE his stress-filled day, Ronin slept like a log.

He woke to an empty bed. After he donned a clean pair of gi pants and a T-shirt, he tracked her down.

He didn't find her mainlining coffee in the kitchen or gazing out the windows in the dining area. But he spied her purse on the couch and realized she hadn't gone far.

Just as he headed to the elevator, the door opened and she

stepped out fully dressed for work. Before she uttered a word, his mouth was on hers. He loved that surprised *eep* she made. He cupped her face in his palms and kissed her thoroughly.

"Happy morning to you too," she panted against his neck.

"I don't like waking up alone. Been three very long days that I've suffered through that."

"Sorry. I peeked out the window and saw all the swirling black and gray clouds, so I went to the roof for a closer look." She pecked his mouth. "The brooding sky reminds me of you."

Ronin stroked her cheek. "Brooding man didn't scare you away this time."

"No. This time I was prepared. This time I came to you."

He murmured, "And so you did." She had no idea how happy that made him.

"We need to talk, but not without coffee."

He let her do her thing in his kitchen. She'd added homey touches, including a grain silo–shaped cookie jar and new oven mitts. He'd tamped down his impatience to have her in his home and in his bed as soon as possible. If it was easier for her to get here piece by piece, then he'd let it happen her way. "I was surprised to see you last night."

"I figured you weren't expecting company when I watched you swimming laps as if you were racing Michael Phelps."

"How long did you watch?"

"Long enough to know to leave you alone."

"So you just sensed my cosmic distress?"

She shook her head. "Shiori came by. It freaked me out because I worried something bad had happened to you. Then, after talking to her, I realized something bad had happened to you, just not what I'd expected."

"Not what I'd expected either."

Amery poured two mugs and slid one across the counter. "What was it like seeing Naomi?"

The hot coffee scalded his tongue. "No different from the last time I saw her. She talked shit, made threats. Trying to rile me and to get people to notice her." He watched the steam rising from her cup. "What did Shiori tell you?"

"She didn't say anything about what went on last night because she didn't know."

"But she did fill you in on how it played out three and a half years ago between Naomi and me," he said curtly.

When Amery didn't respond right away, his gut clenched at the thought of digging up this mess again. Of Amery knowing. "Did Shiori divulge all the dirty details?"

"I don't know. That's why I thought we needed to talk about it."

Ronin glanced up. "You know that Naomi was a plant from my grandfather to align her family's business interests with ours. You know that I spent two goddamn years of my life with her, believing we had something . . . when it was all a lie. Everything was a lie."

"That's not what you initially told me," she said softly. "Why?"

"Do you think I wanted you to know that my family *paid* a woman to be with me? To love me? And that I was so stupid and so goddamn desperate for it that I believed it was real? It appeared that Naomi accepted everything about me, and she never cared about my financial status. Surely a gold digger would've asked for money or support, but she never broached the subject. Which made it so fucking . . . humiliating when she told me that my grandfather had been giving her money every month as an incentive to stay with me."

Amery moved in behind him and wrapped her arms around his neck. "Don't let her back in your head. She doesn't get to fuck up your life again. I won't let that happen. It's my life now too."

He closed his eyes.

"And fuck the negative train of thought that women would only love you because you're a billion-dollar baby." She kissed his ear. "Baby, I fell in love with you before I knew you had billions."

Shocked, Ronin slowly turned around on the barstool. "What did you say?"

"I said I love you. And you were right; I've been holding back on telling you. I don't know why. I fell in love with you months ago. That night I gave you the picture of me bound? I'd planned to confess all, but I chickened out. I believed I had plenty of time, and I wanted the moment to be perfect."

"Then, the next day, you walked out after you discovered—"

She put her fingers over his lips. "That you'd withheld so much from me that I felt like I didn't even know the man I'd fallen in love with."

"So you fell out of love with me?"

"No. But I did hold back from telling you all this time. Not out of spite, but out of fear." Amery pressed her lips to his in a lingering kiss. "Because loving you is a scary thing, Ronin Black."

"Amery. I'm . . ." Speechless. Instead of trying to find the words to fit the moment, he fit his mouth to hers, pouring everything in his heart and soul into the kiss.

When they finally ended the lip-lock, Amery said, "Wow."

He nuzzled her neck. "Say it again."

"Wow."

He smacked her ass. "Say it again."

"I love you."

"I'll never get tired of hearing that."

"I'm sorry you ever doubted how I feel about you, Ronin." She tipped his head back and brushed his hair out of his eyes. "I'm sorry I didn't tell you about taking the Okada job. But I promise it wasn't because I wanted to hurt you. Or that I don't value you or your opinion. I fucked up by not telling you. It won't happen again. And I'd planned to come over last night and apologize before I found out about Naomi."

"Thank you. Apology accepted."

"Now. Don't you have something else to say to me?"

Ronin twined a section of her hair around his finger. "I'm the luckiest man on earth because you love me."

"Not that." She placed her palms on his cheeks and tilted his face back. "You know it scares me that you won't discuss what the doctor said at your follow-up appointment."

Her fingertips brushed the tops of his ears, and he discreetly ducked his head to free himself from her touch. After years of fighting, his slightly disfigured cauliflower ears were a source of embarrassment for him and the main reason he wore his hair long—to cover them up.

"Ronin, I'm not letting this go."

"The neurologist is being overly cautious. He insisted no contact sports and no practice with contact sports for six months. Then in the next breath he said—" He stopped. He didn't want to tell her this.

Because you don't want to believe it.

"Come on. Your life is an open book to me. No secrets, remember?"

Ronin couldn't look at her. "He said that medical science was only now starting to understand the effects of repetitive brain trauma, and hopefully by the time some of those symptoms showed in me—because it was a given that they would—there'd be better drugs and medical options to treat it."

"So you're worried about long-term effects?"

"I wasn't until he brought it up," he said dryly.

"Why didn't you tell me?"

"I hate the thought of you walking away from me now because of how I might be in the future. Jesus, Amery, I realize how goddamn selfish that sounds."

Amery curled her hands around his face. "Let's focus on the short term for now, okay? Just getting you through the next six months without you stepping into the ring or sneaking into underground clubs to prove you're the biggest badass in town, okay?"

He pressed his lips to her forehead. "Okay."

"And if you're worried that I'll think you less than a man because you're temporarily sidelined? Think again. You'll always be more man than I can possibly handle."

Ronin was stunned by the depth of her acceptance.

"I take it you haven't mentioned your doctor's suggestions to your instructors or your sister?"

"No." A soft chuckle rumbled out. "I had this plan to continue to throw myself into Black and Blue Promotions, leave the training schedule as is, with me focusing on working with the lower-belt classes, thinking maybe no one would notice."

"They'll notice. Whether anyone would mention it is another matter. I won't meddle in your business decisions, but when it comes to your health and happiness? I have a personal stake in it, and I expect full disclosure. Even if it scares you."

Ronin wanted to turn the tables and demand full disclosure from her on whether they'd be permanently sharing living space during those six months.

"So now tell me the rest of it."

"The rest of what?"

"What Naomi said last night. Her threats to you."

"Psycho fucking broad wiped her red lipstick off on my shirt."

"Shiori did see that much. She worried Naomi might've gotten violent with you." Amery studied him for a beat and said, "But that isn't what worries you—that I'll find lipstick on your collar."

"No. Evidently Naomi visited Twisted. She talked to the manager, and he mentioned I hadn't done a rope demo in a while." He watched her face carefully. "Naomi said if you weren't willing to be my rope model at the club then she'd volunteer."

Amery paled but rallied with, "What else did she say?"

"Baby, it's not important."

"Yes, it is. So tell me."

Ronin jammed his hand through his hair. "She said your

unwillingness to be publicly bound speaks of your shame and undermines my expertise. She reminded me of something I'd said to her on more than one occasion—that teachers don't let students dictate the lessons."

She paled further, if that were possible.

"Do you see why I didn't want to tell you?" When he reached for her, she backed up.

"Don't."

"Don't let her get inside your head either," he said curtly. "What happens between us—"

"It sounds like what *doesn't* happen between us is an issue." Amery rounded the end of the counter and snagged her coffee cup. Then she walked to the windows at the far side of the dining room and stared out.

Was he supposed to go to her? Or leave her be?

How would you want her to act toward you in this situation?

He'd want her to give him some time to think. So he gave it to her.

Ronin had finished two cups of coffee by the time she wandered back into the kitchen. He waited for her to speak.

"Do you remember when you told me about being a rope master, you said that you are also a teacher? And part of who you are is teaching people who are interested in the art the right way to do things?"

He nodded.

"And regardless if I wanted to participate in your kinbaku or shibari demonstrations, you *would* be giving those demonstrations on another rope model?"

Yes—but that was before he'd fallen in love with her.

"Somehow, in the time we've spent together in the past few weeks, that issue hasn't come up. Maybe I'd hoped it was out of sight, out of mind . . . but it's never that simple. It's also unfair to you if I refuse to be your model in a public venue." Amery affixed her troubled gaze to his. "You know I'm fine with what we do when we're alone together. I didn't even blush too much when your sister made it clear she knew we wouldn't be together if I weren't into your ropes."

"Did Shiori say anything else?"

"Just that you were a record holder and your mother and grandfather are aware of your rope skills."

"But that is not common knowledge. So I figured my grandfather must've mentioned my . . . proclivities to Naomi's family." He paused. "You know how after you figure something out, you think, *Why didn't I see the signs*? Naomi had no qualms about letting me bind her with rope, right away. That should've been my tip-off she'd been warned about my rope master status."

Amery cocked her head thoughtfully. "Maybe her need for . . . more of the S and M side of BDSM should've clued you in that she wasn't a stranger to bondage and sex clubs and that you didn't somehow 'turn' her because she'd been in the lifestyle before she met you."

Why hadn't he considered that?

"I never asked if you went to Twisted when we were apart. Not that I'd hold it against you, but I have to know if you did."

"Yes. I did bind someone else at the club. In a private room, not a public demo."

She stared into her coffee cup. "Who?"

"A model I've used in the past."

"What happened afterward?"

"You know that I don't fuck rope models, Amery."

"Except me," she said softly.

"That's not the same thing. After I tie you, I fuck you because we're alone, because you want me to, because I want to absorb your bound beauty into me, and because I love you, goddammit."

"But that doesn't change the fact that you're a teacher. You want to show off your skills and demonstrate the right way to use shibari and kinbaku. How long before you're demanding that I get on board with it?"

Then Ronin was in front of her, gripping her upper arms and hauling her against his chest. His stomach churned seeing her tears. "I'm not demanding you accept that side of me without discussing compromise."

"The compromise would be mine. You want me to be your rope model in private and in public."

"I want you in my life. That's all I care about right now. Don't cry." He kissed the corners of her eyes. "Please."

"You have to let me go."

He froze. She'd told him she loved him and now she asked him to let her go? No. Fucking. Way. "Amery—"

"Ronin, you're hurting my arms. Let me go."

He released her and gently rubbed on the red spots.

Amery burrowed into him. "I don't want to deny your needs because you'd resent me. Living with that would be worse than being naked and dangling by a rope in a roomful of strangers. And it seems doubly cruel to say no to you when you're already giving up a part of yourself by not fighting for the foreseeable future. I know that practicing kinbaku is a physical need for you as much as fighting is."

Was demonstrating his rope skill really a physical need for him?

Yes.

No.

Maybe.

Fuck.

Should he point out she'd overcome her aversion to being photographed and maybe she'd feel the same about being his rope model for demos?

Should he tell her that no matter if they were alone in his practice room or at the club in a room packed with people, all he'd ever see was her?

As much as it killed him to see her struggling, he had to let her decide her limits on her own. And he had to think about what compromises he'd make to keep her in his life.

"I just wish I had someone to talk to about this."

"What about Molly?"

"It'd scar her. She blushed as red as your ropes when she saw the cover for Cherry's book."

"I thought she'd come out of her shell."

"She has. But knowing her boss is your rope model might put her right back in it. It's not something most people understand. I know I didn't."

"What about the author? She helped you come to an understanding about the lifestyle before."

Amery regarded him. "She's very straightforward. She'd tell me that my trepidation wasn't wrong and I should listen to it."

"Are you looking for someone to tell you something different from that?"

"I don't know. I'd like to talk to someone who's been in the situation."

"Let me see what I can do. If I can think of anyone who can help you make an unbiased decision."

"Thank you. Now I need to get to work." Amery kissed him and disentangled from his arms. "Are you teaching tonight?"

"Depends. Are you working late?"

A strangely guarded look crossed her face.

"I don't want Okada to be the elephant in the room."

"It won't be."

Yeah, with Naomi running around in Denver doing god knows what and Amery's concerns about bondage demos, her job with Okada was the least of their concerns—and wasn't that ironic?

She bent over and picked up her purse; then she kissed his cheek. "I'll keep in touch with you and let you know what's going on."

Her reaction was too dismissive for his taste. He crushed her to his chest. "Less than an hour ago, you told me for the first time that you loved me, so, baby, you *don't* get to storm off without telling me that at least five more times. I've been waiting so damn long to hear it from you."

He felt her smile against his chest. She opened her mouth over his heart and blew a hot breath through his shirt. "I love you, Ronin Black."

Ronin tipped her head back to get at her mouth. He kissed her in the seductive way that turned her into putty, and he couldn't wait to get his hands on her. "I need to be inside you."

"Now?"

"Yes."

Amery didn't protest until he lifted her to the back of the couch and quickly bound her arms behind her with her long leather purse strap. She broke the kiss with, "Seriously?"

"Don't pretend you don't like it," he murmured against her throat as he inched her skirt up her luscious thighs and pulled her panties aside.

"I love it, so it seems silly that it always catches me off guard." Somehow she hooked her toes underneath the waistband of his gi pants and dragged them down his legs.

"Damn, do I love that you're so flexible." Keeping one hand braced on her lower back, he used his other hand to align the head of his cock to the wet opening of her body. He pushed in slowly, savoring every inch of her pussy enveloping his shaft and every soft groan spilling from her lips as he filled her.

When he stayed buried in her to the root without moving, she rubbed her lips across his collarbone. "I love you. Show me how crazy it makes you when I say it over and over as you're fucking me hard."

And he did, secretly satisfied that by the time he finished, she'd said it a dozen times.

Not that he was counting or anything.

CHAPTER SIXTEEN

AMERY was outside, securing the metal drop downs over her windows, when she heard someone call her name. She glanced over to see Shiori leaning against a black limousine. She wandered over, brushing the dust from her hands. "You've stopped by twice in one week. Are you bored?"

Shiori smiled. "As a matter of fact, I am. But that isn't why I'm here. I wanted to see how things went with Ronin last night."

"You didn't talk to him today?"

"No. I've been busy since early this morning, and I'm not teaching at the dojo tonight. So what happened?" When Amery hesitated, Shiori said, "We can discuss this in private, if you like." She opened the limo door.

"Cool." She slid across the gray leather seat to the other side.

Ms. Impeccably Dressed practically floated into the car. Her champagne-colored linen pants didn't have a single wrinkle, and her soft pink silk shirt had zero static. The woman never had a hair out of place. Even the night she'd shown up at the hospital at three in the morning, she'd looked like she'd just stepped away from a fashion shoot.

Amery checked out the interior of the limo. Tinted windows, plush carpet, tons of legroom. Seats that were both firm and cushiony. Beneath the sliding window was a console with a mini fridge. Even the ceiling was upholstered in velvet.

"I've been in a limo only once, when my friend Alyssa got married. I suppose that seems strange to you since having a car and driver at your disposal is your life."

"It's not like I have a choice. I don't know how to drive."

"At all?"

Shiori shook her head. "I don't need to drive in Tokyo. And other countries I do business in frown at an unlicensed driver on their roadways."

Amery laughed. "I suppose that's true. But I can't imagine not being able to climb in my car and drive wherever I want to."

"Where would you like to go now?"

"Oh. I thought we'd just sit curbside and talk. Especially since it's rush hour."

Shiori pushed the intercom button. "We haven't chosen a destination yet, so we'll just stay here for now."

"Let me know when you're ready to go, ma'am."

After winding her long, black tresses into a knot at the back of her head, Shiori secured it with a pair of chopsticks. Then she slid open a door on the face of the console.

"Holy shit. This is a fully stocked limo."

"A requirement for an Okada executive since my job drives me to drink. What's your poison today?"

"Rum and Coke would be great."

"A favorite of mine as well." Shiori flipped open another compartment, which contained ice. She filled two glasses and mixed the drinks like a pro, even adding a wedge of lime.

"Thank you."

"You're welcome. I hate to admit I usually drink alone, so this is nice." She kicked off her heels, five-inch leopard-print Pradas, spreading her bare toes into the carpet with a soft sigh.

Amery sipped her drink. "I appreciate you coming by last night. By the time I got to Ronin's place, he'd worked through some of his anger."

"Did he tell you what Naomi said to him?"

"We discussed it this morning, which brought up some issues between us that we'd both conveniently shoved aside."

"Can you talk about those issues?"

She studied Ronin's sister. The big bad international corporate executive with tremendous sway in Amery's career didn't look so scary with her shoes off and her hair twisted into a messy bun. It occurred to her that since Shiori knew Ronin's proclivities, she'd be a good one to talk to about her fears.

"Why are you sizing me up?" Shiori asked with that haughty edge.

"Relax. I'm just wondering if we're off the record right now. I work for you, and I want to keep things professional."

"Technically you don't work for me since I . . ." She stopped. "Not important. But you're also involved with my only sibling, so we'll have a personal crossover regardless. I'm sure I'm probably the last person you'd trust, but I'd like to prove you can trust me. Obviously my first loyalty is to Ronin, and if you do or say anything that would put him in physical or emotional jeopardy, naturally I'd tell him."

Good to know that after all the trauma Shiori had helped create in Ronin's life that now she looked out for her brother's well-being. "Fair enough. Our off-the-record time is just girl talk. But if you say or do something that might hurt him, same goes. I'll tattle on you like a six-year-old girl."

Shiori laughed. "Deal. And off the clock, my friends call me Shi." She held her glass up for a toast. "May our shared secrets be as juicy as the men in our lives."

Amery clinked her glass to Shiori's. "Oh, I got that covered."

"Did Ronin attack a heavy bag last night to work out his frustrations?"

"He was in the pool when I got there. His knuckles weren't scuffed up like other times when he used his fists. But he was exhausted, so I imagine he did some punishing activity in the dojo." Amery was a little clinical when she summarized what Ronin had told her.

"That's not all of it, Amery. Probably not the worst of it."

Why was she surprised Shiori had picked up on what wasn't said? "Naomi told him she'd heard at the club that I refused to be his rope model in public. She asked him how he let a student dictate lessons to the teacher, which when phrased that way . . ." She swallowed a mouthful of courage. "It puts him in a bad light. But the thing is, since we reconciled, we haven't discussed whether he'll continue with demos. Or whether I'd be okay if he used someone else."

Shiori cocked her head. "Being his rope model in public was a hard limit for you?" When Amery blinked with confusion, Shiori clarified. "Something you will not do under any circumstances, which means you'll safe-word out."

"We don't use safe words. If I get panicked by a binding, I tell him and we talk through it. We don't um . . . practice any aspects of BDSM."

"Besides the tying-up-with-ropes and having-sex-tied-up aspects," Shiori said dryly.

"We don't practice any other aspects of BDSM besides bondage," Amery clarified. "He told me this morning that he'd gone to the club during our break."

"I'm not surprised, but at least he told you. He could've lied and you wouldn't have ever known."

"I realize that."

"Were you pissed off, or hurt or what?"

"All of the above. But I don't have a right to any of it. We weren't seeing each other at the time, and he told me he didn't fuck her."

"And you believe him?"

Amery looked up. "Yes. Public sex after the binding became an issue between him and Naomi. I don't have to tell you that your brother is a very private man. Sex isn't sacred, but it is the ultimate intimacy. He and I are in agreement on that. But I have the same sense of privacy when it comes to baring all. Not to him. But to people I don't know? That terrifies me."

Shiori reached for her hand and squeezed. "Understandable. Maybe the reason it doesn't seem like a big deal to him is—"

"Because he's not the one who's naked!"

"There is that. But Ronin has been around people in the lifestyle long enough to know they're not judging you. I'm sure he feels that should allay your fears." She smiled. "And as a man, he wants to show you off. He wants to demonstrate how in synch the model can be with the rope master. How beautiful you are bound in his rope designs. He wants every person in attendance to feel the sexual heat between you two, because that, more than anything, will prove to everyone that kinbaku is a sensual art."

"It makes sense . . . Until I imagine myself wrapped wrist to ankle and exposed to the point they could see up into my tonsils."

"There's a visual. Look, you have to set limits. Ronin won't know where to start unless you tell him what you won't do. It's give and take. I can't imagine he wouldn't let you wear a thong if he was focusing on chest harness techniques. It'd be different if he was teaching a class of basic rope knots rather than giving a demonstration of a full binding."

She hadn't considered that. Heck, she hadn't thought beyond *no*, and yet she remembered her irrational jealousy when Ronin had bound that woman at the club. That brought her full circle. "The other reason Ronin was so angry yesterday? Naomi offered herself as his model if I wasn't up to the task. I think that made him wonder if I'm right for him." Amery finished her drink. "When it's just us . . . it's beautiful and sensual, and I don't know why my willingness to hand him the ropes behind closed doors isn't enough for him. But I'd never give him an ultimatum because I'd definitely lose him."

Shiori thoughtfully tapped her fingers on the back of the seat.

"What?"

"Wearing a mask wouldn't solve anything either. And I would imagine, like most men, he prefers to look at your face while you're in the scene."

"Unless he's directly in my face, I doubt that's where either one of his heads is focused."

"True. It's just too bad you can't wear a wig and a mask. You'd be amazed by how many people you'd fool and how freeing anonymity can be."

"Speaking from personal experience, Shi?"

"Yes. But to get the real scoop on that secret?" She rattled her empty glass. "I'll need several more of these."

"Fill 'er up. It's not like we're driving."

AND that's how they ended up club hopping—after zipping through the McDonald's drive-through for burgers and fries to soak up some of the alcohol.

Amery wished she'd invited Chaz along since he knew all the hottest clubs. Once Shiori let her hair down, she really let it down. With her exotic looks, men flocked to her. She took it all in stride, not acting like a billionaire heiress, a badass ninja, or the VP of a global corporation.

They danced and laughed and drank. Amery tried to pick a guy for Shiori, but every guy had a flaw that precluded Shiori from approaching him.

"What about him?" Amery asked. "Brown shirt."

"The one who looks like Curly from *The Three Stooges*? Pass."

"How about his friend? The tall blond?"

"Possibly. He looks European. Had enough of those types. I hate competing for the mirror the morning after a hookup." She shuddered. "I actually had one guy get out of bed after we finished banging the headboard, so he could complete his nightly skin-care regimen before he fell asleep."

"Bullshit."

Shiori held up her hand. "True story. As soon as he slipped on the cooling eye mask? I was gone."

"I definitely have to introduce you to Chaz. You two can try to one-up each other on bizarre hookup stories." Amery's phone buzzed on the table again.

"Is that my brother?"

"Yes."

"How many times has he called tonight?"

"A few." She squinted at the recent calls list. "Wow. He's called eight times before the last two times."

"Why didn't you answer it?"

"Been having fun with you. If I tell him I'm hanging with you, he'd try to horn in."

Shiori leaned closer. "You're really having fun with me?"

"Of course. Why? Am I holding you back from hitting something like that?" She angled her chin to a guy with long hair decked out in biker gear who'd been hovering near their table.

"You suck at trying to nail my type," Shiori said. Then she laughed. "But I suck worse at nailing my type." She squeezed Amery's forearm. "It's been a very long time since I've had a girls' night out. Thank you."

"You start in with the 'I love you, man' stuff and I'm decking you. Wait. You're a ninja badass like your brother. You'd whale on my sorry butt."

"He'd shudder to hear you say that."

Amery picked up her phone. "How do you say 'I love you' in Japanese?"

"Aishiteru wa." Shiori took a sip of her drink. "One thing to remember. Japanese people don't feel comfortable verbally expressing their feelings like Americans do. So that's said only on rare occasions. Telling Ronin you love him in English would probably mean more to him."

"If it's rarely said, then they're definitely words I need to know. So say it one more time. Slowly. Phonetically."

"Eye-she-teh-rue wah."

Amery repeated it four times.

"You want another round?" Shiori asked.

The music had dropped a decibel, allowing Amery to call Ronin. "Probably not. But I'd take a Coke straight up."

A devilish look entered Shiori's eyes. "Did you say a cock straight up?"

"No, I did not say I wanted a cock straight up. You do need to get laid."

"Amery? What the fuck?"

"Oh, hey, ah . . . hi, baby. I was just . . . you know . . . talking." She flipped Shiori off. "What's up? I see you called a few times."

"A few? Try ten times. And where are you that you can't answer your fucking phone?"

"A club."

"What club?"

"Not the kind of club you prefer."

Shiori choked on her drink.

"Where. Are. You?"

Ooh, that was his *not amused* tone. "Shi, what's the name of this place?"

"Shi?" Ronin repeated. "Who are you with?"

"Your sister."

"Since when are you and *Shi* drinking buddies?"

"Since today. And we're not only drinking buddies; we're club-hopping buddies."

"Where are you?"

"A strip club," Shiori shouted into the phone.

"Shi! He's making that pissed-off sound, so knock it off."

"Amery. Focus. For the last fucking time. Where. Are. You?"

"We're at this sixties-themed club. It's on—"

"I know where it is. I'm on my way. Be ready."

"For what? Let's get ready to . . . rumble!" She snickered at her lousy cage announcer impression. "Oh, come on, Ronin, that was a funny MMA joke!"

No response.

She squinted at her screen. He'd hung up.

"So how pissed off is my big brother?"

"Some." She smirked. "Nothing I can't handle."

"Or submit to," Shiori said with a grin.

"Shut. Up."

"You blink at him with those big blue eyes and you get pretty much whatever you want?"

She shook her head. "Sadly, I never learned to use the whole 'feminine wiles thing.' What about you?"

"I'd claim to be a rebel, but everyone knows I follow the rules."

"I hardly think that you being a—"

"Look at you two, hitting all the classy clubs in town. Or is it just the limo that makes you think you're classy?"

Amery turned toward the voice to see if the woman's face matched her sneering tone. Yep. The ugly twist to her lips marred the slender Asian woman's beauty. A niggling warning started at the back of her neck. She scrutinized her. Could this be Naomi?

Nah. What were the odds that out of all the clubs in Denver, they'd end up at the same one? She glanced at Shiori. But her angry eyes confirmed Amery's suspicions, and her pulse quickened.

"Quite the little adventure you two have had tonight."

"And how would you know that?" Amery asked. She didn't try to keep the loathing out of her voice.

"Because I've been following your trail of empty lowball glasses since you left Lodo. I'd hoped to have a word with you alone, Amery, but you closed up shop early today. When I saw you and Ronin's traitor sister partaking of the Denver nightlife, I thought I'd see what you two consider fun." She waggled her cell phone. "Maybe videotape the shenanigans. Put the clips up on YouTube. The VP of Okada getting her drink on."

Shiori froze.

Then Naomi focused on Amery. "If I know Ronin—and trust me, I *do* know the man better than you ever will—he'll be livid at the footage of you dancing, seeing how you let your male dance partners put their hands all over you."

Amery laughed. "Your life really must suck big hairy donkey balls if the only way you get your kicks is by spying on other people."

"Ronin and I never had to go out to have fun," Naomi cooed.

Don't fall for her stupid taunts. But that didn't mean she'd allow herself to be verbally assaulted. "That's right; you preferred to go to the club on your own without Ronin. How did that work out for you?"

"Fine for several years. How long have you been with him?"

Amery ignored the last comment and focused on the first part. "Fine? Really?" She leaned closer. "Oh, right, then he figured out that you were desperate to be whipped and humiliated before some strange man fucked you. No wonder Ronin dumped your dumb ass."

The crack across Amery's face landed so hard it snapped her head back. Before the shock registered, she saw that hand flying toward her face again.

She reacted instinctively. She grabbed Naomi's wrist and twisted her arm, standing up to put her body weight into it. Then she kicked the back of Naomi's knee. As soon as the woman lost her balance, Amery was on her, bringing her to the ground. Keeping Naomi's arm behind her back, she pushed the side of her face into the ground and stepped on her other hand.

Naomi screamed.

When bar patrons circled them, Shiori warned them off.

"You disgust me, and that was even before I met you in person," Amery said with pure venom. "Stay the fuck away from Ronin. Go back to whatever hellhole you climbed out of. You're a fucking idiot for what you did to him, and that eats at you, doesn't it? Knowing what your big mouth and your greedy pussy cost you. No one cares about you anymore. Out of sight, out of mind, bitch. And if you ever touch me or what's mine again?" She leaned down to whisper, "I'm from North Dakota. Which means I know how to use a goddamn gun." Amery released her, but she backed away slowly, keeping an eye on Naomi in case she tried to attack her.

A heavyset Japanese man cut through the crowd and helped Naomi to her feet.

Amery and Naomi glared at each other, hatred burning the air between them.

A hand landed on the back of Amery's neck. With adrenaline coursing through her, she just about started throwing elbows, when his hard body pressed against hers.

Ronin.

Naomi's eyes stayed on Ronin. Her lip curled when he placed a soft kiss on Amery's burning cheek. "You'll never keep him."

"Luckily he doesn't want to be a kept man."

Her face turned red and she shook with rage.

"Oh, and for the record? I *am* Ronin's rope model. His *only* rope model. In private and in public. Someone at the club fed you what you wanted to hear. So next time get your facts straight before you start offering your"—Amery gave Naomi a sneering head-to-toe perusal—"second-rate services to my man. We will be doing a demonstration soon. And trust me; it'll be something they'll be talking about for years to come."

Ronin's hand tightened on the back of her neck.

Shiori stepped forward. "And also for the record?" She waggled her cell phone. "You're not the only one with videotape capabilities. If a single image from tonight ever shows up anywhere—and trust me; I'll know since I have teams of computer techs who live for this kind of shit—I will upload this to every media outlet. You're done fucking with my family forever, Naomi."

Her bodyguard or whatever he was stepped between them and ushered Naomi out.

After Naomi disappeared into the crowd, Shiori launched herself at Amery. "You are the shit! We are drinking to celebrate."

"She's had plenty to drink. I'm taking her home."

Before Amery could remind Ronin he didn't speak for her, Deacon tugged her away from Ronin and hugged her.

"I am so freakin' proud of you, darlin'! You reacted to the situation calmly and showed adaptability. Score one for Black Arts and the girl who paid attention in class."

"Don't you mean the flavor of the month who paid attention in class?"

"I only said that to get you to punch harder."

"You are a sadistic asshole."

"Yep, but it worked, didn't it?"

Ronin gently maneuvered Amery away from Deacon and slanted her head back to scrutinize the raised welt on her face.

"I'm fine."

His eyes were black with fury. "She marked you."

"I marked her back worse."

"We need to get you home and ice this before it swells."

"Killer here," Deacon said slyly, "ain't leavin' until we get to toast her victory. The girl deserves it."

"One drink." Then Ronin hauled her body against his, right

there in the middle of the bar, and pressed kisses over every inch of the red mark. Twice.

After the toast, Ronin towed her to the dance floor. He entwined their bodies, and they swayed to the sultry song. He kissed her with sweet heat and the urgency that made her girl parts tingly and her panties slick.

"I'm sorry you had to deal with her."

"I'm not. Now she knows I'm not afraid of her." She nuzzled his neck and inhaled Ronin's scent: salt and clean cotton. "How much did you see?"

"All of it. Deacon kept me from jumping in. I saw some of the self-defense training stuck with you."

"I can't believe I won my first fight."

"Got the fever now?" he whispered in her ear.

"Just for you." Amery kissed him. "Because you are worth fighting for." She whispered, "*Aishiteru wa.*"

His eyes softened, turning that beautiful liquid gold. "Baby."

They danced in silence for a while, just holding each other.

Then Ronin said, "Were you high on victory when you threw down the gauntlet about doing a rope demo at the club?"

"Maybe. She pissed me off. I've been mad at her since this morning when I heard what she said to you last night. And her look of shock when I informed her she was wrong? Totally worth it."

Ronin stopped dancing. "What won't be worth it? Your look of shock in the club when I'm binding you in front of a crowd. Letting her push you into doing something that scares you gives her power."

"No, I *took* the power. I talked to Shiori about my concerns about a public binding."

At first it looked like he might protest about her choice of confidante, but he said, "I'm glad you talked to someone."

"Shiori also said depending on the type of technique, maybe I wouldn't have to be naked."

He gave her that patient Sensei stare.

"Aren't demos more about the completed rope configuration instead of the individual knot techniques?" She swallowed hard at the coolness in his eyes. "In a few of the books you had me look at, the rope models were partially clothed. The clothing even adds to the rope configuration."

"But you are serious about letting me bind you at the club?"

Amery inhaled and exhaled before she spoke. "I'm willing to take it situation by situation. I don't want to lose you, Ronin. And I meant what I said to Naomi. I want to be your only rope model. Giving people a glimpse of the passion between us, the sensuality of how you tie me . . . maybe that's not a bad thing to show off, since I know you respect the intimacy between us."

His mouth crashed down on hers hard. The blistering kiss set every nerve receptor in her body into overdrive. "Need you." He barely brushed his lips over hers. "Come home with me."

"Yes."

"I may fuck you in my car just to take the edge off."

Amery smiled against his lips.

"You like that idea."

"Actually, I've always wanted to fuck in a limo, and your sister has one parked outside. What do you say we ask if we can borrow it?"

CHAPTER SEVENTEEN

"AMERY is really letting you bind her at the club?" Knox asked.

"Yes." Ronin stared out the window at the falling snow. The sky remained a murky gray even at two in the afternoon. An abrupt temperature change always wreaked havoc in the dojo—put the kids on edge, made them energetic and sometimes careless. Thankfully his instructors were clued in enough to pay attention to those types of changes so he didn't have to warn them about his extra safety concerns.

"Do you know which binding you're demonstrating?"

"I know what style and components I'll use, but I'm still working out specifics." Specifically why Amery insisted she'd wear a traditional kimono or a bodysuit and not be bound naked.

You let your student dictate the rules to the master, pussycat?

He shook his head, trying to exorcise Naomi's phantom voice. The thought of anyone but him seeing Amery's bound beauty, the glow of her skin, the serenity on her face when she was at his mercy, the constriction of her nipples and ropes framing the secret heart of her, didn't bring him a sense of pride but a fierceness to protect it. He'd never felt that way. And he sure as fuck didn't know what to do about it.

So the irony was, now that Amery had initiated a demo night at the club, he was the one feeling unsure about going forward with it. But there was no way to stop it.

"Ronin?" Knox said behind him.

He turned. "Sorry. Lost in thought. What did you say?"

"Naomi has always fucked you up. I wanted to throw a freakin' party when you said you were done with that psychotic bitch. I never trusted her. I hated the way she'd burrowed herself into your life, with her controlling, needy bullshit."

Ronin studied Knox.

"What?"

"Is there a reason you didn't mention any of this to me when I was with her?"

Knox scrubbed his hand over his face. "Truth? You'd just hired me. I needed the job—hell, it was my dream job—and at that time we weren't friends. You were too fucking wrapped up in her to have any friends. And what would you have done if I'd said the two of you were in a dysfunctional relationship and the only way it'd end was badly? You would've canned my ass. After you found out how your grandfather had manipulated you, I was the only guy left standing in the dojo. It was only after you handed Naomi her walking papers that you and I established a friendship outside of boss and employee. Deacon gives me shit for saying stuff like this, but you guys are my brothers. I don't hesitate to speak my mind now. But we both know if I would've confronted you about the fucked-up situation between you and Naomi years ago, I wouldn't be here now."

Ronin exhaled slowly. Why had he geared up to level Knox with a verbal smackdown? Because he hated to admit that Knox was right? He needed Knox in his life, not only as his right-hand man in business, but without Knox's friendship he'd be on a different path—a destructive path. "You're right. That pisses me off."

Knox smiled. "I know."

"So to answer your original question, I've been working on a suspension demonstration. More performance-art type of shibari, rather than straight kinbaku, which you know I fucking hate, but that's what best fits this situation."

Shiori walked in without knocking. Her face was pale, her eyes glazed.

Ronin's stomach dropped. "What?"

"Amery. She's . . ."

Immediately he was in Shiori's face. "What about her?"

"She was attacked a little while ago."

He gaped at her, mouth open and body frozen.

"Tell us what happened," Knox said.

"She was meeting a new client. Before she got to the elevator in the parking garage, she was attacked."

Rage and fear roared in his head.

"There were two guys, so she couldn't fight them off. They roughed her up and left her." Shiori put her hand on Ronin's chest. "She called me because evidently Molly was attacked a few months ago and she didn't want to bring back those bad memories for her."

Even beat-to-shit Amery was thinking of others.

Why didn't she think of you?

"Ronin, take a breath, so I can tell you the rest."

He forced his lungs to work, and some of the dizzying rage dissipated.

"Amery didn't call you because she recognized her attackers."

"Who?"

"The guy who was with Naomi the other night. And another guy who'd been lingering around our table."

"Where is Amery now? Did you take her to the hospital?"

"No. She's banged up but swore she didn't need medical treatment. I took her to the penthouse."

Ronin ran out the door and down the hallway.

Behind him he heard Shiori yell, "Wait—" and then Knox saying, "Let him go."

He forced himself to breathe steadily instead of beating the fuck out of the too-slow elevator.

When he finally reached the penthouse level, he took a moment to try to find his calm center. If only for a little while, if only for her.

Amery wasn't in the living room or kitchen or by the bar. He saw the door to his room was ajar and completely dark. The scent of her shampoo lingered in a humid cloud throughout the space as he moved to the dresser and flipped on the lamp. Then he crawled right up beside her. "Amery?"

She'd pulled the covers over her head, but her response was clear. "Go away. I'm fine. I just need to sleep."

"I'm not going anywhere. Let me see."

"No."

"Not doing this with you." Heart pounding, he gently peeled the comforter back. She was curled into a ball, her cheek pressed into the pillow and her hair obscuring her face. "Look at me."

She shook her head and tried to curl deeper into herself.

Ronin slid off the mattress and headed for the door. He flipped the overhead lights on and climbed up next to her again. "Let me see what they did to you."

"I'm afraid to show you."

He jerked back as if she'd taken a swing at him. "Show me anyway."

When Amery didn't move, he leaned over her and started brushing the hair away from her face. First thing he noticed was the bruise on her left cheekbone. His stomach churned at seeing that dark spot as well as the damp track of her tears. "Please, baby. This is killing me. Look at me."

She slowly faced him. Her hair still concealed her face.

Please let it be stuck there by tears and not blood. Her tears weren't easy to handle, but he could do it. But Amery's blood? Might as well shoot him with a tranq gun. He wouldn't handle that. At all.

Ronin lifted her hair, small sections at a time until she made an annoyed sound and sat up.

He knew she was staring at him, but he couldn't look away from the marks marring her beautiful face. The bruises already turning her pale skin a mottled black from the bridge of her nose to the outer edge of her eye. Her upper lip was puffy. Same with her lower lip. The right side of her jaw held a shadowed shape of a thumb. On the opposite side, in a line down her neck, were three big dots. Indicating she'd been grabbed by the jaw and the guy had squeezed until he'd left marks.

Breathe.

Fuck. He couldn't breathe. Rage supplanted air.

"I'm really hideous looking, aren't I?"

Her soft, almost apologetic tone snapped him out of it.

Breathe.

In. Out.

Better.

"No, baby, you are beautiful. What was done to you is ugly."

Tears filled her eyes. "I'm sorry. The training didn't kick in this time. I was so cocky after knocking Naomi down a peg. But these guys . . . caught me by surprise, and I just froze—"

"Ssh. Two against one is never a fair fight." It absolutely fucking shredded him she felt any type of guilt about the attack. "Did they hurt you anywhere else?"

"First the guy punched me in the stomach, probably so I didn't see the fist coming toward my face."

Ronin forced himself to focus on her eyes. The pain in them would be his calm center. "Tell me how this started."

"I got a call from a potential client yesterday. We set up the meeting time for today. He told me where to park and what elevator to take for the quickest access to their floor. Which didn't seem weird at the time, because it is a big building, but now . . ."

"You're a businesswoman. You meet with new clients all the time. There's no way you could've known." He picked up her hand and kissed her knuckles. "Tell me the rest."

"I'd just taken my portfolio out of the backseat when this scary-looking biker dude approached me and asked if I had five bucks for food. I remembered Molly telling me she'd gotten asked the same question before her attack. Then I recognized him; he'd been hanging around us in the bar the other night. Next thing I knew, someone grabbed me from behind and wrenched my arms straight back. The biker guy punched me in the stomach. I think I must've fallen forward, and his knee smacked into my eye. Then he grabbed me by the throat and lifted me up." She began to shake.

"It's okay. I'm here. Take a breath."

She nodded. "The rest is a little blurry. I think he backhanded me. He said something about keeping my mouth shut before he hit me there. Then he hit me again, two, maybe three times."

Stay fucking steady.

"When the other guy let me go, biker dude pushed me into the car and I fell down."

"Did it knock you out?"

"No. It disoriented me—don't know how long I huddled next to my car. When I looked up, the Japanese guy who was with Naomi stood by my bumper, making sure I saw him. That scared me, so somehow I got into my car, locked the doors, and called Shiori."

He would not add to her misery and ask her why she hadn't called him. Would. Not.

Amery lowered herself back to the pillows and closed her eyes.

"How bad does it hurt?"

"More than I thought it would." Tears trickled out of the corners of her eyes. "How can you do this, Ronin? Live with this kind of pain? They barely touched me, and I'm curled up in bed weeping like a baby."

"Barely touched you—baby, he hit you in the face more than once." He inhaled, still searching for a way to settle down the emotions seething inside him. "I go into the cage aware of what awaits me. You didn't ask for this." He pressed his lips to her forehead. "It's my fault."

"No, it's not."

He brushed soft kisses across her eyes, her nose, her cheeks, her temples, that mouse under her eye. He forced himself to stay gentle when his lips reached hers. He forced himself to view the bruises marring her skin as a chance to show his love and care of her and not a reason to go into a killing rage.

Yet.

After he'd kissed every mark, he whispered, "I love you. If I could take the pain for you, I would."

"I know. But it's not your fault. I was feeling cocky for showing that bitch I can take care of myself, and she proved I can't. I humiliated her; she returned the favor." Amery cupped her hands around his face. "She knew hurting me would hurt you."

"I'd rather suffer through a thousand concussions than see one single mark on you."

She blinked at him. "It hurts, seeing someone you love hurt."

That's when he understood Amery's standoffish behavior after seeing him beat-up. She'd felt guilty—like he felt guilty now. "What can I do for you to make this better? I've got a couple of pain pills left."

"Just stay with me until I fall asleep." She pressed her swollen lips to his. "Be here when I wake up."

"Done."

"And don't kill anyone. Please. I can't stand the thought of losing you now that I finally found you."

"Amery, I'm not going anywhere." He kissed her cheek. "Get some rest."

BUT Ronin did leave her. After she crashed and he was sure she'd be asleep for a while, he headed down to the dojo.

Knox and Shiori were in his office, ignoring each other, which was better than their constant sniping.

Shiori stopped pacing as soon as she saw him. "How's Amery?"

"Sleeping. She's shaken up and yet she somehow thinks she deserves it because she started crap with Naomi."

"That is a load of crap."

"Yes, it is." Then Ronin did something that shocked himself and Shiori both. He hugged her. "Thank you for getting her here and being the cool head when you both knew I wouldn't be."

"So you're not mad she didn't call you?"

"No. I'm grateful." Ronin stepped back, feigning a calmness he didn't feel. "I need you to do two things for me."

"Name them."

"Use your resources to find out the name of Naomi's bodyguard. Find out where she's staying in Denver. Find out why the fuck she's here. Find out if there's surveillance tape on that level of the parking garage. I want to figure out who the bodyguard's accomplice was."

Shiori smiled. "It'd be my pleasure. What else?"

"Pick up Amery's car and bring it back here." He tossed Knox the keys. "You'll have to take a limo ride, Shihan. You okay with that?"

Knox grinned. "Hell yeah. Now I'll be thinking of places to stop, so people I know will see me climbing out of a limo."

"Is the city dump open? Maybe we can pick up your girlfriend," Shiori suggested.

"Ooh, good one, She-Cat. Maybe if you do everything you're

told, when you're fifty, your grandfather will let you learn how to drive."

Just as Ronin was about to bark, *Enough*, they took the back-and-forth out of his office.

Almost on autopilot, he changed into workout clothes. He wrapped his hands on his way to the training room. He knew it'd be empty this time of day. While he usually practiced in silence, focusing on the sound of his breath, gauging the pressure of his hits and kicks by the thwack and crack of his feet and fists connecting with the practice dummy, today he needed noise. Loud distortion that fueled and fed the angry clawing beast inside him.

He found the CD with the mix of music that had one commonality: every time he listened to it, he got mad. He cranked the tunes and freed the rage.

Ronin hadn't worked his body this hard since before his last fight injury. Concentrating on the flex and release of his muscles for maximum power. Falling back on his training and becoming the persona that demanded respect and pride.

He dripped sweat. And still he pushed through. Switching from punching to kicking to jumping rope to kettle balls to practicing orchestrated falls.

During a break in the music, he glanced at the clock. An hour and a half had passed. At some point, he'd slicked his hair into a ponytail. He didn't remember. When he hit this zone, his violent Zen, he literally lived in the moment—from punch to punch, kick to kick.

Gil knocked twice before he entered.

Godsmack's "I Stand Alone" started, and Ronin jogged over to lower the volume. "Are you looking for me?"

"I'm looking for Terrel. Have you seen him?"

"No. Why?"

"I came early so we could grapple."

Ronin didn't hesitate to offer, "I'll grapple with you."

Gil's face showed shock. Then trepidation. "I appreciate the offer, Sensei, but—"

"But you're afraid. Of what? That you'll kick my ass? Or that you won't?"

"I, ah . . ." Gil sighed. "Don't put me in this position."

"What position? I'm offering to grapple with you. That's it. I do it with my guys all the time."

Gil stared at him for a long moment before he nodded. "Come up to the ABC training room."

Ronin wanted to ask what was wrong with this training room. But he realized his instructors would start showing up before too long, and chances were good they'd put a stop to the practice. "I'll grab my gi."

It was quiet on the third floor except for the office, where he heard Katie yakking on the phone. Didn't sound like a business call. But she'd settled into being a decent worker, so he'd let it slide. Besides, he'd scare her in his current frame of mind.

Gil was doing warm-ups. Ronin watched him with a critical eye. He hadn't grappled with any of the ABC guys except for Blue, and most of that fight was a blur.

When Gil motioned he was ready, Ronin bowed at the edge of the mat and stepped on.

"Standard tournament rules."

They bowed to each other.

Like Ronin expected, Gil immediately went for the takedown. So he let it happen and ended up in guard. In most cases, top position had control. He intended to show Gil that wasn't always true.

And prove it he did.

First round, he'd put Gil in a headlock.

Second round, he'd locked Gil into an arm bar.

Third round, he'd maneuvered Gil into a rear choke.

They circled each other, ready for round four.

Terrel interrupted. "I'm fifteen minutes late and y'all start without me? That shit sucks."

Terrel was normally so quiet, Ronin had heard him speak only once. He had twenty pounds, several inches and belt levels on the guy, but he tossed out, "I think I wore Gil out."

"Great. Now who'm I gonna grapple with?"

He stood and said, "Me. And you'd better bring it."

Terrel grinned. "Cool, man. I love a challenge." He bowed in as Gil bowed out.

Ronin bounced foot to foot, beyond impatient. In that zone where he felt invincible.

And Terrel wasn't much challenge either.

First round, he put Terrel in an Americana lock.

Second round, he put Terrel in a scarf hold.

Third round, he put Terrel in a Brabo choke.

That's when Blue showed up.

Ronin released Terrel and helped him to his feet. They bowed to each other, and Ronin faced Blue.

"Are you going to tell me that my instructors' groundwork needs work, Sensei?"

"No. I was just helping out. Sometimes I fail to see the differences between BJJ and traditional jujitsu."

"Superior training in BJJ," Blue said.

"Prove it." Ronin's gaze moved over Blue. "You're dressed."

"You've got a dangerous look in your eye, my friend."

"Don't want to grapple? Fine. Let's fight. Give me a chance to reclaim my honor."

Blue snorted. "Your honor isn't in question. Just your sanity."

Ronin had reached that point of a reckless high. "If you're afraid to fight me, Curacao, say so."

"I am not afraid. And you've just gone grappling rounds with both of my top instructors. I hardly think this is the time to offer challenges."

"Or maybe, with me being tired out, it'll be a fair fight for a change."

That got Blue's back up just as Ronin expected it would.

"I knocked you out last time we fought."

Ronin shrugged. "Lucky shot."

Blue spoke in Portuguese to Gil and then he faced Ronin. "I'll need to warm up while it looks like you could cool down."

Ronin's adrenaline spiked again, and he had a difficult time standing still.

By the time they met in the ring, gi tops gone, gloves on, mouth guards in, Ronin's pulse was tripping triple time.

"Amateur parameters?" Terrel asked, serving as referee.

They both nodded.

"You know the rules."

Ronin came out swinging, trying to keep this fight off the ground so he could hear the satisfying smack of his fist on flesh. He let fly and punched Blue in the face.

Just like that son of a bitch did to Amery today.

What kind of sick motherfucker hit a woman? His cross jab landed on Blue's ear and knocked him back a step.

Ronin kept coming. A knee jump that connected to Blue's chin followed by a spinning back elbow that caught Blue in the shoulder.

And when Blue went for the takedown, Ronin relished it and allowed himself to be brought down hard. He got in two head punches before performing a rolling press to get out of half guard.

Blue wasn't expecting that. Or the side mount that allowed Ronin a perfect gut punch.

Just like that son of a bitch did to Amery today.

What kind of sick motherfucker hit a woman? He angled his hand and pummeled Blue—from his chest to his chin.

Terrel yelled, "Time!"

Ronin rolled to his feet and walked to his corner, mopping his face with a towel and taking out his mouth guard for a second. He leveled his breathing and scrolled back through the fight, trying to remember his opponent's weaknesses. He wasn't interested in a tap out; he wanted the fight to go all three rounds. He wanted to deliver pain.

So when the second round started, Ronin didn't see Blue, his business partner, he saw . . . red.

He became methodical in his fury. Cunning. Able to keep his opponent on his feet until that moment he charged, and they hit the mat with a bone-jarring *whump.* Then he was fighting for dominance. Keeping legs and arms in constant motion. Getting away from his opponent's hold by utilizing the running sweep just as the referee yelled, "Time!"

Ronin was starting to feel exhaustion set in as the third round started. Which is probably why his opponent was able to connect with a side kick that caught him in the gut and sent him flying against the net. Pissed off, he charged, knocking him to the mat with a wrestling takedown.

Once Ronin was on top, he utilized jab after jab, feeling a burst of satisfaction at seeing the blood . . .

"Stop! Omigod, Ronin, stop it right now!"

He was abruptly yanked upright. Two steel bands circled his upper body, and he welcomed the chance to rest.

Then Amery was in his face.

Amery?

What the fuck was she doing in the goddamn cage?

Her face looked like she'd gone a round.

Then he remembered and his stomach clenched. That burst of rage exploded inside him again. *My fault, my fault, my fault. Baby, I'm sorry.*

Amery placed her hand on his heart. "Ronin. It's okay. I'm okay. Don't do this. You're not supposed to do this."

He glanced at his opponent—holy shit, that was Blue—holding a bloody towel to his face as he sat in the middle of the practice ring.

What the fuck had he been thinking?

His mouth guard fell out when he started to speak. "Blue. Jesus. I'm so sorry."

Blue rose to his feet with a grunt and shuffled over. His gaze slowly roamed over Amery's face, and he murmured something in Portuguese. Then his eyes met Ronin's. "I don't blame you for the anger, my friend. But now we are even for our first fight."

While Ronin's lungs billowed, fighting for more air, his eyes followed Blue's progress out of the room.

"I'm gonna let go of you now," Knox said.

"Amery, baby, step back in case I fall."

The woman didn't budge. "Then I'll catch you."

He just about lost it again right then.

AMERY watched Ronin closely. He didn't act like he'd gone three rounds with Blue. Evidently he'd gone six grappling rounds with two other ABC black belts before that. Seeing the man was still standing spoke volumes about his strength.

And about his heart.

He didn't speak until they were in the private elevator. "How'd you know?" Ronin asked her.

"Blue sent Gil to find Knox when the fight started. Knox came and got me."

"I'm sorry. You didn't need to see that—or deal with me after what you've been through today."

Amery pressed her cheek to his still sweaty chest. "You put yourself through that because of me. Did it help?"

"Some."

"Did you get hit in the head?"

Ronin kissed her crown. "No. I just needed . . ."

"You don't have to explain. I accept all parts of you, sweetheart." She brushed her lips across his pectoral. "Even the parts I don't understand. But that doesn't mean I can't worry you took it too far."

He said nothing.

The elevator door opened to the penthouse, and she stayed glued to his side, even when he tried to shake her free.

"Look, Amery, I need a shower."

"So do I. I'll scrub your back; you scrub mine."

Once they were in the master bathroom together, not happily, according to Ronin's expression, she realized in all the times and all the places they'd had sex, they'd missed the shower.

The water kicked on. Steam filled the air. Ronin had been in the glass enclosure for a couple of minutes before she slipped in, plastering her body to his.

"I'll be out in a minute," he said, vigorously shampooing his hair.

"No, you won't." Nestling her face against his chest, she ran her fingertips up and down his sides.

"Amery—"

"Why won't you look at me?"

"What? I've looked at you."

"Not since earlier. Right after you saw—"

Ronin whirled around and faced the water. Rivers of bubbles raced down the hard planes of his shoulder blades and arrowed into the dip in his spine, between his buttocks.

Wasn't like him to be intentionally rude, but turning his back to her seemed dismissive.

Amery snagged her loofah. Using the bubbles still coursing down his back, she began to draw small circles from his left shoulder to his right. His golden skin didn't have any freckles or moles. No past or present blemishes that marred his muscled flesh. He had a few scars here and there. But mostly he was just beautiful.

And that ass. The man had an ass to die for. Not too much of a bubble butt, not too flat, those taut muscles creating a perfect mix of round and hard.

In a split second, Amery went from ogling his ass to ogling his cock.

His fully erect cock.

She glanced up at him.

But his eyes wouldn't meet hers. They were too busy assessing the marks and bruises on her face. "Did you put ice on your eye to keep the swelling down?"

"Really, Ronin? I'm naked, touching your naked body, and you'd rather swap first aid tips?"

His eyes were so bleak when he finally looked at her.

Amery moved forward until his cock brushed her belly and her nipples touched his chest. "You're failing my test." He didn't retreat, which was a good sign.

"What test is that?"

"You asked me to move in with you. And my answer will be a solid *no* if you deny me shower sex whenever I want it."

"All it will take for you to move in with me is one round of shower sex?"

She twined her arms around his neck. "Yes. We've never done it in your shower. Maybe the reason is because your technique is lacking or something. So I can't fully commit to living with you unless I'm assured you are up for getting down and dirty when we're getting clean in the shower."

"I feel dirty right now."

Not the type of answer she wanted. "Talk to me."

Ronin rested his forehead to hers. "I hate that someone hurt you."

"I hate that you decided to punish yourself for someone hurting me. You could offer to kiss it and make it better."

"I'm afraid I'll hurt you if I kiss you."

"So pin me against the shower wall and fuck me. Kiss me next time. And the time after that. And talking hurts more than anything because my teeth rub—"

"On the underside. Then your tongue keeps going to that sore spot and making it worse." He feathered kisses over the side of her mouth that wasn't swollen. Then he lightly slipped the tip of his tongue across the seam of her lips, tasting the bruised skin on the inner rim, showing utmost tenderness.

Then he was backing her into the tile wall.

Steam swirled around them. Water spattered against his back.

"Bruises on your beautiful neck. That kills me." Soft, wet kisses followed the arc of her throat, and he followed the sweetness with heat, gifting her with a shiver-inducing pass of his warm breath on the spots he'd just kissed.

"Ronin, I'm fine."

"I'm not fine. Not even fucking close to fine."

"Then let's make it fine. Better than fine." Amery reached between them and jacked his shaft until he hissed with pleasure. "Good. I just want to make sure you're as pumped for this as I am."

He groaned against her throat when she repeatedly rubbed her thumb over the sweet spot beneath the head. "I am. Grab the shower bar." Ronin slipped his hand behind her knee and pressed it into the wall. "Lift your leg. Higher. Come on. You practice yoga."

There was her bossy man. She kept her eyes on his face as he raised her thigh so her kneecap was parallel to her shoulder.

"Hang on to me." He moved in until they were groin to groin. Then he finally stroked her pussy. "You're wet."

"Being naked with you does that to me."

He slowly fed his cock into her. He circled his fingers around her ankle, sliding her leg up, and pushed farther inside her.

"Omigod. That's like . . ." She gasped when he did it again.

"Like what?"

"Stretching me so much that I can feel you on me and in me."

"I want you wide open so I can hear that sexy little fucking moan when I do this." He withdrew his cock and ground against her as he slid in deep again.

Amery moaned.

"That sound right there means I'm doing something right."

"You're doing everything right."

His lips followed the shape of her ear from the lobe to the upper shell. "Fast, slow, sweet, rough . . . it's so good every time. When I'm with you like this, it feels like I'm where I belong."

Words like that . . . Even with the passion flowing between them so strongly she could scarcely think of anything else, his admission brought a quick sheen of tears.

The heat between them took time to build. And Ronin dragged every bit of anticipation out of them both.

His hand gripping her ankle, his mouth licking and sucking on her skin. His cock powering into her. Every stroke created friction on her clit. Every brush of her nipples against his chest sent more tingles skittering across her flesh.

"Amery."

"I know. Me too." Her hand curled around the back of his neck. "Take us there."

And he did, with the erotic precision he'd mastered. They came at the same time, which didn't always happen. But when it did? Holy shit.

"Okay," she panted. "You don't suck at shower sex."

Ronin chuckled against her throat. "Neither do you." He slowly lowered her leg to the floor and eased out of her body. Those wonderfully rough hands skated up the curve of her hip, the bend in her waist, and over her breast. "Thank you, baby, for knowing what I needed and pushing me to take it."

She traced the edge of his collarbone up to his throat and tipped his chin back to look into his face. Some of the tension had lessened, but not all. Not enough. "I know something else you need."

He blinked in that measured way that let her know he was still thinking about sex. "What would that be?"

"You need to create something beautiful with these hands. And I need the connection with you and how you make me feel."

"How's that?"

"Like it's more than just rope binding us."

"It is more. A lot more. And yes, after all that's gone on today, I could use the concentration and the focus entirely on you." He twisted a section of her damp hair around his finger. "Would you give me that?"

"Of course. Should we make this a formal binding?"

His eyes searched hers. "You wouldn't mind?"

"No. We haven't done that in a while. Won't it be more formal between us at the club?"

"It doesn't have to be."

"Okay."

"Your robe is in the guest bedroom." Ronin kissed her cheek. "Ten minutes."

Amery quickly dried off. After slipping on her cherry blossom robe, she arranged her hair in a messy knot on the top of her head, securing it with a pair of ornamental chopsticks Shiori had given her.

Closing her eyes, she breathed deeply for ten breaths before she moved into the practice room.

Ronin had lit candles on the small altar in the corner. Rope work was a deeper kind of meditation for him even when he claimed it was all about her.

Amery was aware that Ronin meditated in his Zen garden as well as at the altar he'd installed in this room. Since she'd never dated a man who wasn't Christian, she'd read up on Shintoism so she wasn't so freakin' clueless. It wasn't an organized religion that expected followers to profess faith and adhere to strict rituals, but a spiritual way of life that celebrated Japanese traditions and history, as well as belief in *kami*—a sacred life force that dwells within all humans and nature.

Of all the people she'd met in her life who professed to live by the tenets of their belief system, Ronin Black actually did.

Waiting on her knees, facing the wall of ropes, was a form of meditation for her. She never felt subservient in this position. It allowed her anticipation to build, reminding her of the *savasana* pose at the end of yoga practice—where her mind floated and her body was still.

Ronin normally moved with such stealth, but he made a point of entering the practice room with enough noise to keep her from being startled. Usually their sessions or scenes were done in silence. She loved the auditory part of the connection before the binding. Hearing his ragged breathing. The thump of rope coils as they hit the floor. The rasping sound of the rope moving through his rough-skinned hands and the friction between two pieces when he crafted knots. Sometimes he pulled the rope back almost like a rubber band, so it made a resounding thud against her skin. Throughout the binding process, the whisper of his gi pants and the scratch of his callused hands on the satiny robe added to her already heightened sensations.

So today it surprised her when the soft, soothing sounds of music drifted from the corner.

"I'm glad you wore your hair up," he murmured against her ear.

She said nothing.

"Aren't you talking to me?"

"We don't usually talk during a formal binding."

"I thought we'd mix it up today."

"Is that why there's music?"

"Yes."

The change in him made her nervous. "What is this music?"

"Ensemble pieces using a samisen, a koto, and a shakuhachi—traditional Japanese instruments."

Very, very slowly, Ronin began to slip the robe off her shoulders.

"Is this in preparation for the club demo? Do you play music then?"

"No, it's just background noise. Reminds me of the years I spent in the monastery."

"Did you play an instrument?"

"I learned the basics of a shakuhachi—the bamboo flute."

"Why that one?"

"Because it's also a weapon."

"Why—"

"Amery." His hand on her lower back and his heated breath on her bared shoulder stopped the rapid-fire flow of words. "Why are you babbling?"

"Because this is so different from every other time we've been in this room, and I don't know what to expect," she blurted out.

"That's not a bad thing. Can you face me please?"

Amery rose to her feet and turned around to see Ronin still on his knees. "Oh. Was I supposed to—"

"No, baby, stay like that. I wanted to see if you had bruising or marks on your stomach. Tell me where it hurts."

She had the childish urge to push him away, but she tamped it down. "He hit me kind of dead center."

"Did it knock the wind out of you?"

"No."

He scooted closer and spanned her waist with his big hands. "Soreness by your ribs?"

"Mostly my face hurts."

Ronin strung kisses from one side of her belly to the other. He wrapped his arms around her, pressing his palms into her shoulder blades. "I want to do a modified chest harness on you. It's a complex pattern, and it'll take some time. Are you up for that?"

"Whatever you want, rope master Black."

He rocked to his feet. "This binding will be face-to-face."

Amery wanted to ask why but refrained. "So do I get to ask what kind of rope you're using?"

"Plain jute. Fairly small diameter."

Ronin sauntered to the wall with the ropes and snagged four bundles from the top row.

Seemed like a lot of rope for just an upper-body binding. But again, for as talkative as he seemed, she worried if she started questioning him about his techniques, he'd clam up.

He pointed to the bench. "Straddle the bench."

"Where will you be?"

"Sitting in front of you."

A seated binding? That was novel.

They sat knee to knee, and Amery had the urge to cover herself. Normally she barely noticed her nakedness when he was tying her. But being this close to him, with her sex bared and him wearing gi pants, she felt more exposed than ever.

Ronin undid the rope, and it made a soft swish as the length brushed the wooden bench. He leaned forward, burying his face in her neck and breathing her in.

Just that small intimacy allowed her to relax.

"Wrists together, palms facing toward you," he murmured, placing a soft kiss on the pulse point on her throat.

Amery watched his focus take over. Eyes dark, full mouth pursed, a bit of color highlighting his cheekbones.

He did a hojojutsu quick tie—she'd come to differentiate them from other ties—each wrap perfectly placed. Then he pressed her wrists against her chest, her palms over the tops of her breasts. "Hold like that."

She couldn't take her eyes off him. Every brush of his fingertips as he wound the rope around her back, every hard tug of the rope over her crisscrossed arms. Every loop and knot precisely placed with such a loving touch. He even stopped to kiss her shoulder, which was a rare reaction from him when he was in the Zen zone as he bound her. Then he kissed the tips of each of her fingers, spread out like starfish over her chest. He caressed her thighs every time he reached for a new rope.

Normally the binding process sent her into a fuzzy headspace. Not tonight. Tonight it wasn't about sensuality, but comfort.

Not comfort for her, but for him. Putting him in a place where he had total control over her. Where he could soothe her, cherish her, protect her.

With each new section he added, Amery saw him coming back to himself.

Her arms were numb, but she couldn't break the unity between them.

Finally Ronin lifted his head and gazed into her eyes. "Done."

Amery glanced down at the plain tan ropes that covered her from shoulders to belly. On the outside, the design resembled a messy, misshapen spiderweb, but on the inside, over the center of her torso, was an exquisite flower, with perfectly shaped petals.

Ronin stared at her bound, pleasure and gratitude on his face.

She blinked back tears. She did this for him. Letting him use her body as a canvas, as a cushion, as a haven, as the chance to create something beautiful and special.

"So unbelievably lovely," he said softly.

"The rope work is stunning. Does the pattern have a name?"

His darkly golden haze hooked hers. "No. I combined two patterns. But I'm thinking of naming it . . . Absolution."

"Ronin. You don't need absolution for anything."

"But you gave it to me anyway." He softly kissed her swollen mouth. "Thank you."

CHAPTER EIGHTEEN

RONIN and Amery arrived at Twisted an hour before the demonstration. His mind was on setting up the riggings since it'd been a while since he'd done a suspension.

But walking through the club took time. Not because they stopped to observe the various scenes in progress, but due to the curiosity from other members about where he'd been in recent months. After the third such question, Amery sweetly piped in, "He's just been so darn busy with his new rope partner. I've got him all tied up in knots."

Crazy, wonderful woman.

Amery remained close to his side, not as tense as he'd expected, until some of his former rope partners approached him—in the guise of checking her out.

"Master Black. You've been missed."

"Thank you for saying so, but I'm certain you've not been lacking partners in my absence."

"I'd hoped to be on your call list when you decided to give another demonstration."

"I'll let Knox know you're interested."

The voluptuous blonde never glanced at Amery, but not as a sign of respect. "Thank you."

Amery turned and put her lips on his ear.

Before she could speak, he said, "She is exactly Knox's type, and he dabbles in shibari."

"Good. I don't like the way these women fawn all over you."

"I didn't notice." He kissed her temple. "I don't see anyone but you."

"That comment is *so* getting you laid later," she murmured.

The small ready room had been set up the way he preferred. Usually he prepared alone and he met the model on stage. Or if he'd needed a binding and sex encounter, he booked a different, private room. So it was a little strange he and Amery were in here together.

He dropped his bag of ropes by the door and watched as she hung up the suit bag with the two outfit choices.

She rubbed her arms and checked out the space.

"Are you cold? There's a blanket on the table."

"Ronin, I'm fine."

He stepped in front of her and nudged her face up to look into her eyes. "Tonight, more than ever, you need to be completely honest with me about how you're feeling. This is a suspension binding. There comes a point that it will be unsafe to untie you if you're having an issue."

"I've come up with a way around that." She lowered her lashes. "If it pleases Master Black."

Such a smart-ass. "Tell me."

"I know in many traditional shibari and kinbaku bindings, the model is blindfolded. You should blindfold me."

Once again he tipped her face up. "You sure? You've never wanted that before."

"It'll be easier to concentrate on what you're doing to me if I'm not looking wide-eyed at the audience." She placed her hand on his chest. "I realize this won't be like other times between us. Not only because I won't be naked."

"At least this time you didn't say naked and dangling in the air like a slab of beef."

She smiled. "So whichever outfit you choose for me to wear, I have a blindfold."

"Amery, I told you I'd let you choose."

She shook her head. "I don't want to pick."

The one he chose was a no-brainer. "The bodysuit."

"Would you like the blindfold now?"

"Yes, because I need to check out the stage."

Amery unzipped the suit bag and pulled out a long section of white satin.

His gaze locked on to the wide strip, and he realized it was the tie from her robe she wore into the practice room. Touched by her need to stay connected to him outside of this public display, he closed his eyes and rubbed the satin against his lips. "Perfect."

"Are you nervous?"

"Anxious. I always look forward to binding you." He kissed her forehead. "I'll see you out there."

He bowed to her. Then he grabbed his duffel bag and headed to the big room that contained a staging area.

Ronin had utilized the space dozens of times over the past few years. Hardware had been provided, but he preferred to use his own. He double-checked the lighting, glad to see the owner had installed Ronin's requested changes. Merrick McBride ran a top-notch club. He'd apologized repeatedly for his manager's indiscretion with Naomi and had assured Ronin any breach in club security had been fixed.

He grabbed a ladder and climbed up to affix the rings to the chains for this suspension. He tested the swing ratio before pushing the remaining chains out of the way.

All set.

Now he had to decide whether to bind her hands above her head in a gauntlet with the dedicated body rope or just bind them in a quick tie with plain rope. He crouched down and unloaded his rope bundles from his duffel bag. He'd already seared the rope ends and folded each length in half to ensure faster connection times when he needed to add more rope. He preferred to work with shorter sections, especially in this case, since he intended to create the knotted version of the full-body tortoise.

If he wrapped the gauntlet-type tie on her from the ankle down, completely around each foot, she'd have no balance. But that played perfectly into the theme.

That decided, he divided the rope coils for easy access. Then he retreated to the far corner of the staging area hidden by a curtain and searched for his calm center.

In this situation, Ronin had mastered the ability to block everything out. So he heard nothing but the sound of his own breathing. His mind stayed focused on the pattern, so he wouldn't be thinking about it when he bound her. He mentally finished the tie twice before Knox approached him.

"The room is full. They're ready for you."

"Merrick approved the camera?" The club owner had asked if there was anything he could do for Ronin to make up for the Naomi situation, and Ronin had requested that he be allowed a video camera in the room for this binding. Cameras, phones, any type of device that could send images outside the club were expressly forbidden.

Knox crossed his arms over his chest. "Yes. But I'm uncomfortable with this, so I can't imagine how upset Amery will be when she finds out. You should've asked her permission."

"I don't need her worried about being on film. She and I are the only ones who will ever see the video. Now that she's decided she wants to be blindfolded, it'll be her chance to see how exquisite she looks in this binding."

"Still think this is gonna come back on you, Sensei. But Merrick agreed—just this one time—and provided a camera that is encrypted. I'll show you where the recorder is." He took Ronin to the side and pointed to a chair in the front row marked off as *reserved*. "There."

"I don't see it."

"That's the point." Knox pulled a small fob out of his pocket. "The recording is going and has a limit of two hours. Push the yellow button when you're ready to change the lighting. I'm bringing Amery in now."

Ronin stretched out his muscles, rolling his shoulders and bending forward and sideways. He performed a couple of jumping frogs as the lights dimmed. Closing his eyes, he inhaled. On the exhale, he opened his eyes and walked onto the stage. He heard the murmurs of the crowd, but their faces were a blur in the darkness.

When he saw Amery on her knees on the mat, her head bowed, wearing a kimono, his body stirred, his heart leaped, and his head swam with one thought: *That beautiful woman is mine.*

The bright stage lights came up, and the audience faded away; it was just the two of them, ready to get tangled up together. He studied her. The overhead lights put an extra sheen on her red-gold hair. Her chest heaved as she breathed much too quickly. The tight clasp of her fingers resting on her lap revealed her nervousness—but only to him.

He circled her twice before softly commanding, "Stand."

Amery pushed to her feet.

He moved in behind her and suddenly wrapped his arm around her chest above her breasts, pulling her hard against his body. He whispered, "Ready?"

She nodded, angling her head against his.

Ronin stepped back and peeled the kimono away, revealing her body in a flesh-colored leotard, which enhanced her curves and gave the appearance of complete nakedness.

He draped the kimono over the back of the chair. Then he removed his gi top, placing it over her clothing, and he reached for the robe tie.

Amery trembled when he trailed his fingertips over the slope of her shoulder. He knew her reaction wasn't from fear but from his erotic touch.

After he secured the blindfold at the back of her head beneath her hair, he followed the line of white satin beneath her eye and across her face. He murmured, "Arms loose at your sides. Feet slightly apart. In a yoga position rather than a defensive position."

She inched her toes out, creating a small gap between her legs.

He pressed a kiss to the side of her neck—his signal the binding would begin.

The rope was smoother than he usually used. He placed the midpoint of the rope at the base of her neck and pulled the two lengths forward so they draped across her collarbone. He tied an overhand knot at the V of her cleavage and continued down her body, placing a new knot every four inches.

As much as he liked that the rope wouldn't chafe her skin, Ronin missed the feel of her flesh beneath his fingertips. Once he passed the apex of her thighs, he spent extra time letting his knuckles rub on her inner legs as he tied knots.

The heat and scent of her body soothed him, incited him.

When he reached her anklebones, he shifted behind her, resting on his haunches as he created knots running up the back of her body that mimicked the knots on the front. As soon as he reached the center point at the base of Amery's neck, he passed the two rope ends through, then tied them together before separating the sections and pulling each line against the swells of her breasts above her armpits.

Once again Ronin moved in front of her, holding the two ropes in his left hand. Before he started on the next step, he studied her face and her reactions. She'd slowed her breathing, yet the pulse point in her throat throbbed beneath his thumb. Her upper teeth were digging into her lower lip. So sexy.

He couldn't resist rubbing his mouth over hers, just a brush of lips and a sweep of his breath. "You are doing great, baby." The whispered words sounded as loud to him as a shout, since he rarely spoke during a public scene, but the only person he cared to hear them offered him a soft sigh of gratitude.

Ronin nuzzled her temple as he tucked the rope ends through the space between the first and second knot. He pulled hard, creating a diamond shape. He slipped his fingers across the curve of her side and around back, tucking the rope ends once again through between the first and second knots in the rope against her spine. Another tug and he checked to made sure he hadn't cinched it too tightly before he expanded the diamond shape and returned both sections of rope to the front.

As he added more rope, the diamond shapes ran in a straight line down her body. The connecting sections kept the smooth, clean look of a tortoiseshell. He added more force so she could feel the impression of the ropes digging deeper into her skin.

With her rounded hips and thighs, the narrow line of her knees and calves made her a gorgeous sight. Ronin knew he'd bind her wrists in a gauntlet from behind her so everyone could see how exquisite she looked in the front.

After he secured the final diamond shape between her shins, he left the remaining rope pooled on the floor and rolled to his feet. Letting his hands roam over the bindings and her body, ever so slowly, he enjoyed the tactile experience of the ropes beneath his palms and feeling the heat from her skin.

He snagged another bundle of rope and reached up to slide the O-ring over Amery's position. Holding the folded end of the rope in his teeth, he circled each of her wrists and held them together above her head with her palms touching. As soon as she held the pose on her own, he started to craft the gauntlet. Threading and wrapping the rope from her wrists to her forearms, leaving enough room between the columns to attach the suspending section of rope.

Ronin hooked her to the O-ring before he stepped back to scrutinize his handiwork.

Gorgeous. Now he needed to wrap her feet and the binding would be complete.

But before he reached that final stage, Ronin followed the sensuous arc of her arms down to her shoulders. He smoothed her hair and fanned it out across her upper back, stopping for a second to bury his face in the softness and sweetness. To ground himself in the knowledge the woman he loved was putting herself out there for him—he would celebrate that.

He stepped back and pulled the rigging, lifting Amery off the floor about a foot. He tied her off into a stable hanging position and snatched another bundle of rope. He knelt, making a loop around her big toe. Then he proceeded to wrap the rope up her foot. When he reached the leftover ends from the body binding, he quickly looped them around her shins to her ankles.

A hard shudder rolled through her, and he glanced up.

Amery's head had fallen back. Her lips were parted, and Ronin saw she'd drifted into the floaty headspace of a bondage high and she'd been there awhile.

He lost all track of time when he had ropes in his hands and inches of pliant flesh waiting to be tied and touched. He secured the last of the rope around her left foot and tucked the remainder underneath the wrap, which caused her whole body to jerk and him to smile; he'd forgotten her feet were ticklish.

Ronin made some last-minute adjustments before he cupped Amery's face in his hands.

"You humble me with your beauty." He kissed her—another first in a demo—and it wasn't a gentle tease or a quick peck, but a kiss full of the passion she brought out in him.

When she wiggled her body, as if reaching for him, he broke the seal of their mouths and jerked on the rigging, lifting her higher off the floor. Then Ronin spun her slowly around and around, showing the rope work on the backside.

Amery's hair flowed out as if she were underwater.

Time for the finale.

He twisted the free rope dangling from the second chain through the back of the gauntlet binding her feet.

Then he clicked off the overhead lights and the black lights came on.

A collective gasp echoed in the room as the neon green glow-in-the-dark rope he used on Amery outlined her body in luminescence, creating the effect of a mermaid.

He pulled on the second rigging, raising her feet to hip level so it appeared she was swimming. The bindings on her feet created the effect of a mermaid's split tail. The way her hands were raised above her head looked as if she were swimming to the surface.

The woman was absolutely fucking stunning. An ethereal, mythical creature come to life. The diamond pattern gave the appearance of scales, and the cinched binding at her waist divided her body. The swishing motion of her hair added to the illusion of a mermaid in motion.

Applause broke out and startled him. Ronin was so mesmerized by her that he'd forgotten for a moment they weren't alone.

And suddenly he wished they were. He wanted to marvel at this bound woman who owned him body, heart, and soul.

He didn't want club members touching her or asking questions or breaking this spell. He allowed himself another long look at her. This wasn't about anyone else but them; he wouldn't treat this any differently than if they were in the practice room when he finished the binding. He held on to her as he lowered the rigging. Once he had her unhooked, he brought them both to the floor.

She sighed and remained pliant no matter how he manipulated her body.

Ronin left the black lights on as he cradled her in his arms. First thing he did was slip off the blindfold. He kissed her as he unwrapped her wrists.

She blinked at him, and then her gaze drifted to the glowing rope crisscrossing her body. She smiled at him with that sweet quirk on her lips.

Next he unfastened the ties around her feet. "How's your circulation?"

"A little tingly but good."

As Ronin slipped the knotted ends of rope free from the tucks and ties, he let the rope zigzag across her skin.

Amery trembled and arched. Then on the next pass, she would try to move away.

So he took his time unbinding her. Touching and kissing to his heart's content. He hadn't even noticed that they'd brought the lights up halfway until he pulled back away from her mouth after another drugging kiss. "Baby. I love you."

"I know."

Then he swept her up into his arms and carried her out the side door, striding down the hallway.

Inside their private room, Ronin set her on her feet only long enough to wrap a blanket around her. Then he picked her up again and settled them on the couch.

The first noise she made was a laugh. "Glow-in-the-dark shibari ropes, Master Black? You are certainly full of surprises."

He pressed his lips into her hair. "I've never used them before."

"Why not?"

"They seemed a little . . . stage showish."

"At least you didn't play the theme song from *The Little Mermaid* while you were binding me."

That made Ronin laugh. "You must be down from your bondage high if you're cracking jokes."

Amery twisted to look at him. "I'm fine. Were you worried I'd be weepy and shaky afterward or something?"

"I honestly didn't know how you'd react."

"And?"

"And you reacted perfectly." Ronin took her mouth in a kiss that was a lazy exploration.

After he ended the kiss, Amery murmured, "Unwrap me so I can touch you."

"You can touch me all you want when we get back to the penthouse. But not here in the club."

"Because that's the way you've always done it?"

He stared into her eyes. The blue so deep and pure it was easy to get lost in them.

"Ronin? Are you okay?"

"Sorry. I'm great. My mind just traveled off track for a bit."

"To where?"

"To how lucky I am that you're in my life."

She pressed her face into his neck. "I'm glad I didn't do something weird and embarrass you."

Ronin kissed the top of her head. "If you decide you don't want to do a demo again, I'm fine with that."

"Really?" Amery tipped her head back and looked at him. "Why?"

He wondered how honest he could be with her.

Or maybe it was how honest he could be with himself.

He tried to arrange his thoughts into some semblance of coherency.

"Sweetheart, talk to me. Don't hold back how you feel—even if you think it's something I might not like."

"That's the thing. It doesn't have anything to do with you. Or your initial fear of being publicly bound."

"Then what?"

"It's been a while since I've done a demo with a woman I'm involved with. Now that I know what real love feels like, I realized I've never done a demo with a woman I love. When we're in the practice room or anywhere we're together, it feels right. Our being together like that is Zen for me. Tonight, it wasn't . . . pure. And, baby, it didn't have anything to do with you. What happened tonight was performance art. While that has its place, I am not a performer." Ronin closed his eyes. "In the past few months with you? I really found the heart of what kinbaku is. It's not about teaching others. It's about teaching myself. It's about creating art and beauty with love and trust. I never got that until you."

"Are you trying to make me cry?" she asked softly.

"No." Ronin tucked a hair behind her ear. "I'm trying to explain that tonight was more of an awakening for me than for you."

"So you really aren't okay."

He sighed. "The only reason I joined this club was for access to rope models who wouldn't freak out about what I needed. Any sexual contact would be safe because a health certificate is required to be a member of Twisted. After Naomi . . . it took me several months to want to do anything but the most basic configurations on a live model. And even then, I had to have some connection to the model to consider taking it further, and honestly it was so rare that I found that." Ronin locked his gaze to hers. "Are you sure you want to hear this now?"

"If you're ready to talk, I'm ready to listen."

"Now I don't know what else to say."

"Are you afraid that now that I've done the public demo once and it didn't cause me to freak out, it's something I'll want to be part of on a regular basis? Because that situation happened with Naomi?"

"Maybe. Are you?"

Amery shook her head. "I'd rather it just be the two of us. But

I'll admit it didn't feel any different to me because I was blindfolded. In my mind, we were in the practice room."

"In my mind too." Ronin feathered his thumb across the dark mark beneath her eye that hadn't completely faded in the past ten days. She'd done well covering it up with makeup, but he knew it was there.

"Stop staring. It's almost gone. And I don't want her here in this room with us any more than she already is."

Ronin smoothed her hair back from her face. "Get dressed. I've got to talk to Knox about one thing before we go home."

She gifted him with a fierce kiss, a claiming kiss that let him know he was hers just as much she belonged to him.

HIS need for her raged through his body like a fever.

The instant they stepped off the elevator, Ronin was on her. She made a surprised *eep* when he pushed her against the wall. Then his mouth covered hers in a kiss born of fire.

She tasted so damn sweet and hot. Like heaven, like home—like *his*. She clutched his shirt, returning his kiss with unrestrained passion.

"Baby," he whispered against her throat. "You're like a goddamn drug."

"So take me." She reached under his shirt and scraped her nails up his chest, pausing at his nipples. "Use me." She pinched the tiny tips hard. "Let me have the raw side of the rope master."

Amery nuzzled his ear, outlining it from lobe to the inner shell, her tongue licking at the scar tissue with such wicked sensuality that he forgot he never let anyone mess with his ears.

"Every dirty, raunchy, nasty thing on your sexual arsenal . . ." She sucked the air clean out of his head, and his skin erupted in gooseflesh. "Do it to me. Without warning, without apology. We'll make this a night we'll never forget." She nipped his earlobe hard enough to leave a sharp sting. "I'm yours. Prove it to me. Prove it to yourself."

"Knees." He pushed on her shoulders until she was on the floor before him. He tugged his gi pants down and clamped his hands on either side of her head, pulling her mouth to his cock. The head breached her lips, and he started to work himself deeper into her mouth with every pass.

Her hands gripped his thighs. She didn't look up at him; she just let him fuck her mouth. Her saliva coated his cock and made her chin and neck shiny and wet.

The visual of his shaft disappearing between her lips . . . Christ. Talk about fucking sexy. This hot, wet mouth of hers could bring a man to his goddamn knees. She sucked hard as he pulled his length out completely past her teeth, and she opened her throat when he shoved in so deep his balls hit her chin.

His legs began to tremble. The electric tingle started at the base of his skull and zipped down his spine. Too fast, but he couldn't stop it. Didn't want to fucking stop it. Ronin hammered his hips into her face with shorter strokes.

Yes. Fuck. Almost there.

He rammed in, feeling the head of his cock against the back of her throat. He slid his hands down to cup her jaw, his thumbs on the pulse point in her neck. In that split second before he shot his load, he growled, "Swallow. All of it." He looked down, her head tilted back, her eyes on his. Her throat muscles working him with an intimate kiss, and every fucking time she swallowed, he felt as if his body were being zapped with a live wire.

And he didn't look away. He let her see his pleasure. He let her feel every twitch of his body until he had nothing left. Then he let his fingers caress her face, tracing the outline of her lips still enclosed around his cock. "So fucking hot with you on your knees and my dick buried in this mouth I can't get enough of."

Amery closed her eyes and made a soft moan when he slowly eased his dick out, as if she were savoring every inch as she let him go.

As soon as she sat back on her haunches, he kicked off his gi pants. He ran his thumb over her swollen lips. "Strip. Then come find me." He made a quick stop in the bedroom before he strode to the dining room and took the seat at the head of the table.

She appeared a couple minutes later.

Ronin patted his lap. "Come. Here."

She sauntered over. But before she could sit down, Ronin said, "On second thought, get up on the table."

Amery perched on the edge and watching him warily with those big blue eyes.

"I've got a surprise for you." He reached behind him and showed her a small rectangular box.

"What's that?"

"Something I saw online that made me think of you. Open it."

She lifted the lid and looked at him with confusion. "What are these? Some kind of paperweights?"

He laughed. "No. They're geisha balls." He ran his finger over the glass. "The flower inside is a cherry blossom."

"They're, ah, very pretty. What do you do with them?"

Ronin lifted them out by the silken tie that tethered the two glass orbs together. "I'll show you. Lie back and bring your heels to the edge of the table."

Amery bit her lip.

He got right in her face. "Don't go all shy on me now. Lie back on the table. I want to see every inch of your pussy, spread wide for my enjoyment."

She muttered something, which earned her a punishing kiss—a kiss he knew she thoroughly enjoyed—before she stretched out on the table.

He scooted the chair up and pressed his face between her thighs. Perfect height. He glanced up to see Amery resting on her elbows. In that position, the gap in her knees narrowed. "Baby. If you can't follow directions, I will get out the restraints."

"Don't you think we've had enough rope play tonight?"

Oh, such a sassy little thing. Ronin reached behind him. Then he dangled the leather straps above her belly. "What's the rule about questioning me?"

This time she didn't say anything.

"Tell. Me."

"Any challenge will be answered. Sir."

He secured the looped end around her ankle and widened her seated stance by fastening the strap to the table leg. He did the same thing to the other leg and stepped back to look at his handiwork. "You're beautiful open to me like this." Placing his hands on the inside of her thighs, he pressed down and licked her slick cunt.

She groaned.

"So fucking wet." Another short lick right over her clit. "I'm going to fuck this hot pussy of mine with my tongue, with my fingers, with my cock. As many fucking times as I want to tonight."

"Yes."

"Reach down and hold yourself open for me so I can suck on that sweet little clit until you come against my mouth."

And it was erotic as hell, seeing her slender fingers exposing the soft flesh. He let his tongue tease those helpful digits every time he made a sweeping pass from her pussy lips and up her slit.

He settled his mouth over her hot spot and pushed one finger inside her pussy. Then two. He lightly flicked his tongue over her clit and began to rub both fingers on her G-spot.

"Goddamn you have . . . yes, more."

"More?" He added a third finger and continued to torture her.

Amery begged. Then she threatened.

Just before he let her come, he plucked the geisha balls from the case and pushed them in her wet pussy.

"What is that . . . ? Omigod, are those the flower thingies?"

Ronin lifted his mouth long enough to say, "Yes." Then he settled his mouth over her clit and flicked his tongue over that swollen nub until she started making that soft wail. He switched to full suction and let her fly.

He knew the instant the balls began to vibrate from the strong pull of her pussy muscles squeezing around them. He continued to suck in time to the clit pulsing against his lips.

Amery's legs twitched, her body shook, and she expelled those silent breathy moans that indicated she'd gone beyond speech.

While she came in a wet rush all over his face, his cock rallied for the next round.

After the shaking stopped and she went lax, he pressed kisses over her mound. He rubbed his lips from the ticklish spot he'd discovered mid-thigh to her hip bone. The overwhelming urge to mark her arose. On a night like tonight, when he skated on that edge, he didn't deny the instinct. He sucked love bruises from the inside of her knee, up to the crease of her thigh and back down the other side.

"What are you . . . ?"

"Whatever I want." Ronin pushed to his feet and stood, placing his hands by her head, stretching his body over hers until they were nose to nose. "You're mine. And I intend to make that perfectly clear tonight."

Amery grabbed a handful of his hair. "Bring it, tough guy."

"Good thing you don't have to work tomorrow, because it'll be goddamn difficult for you to walk." He unhooked the straps from the table and moved her legs to dangle over the edge. He clamped his hands on her ass and lifted her. Keeping his gaze locked to hers as he carried her into the bedroom and tossed her on the bed.

"Hands and knees."

After Ronin grabbed the lube, he noticed Amery had pulled back the comforter. He lifted an eyebrow.

"It's slippery. I figured with as hard as you'll be fucking me, I need to be on a surface that won't send me flying."

He caged her body beneath his, his pelvis against her ass. He stayed like that for several long, deep breaths. Hard skin to soft skin, the scent of her filling his nostrils. His lips found her ear, and he rocked his hips into her.

She gasped softly.

"What's that feel like, baby?"

"I feel full. When I move, those . . . things inside the ball vibrate like a tuning fork, starting strong and then tapering off."

"Do you like it?"

Amery angled her cheek to rub against his. "The fact that I creamed all over your face points to . . . yes."

"Such dirty talk," he murmured and latched on to the skin at the nape of her neck. He sucked hard and drank in her quick gasp and full-body shudder like a shot of adrenaline that traveled straight to his cock.

When he snapped his hips again, her torso was thrust forward. His arms bore the brunt of the motion, and he pushed back.

"Oh god."

"Widen your knees." Once she had a solid stance, he planted kisses down her spine, to her tailbone, letting his tongue follow the crack in her ass down to that tiny rosette. He flicked his tongue across it a couple times and felt the muscles relax.

She groaned.

Ronin pushed to his knees and grabbed the lube. He squirted a thick dollop on his fingers and reached between those soft butt cheeks until he found her damp, puckered hole. He smeared the lube around and worked a finger in past that tight ring, then another, scissoring his fingers to open her up.

Then he pressed the tip of his lube-slicked cock to the spot and pushed through the resistance. The sphincter muscle closed around the head. He let it rest there, feeling the lure of her back channel, so hot and so fucking tight.

Goddamn. He couldn't resist that lure. He plowed into her to the hilt.

Her body moved forward, and she dropped her head down.

Ronin built a hard, driving rhythm. Vigorous enough to dampen his hair and coat his body with sweat.

He'd come once, and that usually meant the second round would take him longer. But the clasp of her anal passage and the sensation from the geisha balls swaying inside her cunt put him on the fast track to orgasm again.

Amery was panting, and he noticed she'd clutched the sheets in her hands.

"Give me one more."

"I need . . ."

He returned to the caged position, his chest on her back, his pelvis pumping. "Not done with you. Never going to be done with you." He dragged openmouthed kisses across her shoulder, then stopped and bit down, gifting her with another mark.

That sent her spiraling into the abyss again.

The squeeze and pull of her orgasm propelled him into thrusting harder, deeper until he came in a scalding rush of heat that momentarily struck him stupid. When he realized he'd kept up that punishing rhythm even after he'd come, he worried for the first time he might've taken her too hard. He slowed and stopped. "Amery. I got carried away. I'm—"

"Don't you dare say you're sorry," she warned. "It's a rush that I can make you lose control like that, so don't apologize."

He followed the arch of her spine with kisses as he slowly withdrew. When he reached her buttocks, he gave her a big hickey on each cheek.

"You weren't kidding about marking me everywhere."

"No, I wasn't. Loosen your grip on the geisha balls so I can take them out." Ronin found the string and tugged them free.

Amery caught him off guard and pushed his elbow, rolling him to his back. She scooted off the bed until her feet hit the floor, and she sauntered to the bathroom. Her eyes glittered with lust when she stopped in the doorway and looked over her shoulder at him. "You promised to fuck me until I can't walk. I'm still standing. What are you gonna do about that?"

Growling at her challenge, Ronin chased after her.

He fucked her in the shower.

Then he fucked her in the living room.

Then he fucked her over the bar.

After that, she couldn't walk, so he carried her to bed.

Hard not to feel cocky about that.

CHAPTER NINETEEN

AMERY adjusted the lighting on the objects scattered on the black velvet for the twentieth time. Over the past two weeks, since the demo in the club, she'd been inundated with new clients. Between that and the Okada project, she could work nonstop seven days a week, and she knew she had to settle on whom to hire. The dynamic between her and Molly was so good she didn't want to upset the balance and make a bad decision, so she'd been lax on making her final choice.

She'd moved a few of her things to Ronin's penthouse. Cooking utensils, clothes, a few quirky knickknacks that looked wildly out of place amid Ronin's structured furniture and minimalist furnishings. Ronin hadn't complained—just the opposite. He wanted the mix of their pieces to make it seem more theirs. She was the one who'd been dragging her feet.

Amery didn't doubt her feelings for him. She spent her nights and weekends with him anyway, so it shouldn't have been such a big deal. But anytime she brought up paying rent and splitting the grocery and utility bills, Ronin said he'd cover it. She'd been too independent for too long just to let him take care of her. Especially financially.

She refocused on the items on the table. It was harder than she'd imagined to make homemade sex toys appear sexy and not weird. The paddle with the tacks on it looked painful. What part of the body was that used on?

Ronin's voice popped into her head. *Any part I want to use it on, baby.*

She bit back a grin and wondered what he'd think if she used the modified Wartenberg wheel on him. She crouched down and snapped off a couple of shots, using the edge of the velvet-covered table to steady the camera. She'd been jumpy all damn day. She couldn't attribute her jitteriness to caffeine since she hadn't had a single cup.

"Amery?"

"Hang on a second, Molly. I'm trying to get the angle on this right. Would it be too over the top for this catalogue if the edgier sex toys had a glint coming off the metal?"

"Uh . . ."

"Would that defeat the purpose of getting people to try something new and kinky?"

"Amery!"

"What?" she said testily and whirled around to find herself face-to-face with her parents.

Her parents?

What the hell?

"What are you doing here?" A sick feeling nearly knocked her to her knees. "What happened to Aiden?"

"Nothing, as far as we know. He's still in Afghanistan."

"Thank god. I mean, I wish he'd be done with this tour, but I'm glad he isn't the reason you're here."

"No, something has been brought to our attention. Something we need to discuss with you in person. Alone." They both turned and glared at Molly.

"I'll see you're not disturbed." Molly left and shut the door.

Amery wasn't surprised her parents hadn't hugged her. They

weren't much on public displays of affection. But that'd also mean they'd have to feel some type of affection first in order to display it.

"Okay. Wow. This has caught me off guard."

Her mother shot a disgusted look at the prop table. "We can see that. This is how you make money? Taking photos of perverted things?"

She blushed. Goddammit—she tried to stop it, but her body still reacted instinctively to her mother's condescending tone, and that annoyed the piss out of her.

"Put them away," her father demanded. "They're upsetting your mother."

"Then maybe you should both wait outside," she snapped.

"In this case, out of sight does not equal out of mind. You can no longer hide the sick things you're doing, Amery Lee Hardwick." Her father marched up to her. "And we will stay right here. We will not be brushed aside so you can call this Ronin Black, the man who has exerted some kind of control over you."

How had they found out about Ronin?

"Yes, we know about him. We know the type of sick, dangerous things he's involved in, things he's tricked you into getting involved with too, brainwashing you into thinking those types of activities are normal. We're here to put a stop to it."

"Whoa. I don't know where you've gotten your misinformation, but Ronin Black is a respected businessman."

"He's a deviant, promoting deviant behavior. He's violent and uses violence as a weapon to further his control over you."

Amery had the overwhelming urge to laugh, and she couldn't stop one quick giggle.

"This is not funny. And that you think it is shows us how far you've fallen into his web of deceit," her father said hotly.

"Where did you get this information?" When they stared at her stoically, she said, "It's all hearsay, isn't it? You're assuming a lot because Ronin runs a martial arts studio."

Her parents exchanged a look. Then her father said, "It's not hearsay. Marion, show her."

Show her. Amery watched as her mother removed a thick manila envelope from her purse. "What is that?"

"This is what was sent to us. It contains a letter telling us all about this Ronin Black"—she grimaced at his name—"who he is, what sick things he does, and pictures of the two of you together. As well as this." Her mother pulled out a DVD and shook it at her. "Do you have any idea how disturbed we were to discover that you're involved with the man in this piece of filth? After viewing it, we understood why you never mentioned him. Because you know what he does is wrong."

"He does it to you, too, doesn't he?" her father said angrily. "He has convinced you that it's normal? That if you want him to love you, you need to be this type of woman for him?"

Amery asked, "What's on the DVD?" even when she had a pretty good idea.

Her father got right in her face. "You'll see. We want you to watch it. Every second of it."

"Fine. Hand it over."

He shook his head. "We will watch it together."

Her stomach turned. "Why?"

"So we know you've suffered through it like we had to. So you'll understand our concern."

"Give it to me. I'll watch it."

"There's more than just one DVD," her mother added. "There are two and pictures."

"Pictures?" she repeated. "Of what?"

"One thing at a time. Where's your DVD player?"

They were serious. They were going to force her to watch whatever was on that DVD with them in the room.

"I'm sure she has one in her apartment."

No way was she taking her sour-faced judgmental parents to

her loft, the place that'd always been her sanctuary. Amery grabbed her laptop off the prop table. "I can watch it right here."

"I want to warn you that it won't matter if you try to destroy it. We've made copies of everything." Her mother placed the plastic case in Amery's hand.

"Of course you have." She pointed to the folding chairs. "If you want to sit." She pushed the rolling chair up to the table and popped open the DVD slot. When she felt her parents behind her, she wheeled around. "Do not stand over my shoulder, or I will take this in another room."

Her mother harrumphed. "You do not get to decide—"

"Yes, I do. And besides, aren't you supposed to be studying my face and body language to see how I react to what I see?"

"Now, sweetheart, we understand why you'd be defensive—"

"Don't you *ever* call me sweetheart, Dad. *Ever.* You couldn't show love and compassion when I was growing up, so you have no right to it now. I'd rather have your fucking contempt, which apparently I've got, so stick with that. Now, sit down."

Her parents were shocked into complete silence for once.

Amery loaded the DVD. It was more than an hour long. "Do you expect me to watch the entire thing? Right now?"

"Yes. Why do you think we drove all the way from North Dakota?"

To shame me in person.

Before Amery hit PLAY, she wondered if someone had gotten a copy of the shibari demo they'd done at the club. At first she'd been annoyed Ronin had taped her without her knowledge. But after she'd seen it, she understood that Ronin needed her to see the demo from a different perspective. She'd actually cried during the part where he'd so lovingly removed the rope. Amery knew there was an amazing sexual chemistry between them; she felt it every time the man touched her. But to see it on-screen? To see the passion and tenderness in Ronin's hands and on his face as he'd bound her and then untied her? That had unwound her completely. She had no defenses left where Ronin was concerned.

Somehow she didn't think she'd see that on this DVD, and her pulse spiked when she clicked the start button.

The images were grainy, like a home movie with crappy video. But she knew the man she was seeing was Ronin. A younger Ronin.

There wasn't any sound in the first segment as he bound an unknown naked woman. The focus was on the binding itself, not the sensuality of the act. The next two scenes were clearer, but the atmosphere had changed along with his rope partners to a harsher scene. The women were more intimately displayed. One even asked him to stop, at which Ronin crouched down and talked to her. Then he resumed his binding.

She might not have recognized Naomi after the first fifteen minutes of viewing if she hadn't seen that annoying smirk up close and personal and heard that cooing baby talk voice.

The queasy sensation rolled over her as she watched Ronin binding Naomi. Not in the clinical manner as in the previous scenes, but with the loving touch she knew firsthand.

It shouldn't have shocked her when Ronin stripped and started having sex with Naomi after finishing the binding. The shock, coupled with Naomi's betrayal in taking something so intensely personal and almost . . . sacred to Ronin and using it to hurt him, sent her thoughts spiraling toward desolation.

To think her parents had watched this didn't embarrass her; it infuriated her. This side of Ronin wasn't Naomi's to share. It never had been. Add in that she'd secretly taped them, and it spoke of her absolute evilness, vileness, and vindictiveness on a different plane.

By the third scene with Naomi, tears coursed down Amery's face. She ached from the very bottom of her soul. Ached to see that the tenderness and care in Ronin's beautiful eyes had been so wholly undeserved for this woman. Knowing when he saw this, he'd be mortified. Would he close himself off to her all over again?

To the untrained eye, or maybe to anyone who didn't know Ronin on the level she did, the scenes that followed were harsher. The love and gratitude for the experience that shone in his eyes was gone. He tied Naomi in intricate configurations that took an incredible amount of time. The sex afterward was perfunctory at best, one-sided at worst. Ronin got off and didn't seem to care if Naomi did. Their conversations were in Japanese, so Amery couldn't decipher them, but she understood begging. Not the sexy kind of begging, but the desperate kind. Ronin's reluctance was apparent when Naomi grabbed his hand and tried to make him spank her.

And he did—not with his hand. He used a paddle.

And then a belt.

In the next scene, Ronin splayed Naomi's pussy wide open and flogged it. Her screams were audible even behind the ball gag. But they weren't screams of pain. She recognized the difference; she doubted her parents did.

She wanted to stop the DVD—she'd seen enough—but she knew if her parents had driven all the way down here expecting her to watch it in its entirety, her telling them she'd seen enough would only drag this out longer, and she just wanted to be done with it. So she said nothing, just kept her eyes on the screen and let the tears fall.

The scenes became more violent. He slapped Naomi across the face.

That jarred her, seeing the man who needed kinbaku as beauty in his life to have to resort to ugliness.

She was still crying after the DVD went dark. Crying and heartsick and embarrassed.

Her father cleared his throat.

Please don't say anything.

"You see why we're concerned."

"You don't understand." The instant she said it, she realized she should've kept her mouth shut.

Her mother stomped forward. "This man has you brainwashed. How can you watch something so filthy and not be absolutely disgusted?"

She was disgusted, but not for the reasons they were.

"Do you let him treat you like that?" her mother demanded. "String you up like you're his piece of property and let him hurt you?"

Amery gazed up into her mother's angry face. "It's not like that."

She grabbed hold of Amery and yanked her out of the chair, pinching the tender flesh of her upper arm hard as she dragged Amery forward. Spittle flew from her mouth. "You watched it. How can you defend him? Especially when you know what kind of a violent pervert he is. That woman in the video was crying and begging him to stop, and yet he still hit her. He is a horrible, awful man."

"Let go of my arm."

But her mother had gone into meltdown phase. "We know this Ronin Black has money. You let him tie you up like a dog and do unspeakable things to you while you cry? But then he buys you pretty, expensive things and you just forgive him? And you let him do it all over again? What is wrong with you?"

"Let go of my arm."

"I tell you what, little girl. You always were a willful child who needed discipline. Maybe that's why this unholy type of behavior appeals to you. You think you deserve to get abused—"

"Shut up." Amery used a pressure point technique on her mother's elbow to force her to release her arm.

Her mother whimpered and stepped back.

Her father was right by his wife's side. "What did you do?"

"I told her to let go of me. She was hurting me." She lifted her sleeve and looked at the angry red marks. Guaranteed she'd have bruises tomorrow.

"Isn't that what you like? Or is it only when a man with a big bank account does it to you that it's acceptable?"

Hearing the crack of her hand across her mother's cheek would be momentarily satisfying, but not worth it in the long run.

"Marion, curb your tongue."

Her mother glanced at her husband meekly, with tears in her eyes.

"We needed to shock you, Amery. We wanted you to see from an outsider's perspective just how wrong all of this is."

Amery folded her arms across her chest, unsure what to say or what to do.

Her father's gaze landed on her wrist—specifically the rope burn on her wrist. His face paled. Then his mouth tightened. "This man has you so in his thrall that you won't listen to reason."

"I've listened to everything both of you have said. Everything. Now you need to listen to me. You need to meet Ronin and see for yourself—"

"Absolutely not. I'm a man of God, a man of faith, but I might just forget that if I'm in the same room with that heathen monster. Not only is he sick in the head, this Ronin Black isn't even a Christian."

Amery would ask how he knew that, but probably the package included that info, along with other choice bits such as Ronin's financial status.

"And he's part Japanese. That right there is an affront to everything in our family. Your grandpa Joe was a POW during World War Two. Did you forget he was tortured at the hands of the Japanese for more than a year?"

"It's highly unlikely that Ronin's grandfather was personally responsible for Grandpa Joe's capture and his torture."

"You watch your mouth," her mother warned. "Your grandfather was a war hero. A *hero*."

"Which has nothing to do with Ronin or his family. Ronin's father was a hero too—in the United States Air Force. Ronin is a US citizen."

"You are trying to distract us from the real issue at hand," her father said. "Give me the package, Marion. Then you'll see."

Her mother retreated and fished out the envelope again. Then she passed it off to Amery like it was coated in poison.

Amery dumped the contents on the table. She moved the DVD aside to pick up the stack of photos. She leafed through them, not really seeing them other than noting they were bondage shots. But she spied a picture with a yellow sticky note on the top, and she pulled that one from the pile.

She froze. It was a picture of her and Ronin, taken the night she'd had the altercation with Naomi. In this shot, Ronin was pressing her body against the limo so completely, her upper back was bowed away from him. His face was hidden because he'd been whispering in her ear. But the red handprint on her face was still visible. It appeared to be an angry shot.

But that couldn't be further from the truth. He'd been saying such deliciously naughty things, so sweet and hot, that she'd closed her eyes to savor every word.

"Can you explain that away?" her mother demanded, shoving another picture at her where it looked like she was crying as she climbed out of the limo alone. "Or were you so impressed by the limo you didn't care what he did to you or how he hurt you?"

No. The only thing I cared about in that moment was twining myself around him, feeling his breath in my ear, his mouth on my skin as he showed me how precious I was to him. The tears hadn't been because he hurt her but because he loved her.

When she looked from her father's face to her mother's, she had a sense of loss. They'd never understand. And part of her didn't care if they did.

"Was that a supportive, Christian thing to say, Mom? Berating me? Making me feel like some kind of materialistic bitch?"

"Don't you talk to me like that. We're here to help you."

Amery sighed. Counted to twenty. "Then please don't judge me before you let me speak." She waved the picture. "I don't know who took this, or why, but that wasn't Ronin's limo—not that it matters. And the red mark on my face? Was from Ronin's ex-girlfriend, the one I assume sent you this package of stuff."

"So you're saying it's all lies? That she somehow digitally altered his face into the shots?" Her father pointed to the stack of photos. "There are well over a dozen different women in those pictures. Whoever did this couldn't have faked that."

"I didn't say they were faked. Those are pictures from a long time ago." Amery had seen some of those pictures—they were in Ronin's photo albums, visual records of his previous bindings. So that snake Naomi had somehow copied the photos without Ronin knowing, which was just another breach of trust.

"What about this one?" he demanded, pulling out a shot of Amery leaving the dojo the day after the parking garage attack, her lip still swollen, her eye a hideous shade of black. With the hunched-over posture, she looked . . . beaten down. The next shot, a close-up of her face, showed every mark in detail, including the bruises on her neck.

"So you're not denying anything we've said about this man?"

"I'm telling you that you don't know him. He would never hurt me. And you have no right to judge him."

A long pause settled between them.

"Who are you?" her father said hoarsely. "This is not how we raised you. We provided you with a moral compass. How did you veer so far off the right path?"

"Here you are, living in the big city, living a life of sin and depravity." Her mother picked up the argument. "This is why she doesn't come home more often—she knew we'd see the ugly truth about her life. She's so caught up in it that she can't see she's allowing herself to be fed a line of lies. Where will she be when she's been used up and discarded? No one will want her then. No one will care to help a woman who refuses to help herself."

Don't cry. Goddammit, don't cry. "Not even you?" she managed to choke out.

"We can only do so much," her father added, slipping an arm around his wife's shoulder. "We want to help you. Will you come with us to church service tonight and pray about it?"

Help her their way. Amery shook her head.

"Are you running straight to him?" her mother demanded.

She shook her head again.

Her father appeared relieved. "At least give this some thought, okay? We're staying at the Holiday Inn Express out by the airport."

"For how long?"

"That depends on you."

"Meaning what?"

"Meaning we've been in contact with a Christian center here in Colorado that runs a retreat for abused women. We've secured a place for you for a few weeks. We'll take you there and check you in."

She clenched her jaw to keep it from dropping. They thought she was a victim? That Ronin was some kind of abuser?

Why would they think differently? Your assumption about what kind of man Ronin was the first time you were in his practice room was similar to theirs.

Amery refused to let that voice she'd worked so damn hard to exorcise from her mind and her life get a foothold again.

"Watch the other DVD. You need to see it."

"What's on it?"

"Just watch it," her mother said shortly.

Fuck. Amery didn't want to do this, but it appeared they wouldn't leave until she met their demands. She switched out the discs, but didn't sit down when she hit PLAY.

Two fighters circled each other on-screen. One was Ronin. Immediately he was the aggressor, cornering his opponent, getting him on the ground. Keeping the guy locked down. The round ended when Ronin got the guy to tap out after an arm bar.

Another fight started. This one was more physical on the

boxing and kicking side. Ronin's opponent refused to stay down. But Ronin adapted. He brought out his punching and kicking game. And he beat the guy bloody. The final move that ended the fight was when he performed a spinning back kick that connected with his opponent's head.

Straight knockout.

After she watched the third fight, where once again Ronin was victorious, she didn't see the point to watching this DVD. Was she supposed to believe that he'd take this behavior outside the cage? Direct it at her? Just as she opened her mouth to ask the purpose, another fight started.

But this wasn't like the others. This fight found Ronin on the receiving end of rapid-fire fists. His opponent absolutely brutalized Ronin. The skin above his eye was sliced open and bleeding. His mouth was cut and swollen. The camera had zeroed in on him, and the look in his eye was complete blankness. Bleakness. And she knew, in that moment, this was the fight he'd been in the night he'd shown up at her loft beat to crap.

Where had Naomi gotten footage of this? Had she been there? Taking joy in watching Ronin getting pummeled?

Ronin had come to her to help him become whole again. He needed her. Amery bit her lip and tasted the salt from her tears in the back of her throat.

She opened the DVD drive and removed the disk.

"Well?"

"I don't know what you want me to say."

"I told you this was a waste of time," her mother snapped.

"Say that our concerns are justified."

Amery shook her head. "You are off base on this. Ronin isn't a monster. Not even close."

"You will never convince us of that. And we won't stand by and watch your life destroyed, young lady."

"You're telling me if I stay with Ronin, you'll disown me?"

"We cannot support you in this life choice, Amery. We will not."

"You've never supported me in any choices. From what dress I wore to prom, to what college I chose, to moving to Denver."

"We'll be waiting to hear from you. If we don't, we'll be on our way and you won't hear from us again until you prove you've gotten your life straightened out."

Amery clutched the manila envelope to her chest and didn't even get up when they walked out the door.

CHAPTER TWENTY

RONIN couldn't get ahold of Amery.

Normally even if she was busy she'd at least text him back and let him know she'd call him when she had a chance.

So why hadn't he heard from her in more than seven hours?

Don't be a possessive asshole who needs to know where your woman is at all times.

He'd finished teaching the class of blue and green belts—what a trip that'd been—and was taking a breather in his office when Deacon poked his head in.

"Got a minute, Sensei?"

"What's up?"

"Molly is here for my kickboxing class, and she wants to talk to you."

There went Ronin's theory that Amery had kept Molly late to work on the Okada project and had lost track of time. "Send her in." As soon as he saw Molly's face, he knew something was wrong.

"Sorry to bother you, but have you talked to Amery in the last few hours?"

He shook his head.

"Well, I sort of hoped she'd snuck out the back and just come here after . . ."

He fought his impatient response to tell her he didn't have time to play these games. "After what?"

"After her parents' surprise visit today."

"Amery's parents are in town?" His gaze sharpened. "Did something happen to her brother?"

"I don't think so. They spent a long time in her office."

"How long?"

"Two hours. I heard some arguing, but couldn't make out specifics. Then her parents left. Amery didn't walk them out or introduce them to me or Chaz. She just stayed in her office with the door closed. I didn't want to bug her, you know?" Molly squeezed her training gloves in her hands. "So when it was time to shut down, I saw she wasn't in her office. I checked her loft, just to be sure, and she wasn't there either."

"What time did her parents leave?"

"About four. I think if she would've been meeting them for supper or something, she would've told me. Or you would know, right?"

"I haven't heard from Amery since before lunch." Ronin glanced at the clock. Seven fifteen. No one had heard from her for more than three hours. That wasn't like her.

"So you have any idea where she could've gone?" Molly asked. "I'm worried."

The last time she'd suffered through a bad day . . . she'd at least texted him where she was. That she'd fallen off the grid didn't bode well.

In that moment he knew exactly where he'd find her.

At least he hoped.

Ronin stood. "Thanks, Molly. I appreciate you coming to me with this."

In the doorway, Molly stopped and faced him. "You should know that the weeks you guys were apart, she was a mess. Now . . . she's happy with you. I know you're happy with her. It makes me sick someone would try to ruin that. First someone from your past and then someone from hers."

Deacon stepped aside as Molly walked out.

Ronin shoved his hand through his hair. "I'll be gone the rest of the night."

"Do you know where Amery is?"

"I've got a pretty good idea."

HE found her in a back booth at the Rialto Lounge, knocking back two-for-one happy-hour specials.

An immense feeling of relief flowed through him. She didn't notice him at first, so he had a minute to study her, his beautiful troubled woman. Her hair was loose; a few sections were twisted from her habit of twirling it around her finger when she was upset. Five empty lowball glasses were pushed against the wall, and the sixth sat in front of her, half empty.

Ronin slid into her side of the booth.

Amery looked at him, but didn't seem all that startled to see him. He pushed her hair over her shoulder and leaned in to kiss her, tasting the tartness of the gin and the sweetness that was just her. The kiss went on and on, soft and slow, until her face became damp, and he caught the salty taste of her tears. He slipped his mouth free and brushed even softer kisses over her trembling lips as he tenderly wicked away the tears from the corners of her eyes. "Baby. It's okay. I'm here."

"I knew you'd find me."

"I'll always find you." He nuzzled her ear. "I'll always come running after you. Always."

Her shoulders started to shake, and the real tears started.

Ronin pushed the table back and picked her up, cradling her to his chest and holding her tightly as she cried. He rubbed his lips over the crown of her head, breathing her in, offering her his strength, his heart breaking that this strong, independent woman needed it.

After the storm of tears subsided, she placed a soft kiss on his neck. "Thank you. Will you take me home? To my place?"

He shoved aside the reality that she didn't consider his penthouse home. "Sure. Is your car here?"

"No. I walked. I needed the fresh air to try to clear my head."

He kept an arm around her shoulder as he led her outside. Tiny flakes of snow had started to fall, and Amery hadn't worn a coat. He unzipped his leather jacket and stopped to put it on her. After zipping it up to her chin, Ronin noticed she was crying again. "What?"

"You take good care of me. If no one else ever sees that or ever knows that but me, it's enough. I don't want to explain it. I don't need to explain it or defend it because it belongs to us."

He framed her face with his hands. "You and me? This matters. Nothing else does."

She closed her eyes and curled in to him.

Ronin bundled her into his car and found a parking place close to her building. He unlocked her alley door with his key and followed her upstairs.

Amery immediately went into the kitchen and took a bottle of gin out of the cupboard and one glass.

Ronin raised an eyebrow at her, as if to say, *Don't you think you've had enough to drink?*

She poured and slid it across the countertop. "For you."

He opened his mouth to protest and she shook her head. "Trust me. You'll need it."

That bad feeling reappeared, stronger than ever. "Amery. What's going on?"

"Let me get warmer clothes on and then we'll talk."

She swayed on the way to her bedroom.

Ronin didn't touch the booze. He stopped in front of the living room window and watched it snow.

With Amery having downed six drinks, he wasn't confident they'd be doing much talking. Sure enough, when he went to check on her, she'd put on her pajamas and slipped into bed.

He swept her hair from her face. "Baby, I know you're tired, but we need to talk about what happened when your parents came to visit you today."

"They brought me something."

"What?"

"Some stuff. It's in an envelope."

"Where?"

"I put it under the sink in the kitchen."

"Why?"

She frowned. "To hide it. I wanted to burn it . . . or smash it. Not even show it to you."

It was bad enough she wanted to hide it? "Tell me what it is."

Amery turned away from him, snuggling deeper into her pillow.

"Don't go to sleep yet."

"I'm tired. So fucking tired of all of this."

"Amery. Please get up and show me—"

"I can't watch it again."

Watch it?

He waited for her to say more, but her breathing slowed almost immediately.

Ronin found the thick envelope addressed to Mr. and Mrs. James Hardwick. The postmark date had been smeared. He dumped the contents on the counter. Two DVDs, a stack of photos, and a typewritten note about . . . him.

He thumbed through the photos, his sense of dread growing.

These had been sent to Amery's parents? The poses weren't as explicit as some he'd done. But there were a lot of different women.

He made it through the stack, more than a little rattled. Then he grabbed the gin and the DVDs before he returned to the living room to see what was on the discs.

After the first scene with Naomi, Ronin had to keep from putting his fist through the TV.

His ex had done some seriously fucked-up shit, but this went beyond anything he could've imagined. Looking at the footage, he could tell she'd set up cameras not only in her bedroom, but in Ronin's bedroom. He'd never consented to that. Never.

He seemed stuck in an out-of-body experience as he watched himself on-screen, binding Naomi. Fucking Naomi. He cringed in the scene where he'd slapped her across the face. He had to pause and curb his anger. Why hadn't he said no to her that time? Afterward, he'd felt so ashamed. He closed his eyes, wishing he could just fucking erase that memory.

"I don't see the big deal. You use forcible contact all the time in your role as Sensei. In your role as master, you are supposed to take into account what I, as your submissive, want. I need this."

"Don't call me master. We are not in the Dominant and submissive roles. Naomi, you are my rope model and my lover. You aren't even my student, so you don't understand the role of violence. And yet you're demanding I use it against you during an intimate moment?"

"You use me anyway. I'm nothing more than a mannequin for you to bind and a hole to stick your cock in when you're done."

She'd started to cry then. Manipulating him. Demanding to know why she had no say in their public or private play. And like a fucking idiot, he'd given in. Afterward, he drank until he'd passed out. And he stayed away from her for three weeks.

That's when he'd decided to convert the third bedroom into a play room.

That'd also been the beginning of the end.

Was this the beginning of the end for him and Amery?

No way. No *fucking* way.

Ronin couldn't imagine how upset she'd been at seeing this display of him with his former lover. Especially when that wasn't really him at all.

But to find out her parents had also seen it? That this was their first—hell, their *only* impression of him? He was shocked Amery hadn't ordered him out of her life.

"Naomi goes for the jugular, doesn't she?" Amery said softly behind him.

He closed his eyes and prayed he wasn't about to lose this woman. "A nick, rather than a slice just to see how fast you'll bleed out." *Or see if someone will notice and save you.* "I had no idea she'd . . ."

"I guessed that. But I'm surprised you hadn't expected something like this from her. Do you think she kept it all these years to blackmail you?"

"Not for money when humiliation is so much more damaging." He ejected the disk. "Do I even want to know what's on the other DVD?"

"It's outtakes from some of your fights."

Fucking awesome. "This is why your parents showed up unannounced. Naomi sent them a hate package."

"Yes." Amery sighed. "They forced me to watch it with them in the room."

Then Ronin was on his feet, standing in front of her, but he hesitated to touch her. "I . . ." What the fuck did he even say to that?

"It was horrible." Amery wrapped her arms around herself. "They kept asking questions and treating me like some kind of victim of abuse."

He just stared at her helplessly as she matter of factly relayed every ugly accusation her parents had hurled at her for being involved with someone like him. By the time she finished speaking, she was crying so hard he couldn't understand her. Regardless of whether she wanted it or not, Ronin hauled her into his arms and held her.

She clung to him. He waited for the moment her embarrassment would turn into anger and she'd lash out at him. He steeled himself against it.

But it didn't happen.

He had no idea how long they remained like that, Amery sobbing against his chest while his self-recriminations paralyzed him.

"So after they left, I needed some time alone to try to process everything."

"Where did you get to in that process?"

"Same place I started—except the booze gave me a buzz. I tried to look at it from both sides. From their side. How I'd feel if I'd gotten something like that in the mail."

"And?"

"And it didn't matter. I couldn't separate myself enough."

"Separate yourself from what?"

"From the anger and humiliation."

Ronin tipped her head back to look into her eyes. "I can't imagine the anger you're feeling toward me right now."

Amery's eyes searched his. "Ronin, I'm not angry at you. I'm angry *for* you. No matter how it ended between you and Naomi, she doesn't have the right to humiliate you. The only anger on my side is directed at my parents. They came here for two things. To judge me for my involvement with you and to show me your humiliation. When I tried to explain that they didn't understand you, or our relationship, they insisted I'd been brainwashed. That I was excusing my abuser's behavior."

Abuser. That twisted his stomach.

She touched his face. "So according to them, I've been abused by the man who taught me how to defend myself against a real threat. Abused by the man who respects my career aspirations and asked his family to consider giving my designs a shot. Abused by the man who won't let me hide my wants and desires from him. Abused by the man who knows me, as well as my heart and my body. Abused by the man who gives me his coat when it's cold, who feeds me when I'm hungry, who nourishes my soul just by his existence. I can't stand by and let them tell me that I'm abused . . . by the one man who taught me what it really means to love someone."

He closed his eyes against the surge of emotion. This is what she meant when she said no one else mattered. She knew the truth about them and it was enough. God. He loved this woman with everything he had.

Amery tapped his cheek. "Look. At. Me."

Ronin slowly lifted his lids, but two tears escaped anyway.

"Don't," she whispered. "It's not worth your tears."

"But you are."

"You didn't even cry when you were beat to shit."

"This hurts me so much worse than that, because it's hurting you."

She sniffled. "But it's not. That's what I'm trying to tell you."

"So your anger, humiliation, and indignation is all for me?"

"Who else would it be for?"

"For you for having to deal with it because you're involved with me."

"Oh, Ronin. No." Her eyes filled with tears again. "I hate that she's still fucking with you. With us."

What had he ever done to deserve this beautiful, wonderful woman? She should be running from him. Instead, here she was, crying for him. Hurting for him. Ronin caressed her cheek. "She brought your parents into it, thinking it'd mortify you, and you'd lash out and blame me. Naomi wants to hurt you because she knows that will hurt me."

She rested her forehead to his chest. "What a mess."

"And yet you're still here."

"Because you and I aren't in the wrong. You were wronged.

What happened between you two doesn't concern me, and it sure as hell doesn't concern my parents."

He stroked her hair, unsure where she was going with this.

"If someone had sent them pictures from the demo we did at the club, or if they'd placed cameras here or at your place and had shots of us in intimate moments, that might've given my parents the idea I was in an unhealthy relationship. Then I could understand their need for a face-to-face visit with me."

"But?"

"But they chose to come here and confront me and demand . . ." She made a hiccupping sob. "They gave me an ultimatum. Break it off with you and get some help. If I choose to stay with you, then they're washing their hands of me. I can't go crying to them when it's goes bad."

"God. Baby. That's harsh."

"I know. I just can't help but wonder how sad it'd be if I was in an abusive situation. They'd turn me away and say 'we told you so' rather than helping me because I didn't take *their* help on *their* time frame."

"Luckily you'll never have to test those fears. You'll never need to go crying to them because this won't go bad between us when it's so good."

"You know what bothers me? The only time they show up during the six years I've lived in Denver is to cram yet another thing they perceive I've done wrong down my throat. They don't know me at all, Ronin. They never have."

"Their loss. I know you. I know this big heart of yours, and I know this is hurting you. No matter how different your life philosophies are from theirs, they are still your parents. There's part of you that wants their acceptance. Not necessarily their unconditional love, because it doesn't sound like they've ever been capable of giving that. But at least their acknowledgment that you're happy in your own life."

"Do you ever think you'll get that acceptance about your life choices from your grandfather?"

What a question. He didn't think Amery asked just to deflect the conversation from her own situation, but because her confrontation had brought family issues front and center. She'd respected his boundaries and hadn't asked specifics on his current relationship with his grandfather. But now those boundaries had been tested, and he felt, maybe for the first time, he could be honest with her—and himself—about his complicated relationship with the man he both admired and resented. "He's been different since everything happened with Naomi. I know he feels guilty—as he should. He stopped putting pressure on me to take over the company. But because of our history, I've wondered if he was using reverse psychology on me."

"Sometimes when you talk about him it's with . . . disdain, like he's the evil, controlling emperor. And other times you almost sound fond of him."

Ronin threaded their fingers together. "There have been times when I've disliked what he's done or the parameters he's set, but I don't hate him. I respect him too much."

"Do you think he respects you?"

"I know he does. That's why he was after me to run Okada—he knew I wouldn't run it into the ground." Ronin kissed her knuckles. "How did we get on this topic?"

"I'm tired of talking about my fucked-up family situation." She sighed. "In fact, I'm just plain tired. Too much booze, too much angst. Can we just crawl into bed and put this day behind us?"

"Whatever you want."

Amery shed her clothes and slipped between the sheets naked. "It's been a while since you stayed over here."

Ronin spooned her. It'd be thoughtless, given the state of her emotions, to say he hoped it'd be the last time either one of them crashed here. He was damn near desperate for her to make the final leap, but she needed to do it on her own time frame.

THE next morning, Amery smelled coffee, and that enticed her to get out of bed. She saw Ronin at the breakfast bar with a baker's box. "Am I witnessing Ronin Black holding a box of doughnuts?"

"Of course not. These are seven-nut, whole-grain pumpkin muffins sweetened with organic honey and raw sugar."

"Is it wrong to hope one day I'll see you with powdered sugar all over your face and frosting in your teeth?"

"Yes." He kissed her, but not a pleasant good-morning smooch. A whole-body kiss with one hand clamped on her butt cheek, the other on the back of her head as he devoured her mouth.

Dizzy and panting from the sheer passion of Ronin's kiss was a perfect way to start her day.

He growled against her lips, "For as poorly as the evening started out, it sure ended with a bang."

"Mmm-hmm." As many times as they'd had sex, made love, fucked each other raw during their relationship, the joining of their bodies had gone beyond that last night, when they'd turned to each other in the night. Clichéd for sure, but they'd reached another level of intimacy and deepened their connection.

"I love waking up with the taste of you on my tongue." He zeroed in on the sweep of skin between her shoulder and neck. "I let you sleep in, but now I can't think of anything but dragging you back to bed," he murmured.

"I can't. I'm already late. We're interviewing office help today." She disentangled from him and grabbed the mug he'd filled for her. "What inspired you to get breakfast?"

"I stopped by the hotel your parents are staying in and introduced myself."

Amery choked on her coffee. "Why did you do that?"

His eyes were unreadable. "I wanted to head off another confrontation with them for you."

"And?"

"And I also dropped off a prepaid Fed-Ex box and asked them to mail the extra set of copies they'd made because I need all of it for evidence against Naomi."

"You're taking her to court?"

"I don't know what my legal options are, but I can't ignore it." Ronin ran his hand through his hair. "At first I was inclined to follow your suggestion and blow the whole thing off. Staying strong together is the best revenge. But what if that just pisses her off more and she uploads one of those DVDs to YouTube? Or if she sends copies to the parents of my students? I have no problem telling people about my rope expertise, but those pictures and DVDs are only about my humiliation. I can't help but fear if that DVD did get out, she could ruin my dojo.

"So I'm taking precautions against that. The Okada tech team is scouring the Internet for anything untoward regarding me. The legal team is crafting a letter. A copy of it will go to Naomi's family, so they understand the seriousness of the situation." His smile was decidedly sharklike. "No one wants to cross Okada's legal department. One of the best in Japan."

"What did my parents say?"

"I told them they didn't need to wait around today to hear your answer. That you'd made the choice to stay with me long before my vengeful ex-girlfriend attempted to wreak havoc with our lives."

"That's it?"

Ronin cornered her. "No, baby, that's not it. I told them I loved you and I'd never hurt you. Which is the truth."

"How did they respond?"

"I didn't give them a chance to pull me into a pointless argument. I said if they wanted to cut you out of their lives, it was their loss. Because I would be in your life for good."

Amery stared at the fierceness coloring his eyes.

"The only thing that matters to me is that you love me and trust in me."

"I do. You know I do. You're the best thing that's ever happened to me."

He twined a section of her hair around his finger. "How did I get so lucky to have a woman like you fall in love with a man like me?"

"Ronin, I think the luck is all on my side."

"How about if I pick you up after work and take you to dinner? We've haven't done any of that couple stuff you're so fond of."

"I'd love that."

"It's a date." He brushed his lips over hers. "Let's eat breakfast."

She eyed the muffins. They looked utterly disgusting. "I'm not really hungry."

He laughed. "As soon as I'm gone, you'll sneak back up here and have a cookies-and-cream Pop-Tart, won't you?"

Amery smiled. "Busted. I don't see why every meal of the day has to be healthy."

"What you feed the body, feeds the mind and feeds the soul."

"Your body might be a temple, but mine isn't," she retorted.

"Wrong. I worship your body plenty." He kissed her in that thoroughly mind-boggling way that left her clinging to him and cursing him. Her tingling lips made her tingling body parts very jealous.

"Are we okay?"

"I am. I really am." She blew out a slow breath. "Maybe before you take off we should load some of my stuff into your car for you to take up to the penthouse."

Pure satisfaction shone in his eyes. "It would be my greatest pleasure."

CHAPTER TWENTY-ONE

"WHAT was that swivel thing you did with your tongue?"

Ronin smiled against Amery's neck. "Liked that?"

"I think my scream indicated that I did."

"I wish I could tell you it was from the *Kama Sutra* or something I saw in a shunga print, but I think I saw it in porn."

Amery pushed back and looked at him. "You watch porn?"

"Baby, every man under the age of seventy watches porn. Those who claim they don't? Are lying." He twisted a chunk of her hair around his finger. "It doesn't reflect on you, that you aren't giving me what I need in bed. I just like watching people have sex. It's fucking hot; it turns me on, and the added bonus? I pick up new things to do for you."

"So I shouldn't feel threatened or like you're imagining me with another guy? Or maybe another girl?"

Ronin tugged her hair, bringing her closer. "I don't share. Ever. And the thought of anyone ever putting their hands on this body? I'm deciding which bone-breaking techniques I've learned that would bring the most pain."

"But you don't mind people looking at me?"

"On those sexy book covers? No." Amery had just finished the preliminary mock-up cover for *Tangled Together*, the third book in Cherry Starr's erotic series. "I'm still blown away that you reworked a still shot from the club demo video and kept the sensuality of the scene without exposing our faces. So not only are you cover-model hot, you're very talented."

"Thank you. So are you. Your rope work is stunning." She paused. "It's really a shame you've sworn off public demos."

Shocked, he said, "What?"

Her eyes turned serious. "Look, I've wrestled with bringing this up with you, so I'm just going to say it straight out; I don't want you to give up such an integral part of who you are."

Ronin stared at her silently, unsure if he'd heard her correctly.

"I'm not saying this because I've got some secret desire for you to bind me in front of large crowds at a sex club on a regular basis. But, sweetheart, a sex club isn't the only place you can teach and give demos. You have plenty of space at the dojo to offer private lessons. You could hold basic beginner classes on tying techniques for couples, or offer classes to Doms and Dommes who want to learn advanced techniques. You are a master—and that comes with responsibilities. You have to teach and pass on those skills. I would feel guilty if your hesitation to continue demo teaching was solely because of me."

"It's not." He brushed his knuckles across her jaw. "Haven't you noticed that I tend to have the all-or-nothing mind-set?"

She gasped with total sarcasm. "No. Really?"

He playfully swatted her rear.

"There is a catch, however." Amery smiled—all teeth. "I am your rope model. Your only rope model, whether we do a full demo or a simple chest harness. I'll be whatever you need."

"Baby, you already are what I need." And she was. He slanted his lips over hers, starting the kiss out at a slow pace, reveling in how she unraveled him. He'd just cranked up the intensity when he heard the *ping* of the elevator doors.

That ripped him out of the moment. "What the hell?" No one breached his inner sanctum.

"Maybe there's an emergency at the dojo." Amery was looking over her shoulder, and the movement caused the gap in her robe to widen.

Momentarily distracted by the sight of her taut nipple, he glanced up when Amery stiffened. Then his gaze followed hers to the woman standing in the entrance to the living room.

"Mother? What are you doing here?"

At the word *mother*, Amery scooted off his lap so quickly she nearly fell.

His mother answered in Japanese and crossed the room.

Protocol demanded he stand. He met his mother halfway. After pressing his cheek to hers, he offered her a slight bow. "What a surprise."

"Not an unpleasant surprise, I hope."

"Never."

She laid her hand on his cheek, and her eyes scrutinized every inch of his face. "Ronin-san. You look wonderful."

"As do you, Okasan." At age sixty-three, his mother was still an attractive woman.

"Who let you up here?"

"Your sister. Her greeting was less . . . enthusiastic than yours."

"Is everything okay? You never—"

"Everything is fine with me and your grandfather."

"So would you like to sit?" *And tell me why the hell you're here?*

"In a bit. I'd like a tour of your home first."

Amery secured the robe. "I'll just ah, go . . . get dressed."

Ronin tugged her to his side. "Amery, this is my mother, Tamara Okada. Okasan, this is my"—everything—"Amery."

Amery acted unsure on whether she should offer her hand, but she clasped his mother's when she offered it. "It's a pleasure."

"For me as well."

Before Amery fled, Ronin kissed her temple.

He led his mother to the elevator and eyed her outfit. Some flowing silk thing and a pair of ankle-breaking heels. "We'll start on the roof. Should I get you a jacket? It's chilly up here."

"I will be fine."

They ducked inside the bubble, and she wandered from poolside to garden side. "I imagine this is lovely in the summer months."

"The view is great too."

She perched on the end of a chaise and gestured for him to sit across from her.

"So why the impromptu visit?" In the fourteen years he'd lived in the United States, his mother hadn't visited. It hadn't seemed like a big deal because he saw her at least once a year in Japan, and she was so busy traveling with his grandfather, she preferred to stay home in her down time.

"Both of my children are here. Plus I was worried." She remained perfectly still, her hands clasped in her lap. "I'll get right to it. You never talk about this kind of thing with me, but Shiori indicated that you went back into the ring after Amery ended your relationship and you ended up injured? On multiple occasions?"

Rather than confess the extent of his injuries because his mother would have a mini meltdown that he hadn't told her, he countered with, "Did *she* tell you why Amery broke it off? It was Shiori's fault." He sounded like a petulant kid.

"Yes, she summarized the situation, but I do agree with your sister on this. You should've told Amery about your family connection."

Ronin opened his mouth, and she did the one-finger silencing action he remembered from his childhood.

"You've chosen a different path. Your grandfather never believed you'd stay on it. I knew you wouldn't deviate. That's what defines a family—accepting those divergent paths in those we care about. Your grandfather and I both worried when we hadn't heard from you personally in weeks . . . I came to check on you."

He thought back to the ugly scene with Amery's parents. Their accusations, ultimatums, and embarrassment about the path Amery had taken. He'd watched her crumble after swearing it didn't matter. But that kind of rejection is hard, no matter how old you get.

Then he had a pang of awareness—had he done the same thing to his family? Rejected them because he believed they wouldn't understand his life choices?

Sobering thought.

"Ronin-san?"

He smiled at her and the only term of endearment she ever used. "How is Grandfather?"

"Old." She ran her hand through her hair. "I've never said that about him because he's always seemed so invincible. But he's had some health issues in the last year. Which doesn't sit well with him."

"And you are bearing the brunt of that?"

She shrugged. "It's what I do."

"Why didn't you ever remarry? Then you wouldn't have to be at your father's command."

"He doesn't command me." She sounded affronted. Then she sighed. "I wondered if you'd ever ask me about this."

Ronin waited.

"None of the men in my social circle hold a candle to your father. He was an electric charge; other men were dim bulbs. My father kept trying to fix me up because he didn't want me to spend my life without a companion like he had."

"But I thought Grandfather was mad that you eloped."

She frowned. "He was upset because he couldn't give me a proper society wedding. I eloped because I couldn't imagine my life without your father. And after he died, your grandfather understood what I was going through and he begged me to return to Japan."

"I didn't know that."

"How could you have? You were eight. I grieved. I grieved to the point I couldn't care for you or your sister. He had to step in."

She squinted at him. "Don't you remember him working with you on your Japanese language issues?"

An image jumped into Ronin's head of sitting at the table with paper and pens, Shiori curled up in their grandfather's lap while he patiently drilled Ronin on reading and writing. "I'd forgotten that."

"I'm not trying to paint Nureki Okada as a saint. But he's not a villain either." She smiled softly. "Well, not all days."

"Why are you telling me this?"

She stood. "Because you, your sister, and I need to discuss some family things."

"What things?"

"I'll go into more detail tomorrow. Lunch will work, since you're not teaching during the day, and who knows what Shiori is doing with her time since she quit."

"She quit? Quit what?"

Her eyes turned shrewd. "Your sister resigned from Okada weeks ago. How else could she spend all this time here?"

His jaw dropped. "She never even fucking mentioned that."

For once his mother didn't give him a pinched look about his language. "I'm not surprised. But you've been so wrapped up in your own life that you hadn't noticed all her free time?"

Chastised, he retorted, "I had a couple of life-changing events, a couple of health issues, so I wasn't as aware as I might've otherwise been."

She offered him the half smile that signified the conversation was over. "It appears you and Amery worked things out."

"Mostly. The rest will be handled after she's living here permanently."

"Your Amery is a beautiful girl. I can see she makes you happy."

"She does. She also has that electric spark that lights my life."

The remaining house tour didn't take much time. Amery had made the bed in their room and put away the silk scarves. When they finished the tour in the kitchen, he saw Amery had fixed her hair and put on makeup. He found it sweet she wanted to make a good impression on his mother.

"Would you like something to drink?" Amery asked.

"Tea?"

"We have pretty much everything except for that."

"Of course. Do you share Ronin's dislike of tea?"

"No. After I move in, I'll stock it for when you visit."

Message received: Amery wasn't going anywhere.

That pleased rather than annoyed his mother. "Excellent. I look forward to having tea with you, Amery." She faced Ronin. "I apologize for dropping in and interrupting your evening. I'll see you tomorrow for lunch."

"Where are you staying?"

"With Shiori at the Ritz. She's got an extra bedroom in the penthouse suite she insists on." She patted his cheek. "So much more fun to cramp her style than yours, Ronin-san."

He grinned and walked her to the elevator. "Want me to ride down with you?"

"Not necessary." Right before the doors closed, she said, "Sweet dreams, my handsome boy," in Japanese, like she used to when she tucked him in at night.

Amery's arms circled his waist. She rested the side of her face against his back. "You okay?"

"Oddly enough, yes. But that was bizarre. Must be the month for surprise parental visits."

"Looks like yours went better than mine. You two were on the roof for a long time."

"She gave me a few things to think about."

"Like?"

Ronin turned around. "Like I wondered why Shiori was still here, but she hedged every time I asked. Come to find out, she quit Okada several weeks ago."

Amery dropped her gaze.

He grabbed on to her chin and tipped her face up. "You knew."

"Yes, but—"

"No buts."

"After I decided to sign the contract, Shiori warned me I wouldn't be working with her. A week or so later I got to thinking about how suspicious that sounded, so I called her on it, so she told me the truth. It's been hard not telling you because my loyalty to you will always come first. But she begged me not to say anything because she needed to wait until the timing was right."

"And for you, did that loyalty start before or after Okada cut you a big fat check?"

Immediately after he said it, he knew it was a dick move.

She stepped back. The hurt on her face sliced into him, and he reached for her, but she dodged him. "Did you ever consider the reason that your sister doesn't share anything personal with you is because you can be such a judgmental asshole when it comes to family stuff?"

Keep your goddamn mouth shut for once, before you make it worse.

"I didn't ask to be her confidante. But I like her. I don't hold a grudge against her for your mistake. Granted, I don't know everything that's gone on in your family saga—frankly I don't want to know. But if we're going to be together, then your sister will be in my life. I intend to have her as a good part of it because god knows I don't have anything like that with my family."

"What the fuck does *if we're going to be together* mean?" he demanded. "We are together. We goddamn *live* together."

"Not yet we don't. And right now, I don't want to be in the same apartment with you, let alone the same bed." Amery snatched her purse off the end table. "Unfuckingbelievable."

"Amery—"

She whirled around. "That's what you took from everything I just said? You made it about you? Why don't you think of someone else for a change? You really believe that Shiori is hanging out in the dojo because she needs a place to train? Wrong. She's there because she wants to rebuild her relationship with you."

"Then why didn't she just say that?" he bellowed.

She poked him in the chest. "For that reason, right there."

He couldn't think of a damn thing to say as the elevator doors closed in his face.

THAT'S how Ronin found himself at the Ritz-Carlton at nine o'clock at night.

Maybe it'd been typical behavior for him, commanding his sister meet him in the bar. But she'd agreed, so he must not have been too much of a raging asshole.

He'd taken a booth in the corner and ordered. He'd barely had a chance to savor the subtle notes in the scotch before Shiori slid across from him.

The waiter was immediately tableside, wearing a big smile. "Ms. Hirano, it's wonderful to have you back. What are you drinking this evening?"

Shiori pointed to Ronin's glass. "Whatever he's having."

"The Highland Park 1958 single-malt scotch coming right up."

"You're hitting the good stuff tonight."

"Life is too short to drink shitty scotch."

She smiled. "You've developed a sophisticated palate simply because you don't *have* to drink cheap, shitty scotch."

"I'll admit it's an indulgence."

Neither said anything until she received her drink.

Shiori raised her glass for a toast. "To the finer things in life—good booze and good company."

Ronin touched his glass to hers and drank. "The last part is up in the air."

"Lucky me, summoned when you're in a lousy mood."

"Then put me in a good mood. Tell me if you found out anything about Naomi's accomplices."

Shiori delicately sipped. "I spoke to Jenko. The protection business in Japan can be incestuous, so he knows the guy. Hiko Tamagachi. Jenko says he's not surprised Hiko threw in with someone like Naomi."

"That son of a bitch held Amery while that other fucker hit her. Hit her in the face," he repeated as if Shiori didn't know.

"Jenko has put the word out about what Hiko did and to whom. Trust me—Hiko's protection days are over. At least with the clientele that used to hire him."

"What else?"

"Nothing on the other guy. We're betting the biker look was a disguise. As far as Naomi and her motivation to screw with you . . . we did a little digging and found out that after you put Naomi on an Okada jet to Tokyo almost four years ago, her family picked her up and she vanished. We also discovered her background had been completely fabricated—even our investigative team had been fooled."

"That had to sit well with Grandfather," he said dryly.

"Ronin, he didn't know back then, and I'm not going to tell him now."

"So you're keeping it from him out of sibling solidarity?"

"Yes. Although I'm sure you find that hard to swallow."

Just for an instant, Ronin saw a glimpse of his baby sister—the sweet-faced tomboy who'd trailed after him from the moment she could toddle along—and not the cut-throat business mogul she'd become.

"He wouldn't have wanted you anywhere near such a psycho bitch. Ojisan adores you. I know you see everything he's ever done as manipulation, but control isn't his only motivation. He doesn't show affection well, and he sees meddling in your life as a way to show he cares about you."

"I'm starting to understand that. Go on."

"But Ojisan's reason for getting into business with Naomi's family wasn't solely for you; it greatly benefitted Okada too." Shiori leaned forward. "Contrary to what Naomi told you, he never paid Naomi to be with you. He pulled a few strings with her visa to keep her in the United States with you, but that's it."

Part of Ronin had suspected Naomi lied about that, but he'd been too infuriated with his family to ask how much of what Naomi had told him was true. "Did it ever occur to you how fucking weird it is that Grandfather was so damn concerned about my romantic life? When he never married again after age twenty?"

Shiori rolled her eyes. "Why would he marry? Up until five years ago, he had four mistresses to satisfy him and our mother to tend to his social responsibilities."

"How the hell did he keep four mistresses happy?"

"You should ask him."

"No, thanks. Finish the Naomi story."

"After she screwed things up with you, her family put her under lock and key. The only person she had contact with was . . ."

"Her friend Kiki."

"Evidently after Kiki saw you with Amery, she immediately called Naomi in Japan. And Naomi dragged Hiko, her bodyguard, lover, and muscle for hire into her revenge drama. Cut to Kiki, who'd stored all of Naomi's things after you'd sent her away so suddenly."

"Does Kiki know where Naomi is now?"

"The PIs here questioned Kiki, and she swears she saw Naomi only briefly—long enough to give her the two boxes of stuff. After Ojisan found out about a potential blackmail situation, he personally contacted Naomi's family and warned them if a single image surfaces anywhere in the world, he'd ruin them permanently. We both know he has the juice to back it up, so I don't think Naomi will ever be a problem again."

He bit back his question on how their grandfather had heard about the new situation. Had he gotten the same kind of package that Amery's parents had? "Thank you for checking into all that for me. I hope you're right." He swirled the liquid in his glass. "You didn't have an issue utilizing Okada's resources even when you no longer work there?"

Shiori's expression didn't change. "So Mother told you that I'm unemployed?"

"Yes. I wondered why you were here for so long. And, yeah, I probably should've asked."

"I believe you did. I believe I hedged."

Ronin rested his forearms on the table. "What happened?"

"I wish I could blame Grandfather for unfair treatment, or that Okada got involved with a company that displayed poor business practices and I left in protest, but the truth is, I'm thirty-five, I'm single, and I'm tired of being alone."

That jarred him.

"I work too much; my friends are all in relationships and have children. They look at me with envy because I can hop on a plane and go anywhere in the world. I look at them and think if I had a husband and a baby, I'd never leave home." She held up her hand. "Please don't say I don't seem like the maternal type."

"Shiori, I don't know you well enough anymore to make that kind of observation."

"Thank you." She took a sip of her drink and sighed. "That scotch really is worth every penny. The only other time I've had it is at Ojisan's house."

Just another reminder he had absorbed some of his grandfather's habits without conscious effort.

"Anyway, I realized on the night of my thirty-fifth birthday—which I spent alone incidentally—I've been trying to prove that I deserve the CEO status at Okada, and I lost sight of everything else. Within a week after all my doubts surfaced, I came across an inner-office memo I wasn't supposed to see. Okada is trying to hire Inichi Matso away from Satzu to name him interim CEO because Grandfather wants to step down."

"You have got to be shitting me."

Shiori shook her head. "No, and here's the reality: he would be excellent for Okada."

"But that position has always been yours. Or at least your dream."

"I realized I'm not ready for the top spot. Just because I'm Nureki Okada's granddaughter doesn't mean I deserve to take control. So if he offered it to me right now, I don't think I'd take it. More work for the next forty years?" Shiori leaned forward. "Ojisan will be eighty-six. I don't want to look back at my life when I'm his age and wonder what I'd done with it besides work. Even without our inheritance, I have more money than I can possibly spend. So I quit and came here, hoping you'd have wisdom to guide me through this. But I didn't have the guts to even tell you the truth."

"You're totally screwed."

"Fantastic. Thank you."

"All joking aside, on a business level, I've made some changes with the dojo, but I wouldn't have done it if not for Amery." He met his sister's gaze. "But on a personal level, I've had that same epiphany, wanting a life outside of being Sensei Black. Even with the new projects that I've taken on, it'd be ideal if I could hand off some responsibilities and enjoy having found this amazing woman who gets everything about me."

Tears pooled in Shiori's eyes. "I'm happy for you. I mean that. Amery is just what you need in your life." She sniffled and wiped her eyes. "Damn scotch."

He hid his smile behind his glass.

"So does handing off some responsibilities mean I can keep teaching at Black Arts?"

"As long as you're interested in taking on a supervisory role in training our advanced students too."

"I noticed you've passed off all your upper-level classes to other instructors. The only reason you'd relinquish control was if you didn't have a choice." Her gaze sharpened. "What did the doctor say?"

Of course she'd pick up on that. Ronin was actually relieved to tell her everything. After he finished, he added, "Without coming across as self-serving, I'm glad you're not gainfully employed, because I could use your help running the dojo."

"What about Knox? He's your second-in-command and general manager."

"Knox is great with people—students, parents, all that glad-handing stuff I hate. Until I know if I'll ever be able to return to contact training, I'll need an advanced belt to teach my instructors and oversee their training methods. I trust you—not only because you're my highest-ranking belt."

"Then why?"

"Because we're alike in many ways. Plus you do the hardass, dragon-lady bit so well."

She snorted delicately.

"And it is a temporary position." He studied her. "I don't have to worry that you'll implement a hostile takeover, do I?"

She laughed. "No."

"So how did Grandfather react when you quit?"

"Not well, given her method of delivery," their mother said as she slid into the booth next to Shiori. She raised her hand to the waiter and signaled for three more drinks. "She sent him a text message."

"Okasan, we were just—"

"Do you remember how many times you said that when I caught you two doing something wrong?"

Ronin's gaze winged between his mother and Shiori. They looked enough alike they could be sisters. "You're mistaken. We never did anything wrong."

She laughed—loudly for their mother, especially in a public place.

He exchanged a WTF? look with his sister.

"That's right. I had perfect children," she said, switching to Japanese. "Neither of you were criminals or psychopaths, and I'm immensely grateful for that."

The waiter dropped off the drinks.

"I wanted to have this conversation tomorrow over lunch, but this is as good a time as any to tell you of the upcoming changes in my life."

"Maybe we should just have the waiter leave the bottle," Ronin muttered.

Shiori kicked him under the table.

Their mother held her glass aloft. "Raise your glasses to the new interim director of Okada Food Conglomerate."

He looked at Shiori who was looking at him blankly. He managed to say, "Who is the new interim director?"

"Me," their mother stated.

Ronin almost dropped his glass. He and Shiori said, "What?" simultaneously.

"Drink your toast."

Shiori and Ronin drank.

"Okay. What the hell is going on? I feel as if I've stepped into an alternate universe. Shiori quits. And you're taking over?"

"Yes. My father is ready to retire. I knew Shiori wasn't ready for the CEO chair. I knew you didn't want it," she said to Ronin. "And some guy who looks good on paper doesn't deserve it sight unseen. I've been around this food business my entire life. For close to thirty years, I've served as my father's hostess for business events as well as his business confidante. As his only child, I *am* the first heir. Something many people have forgotten."

"But you've never had any interest in taking the mantle," Ronin said.

"Not publicly, no. So after your sister's charming text message to your grandfather, giving the reasons why she's stepping down, I'm stepping up."

"You're really taking over?" Shiori said with equal shock.

"Yes. Okada is hiring Inichi Matso, except he will answer to me. Even if he passes the probationary period, he will still answer to me. We've revised the legal documentation in the past few weeks for the board of directors. A member of the Okada family will always have oversight of the company and will always have at least one seat on the board. For now, that's me. I have my own team to run checks on every aspect of the business anytime I deem it so."

"And Inichi Matso agreed to this?"

"Of course. He wants to get control of a five-billion-dollar business and turn it into more."

"But what about all your free time? You're a few years from retirement."

"I like to do things differently—get a job when most people retire. Your grandfather is feeling remorseful for some of the things he's done." She offered them a sad but surprisingly sneaky smile. "I played on that mercilessly. I did demand that he make both of your trust funds fully accessible—without strings."

That seemed too good to be true, even when Ronin had no idea what he'd do with that much money. "No strings? At all? Ever?"

"Just the usual inheritance tax issues. But besides that? No. The only strings that should come with a gift are on the outside of the package when you open it."

Such a smart woman.

"After our earlier discussion, I got to thinking about your father. How much I loved being with him." She slid her hands across the table and squeezed both Ronin's and Shiori's forearms. "I want that kind of happiness for both of you."

"Doesn't love like that just break your heart? You loved him and you lost him," Shiori said softly. "Who wants that kind of forever pain?"

"I did. I miss him every day. But I see him in both of you, so he's not completely gone. I would rather have that all-encompassing love for a short time than never have had it at all." She patted Shiori's hand. "Keep looking, Shiori-san. You'll find it. Probably where you least expect it." Their mother stood and she focused on Ronin. "Don't waste another minute of your life without her. You never know how many minutes you'll get."

CHAPTER TWENTY-TWO

RONIN broke damn near every traffic law getting to Amery's. He parked his motorcycle in the alley. He rapped on the door four times before unlocking it. Inside, he tossed his helmet aside and yelled, "Amery?" as he started up the circular stairs.

"I'm right here, Ronin. You don't have to yell."

As soon as he reached the top, he yanked her body to his and kissed her.

Either she'd cooled off or the kiss knocked the fight out of her because Amery wrapped herself around him, returning his passion with equal zeal.

He clamped his hands on her ass and hoisted her against the brick wall separating the bathroom from her bedroom. "I love you. And I never want you to walk out on me again like you did tonight. Never want to hear you say *if we're together.* We are together, and I want to make it permanent. Before you move in."

"Have you been drinking?"

He laughed. "A little bit during our family 'come to Buddha' meeting."

She blinked at him with confusion.

"But the conversation with my mother and my sister led me

to the realization that I don't want to just live with you. I want to marry you. I want you as mine officially, permanently, legally, all that."

"Seriously, Ronin, have you lost your mind?"

"I lost you once, and that put me out of my mind. When you left tonight because you were mad at me, you had someplace else to go. It might make me a selfish dick, but I don't want you to have that. So when we fight, which we invariably will, you can slam the door to the den, or to the practice room, or to the guest bedroom if you need time away from me." Ronin pushed a strand of hair from her cheek. "But I want to walk down the hallway to hash things out, not across town. And I'll always come after you, Amery. Always. I will be your safe haven. Because you're already mine."

"Um, that's sweet, but I'd like to point out that you're telling me to marry you rather than asking me."

"Is that what you want, baby? Me on one knee? Holding a diamond ring? Begging you to be mine forever? Because I'll do it."

"A big diamond would be an indication of how much you loved me," she joked.

Ronin swept his fingertips across her cheeks, strangely touched by her nervous babbling. "The size of a diamond doesn't indicate the size of my love for you. The earth hasn't produced a diamond that big because my love for you knows no bounds."

Her eyes swam with tears. "I don't care about the ring. I just want you."

"You've got me." His eyes searched hers. "So is that a yes on marrying me?"

"Yes."

Their mouths met, and the kiss was so loving and perfect; a silent promise. In that moment he felt the shift between them. It took every bit of Ronin's willpower not to beat on his chest and snarl, *Mine.*

He pulled back and set her on her feet. He said, "I have something for you. Keep your eyes closed and hold out your arm," while continuing to tease her addictive lips.

Amery complied.

After he fished a section of twine from his pocket, he took his time fashioning a bracelet. He placed a soft kiss on the inside of her wrist. "Okay. You can look."

Her eyebrows drew together as she squinted at the thin rope circling her wrist. "What is it?"

"A placeholder until I can get you a real ring." Ronin traced the intricate knot at the center. "This is an eternity tie." He gently turned her arm so she could see the backside of the bracelet. "You can't see where it begins or ends. That's how my love for you is."

"It's beautiful. I may never take it off."

He caught her exaggerated sigh in a long, steamy kiss. "So," he asked between nuzzles and soft smooches, "how soon can we do this? Because I'm ready to marry you right fucking now."

"What's the rush? Are you pregnant or something?"

He loved her smart mouth, but he pinched her ass anyway.

She yelped and swatted at him. "In all seriousness, there are several things to consider before we even think about taking that permanent step."

"Like what? I love you; you love me. The next step is promising to spend our life together. Simple."

"Well, like it or not, you are an Okada heir . . . I imagine you want your team of financial advisers to draft a pre-nup?"

"No," he said with an emphatic shake of his head.

Her eyes narrowed suspiciously. "May I remind you that you had me investigated *before* we went out on a date? Why wouldn't you want to protect yourself now when we're talking long-term?"

"For that very reason. I trust you. With everything I am and with everything I have."

"That's it?"

"That's it."

"So what if *I* want a pre-nup?"

Ronin carried her to her bedroom and fell onto the bed with her. "What would be in your pre-nup?"

She twisted a hank of his hair. "Oh, I don't know. I just wanted to sound cool, so you didn't think I wasn't bringing anything of value into this marriage."

"You're bringing everything I'll ever need into this marriage. You're bringing you."

"I love you so much."

"I love you too. So that's why I need to know about the wedding. Big? Small?"

"A civil ceremony will be fine." Amery turned her head and looked at him. "How soon you want to do this?"

"You busy tomorrow?"

"Ronin Black, just because I'm not the fancy wedding type doesn't mean I'll get married in jeans and a T-shirt; nor will I let you wear your damn gi. Besides, Chaz would never forgive me if he didn't get to go dress shopping with me."

"This is about making Chaz happy?"

"No, sweetheart. It's about making me happy. I'm getting married once. With a once-in-a-lifetime event, I deserve to spend a little time *ooh*ing and *aah*ing over sequins, lace, satin, and tulle."

"Whatever you want. It'd be nice if we had a date picked, so my mother can be here."

Amery looked away.

"If you want to wait and see how things go with your parents so they can be here too—"

"No," she said quickly. "I don't. They'd ruin it by demanding we had a ceremony of their choosing. And I don't really care who's there other than you."

"Me either." He kissed her. "Besides. I'm all about the honeymoon."

"Nothing extravagant," she warned him.

"It's cute how you think you get a say in that." He kissed her on the nose. "Fair warning: I plan to spoil the hell out of you when you're my wife, and you will have to just deal with it."

EPILOGUE

Three months later

RONIN'S spinning back kick connected with Bob's head. He kept his balance as he reversed the move, coming from the opposite side this time. Focusing on rapid-fire blows to the knee, then feeling the connection of his heel to the jaw. Another satisfying crack of flesh on flesh.

Or what passed as flesh. Although "Bob," the full-sized training dummy, wobbled, it remained stationary. The high-tech piece of equipment allowed Ronin to continue to train at his advanced level—he literally didn't have to pull any punches or worry that punches would come flying back at him.

Still, it wasn't the same as being in a real fight.

You're not ready for that. You're not rushing this.

His future as far as contact sports remained up in the air. He'd postponed his annual trip to train with his sensei even when he'd feared his teacher would release him if he couldn't keep up with the requirements for his belt level. What sucked was his teacher had refused to discuss it until after Ronin's next doctor's appointment.

These last three months had been frustrating with so much in limbo. The only thing he could do was push forward. Focus on what he could do instead of what he couldn't. That thought made him smile. For all the times Amery had commended him on his Zen attitude in the past, now she was the one who'd kept him upbeat about his future on the combat side of martial arts.

"Wearing that shit-eating grin while you're beating the fuck outta poor Bob is some scary stuff, Sensei."

Ronin leveled one more kick to Bob's midsection before he stopped and looked over at Knox. "Hilarious."

"He's holding up well, considering that you're trying to kill him," Knox added.

"Bob is not much of a challenge." He wiped the sweat from his forehead with his forearm and gave Knox a questioning look. "How long have you been standing there, watching me?"

"I just got here. I know we'd talked about grappling today, but I have a message from your wife."

Ronin couldn't stop his smile. He wondered if he'd ever get used to that feeling of male satisfaction that Amery was his—only his—forever. "What's the message?"

"She broke the 'no observation' rule again. She watched you beating on Bob just to make sure you weren't doing too much. Does that mean anything to you?"

It meant everything to him. He'd been out of sorts the past few days, and his sexy wife knew exactly what would pull him out of it. He began to unwrap his hands. "Yeah. I know what it means." Ronin fished his wedding ring out of the special cup he placed it in when he worked out. He'd gotten so used to the weight of the metal circling his finger he felt naked without it.

"Amery seemed concerned about that." Knox pointed to the large bandage on Ronin's right arm that had started to slip off, revealing a bloody piece of gauze taped to his skin. "What happened?"

Ronin didn't respond.

Knox sighed. "I don't wanna know, do I?"

"Nope. But I'll tell you tomorrow anyway." Ronin slipped on his gi top. "I'm officially off the clock. See you at the meeting in the morning."

By the time he'd reached the penthouse, his arm throbbed. Getting sweaty and putting pressure on the muscles hadn't been the brightest idea, but he'd been anesthetized during the procedure. He needed the pain afterward as a reminder of why he'd done it.

The elevator doors opened and Amery stood there waiting, arms crossed, bare toes tapping on the tile, looking annoyed. Looking beautiful. Looking like home.

He opened his mouth to speak and she shushed him. *Shushed* him. His eyes narrowed.

"Oh, don't give me the evil sensei eye, Master Black." She pointed at his gi top. "Nice try. I already saw the blood. Take it off."

Ronin felt compelled to point out, "Baby, it's not what you think."

"Then explain it to me, *baby*," she retorted. "Because after the last time Shiori took off a layer of your skin, you promised me that you wouldn't sword fight with her anymore."

"It's not an injury from a katana. I promised you I'd steer clear of weapons training." He touched her cheek. "I keep my promises. All of them."

A bewildered look entered her eyes. "Then what happened? You're bleeding."

He glanced down at his arm. Great. Now he was leaking through his gi. He kissed her softly. "Give me five minutes. I'll explain after I grab something to clean this up."

She didn't argue.

In the master bathroom, Ronin ditched his workout shirt and peeled away the gauze. He hissed. It hurt like a motherfucker.

A shocked gasp sounded from the bathroom doorway. He

turned. Amery's face was a ghostly white. "Ronin. We have to get you to the hospital. That needs stitches."

He pressed a cold washcloth on the jagged wound. "No."

"No? But . . . it'll scar."

"Amery. That's what I want."

"Why?"

"Doing it myself with barbed wire seemed a little over the top. The plastic surgeon that stitched me up after my last fight has done this sort of thing before." He removed the washcloth. "Look at it and tell me what you see."

Amery reached out to touch it, but snatched her hand back at the last second. Then she leaned closer. "Okay. It's hard to discern much beneath the, ah, blood, but it looks like a Japanese symbol."

"It is. It's the symbol for your name."

"I don't understand. Why would you maim yourself on purpose?"

With his free hand, he tipped her face up to meet his gaze. "Because your name is already etched into my heart and burned onto my soul. I wanted it carved into my skin." He angled his head and pressed soft kisses over the thin white scars on her right arm—the unintentional marking of his name that had drawn him to her in the first place. Now that he'd chosen to be marked in the same way, he finally felt they'd come full circle.

Her eyes filled with tears. "You crazy, masochistic man. Couldn't you have just gotten a tattoo?"

"Tattoos fade. The scarring will get more prominent with time." He rested his forehead to hers. "Please understand. I needed to do this."

After a moment, Amery said, "Believe it or not, I do understand."

"Good." Ronin released a shuddering breath. "I love you."

"I know. You've got my name gouged into your skin."

He laughed softly and leaned back, his mood lighter. "Now that that's out of the way, there's the issue of you breaking the dojo rules again. You can think about possible consequences as you're waiting for me, on your knees, in the practice room, while I'm bandaging this up."

Amery's mouth dropped open. "But that's not fair! I only did it because I was worried—"

"So you admit that you did it?" He flashed a smile. "Then why are you still standing here arguing with me?"

"Because you tricked me, you jerk."

"Yes, sir, or yes, Sensei, or yes, Master Black is an appropriate response. *You jerk* is not. Is that clear, Amery?"

"Crystal clear, sir." She stood on her tiptoes and kissed him. "But that's Mrs. Black to you."

Don't miss Lorelei James's upcoming release
in her Blacktop Cowboys® series!

HILLBILLY ROCKSTAR

Coming from Signet Eclipse in August 2014

She's protecting his body and guarding her heart. . . .

Country music star Devin McClain understands there's a downside to life in the public eye, but the laidback Wyoming cowboy has never imagined he'd attract crazed fans who would do anything to garner his attention. When veiled threats become real, he agrees to hire a discreet security detail. But Devin is shocked when that bodyguard is a hard-bodied woman. He's even more stunned to be attracted to the steely-eyed stunner.

Former soldier Liberty Masterson's return to civilian life has been wrought with challenges until she lands a job with a prestigious security firm. But when she agrees to provide personal protection during a cross-country tour, she doesn't realize she has signed up to masquerade as the playboy star's girlfriend. Though she's more comfortable in combat boots than high heels, she has no choice but to appear to be the sexy groupie Devin prefers.

Living in close quarters causes the chemistry between them to ignite, and Devin realizes he wants to turn their charade of a romance into reality. Although Liberty surrenders to his every whim behind closed doors, she fears the sexy country star doesn't see the real her; and Devin can't help but worry when the tour ends that there might not be enough between them to build something that won't fade away. . . .